# THE DARK WORLD

# THE DARKWORLD

## CARA LYNN SHULTZ

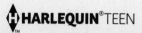

ISBN-13: 978-0-373-21120-3

THE DARK WORLD

HARLEQUIN®TEEN
www.HarlequinTEEN.com

For my husband, Dave,
who makes every day a special event

I PEELED AWAY THE CHEAP, GREENISH-GRAY paint on the wall of the third-floor girls' bathroom. Underneath the dull paint, the wall was a bright robin's-egg-blue. I'd started picking at the chipping paint in September, in the beginning of junior year, with the intention of peeling it all away and returning the wall to its original cheery color. Instead, I'd just made a mess.

Story of my life.

"Paige, are you sure you won't get in trouble for ditching class?" my best friend, Dottie, asked. She stood awkwardly in front of the muddy-brown-painted bathroom stalls—really, whoever picked the colors for this bathroom was in dire need of a hug or some therapy—and nervously pulled the sleeves of her baby-blue cardigan sweater over the heels of her hands.

"Don't stress it, Dots. It's fine," I reassured her as I peeled a satisfyingly large piece of paint off the wall. I tossed it in the wastepaper basket and brushed the chips off my hands. "It's just study hall on the last day of midterms. Tomorrow's Friday. I could flip off Vice Principal Miller and still avoid detention."

"Okay, then," Dottie said, smiling. I was pretty sure I wouldn't get into trouble, but I would happily have served my sentence in detention for some girl time with my best friend. I'd been busy studying for midterms, and I knew she had been lonely. I hopped up to sit on the radiator under the painted-shut window and leaned against the glass, shivering a bit as the cold January air seeped into the back of my uniform shirt.

"So, what are you doing to celebrate no more exams?" Dottie asked in a singsong voice, rocking back and forth on her heels and clasping her hands behind her back. "Thrill me with some exciting stories."

I snorted as I let my feet drum out a dull rhythm on the radiator's barely warm metal coils. "My dad got free tickets to some horrible play, and he's dragging me to it. He thinks it will make me 'cultured.'" I added finger quotes around the word. Saturday night would be spent at an interpretative dance version of *Chicken Little* called *Poultry in Motion*. Seriously. When I explained it to Dottie I thought she would never stop laughing.

"That sounds worse than when he got free tickets to see Cinderella as…what was it again?"

"A hippie," I reminded Dottie, chuckling as I unwrapped a Hershey's Kiss. "And instead of a glass slipper, the prince found a giant platform shoe and instead of the ball, she went to Woodstock."

"Why is that so funny, again?" she asked, her pale blond brows furrowed in confusion. I was halfway through an explanation when the bathroom door swung open.

"Having another one of your riveting conversations, Paige?" sneered Pepper Dennis. Oh, how I loved Pepper. The only thing I loved more than Pepper was sarcasm. Most of the students at Holy Assumption ignored me, writing me off as a weirdo and a freak. But much like her namesake, Pepper was irritating when she was in my face. Before I transferred in at the beginning of sophomore year, Pepper was at the top of the class, the student unanimously recognized as most likely to be valedictorian. But now she was number two, after yours truly. I thought number two suited her—the girl really was a little shit. And right now she was giving me a hard time. Again.

"It's better than talking to you, Paprika," I said, punctuating my words by popping the Hershey's Kiss into my mouth with a flourish. Dottie giggled.

"It's Pepper, and you know it," she grumbled, stopping in front of the mirror to expertly apply her eyeliner. Pepper had been dating Matt, universally considered the hottest guy in our class, since the dawn of time, to hear her tell it. In reality, it was since October. You always knew when they were going out after class, because Pepper was in the bathroom, applying flavored lip gloss with the artistic precision of Michelangelo.

"Well, paprika gives me a rash, so you can understand why I'd confuse you with it," I said matter-of-factly, giving Dottie another giggle fit. But her laughter stopped when the door swung open again, and Pepper's best friend, Andie Ward, walked in.

When Andie saw me, a repulsed look crossed her face. The bathroom door slammed shut behind her, and Andie audibly gasped at the idea of being in a room with me. *Oh, the horror.*

"Pepper," Andie whined, her hands fumbling behind her for the doorknob. "What are you doing in here with…her?" She looked at me like I'd just kicked a kitten. I rolled my eyes.

I'm pretty sure I managed to roll them a full three-hundred-and-sixty degrees.

"She was talking to herself when I came in here, you know," Pepper said with a cackle, throwing her eyelash curler in her oversize, sparkly makeup bag. "She's such a freak."

"Psycho," Andie mouthed before stomping out of the bathroom, slamming the bathroom door behind her for emphasis.

I shrugged. This kind of reaction was to be expected when your best friend was a ghost.

I glanced over at Dottie, and she was slightly transparent, a sad look on her face as she started to shimmer away. Whenever she got upset, her ability to stay here faltered. It was annoying talking to a see-through Dottie; that's when I really felt crazy.

"Don't go," I whispered as quietly as I could to Dottie, but my hushed words echoed around the empty bathroom. Dottie gave me that tortured look again, nervously pulling on her sleeves to hide the ugly red scars on her wrists.

"What did you say to me?" Pepper sneered, taking out a tube of cherry lip gloss and pursing her lips.

"I didn't say anything," I snapped, and Dottie became a shade more transparent. I gave her an exasperated look as I toyed with my bracelet, spinning it on my wrist.

"You better not leave. I'm cutting class for you," I said through gritted teeth, pointing my finger at her for emphasis. I heard Pepper exhale loudly.

"I swear, Paige, I'm going to find out how you're cheating and getting straight A's, and then you're out of this school," Pepper vowed, and I rolled my eyes again. I'm a champion eye roller. I could go Olympic level with my talent.

Suddenly, Dottie was standing in front of me, in solid form, huffing indignantly. "She thinks she can threaten you? Well, why don't you ask Pepper about two weeks ago, when she made out with her ex-boyfriend? You know, the dreamboat senior?" Dottie asked, a devious smile playing on her baby-pink lips as she patted her blond hair.

A wicked, delighted smile spread across my face. Sticks and stones may break my bones, but I have a best friend who's a ghost and sees all. So, nyah-nyah-nyah. Suck on that spicy little number, Pepper.

"Hey, Pepperoni," I called, trying—and failing—to keep the amusement out of my voice. "I'll tell you how I'm getting straight A's when you tell Matt that you hooked up with Diego."

Pepper blanched, and she dropped the wand into the sink, leaving a thick globby line of gloss on her chin.

"What are you talking about?" Pepper shot me her most menacing glare, but her shaking voice made her seem as threatening as a baby otter in a tutu.

"You know what I'm talking about," I replied, nearly howling with laughter as Dottie held her arms around an imaginary person, wiggling her tongue as she mimed, as she would say, a "hot 'n' heavy make-out session."

"There's no way you could know about that," Pepper swore, her eyes wide.

"So you admit there's something to know about?" I asked, and Pepper nervously ran her fingers through her short brown hair, making the carefully arranged layers fall askew.

"No one will believe you," Pepper vowed. "You're crazy, and everyone knows it."

Pepper grabbed her lip gloss out of the sink and angrily wiped her chin, smearing the bright red goop all over her skin.

"That's really not your color," I called, and she let a creative list of expletives flow before opening the bathroom door to storm out. But before she stomped away, Pepper stopped to glare at me.

"You think you're better than me, don't you? Well, I'm going to meet my boyfriend and go to my friend Andie's house to hang out with a bunch of friends," she said, stressing the words. "But you? Where are your friends, Paige? You're alone in the bathroom talking to yourself like a freak. Think about that when you're feeling so superior. You're a loser and the entire school knows it," she barked before stalking out, slamming the door behind her. I flinched at the loud smack of the wood reverberating around the bathroom, but recovered when I saw Dottie's mournful expression.

"Well, that was all kinds of dramatic," I scoffed, but Dottie just shook her head rapidly, almost making her hairdo move—almost. They used an impressive amount of hair spray in 1955, after all.

"I'm so sorry. It's because of me—" she began, and I cut her off.

"Don't, Dots. It's okay," I promised her. "I've got a thick skin. Rhino thick. Chain-mail thick."

"But doesn't it ever bother you that she called you a loser?"

"She called me several things. Whatever," I replied, shrugging nonchalantly and doing my best to alleviate Dottie's guilt. It didn't work: she gave me a regretful smile, reaching out her hand to grasp mine, and her fingers passed through my skin, giving me an eerie chill. We both jumped back.

"Sorry!" she apologized, her pink lips twisted in a frown. "I forget sometimes that, you know…"

"That you're…um—"

"That I'm dead. Yeah. That," she interrupted me bluntly, looking down at her saddle shoes.

"Eh, it happens."

"Does it ever freak you out that you talk to ghosts?" Dottie asked, her voice small. "You can tell me. I won't take it personally."

I smiled at her, shaking my head.

"I did the whole freak-out thing after the accident," I reminded her. "Been there, done that, have the souvenir T-shirt."

I'd told Dottie all about it: the accident sophomore year, when I'd pushed some little kid out of the way of a car and gotten hit instead. I'd told her about how I'd died. I only died a little—just under a minute—but it was enough. I had a tendency to imagine the scene as if it came straight out of one of those medical dramas, where ridiculously attractive doctors with perfect touch-me hair and tortured love lives screamed, "Clear!" before shocking my still heart back to life.

But once I came back, things were…different. Not just physically, although I was pretty banged up after getting slammed by a car. And there was the little matter of me talking to people in the hospital that no one else could see. I went for brain scan after brain scan, tried little white pills, big blue pills, yellow pills—I tasted the rainbow when it came to pills—but the doctors couldn't find anything medically wrong with me.

Since I'd lost so much time recovering from the accident—

and, you know, was talking to invisible people—my parents and doctors thought it would be best if I transferred to another—easier—school and repeated sophomore year. Everyone seemed to think that I had some kind of stress-related mental illness—everyone, including me. So, I didn't put up much of a fight when Mom and Dad plucked me out of the competitive, college-prep Vincent Academy on Manhattan's posh Upper East Side, and sent me to Holy Assumption, across town on the Upper West. The schoolwork was less intense, but the blue plaid uniforms were uglier. And possibly made of low-grade steel wool.

I had been pretty quiet at first—merely another nondescript girl in the back of the classroom, terrified of talking to anyone unless I had tangible proof that they were, in fact, tangible. I fulfilled the ultimate new-girl stereotype. I mean, I could have taught a class in it: Quiet Newbie 101. And then I met Dottie. It was October, the second month of my second sophomore year. I was in the crowded third-floor bathroom and noticed Dottie gazing forlornly through the few scratches in the painted-over window that gave a glimpse outside. She looked so sad, so lost. I couldn't ignore her.

"Are you okay?" I asked her gently, and she turned to face me, her brown eyes wide.

"You're—you're talking to me?" she stammered, astonished. A timid smile spread across her face.

"Sure, why not?" I asked, glancing around the bathroom. One girl elbowed another and tilted her chin in my direction. Considering that everyone in the bathroom had ignored this girl, who stared dejectedly at whatever scraps of the outside world she could see from the bathroom window, I decided that Dottie must be the outcast—just like I had been at Vincent Academy after I talked to a figment of my imagination for twenty minutes on the steps of the Metropolitan Museum of Art. That little display made me about as popular as an onion milkshake.

I wanted to reach out, be a friend—be the person no one at my old school had been to the girl who was a little messed up after a car accident. I mean, I did save a random child's life and all when he somehow got away from his mom and ended up in the middle of Tenth Avenue. Talk about a tough crowd.

"Yeah, sure, I'll talk to you," I said, hopping up on the radiator and holding out my hand.

"I'm Paige. Paige Kelly. I just transferred."

Dottie looked at my hand and hesitantly reached out to shake it, then pulled her hand back.

"Dottie Flanagan. I don't think I should try to shake your hand, sorry," she murmured, tugging at the sleeves of the blue cashmere cardigan she wore over her white uniform shirt. I caught a glimpse of angry red slashes on her wrists before she pulled the soft fabric over the heels of her hands.

"What is she doing?" one of the girls in the bathroom hissed to another. I realized that the once-noisy bathroom had gotten quiet—eerily quiet. You could hear every sharp intake of breath, every rustle of fabric as one student tugged on the arm of another. If jaws made noise when they dropped, we'd all have been struck deaf by the thundering sound.

"Why?" I asked, curious. "Are you sick? You don't look sick. I'll shake your hand."

"She's sick, all right—sick in the head," one of the girls snickered, and I whipped my head to stare coldly at her. It was obvious what had caused the scars on Dottie's wrists. I knew what it was like to be mocked, despairing, and so incredibly scared. I couldn't imagine what had brought Dottie to the point of attempting suicide, but whatever it was, the poor girl didn't need to be ridiculed for it.

"You should be embarrassed of yourself." I glared at the girl angrily.

"Me?" Her eyes fluttered in surprise. "You're the one who's embarrassing yourself."

"You should watch your mouth before I smack you in it." My voice was cold, threatening as I glared at the girl—whom I later learned was Pepper. She paled and shuffled back a few steps, intimidated by me. I exhaled in relief—I'd only ever been in one fight, and that was in fourth grade, but at least I talked a pretty good game.

When I turned to continue talking to my mystery friend, she was gone. The immediate area around me was empty— not a surprise, since I'd just threatened a student in defense of…thin air, apparently. My cheeks burned as if I'd lit them on fire. It'd happened again. Again! I'd made friends with some figment of my imagination. I grabbed my backpack and ran out of the bathroom, pushing my way through the girls—some stunned into silence, others taunting me—and raced to the library to hide.

By the next day, it was all over school: Paige Kelly talks to herself. Paige Kelly is a mental case. Paige Kelly threatens people. Ladies and gentlemen, step right up to stare at Paige D. Kelly, the freak of the week.

During my last few weeks at Vincent Academy, I'd kept my long dark hair pulled in front of my face, trying to hide, trying to not make eye contact with anyone as they whispered stories of my imagined conversations. Well, if I was also going to be considered a freak show at my new school, I might as well own it. I kept my hair pulled back into a ponytail and walked down the halls with my head held high as they whispered my new nickname: "Bellevue Kelly," after the infamous mental hospital.

A few days after my first encounter with Dottie, I was in the third-floor girls' room, washing my hands. Alone. When people saw me in the bathroom, they usually walked out so quickly I practically saw smoke at their heels.

"I'm sorry."

The soft voice caused my shoulders to jerk in surprise, and I glanced up to see Dottie appearing over my shoulder in the mirror. She was still wearing the blue cardigan sweater over her buttoned-to-the-neck uniform shirt, her blond hair curled with bangs, like the hairstyle I'd seen on old comedies from the 1950s.

I kept my eyes downcast, trying not to meet her sad brown gaze. Maybe I could cure myself of these hallucinations if I stopped indulging them. I was tired of going to therapy, tired of being forced to try new medications, tired of my parents hovering over me and my classmates running away from me.

"I know you can see me," she said.

I continued washing my hands, scrubbing at the skin and feeling very Lady Macbeth-y.

"I said sorry," Dottie repeated, and I glanced up to see her tugging at the sleeves of her sweater again. "I shouldn't have spoken to you. I was just so happy to be out of there."

"Out of where?" I blurted, before gripping the soapy edges

of the sink and exhaling in frustration. I couldn't help it; I was curious what she meant. Or what this figment of my imagination was trying to tell me. *Might as well embrace the crazy, Paige. At least it's entertaining.*

"You can still see me?" A hopeful smile spread across her face, and I nodded at her reflection. I spun around to look at her, leaning my back against the sink, ignoring how the wet porcelain soaked the back of my shirt.

"Where were you?" I asked, and she sighed again.

"You don't want to know." Dottie frowned, looking down at her shoes. Whatever she was thinking of caused her to visibly flinch, and when she spoke again, her voice was despondent. "It's a distorted version of here. That's the only way I can describe it. It's dark. It's lonely."

"I don't understand."

"And there are scary things…" she whispered, shutting her eyes tightly. But then her eyes popped open with excitement. "But out of nowhere, I felt this energy, and I had to follow it. Suddenly, I was back here. No one else could see me—but you could."

"What kind of scary things did—" I began to ask, but the bathroom door opened, and Pepper walked in. When she saw me, she stopped short and called over her shoulder.

"Let's go to another bathroom. Bellevue Kelly is in here having a positively enthralling conversation with the sink." Delighted peals of laughter answered her, echoing in the hall until the door slammed shut. I gritted my teeth and stared at the white tile floor.

"You're a figment of my imagination. You're not real," I stated, more as a reminder to myself.

"I'm not a figment of your imagination. I'm—well, I guess I'm a ghost." Dottie cocked her head to one side as a look of awe flashed across her pretty face. "Wow, I've never said that out loud before," she said breathily, before adding, "Then again, I haven't had someone to talk to in a while."

"That's crazy," I scoffed, folding my arms across my chest. "There are no such things as ghosts."

"Well, would you rather that I was a ghost or a product of your fevered mind?" she countered, and I studied her curiously. There was something...different...about Dottie, now that I scrutinized her more closely.

"You do kind of glow." Her skin seemed luminous—she exuded a faint light, as if a soft candle illuminated her from within.

"That's probably just my sparkling personality," she said, giving me a winning smile.

"Look, if you want proof, just look in my freshman yearbook," Dottie said, pointing a pink-manicured nail to the door. "All the past school yearbooks should be in the library. They were when I went here, at least. Look up 1954. I was a freshman then."

I nodded, feeling a little light-headed, before bolting from the bathroom. I felt like running home, but I ran down to the library instead. *Now you're taking orders from the imaginary people, Paige. This is how serial killers get started.*

With shaking hands, I pulled the 1954 yearbook off the shelves and rested it on the nearest table. There, between Margaret Falconi and Donald Foster, I found Dorothy June Flanagan.

My eyes met the black-and-white version of her brown

eyes, and I felt like I was falling—like the room had shifted. I pulled out the nearest chair and collapsed in it, gripping the edge of the table for support. My heart was pounding, and my stomach, well, my stomach was probably somewhere in the basement. Yearbook Dottie had slightly shorter hair, but it was still flawlessly arranged, with little bangs that curled over her forehead. An untroubled, pretty grin brightened her face, as she smiled at me from the page, as if to say, "See? I told you so."

Because it was her.

Because she was real.

Coincidence. It has to be a coincidence, right? Underneath her name, her extracurricular activities were listed—Glee Club, Spring Fling Committee. My fingers fumbled as I flipped through the book, leaving small creases in the glossy photos because my hands were trembling so badly. I quickly found the page devoted to the enchanted garden-themed dance and saw a photo of Dottie. Her corsaged wrist rested on the shoulder of a boy who looked like the fifties ideal of the all-American teen idol: tall, broad-shouldered, deeply dimpled and clean-cut. She gazed up at him with a blissed-out grin as they danced under a poorly made papier-mâché flower arch.

My heart was pounding. Twenty minutes ago, I thought I'd imagined the whole thing. Now I knew my figment had a boyfriend. I wanted to know more. I needed to know more, see more—have more proof in front of me that Dottie existed. I flipped to the Glee Club page and searched it for another photo of the ghost girl. There, in the bottom left, my figment appeared again. In the picture, Dottie stood next to an older girl, who looked remarkably similar. They both held sheet music in front of them, their mouths open in song. The caption read: *The Flanagan sisters, Dottie and Lorraine, rehearse for their solos in the spring choral presentation.*

Whoa. My figment had a family. I set off in search of Lorraine Flanagan, finding her in the juniors section.

I slammed the book shut, the shaking that had overtaken my hands now spreading throughout my entire body.

*My figments are real. They're ghosts.*

My mind reeled, thinking of everyone I'd spoken to that no one else had seen. The older woman at the bus stop. The playful young man outside the Met. The woman in Central Park. I exhaled slowly, not sure of how to feel. Was I relieved that I wasn't crazy, or crazy because I was accepting something otherworldly as an answer? Could I at least be sure I wasn't about to turn into a serial killer? A brief image of myself in court, passionately telling the judge, "The ghosts told me to do it," flickered through my head.

I stood up and carefully slid the book back into its space on the shelf, my fingers brushing the worn blue-and-gold spine of the 1955 yearbook. I yanked the book off the shelf and rapidly flipped through the pages, looking for a photo of Dottie. I needed more evidence that she once lived—that the girl in the bathroom was, indeed, a ghost. But when I didn't find Dottie listed among the sophomores, I found myself looking up her sister, Lorraine. She was beautiful in that polished, fifties way, with blond bangs rolled thickly, eyebrows perfectly plucked and arched. But Lorraine's smile didn't quite reach her eyes—they looked heartsick. Grief-stricken. And where most seniors penned cryptic comments and inside jokes for their yearbook inscriptions, Lorraine's merely said, "Polkadot-tie, I miss you every day."

I grabbed the yearbook and ran back up to the bathroom, but Dottie wasn't there.

"Boo," I heard from behind me, and I dropped the year-book on the floor. The binding hit the white tile with a loud slap that reverberated in the bathroom, and I yelped.

"Sorry, I couldn't help it!" she said with a lighthearted gig-gle, her brown eyes glinting with mischievous joy as I picked up the yearbook.

"This is about you, isn't it?" I asked gingerly, flipping through the book and opening it to her sister's page.

Dottie studied her sister's words, her eyes misting over with what looked like tears, and I wondered if ghosts could cry.

"Oh, Rainey," she murmured, blinking back the mist. "Of course she would do something like that. I should have talked to her before…before I…" Her voice trailed off, her eyes sorrowful. And then Dottie told me her story, about how she rashly decided to kill herself after she found out she was pregnant. I told her my story, which sounded like a fairy tale compared to her heartbreaking, tragic end. I didn't get home until nine o'clock that night, which led my very worried par-ents to ground me.

But I didn't care: it's not like I was going to go anywhere that was more intriguing than the third-floor bathroom at school. It was where Dottie died—where she felt the stron-gest. I spent every free period, every lunch hour, in the bath-room talking with Dottie. When I was in class, she roamed the halls, spying on teachers, sometimes whispering answers to me when I was stuck on a test. It was pretty helpful, since

I couldn't exactly concentrate on my studies while my mind reeled with the fact that I could communicate with spirits. And Dottie made it her personal mission to make sure I'd beat Pepper as valedictorian, since she felt responsible for my social leprosy.

There was only one downside to having a ghost as a best friend—other than people thinking I was insane and all—Dottie couldn't leave the school. When she was in my world, she was tethered to Holy Ass, as they had nicknamed the school when Dottie was a student. When I was away from the building for too long—home sick or on vacation—Dottie was sucked back to that dark world, as she called it. Where it was at once hollow and filled with nightmares. She didn't like to talk about it, no matter how many times I'd tried to wheedle some details out of her.

My cell phone beeped, breaking me out of my reverie. I didn't bother to look at it—I got the same text every day from my father, just "checking in."

"You have to go?"

"Yeah. You'd think I was brought home regularly by the cops or something, the way my parents stalk my every move," I huffed. "I'm not a delinquent. I'm just apparently crazy. But you know my parents."

"No, I actually don't," Dottie reminded me with a wry smile, and I instantly regretted my off-the-cuff comment. "But I wish I did. I wish we could have slumber parties, listen to records, watch color TV and all that." She smiled bashfully. "I get so lonely."

"Me, too," I admitted. My time away from Holy Assumption wasn't an undead nightmare like Dottie's, but Bellevue

Kelly's phone didn't exactly ring a whole lot. I was a little lonely, too.

"Maybe you'll meet a boy soon," Dottie chirped, not-so-subtly segueing to her favorite topic—boys. She was perpetually a boy-crazy fifteen-year-old and, in spite of her crushing experiences with the opposite sex, remained a true romantic.

I, however, was a realist and merely snorted in reply. "Yeah, wish me luck finding a guy that doesn't mind when I have a scintillating conversation with the walls." I'd gotten better at telling the difference between ghosts and humans, but every now and then I screwed up, earning wary glances from anyone within earshot. The last guy I dated—okay, Chris was the only guy I'd dated, for a whopping streak of three dates—was two years ago, back during sophomore year at my first school. On our final date, I'd talked to a ghost by the carousel in Central Park. You could say it was a bit of a romance-killer.

"You should talk more to that new boy. He's quiet, but he seems nice," Dottie mused, "and he's always borrowing pens from you and talking to you about assignments."

"Who, that Logan guy?" I asked, surprised, and Dottie nodded, wagging her arched eyebrows up and down. "He wants my pens. Not my sweet, sweet lovin'."

"Your pens are pink with feathers and glitter and purple paw prints on them," Dottie said, folding her arms, before adding with a saucy tone, "I doubt it's really your pens he wants."

"Oh, please," I scoffed. "He'd use crayons if he didn't have anything to write with. I'm pretty sure I'd use eyeliner if I was pen-less before a pop quiz."

"Look, he's not exactly my type," she said, waving her

hands dismissively, "but he's a potential dreamboat if he got a proper haircut."

"He's a transfer who hasn't heard yet what a psycho I'm supposed to be and suffers from a debilitating inability to bring in school supplies," I countered. I didn't tell Dottie that I'd started bringing in extra pens in case Logan needed to borrow one. Why encourage her? "Besides, Dots, you make it sound like he's fawning all over me when he's merely polite." Logan had slid into the seat across from me in the library only last week while I ate Hershey's Kisses and studied Spanish. He'd quietly asked questions about our assignment as Dottie hovered over me, gushing about him and offering incredibly outdated advice on flirting. She practically had me dropping a handkerchief, leaving me wondering if she was from 1950 or 1850. I'd done my best to tune her out—even casually scratched the side of my cheek with my middle finger to give her the hint—but Dottie wasn't much for subtlety.

I jumped off the radiator, my feet slapping against the white tile floor with a dull thud. I wanted an end to this conversation—quickly. There was no point in getting my hopes up. I was destined to check "forever alone" under my relationship status for the rest of my life.

"Maybe you'll meet a guy who can talk to ghosts," she said, a faraway look on her face. "When you come back to visit me after graduation, you'll have some wonderful stories to share about the dreamy Big Man on Campus who fell for you at college."

Dottie was too busy swooning over the fluffy fairy tale she was spinning about my fictional college life to think about what me going to college really meant: that Dottie would stay trapped on the other side.

Dottie couldn't follow me when I left the confines of our school, and she couldn't seem to materialize in our world unless I stayed close to where she'd died—the third floor of our school.

"I'll walk you down—I want to be near the library," Dottie told me. I nodded, and pulled open the bathroom door for Dottie. She didn't like walking through walls.

"Why the library?" I asked as we slowly made our way through the empty hallway to the staircase. "Do you read the books people leave out or…?"

I trailed off as dread colored Dottie's face, and she shook her head rapidly, as if she were trying to shake off whatever mental image had rattled her.

"The library—it isn't that bad over there," she stammered, looking at the black steps as we slowly thudded down the stairs, her footsteps a faint echo of mine. She was quiet for a bit, and her voice was barely a whisper when she continued. "It's not really scary in the library—just quiet. When I end up getting sucked back into the dark world tonight, I'd rather be in the library."

"I wish you could stay on my side tonight," I said, my heart breaking a little as Dottie smiled wistfully.

"I wish I could stay here permanently," Dottie said with a humorless laugh. She wanted nothing more than a second chance at life—and not to have impulsively decided suicide in the school bathroom was a better option than facing her domineering father and telling him his fifteen-year-old daughter was pregnant. But Dottie's boyfriend—the all-American dreamboat, Bobby—had disappeared. She'd felt all alone. Abandoned. So Dottie had made the worst decision possible. She'd told me she'd regretted it after slicing into her second wrist, but of course by then it was too late. She'd ended her short, promising life before it had even begun.

Dottie stared down at her wrists, her shoulders slumping. I couldn't even give her a hug. I felt the tears begin to prick my eyes as we rounded the corner into the library—just in time for me to smack directly into Logan Bradley.

# 02

"SORRY ABOUT THAT," I MUMBLED, WIPING THE few tears that leaked out on the heel of my hand. Pepper seeing me talk to myself was one thing—I felt a smug satisfaction in her freaking out over it—but getting caught all weepy by the one person who had been halfway decent to me? Embarrassing didn't even cover it—even if he was just using me for my school supplies. I might have to invent a new word to accurately capture the humiliation. I stared down at Logan's scuffed black Converse, unwilling to meet his eyes with my probably bloodshot ones. How he got away without wearing the uniform-mandated brown shoes, I had no idea.

"It's cool— Hey, are you okay?" Logan asked softly. I reluctantly looked up into his warm, light brown eyes, shaded under the brim of his navy Yankees cap—another uniform infraction that went unpunished.

"Yeah. I'm fine," I insisted, doing my best to smile brightly.

"Are you sure?" he asked. "Because you're kind of crying right now."

"Flirt, Paige! Bat your eyelashes at him. Your eyes don't look that puffy, and your nose isn't too red." Dottie barked more not-so-helpful flirting tips, and the corner of Logan's mouth curled into an amused smile, his shoulders rising in silent laughter. I felt like strangling my dead friend—until I remembered that Logan couldn't hear Dottie.

Which meant he was laughing at me. Logan. The one person who had seemed halfway decent.

"Don't worry about it," I snapped, angrily dashing the backs of my hands across my cheeks. "I'm sure you've heard by now that I'm the resident crazy girl. Crying in the hallway's just another sideshow performance by Bellevue Kelly."

Logan's smile promptly vanished. He took a step back, his eyebrows pulling together as a dark look briefly crossed his face. He folded his arms and stared at me.

"I don't think you're crazy. And that's the dumbest nickname I've ever heard," he said, sounding annoyed.

"Then why are you laughing at me?" I countered, narrowing my eyes.

"I'm not laughing at you." Logan's eyes flickered from mine to stare down the hallway behind me.

"Miller's coming. That's who I was laughing at," he added, giving me a pointed look. "He's got his toupee on crooked."

"Oh," I said sheepishly. I toyed with my bracelet, embarrassed by how quickly I had rushed to judge him. What do you know, Logan Bradley's an endangered species: a legitimately nice human being.

"I don't know who he thinks he's fooling with that rug," I muttered.

"An actual rug would look more realistic," Logan said seriously. "It's like he skinned a teddy bear and glued it on his head."

I gaped at him—who knew Logan had jokes?—before bursting into laughter.

"What? It's really bad," he said, and I just nodded in agreement.

"He looks like he's in a bad mood," Logan said, tilting his head as he stared down the hall. "You should probably get out of here before he finds a reason to give you detention."

"I like this one for you, Paige," Dottie gushed next to me. If her eyeballs could have popped out with giant cartoon hearts, they would have. "Now get out of here before you embarrass yourself. We'll talk boy strategy tomorrow. I already have some ideas!" Good thing she was a ghost, because Dottie was about as smooth as gravel.

I mumbled a quick goodbye before heading off to my locker, trying to avoid looking back at Logan as my perpetually boy-crazy friend remained behind, staring goofily up at him. I grabbed my coat and was walking out of the school's thick metal front doors when I heard Miller's unmistakable gruff voice in the hallway behind me. He had four students I'd never seen before in tow, and it looked like he was giving them a tour. There were three girls and a boy—a tall, dark-haired boy who stared after me curiously. He gave me a slow smile before turning his attention back to Miller. That smile sent chills racing down my arms, leaving gooseflesh in their wake, but not in a good way. It was less Mr. Sexypants and more Mr. Windowless Van.

The door wheezed shut behind me with a hiss of the air brake as I stepped out onto the concrete front steps of Holy Assumption, only to see Pepper and her friends clustered on the corner, Pepper smearing her carefully applied lip gloss all over Matt's skin as they sucked face. *You stay classy, Pepper.*

I shoved my gloveless hands in my pockets and changed direction to avoid Pepper's sycophants as I began the long walk home from the Upper West Side to my family's apartment on West Forty-Fourth Street. The subway wasn't an option for me—it was full of ghosts, and not all of them were as pleasant as Dottie.

I replayed my brief encounter with Logan in my mind as I walked. I didn't know much about him. Logan had transferred into Holy Assumption at the beginning of junior year and was pretty quiet in class. He hung in the back, observing everyone. I tried to think of all the times I'd seen him in the halls, and I couldn't recall ever seeing him with a group of friends—or even one friend—although I thought I'd seen Andie sidling up to him a few times. But he shouldn't be so desperate for friends that he needed me, the social pariah, as an ally. Maybe he was merely a legitimately nice person, nonjudgmental and kind. I'd read about those mythical figures in books, although I sure as hell hadn't met any. I'd figured they'd gone extinct with the dodo bird.

And what was up with new kid Smirky McSmileson giving me the eye?

I kicked a coffee-stained paper cup into the gutter, where it rested on top of a stubborn mound of soot-covered snow that refused to melt. I felt a little cruel dismissing Smirky as creepy—hadn't I complained enough about being labeled with that particular epithet? But I brushed that last thought aside quickly. The new kid would hear I was a psycho soon enough, and he'd want to run from me, not flash borderline shady smiles my way.

Shrugging off all thoughts of school, I put my headphones on, cranking up some bootleg live music as I walked home. I daydreamed about the concerts I wish I could have seen until my numb fingers fumbled with the keys to the front door of the five-story apartment building I lived in with my parents. We were on the second floor, in a walk-up apartment. My mom always talked about someday moving—her dream was to be on the fortieth floor of some shiny glass high-rise with majestic views of the Hudson River—but apartment 2W worked for me. I was terrified of heights. Besides, I had a pretty sweet deal: my bedroom was at the opposite end of the apartment from my parents' bedroom, which meant I could blast music as loudly as I wanted without bothering them. My keys had just unlocked the dead bolt when I heard my father cheerfully call my name over the loud screech of the hinges.

I'd been doing so much better lately in my parents' eyes— but they still insisted on babysitting me, even though I should have been wrapping up my high school career and planning for college by now. After a few too many one-sided conversations, Dad had changed his hours at work—he was a driver for a car service, which meant he drove rich people all over town in fancy leather-upholstered town cars—and switched to the night shift so he could be home when I got out of school. But lately, he'd been talking about returning to his old schedule. Which meant my parents were beginning to trust that I could be left alone without cracking up. Which meant—cue the chorus of singing angels—no more 'round-the-clock supervision. I forced a bright smile on my face as I entered the living room, where I promptly began coughing.

"Cooking again, Dad?" I asked, waving my hand in front of my face to dispel some of the acrid-smelling smoke. I crossed the living room and pushed open the narrow window, in spite of the frosty temperatures outside.

"I know it smells funny, but I promise it'll be delicious," my father called from the kitchen, his shock of red hair visible even through the thick smoke billowing up from the stove. Richard Kelly had two weaknesses—cooking and complimentary crap. He'd sign up for a new credit card or take a customer survey faster than you could say "freebie" if it meant he got a T-shirt or towel…or tickets to some horrible play that he'd usually force me to attend with him. I headed into the narrow kitchen, and sure enough, he was wearing an apron splattered with fresh stains that nearly obscured the name of an already-defunct barbecue sauce company on the front, and stirring a pot filled with something that looked like it still had a pulse.

"Food's supposed to make my mouth water, not my eyes," I teased, leaning my back against the scratched white counter where a Thai cookbook was propped up. He rolled his eyes at me, and I grinned. I'd inherited my dad's blue eyes—and his penchant for sarcastic eye rolling—but I had my mom, Anna's, hair, which was thick, wavy and such a dark brown it looked black. I quickly changed the subject—Dad was touchy about his creative Franken-meals, and I didn't want to put him in a bad mood, especially if he was thinking about releasing me from Overprotective Parent Jail.

"What time do you have to be at work tonight?" I asked,

stealing a handful of peanuts from the bowl on the counter and popping a few into my mouth. My dad playfully smacked my hand and grabbed the rest of the nuts, stirring them into the pot. I eyed the creation cautiously. I think he might have invented a new color.

"I was thinking about watching a marathon of old movies to celebrate the end of finals. Watch with me before you're off to work?"

"Probably not, kiddo," Dad said, giving me a wistful smile. "I have an airport pickup, so I have to leave right after dinner. But how did it go today? Any surprises?"

*You could say that.* My odd encounter with Logan flickered through my mind—"I'm not laughing at you...I don't think you're crazy"—and my forced cheerful smile fell a miniscule amount before I brightly said, "Everything was fine."

My father, of course, didn't miss the slight crack in my facade.

"Everything okay?" he asked, searching my face.

"Yeah, everything's great."

"Paige, be honest," my father ordered, setting down his wooden spoon on the counter.

"I am being honest," I insisted, then jerked my chin toward the spoon. "You might want to move that. It looks like your science project is burning a hole in the countertop."

"Don't try to distract me. You looked troubled."

I flinched. I hated that word. *There's nothing medically wrong with Paige, she's just troubled. Take these pills.* It was a warm and fuzzy term for crazy. And I wasn't crazy. I spoke to ghosts. There was a difference.

"Did something happen at school, Paige? Did you, um, have

one of *those* conversations? I know it's been several months since you've had an episode—"

"Everything's fine," I interrupted him, agitated. "I just finished a week of midterms, Dad. What do you want from me, jazz hands? Show me someone who gets thrilled about midterms and I'll show you a masochist."

"There's no need to get snippy, young lady," Dad scolded me before softening his tone, adding, "You just seem a little... upset by something."

I pursed my lips, contemplating how to handle this. I was not about to tell my overprotective father I had been mulling over a confusing conversation with a boy. I'd rather tell him I talked to the mailbox for an hour. He'd probably prefer that, too.

"I had a hard time with a few questions on my history final. I'm just nervous about how I did."

"I'm sure you aced it, honey," my dad said, exhaling in relief. Sure, I aced it, only because my ghost best friend sauntered over to Mr. Malhotra's desk and read the answers over his shoulder.

Whatever was in the pot triggered another coughing fit, so I excused myself and retreated into my bedroom. I stripped off my boxy, blue plaid uniform skirt in favor of black yoga pants and a bright yellow sweatshirt my dad had gotten from some insurance company, and flung myself on the bed. My black-and-white cat, Mercer, curled up at my feet, his chin resting on my ankles.

"At least you don't think I'm crazy," I murmured, and Mercer—named after the street where I found him wandering as a kitten—continued to purr, his throat vibrating against my socks.

I managed to play the part of the perfect, untroubled daughter over dinner—fortunately, my mom brought home Fat Sal's pizza when she returned from her secretarial job, so we didn't have to eat whatever maniacal creation my dad had made. I'm pretty sure it screamed when he threw it in the trash— and I told him so over dinner, which made my mom laugh and my dad pretend to pout before laughing along with us. *Paige is making jokes, look at our funny, witty, un-crazy daughter.* My dad even mentioned he was considering taking my mom to the play on Saturday instead of me, which would leave me with a rare, unsupervised night at home.

I went to bed with a blissful smile on my face, my head filled with the possibilities of being home the day after to-morrow, alone and unsupervised, for the first time in nearly three years. I could dig out my old art books and sketch or paint. At Therapist Number Three's orders, my parents had confiscated my artwork as if it were evidence in a criminal case. They'd inspected it for telltale clues of what was mak-ing me insane. I guess they were looking for grisly illustra-tions of car accidents and bloody murder scenes. Instead, they just found a bunch of pencil portraits and detailed sketches of old buildings around the city that I thought looked cool. The only thing killed was my desire to continue painting or drawing. But this coming Saturday, I could sketch for hours, uninterrupted, without anyone checking on me or looking at my drawings to make sure I wasn't creating some maca-bre scene. Or I could watch TV in my pajamas. Win-win, if you ask me.

It snowed overnight, dusting the streets and sidewalks with a fine, slippery coat, and my walk to school took longer than usual, so I didn't have the chance to rehash things with Dottie first thing in the morning. My first class was gym, and I barely had time to stash my jewelry in my locker and change into my shorts and T-shirt before the first bell. I didn't wear piles of jewelry, but we weren't allowed to wear any during gym. It made Fridays living hell for Tabitha Nakamura, a junior with about ten piercings in each ear.

Aside from a couple of studs in each ear, the only jewelry I wore on Fridays were a ring and the platinum filigree bracelet given to me by Melody, the mother of the kid I saved. It had belonged to Mel's great-grandmother, passed down through generations in their family. I'd insisted that Melody didn't owe me anything, but my mom said it was important to her to give me something.

She didn't understand how Dylan had ended up in the street. He hadn't even remembered how he got there. But Dylan was a rambunctious kid, and it had been Melody's greatest fear that he'd run off into the street and get hurt. She'd insisted that she was holding his hand tightly one second—and then he was in the middle of the intersection at Tenth Avenue and Forty-Ninth Street the next, terrified and frozen in place as a car made a very wide, very dangerous turn from the far lane, nearly hitting the four-year-old. I had been walking home from a friend's house, saw what was about to happen, and shoved Dylan out of the way. The driver had slammed on the brakes and swerved, missing Dylan and ramming right into me. Fortunately for me, we hadn't been far from a hospital. Melody had begged me to accept the bracelet, and finally I did, mostly to make her feel better. Now, I probably couldn't get through a day without it. I wore it every day as a reminder: when someone called me a loser, I could touch the bracelet and remember that there were a few people who were glad I was around.

And after gym class, it was gone.

I knew I'd locked my locker. And I knew I'd left it on the top shelf, right next to my earrings. But now, the space was empty. I pulled everything out, flipped through textbooks and even checked the sleeves of my coat, but I knew I wouldn't find it. I always put it in the same spot, and it was gone. I stared at the empty dark green metal shelf, willing the bracelet to appear.

"I guess she lost something—other than her mind, I mean," Andie Ward sniped from across the locker room, earning a few quiet snickers in reply.

I shut my eyes and took a deep breath. "I can't find my bracelet," I said before turning around to face the locker room. "Has anyone seen it? It's a platinum bracelet, with a lacy, scrolled design. Anyone?"

Silence.

"Is she talking to us?" Andie stage-whispered, and the laughter this time wasn't as muted.

"Yes, Andie, I am talking to you," I said, making an effort to keep my voice steady. "To everyone, actually. I had my bracelet in my locker. Now, it's gone. Please. Has anyone seen it?"

A few girls offered muttered "Sorry's" and "No, I haven't seen it." Tabitha even offered to help me look, and we fell to our knees and peered under the lockers, seeing nothing but dust and—oh, gross—mouse traps.

"Sorry, Paige. I hope you find it," Tabitha said, twisting her last earring in place before grabbing her bag. "I gotta get to class."

I thanked Tabitha and sat down on the bench between the row of lockers, steeling myself to face my next class when all I wanted to do was go home.

The first bell rang, and I put my things back in my locker, resolving to come back at lunch and break into Andie's locker if I needed to. Maybe she took it…maybe she's helping Pepper get revenge for my comment about her extracurricular activities with Diego. I couldn't figure out how someone could get the combination on my lock, though. Hadn't I locked it?

I ran up the stairs to homeroom, my hand automatically reaching for my right wrist to play with the bracelet, and my mood fell even more when I was reminded that it wasn't there.

That's when I heard him.

"Paige—hey, Paige, wait up," Logan called. His footsteps thudded on the stairs as he raced after me. I fumbled in my bag for a pen and grabbed the first one I felt—a pink one with feathers on the top.

"Here," I said quickly, shoving the pen at him as I continued to run up the stairs. Matching my pace, he took the pen and stared at it with confusion.

"What? No, I don't need a pen. Um, you dropped something," he said, his cheeks flushed pink and his voice a little breathy. I stopped short, pulling over to the side of the stairway to make way for the crush of students running up the stairs, and slid my backpack off my shoulder to inspect its contents. I figured I hadn't zipped it shut in my frenzy over my bracelet, but it was closed.

"This is yours, right?" Logan reached into the pocket of his black school pants before extending his hand. There, coiled in his palm, was my bracelet.

Relief flooded through my system, making me almost light-headed. I dropped my backpack from my hands, and it fell down a few steps as I grabbed the delicate bracelet.

"Oh, my God! Where did you find this? Thank you so much!" I grasped the bracelet in my fist and curled it close to my heart. "This is really sentimental, so I was freaking out a little bit," I admitted.

"Oh, I'm sorry," Logan said, and I blinked in surprise.

"Sorry? Why are you sorry?" I asked. "I'd probably be spending tonight listening to depressing music, wearing a black veil and writing poetry to my lost, abandoned bracelet if it weren't for you. So, thanks."

I draped the bracelet over my wrist as I tried to refasten it.

"Wow, you're really..." His voice trailed off as he took his baseball hat off, running one hand through his floppy brown hair before setting the cap back on his head.

"I'm really...?" I repeated, my voice rising in pitch.

"You're really random—but in a good way," he hastily added when he saw the slightly insulted look on my face. "I like it. I mean, it's funny."

"Oh. Um, sorry?" I stammered, thrown by his comment.

"Don't be sorry," Logan said, his lips quirked up in a smile. "So, do you want to get it on?" He held his hand out to me.

My eyebrows shot up as I stared at his outstretched hand before glancing at the students around me. I didn't have a ton of experience with the opposite sex, but things couldn't have changed that much from when I dated Chris two years ago. *Who asks that? People don't just ask that question in public… do they? I thought only Dottie used that term. What the hell had I missed while I was talking to ghosts?*

"Um, what—what did you say?" I sputtered.

Logan flicked his fingers toward my wrist. "The bracelet? You need help getting that on? You want to wear it now, right?"

"Oh, yeah—of course. Thanks," I stammered, handing him the bracelet and holding my wrist out, hoping he didn't see how flustered I was. I said a silent thanks that Dottie wasn't there. She would have told me to grab his hand and kiss it, most likely. Or tell me I should pretend to faint and let him catch me.

"How did you know this was mine?" I asked as he grasped the ends of the bracelet. The tips of his fingers lightly brushed against the skin on the inside of my wrist, and I felt a shiver run down my spine. Who knew the skin on the inside of my wrist was so sensitive?

"I saw it fall off your wrist," Logan said, closing the clasp on my bracelet.

"What?" I shook my head. "No. This was taken from my locker."

"I saw it fall off your wrist just now," Logan insisted. "I just saw it happen. That's how I knew it was yours."

"But I could have sworn…" I began, confused, and Logan just shrugged, giving me a sympathetic smile. The second bell rang—and we both had to run up the stairs, me to homeroom, Logan to whatever class he had next. I twisted the bracelet now that it was safely back on my wrist, satisfying my nervous urge, which was growing stronger. Had I imagined that I took off the bracelet? Why didn't I get yelled at in gym class for wearing it, then? Did I put it on and forget about it?

And then a small, but strong voice in the back of my head whispered my biggest fear.

*Maybe you really are losing your mind.*

I opened my homeroom door, hoping Mrs. Clifton would be late to class so I could silently puzzle over my confusing morning and avoid detention. Instead, she was standing in front of the room, introducing three of the four new students I'd seen with Vice Principal Miller yesterday. Guess Miller managed to scare off the fourth prospective student. Not surprising: he was as inviting as a poison-ivy welcome mat.

"Ah, Miss Kelly, did you take the scenic route?" she asked, raising an eyebrow at me over her glasses. Everything about Mrs. Clifton was severe—she was all hard lines and angles. Her eyebrows were perfectly symmetrical, inverted Vs that peaked just underneath blunt, razor-perfect gray bangs so sharp, they could cut salami.

"Sorry," I mumbled, sliding into my seat and wondering if I'd have detention for the first time in my life or if Mrs. Clifton would give me a break.

"She probably stopped to have a chat with the fire extinguisher," Pepper stage-whispered from the rear of the classroom, eliciting laughter from the back row. I gritted my teeth. But the whisper in the back of my head got louder. *Maybe Pepper is right about you. Maybe you really are insane. You had the bracelet on the entire time, and you forgot about it. Blacking out— isn't that a sign of mental illness?*

I stared at my bracelet, wondering how it had fallen off my wrist. There was no other explanation. It's not like Logan had gone into the girls' locker room and stolen my bracelet. And my lock hadn't been open… I must have forgotten to take it off. Or I put it on after gym and forgot about it. The clasp must be broken. It is an antique, after all. I'm just lucky Logan saw it fall off my wrist.

I inspected the clasp—it looked fine to me—but I didn't want to risk losing the bracelet again. I unfastened it and slid it into the left pocket on my uniform shirt. I would ask my mom to look at it when I got home. She'd been saying she needed to have a new battery put in her watch. Maybe we could get a new clasp put on my bracelet, so I wouldn't lose it. I was so caught up in my thoughts that I didn't even realize Mrs. Clifton was standing over me, handing me a detention slip, a hard smile on her prim face.

I folded the pink scrap of paper and slipped it into the pocket along with my bracelet. *At least you finally have plans on a Friday for once.* The bitter thought bounced around in my head.

"Check in with Vice Principal Miller after school," Mrs. Clifton ordered, shaking her head at me with a disappointed look on her face.

"Now, class, as I was saying, we have three new students today," she said as she strolled to the front of the classroom to stand next to them. "Please welcome Blaise, Della and Aiden. They'll be in your classes, so, please, help them find their way around the school. Preferably on time," she added, casting a look in my direction. *C'mon, lady. It's the day after midterms, cut me a break.* I almost scowled before I realized that would do nothing except earn me more time in detention.

Of course, the three new students were now staring directly at me, thanks to Mrs. Clifton. Blaise was tall and lean, with pin-straight red hair that hung to her waist, and pale, thin legs that stuck out from underneath her skirt. She was bare-legged—and it was twenty degrees outside! I checked out Della's legs, and noticed that she had the good sense to wear tights—but her skirt was so short it was practically a belt. Where Blaise was plain—the only remarkable thing about her being the look of sheer disdain on her face as her dark eyes flitted around the classroom—Della was stunning. She was short and ridiculously gorgeous—and all curves, I noticed a little jealously. I self-consciously folded my arms in front of my own chest, which was only impressive when I was retaining water.

Della cocked an eyebrow and gave Pepper's boyfriend, Matt Vogel, a lusty smile before mouthing "hi" to him. I didn't know whether it was impressive, or tacky, that she managed to zero in on the best-looking guy in school before homeroom was over. I snuck a quick look behind me to see Pepper's reaction, and she was glaring at Della with the "die-die-die" stare she normally reserved for me. I sighed in relief. Finally, someone new for Pepper to hate. I briefly wondered what had happened to the fourth student I had seen—a blonde girl, I think—then turned my attention to the last new student, the one who had given me the Captain Creepy smile yesterday.

Remember when I said Matt was the best-looking guy in school? Now that I had a closer look at Aiden, I knew that Matt's reign was over. Aiden was, without a doubt, beautiful. Tall, angular and black-haired, with eyes that looked vi-olet. I smiled to myself, flattered that someone who looked like that had thrown me such a flirty look yesterday. *Hmm… maybe he's not so creepy. You're just used to people treating you like you're a pariah.*

And then I realized Aiden was looking right at me, notic-ing that I was, essentially, gawking at him in the middle of the classroom. *If he's Captain Creepy, you're the General.* I dropped my eyes immediately, positive that I'd just confirmed what-ever Aiden would eventually hear about me being a weirdo.

I kept my eyes on my notebook for the rest of homeroom and hunched down low in my desk, managing to avoid being called on in all my morning classes. Good thing—I had at least one of the new kids in each of my classes, and they were already staring at me curiously, probably waiting for me to talk to my pencil. Usually Dottie would show up in math—she particularly liked standing behind my teacher, Dr. Walsh, and mimicking the way she waved the ruler around. Walsh looked like she was conducting an orchestra, the way she wielded that thing. But Dottie had been suspiciously absent all morning. Maybe she was giving me a break, since her last words to me were instructions to not embarrass myself, and she was often the unwitting source of my humiliation—usually by making me laugh.

I headed to Dottie's third-floor bathroom during lunch, anxious to talk things over with my best friend. It wasn't like me to be so forgetful—or to not even notice that my bracelet was on my wrist. I played with it enough.

I patted the bracelet in my front pocket, feeling the reas-suring weight of the platinum swirls against my fingertips as I entered the bathroom. It was empty as usual, since most of the students were in the basement cafeteria. I hopped up on my usual perch on the barely warm radiator and pulled the tomato-and-cheese sandwich I'd made the night before out of my backpack, banging my heels on the metal coils as I waited for Dottie to appear.

Finally, she shimmered into existence in front of me and gave me a big, relieved smile as she jumped up and down on the white tile floor.

"Finally made it," she said breathily—an impressive feat, since Dottie didn't exactly need to breathe.

"About time!" I agreed, after I swallowed a mouthful of sandwich. "Where have you been?"

"I've been trying to see you all day, but I couldn't find you," she said, her brow creased with concern. "I was starting to get worried that I couldn't come to this side anymore."

"Well, you're here now," I reassured her—even though my stomach began to churn with worry. Why hadn't Dottie been able to break through? She usually just followed my "energy," she said. It's not like we had maps or directions for crossing between her dark world and mine.

"But it took me long enough," Dottie said, pretending to wipe her forehead with the back of her hand. "And I've been dying to talk to you about Logan."

At the mention of his name, my brow creased—and then I blushed furiously.

"What? Did something happen? Ooh, tell me!" Dottie squealed. I quickly explained about the bracelet—purposefully leaving out when I'd misunderstood what "get it on" meant—and I thought Dottie might faint.

"That is just so romantic!" She sighed, folding her hands against her cheek and smiling sweetly. "Like Prince Charming returning Cinderella's slipper."

"More like a classmate returning a bracelet he saw fall off a girl's wrist," I corrected her, trying to stem Dottie's swoony tidal wave that threatened to knock me right off the radiator.

"Do you like him, though?" Dottie asked, searching my face.

"I don't know him well enough to like him," I replied.

"Well, do you think he's cute?"

I took a massive bite of my sandwich to avoid answering her.

"Paige, tell me." Dottie gave me her best no-nonsense look. "I am older than you are, by tons of decades. Respect your elders!"

I chuckled at her comment as I pulled my hair out of its ponytail and scratched at my roots.

"What do you want me to say?" I asked, my shoulders sagging as I leaned against the chilly window. "Am I attracted to Logan? Honestly, who wouldn't be? He's really cute. But it ends there. It has to."

"It doesn't have to."

"Yes, it does. He's a nice guy who talks to me about assignments and begs for pens when he's missing one. That's all it is. Please, don't try to talk me into thinking it's more," I pleaded with her. "I'm the weird girl. And no one wants to date the weird girl, Dottie," I repeated, brushing the crumbs off my plaid skirt. "And to be honest, I don't blame them. People have enough problems—why would someone want to take that on?"

"Paige, don't be like that! You're not weird! You're funny, and sweet, and loyal—"

"So says the best friend that no one can see or hear."

"But you're also smart, and pretty. Even though I don't quite understand your choices in makeup and hairdos sometimes."

I snorted at that. Dottie's shellacked hair wouldn't move in a hurricane.

"Look, I appreciate the support—really, I do," I said, leaning against the window, then recoiling back when the condensation seeped through my shirt. "And I don't mind being the school's resident weirdo. It's not your fault, and let's be honest, it probably would have happened anyway. I'd have talked to a ghost on a class trip or at a party, and it would all have been downhill one way or another. But it means I have to be a little self-protective, Dots. I can't start crushing on a guy when there's no hope. I can't set myself up for disappointment like that."

Dottie set her petal-pink lips in a frown.

"You can at least flirt," she bargained.

I tried not to snort in reply. My best friend, the eternal romantic, stuck with me, the cynic.

"I wish you'd flirt. At least for practice," Dottie murmured. But all the fight was out of her voice, and I exhaled, relieved that this conversation seemed to be over. "He seems kind of shy but I swear I've caught him looking at you in class. And I thought he was so sweet to you...."

Dottie's voice trailed off and got weaker—as did her appearance. I could see the door to the bathroom appear through her as she became more translucent.

"Dottie?" I called. What if she was right—that her connection to this side was weakening? I saw her mouth my name, and then she disappeared, fading out of sight right as the bathroom door swung open.

The new girl Blaise barged into the bathroom, her long legs making her stride swift and graceful. She crossed the room quickly and stood a few feet from me before folding her arms and running her dark eyes up and down until they settled coldly on my face. I stopped drumming my heels and returned her stare. I was already in a bit of a foul mood, so I didn't have much trouble matching Blaise's scornful attitude.

"Can I help you?" I asked, mimicking her condescending expression.

Blaise snorted, a disdainful look crossing her face.

"This shouldn't take long. Pity," she sniffed. "I was hoping you'd put up a fight, but you're not much, are you? You're kind of pathetic."

I was used to insults and nasty nicknames whispered in the halls, but I'd managed to avoid bullying of the physical kind so far. *Well, guess that streak is over.* I slid off the radiator and raised my chin, meeting her arrogant gaze.

"I'm pathetic? And you just scream 'thug life,' right?" I drawled, doing my best to sound bored as I stretched out my arms and pretended to yawn, even though my heart began to pound. "I'm, like, so totally scared of you, like, oh, my God," I said in my best sarcastic valley-girl accent.

"You will be," she vowed, the corner of her mouth pulling into a half smirk.

"Bring it," I challenged her, mentally taking an inventory of the bathroom for something that could be used as a weapon.

I had a feeling the rolls of toilet paper stacked in the corner wouldn't be of much use, unless I wanted to blot her to death. I hadn't been in a real fistfight since fourth grade, and that had been over pretty quickly; I'd stood up to a fifth-grade boy who'd been harassing one of my friends, and come home with a black eye. You could say it was a pretty one-sided fight.

My eye twitched at the memory, but I squared my shoulders as I glared back at Blaise. She smiled, her lips tightening into thin red lines as her grin stretched unnaturally wide across her face, baring more sharp teeth than anyone should have.

More teeth than any human should have.

Her menacing grin continued to expand, pulling past the corners of her eyes—eyes which opened wider, bulging out until they were massive dark orbs, glittering like black coal speckled with diamonds. She flicked a black tongue between her crimson lips, and I began sweating—and not just out of terror. It was hot in the bathroom, far too hot for late January. My shirt began to stick to my back as Blaise rushed toward me, arms outstretched, a fierce rumble emanating from her chest.

I scrambled backward, stumbling against the radiator as Blaise slapped her palms against the window on either side of my head, condensation escaping as a small hiss and puff of steam from between her fingers. She tilted her head and gazed at me with those large dark eyes, grabbing a fistful of my hair and yanking my head back.

"I can smell your fear," she purred, running her nose along my neck as she inhaled deeply. "It smells like sour cherries. Delicious."

I swung my right fist up, aiming for her exposed neck,

but Blaise caught my wrist with her free hand, jerking my arm sideways at an unnatural angle. I cried out in pain, her touch burning my skin as she bent my arm farther, forcing me to my knees.

"What do you want?" I choked out, clawing at her skin as I tried to pry her fiery grip off my arm. Charcoal plumes of smoke wafted from where my fingernails sank into her skin, and Blaise whined in pain, rows of razor-sharp teeth gleaming in the dull fluorescent light. She released me from her tight hold, and I scrambled away from her, cradling my sore wrist.

"Well, I want to watch you burn, but I've been told I have to take you alive," she pouted, rubbing the dark crescent-shaped marks I'd left in her skin.

The bathroom door pushed open, and Blaise's features snapped back into place, her mouth shrinking to a small frown as three freshmen walked in. The trio gave us both suspicious looks as I cowered in the corner. One took up residence at the sink, vigorously brushing her hair and casting wary looks at us through the mirror as the others hurried to the toilets, chattering loudly to be heard over the divider between the stalls.

"An audience is inconvenient, so we'll resume this later. I'll find you," Blaise promised with a low hiss. They had resumed a normal shape, but her pupils still glittered as she stared at me, challenging me with those narrowed inhuman eyes. She turned on her heel and strode gracefully out of the bathroom, and the freshman at the sink reflexively flinched as Blaise passed by her. I slumped on top of the barely warm radiator, which felt cold against my overheated skin. The chill seeping in through the window was a welcome relief against my sweaty back.

Dottie shimmered back into existence, her face twisted in worry.

"What is going on, Paige?" she asked, frantic. Her brown eyes wildly whirled around the bathroom. I tilted my chin toward the girl now braiding her hair at the sink, and she instantly understood.

"Why do you look upset? Did something happen?" Dottie asked, and I merely nodded. I didn't need everyone in the school to bear witness to my one-sided conversations, after all. Not that I thought I could form a coherent sentence—I was trembling, my mind racing as I tried to make sense of what had just happened.

What *had* just happened?

"Did someone come in?" she asked, and again, I gave her a quick nod, wiping the sweat from my forehead with the cuff of my uniform shirt. The first bell rang, and I felt my stomach twist into knots. My first thought was to ditch class—but what if Blaise followed me home? What would she do to my parents? She swore she'd find me. I ran my fingers through my slightly sweaty hair, trying to figure out what I should do.

"What happened to your wrist? Did someone attack you?" Dottie gaped, and I nodded as I studied the tender, pink impressions that curled around my wrist. That had to prove that I'd just been threatened by the new girl—who may or may not be a girl. That nightmarish, gaping maw, full of sharp teeth, couldn't have been a hallucination, right?

I decided to go to the nurse's office. Maybe I could feign sickness and get sent home—I sure felt like I had a temperature. And I'd go somewhere public—a store, a library, *somewhere* until I was sure Blaise hadn't followed me.

I picked my bag off the floor with shaking fingers. And that's when I saw it—the charred, black tiles which marked the spot where Blaise had stood.

Dottie saw it, too, staring at the spot in the middle of the white tile floor in confusion. The second bell rang, so I ran straight to the nurse's office, Dottie in tow. She pelted me with questions I couldn't answer as ancient Nurse Esposito inspected my wrist with eyeglasses so thick, they were probably bulletproof. The nurse was sympathetic until she checked the computer at her desk—and then she berated me for trying to get out of detention.

"If you went home sick, you'd just have to make up detention on Monday," she scolded, peering at me over her wide tortoiseshell frames before begrudgingly handing me my excuse slip for my next class. Even though the halls were empty, I kept my voice low, telling Dottie what had happened with Blaise as my best friend walked me to English. Dottie— usually a slowpoke—kept up with my brisk pace. I needed to be around people. I needed witnesses.

"All I know is that when she was in the room with you, I couldn't stay here," Dottie whispered when we arrived at my class, even though she didn't have to keep her voice muted. "There's an energy around you that guides me to cross over. You're this beacon—kind of like a lighthouse in the darkness. But I can't keep a hold on it when she's there."

My English teacher saw me hovering by the open doorway and gestured for me to come in, which earned a few snickers from some classmates.

"What was she doing just staring off like that in the hall?" Scott Young whispered, shaking his head and giving me a bemused stare as I handed Mrs. Doyle my excuse slip from the nurse.

"She's one of those idiotic savant people," Andie Ward hissed back. "Good grades, but a psycho."

Normally, I would have corrected Andie, but I had bigger, scarier and deadlier things on my mind. I stayed slouched low in my seat, not even hearing my English teacher drone on and on as I searched my memory for anything I might have read that explained what Blaise was.

When I'd first discovered that my hallucinations were ghosts, I researched the paranormal. I'd gone to any website that looked halfway legitimate. I'd even trekked to the library and checked out every old, dusty book on the supernatural that I could find, secretly hoping to stumble upon some hidden chamber, filled with books unlocking the mysteries of the supernatural world and managed by some kindly old witch who'd take me under her magical wing.

But instead, I'd read textbooks about witches and warlocks and ghosts at communal tables under buzzing fluorescent lights. I'd even taken photos of Dottie, but apart from a few orbs and streaks of light, the pictures just showed the brown bathroom stalls and green-to-blue paint job I'd ruined. Nothing gave me any answers. As a last resort, I'd tried speaking to a few tarot card readers and psychics whose storefronts lined the streets in the East Village. I figured if I was able to talk to Dottie, then I couldn't be the only one, right? But everyone I'd spoken to was a low-rent charlatan angling for my allowance, so I'd eventually assumed I was alone. Until now.

I repeated my slouched-low-in-my-seat routine in Spanish and silently prayed that there would be multiple students with me in detention. Maybe I could walk out of the school with Miller. Maybe I could ditch detention. Maybe I could come up with some sort of plan, if Logan would stop distracting me by trying to get my attention.

"Where's your bracelet?" he mouthed, and I pulled it out of my pocket to show it to him. His eyes widened, and I could have sworn he looked horrified before Travis Moore leaned forward to whisper to someone, blocking my view.

I stared at my bracelet, as it sat coiled in my palm. A hundred thoughts rattled around in my head, until one thought—one loud thought that silenced all the others—echoed in my brain.

*What if I really am crazy?* What if I blacked out and only thought I'd lost my bracelet? What if I hallucinated a student transforming into some kind of monster in front of me, attacking me and bleeding plumes of smoke when my nails punctured her skin? What if I burned my own wrist to make the hallucination seem real? I didn't feel crazy—but I'm pretty sure crazy people don't realize they're nuts.

I put my bracelet back in my shirt pocket and rubbed my eyes with the heels of my hands, exhaling deeply.

*Calm down, Paige. Get yourself together. Get through today. Take a cab home so Blaise can't follow you and hurt Mom or Dad or Mercer. Maybe it's time for another therapist. Or time to sleep with a baseball bat at the ready.*

I looked down at my notebook and shivered: I'd filled the last two pages with horrifying, cartoonish images of Blaise, with her mouth gaping and her eyes glittering with hunger and hate—the kind of sketches that would have had Therapist Number Three calling for a straitjacket. The bell rang, and I yelped, slamming my notebook shut in an effort to force the sight out of my mind. I bolted from class to grab my stuff from my locker—I could have sworn I heard someone call my name as I sped through the halls, but I just chalked it up to more of my neurons misfiring. *Now you're hearing voices.*

I could make it. Just one more hour and a half, and I could make sense of all this. I could go home, curl up with Mercer, and somehow things would make sense again.

They had to make sense again.

When I slid into the fourth-floor classroom used for detention, I was comforted to see that there was at least one other student trapped in after-hours hell with me. Travis Moore sat by the window, not-so-surreptitiously checking sports scores on the phone in his lap. He was perpetually late to school, coming in from Pelham Bay in the North Bronx every morning—so he was a regular in detention. He was practically the detention mascot, much to Dottie's delight. She mooned over Travis every day after school, gushing to me that he was "the most." The most late student, but whatever. She thought he was, and I quote, "choice."

"Take a seat behind Mr. Morris, Miss Keller." True to form, Vice Principal Miller managed to get both of our names wrong as he snatched my detention slip from my fingers. As I headed to the last row, I heard Miller complain under his breath. "Damn kids, can't keep out of trouble one day so I can go home early...."

Miller returned his attention to whatever book he was reading. Judging by how sweaty his face was, I'd guess it was quite porny.

I slid into my chair, staring at the back of Travis's head—he had soft, flaxen hair, the corn silk kind that girls daydreamed about having. Maybe that's why he kept it buzzed so short—any longer and he'd risk looking like a Barbie doll.

"Take out a textbook and start copying the pages," Miller said, and I groaned internally, reaching into my bag for my history textbook. My fingers brushed against the transparent brown bottle of pills I pretended to take every day—the antipsychotic drugs that I told my parents made the hallucinations go away. I curled my fingers around the bottle, considering taking a dose, when I heard Miller exhale angrily.

"You're late," Miller barked, slamming his palm on the table. I turned my head to the doorway, relieved that yet another student had detention—until I saw who it was.

"It's not like you could start without me," Blaise crowed before strolling into the classroom. In one lithe movement, she hopped over the first desk in the first row by the door, her red hair rippling behind her. She gracefully sat down, stretching her long legs in front of her. Her toes nearly touched the beige wall—meaning I'd have to step over her legs to leave.

If she let me leave.

"I wouldn't miss this for the world," Blaise said, twisting in her desk to give me a slow smile.

And then, her eyes began to glitter.

# 03

"WHAT'S UP WITH HER EYES?"

Travis turned in his seat, his face ashen with fright as he whispered to me. I dropped the pills back into my bag, feeling a momentary rush of relief—*he sees it, too*—before panic began to set in.

Travis confirmed it. She's real—this was all real. And right now, she's blocking the only exit to the classroom.

"You see it, right?" he asked, panicked. I nodded, and gulped against the lump in my throat.

"Are those contacts? I don't think those are contacts," he hissed, darting another nervous glance at Blaise, whose large black eyes were dotted with several twinkling facets.

"We need to leave," I said, my voice low, and Travis nodded in agreement, shrugging into the hoodie he'd slung over the back of his desk.

"Stop talking," Miller ordered, glaring at us before returning his attention to his book. "And you—Blythe? Bunny?" he asked, snapping his fingers in the air as he tried to recall her name. Finally, he gave up, shaking his head. "New girl, turn around and hand me your detention slip."

The sparkling facets glittered like crystals as Blaise rolled her black eyes, a surprisingly human gesture for someone so inhuman.

"First things first, let's get rid of this one," she sniffed, turning around to cast a condescending look at Miller as she languidly stretched one slender arm out in front of her. She extended two fingers, as if she were making a sideways peace sign—and then pointed her fingers down, shifting them back and forth to mimic walking.

That's when I noticed Miller stumbling toward her with halted, faltering steps. His face was blank, his eyes hollow and sightless as his limbs jerked forward in time with Blaise's movements, merely a marionette she controlled.

Blaise held her palm up and Miller stopped short in front of her desk just as she slunk out of her seat, resting one knee on top of the desk to crouch, catlike, before him.

"You left this room at four-thirty. These two students left with you." Blaise's seductive voice was almost a purr. Miller nodded woodenly, his eyes unfocused as he staggered to the door, opening it with the same broken movements. I gripped the edges of my history textbook—it was thick and probably would leave Blaise with one hell of a headache when I whacked her with it.

I slowly slid out of my desk, holding my history textbook in front of me as the door slammed shut.

"Now, where were we?" Blaise asked almost cheerfully, striding to the front of the classroom as if she were a teacher.

"What the hell was that? What are you? A witch or something?" Travis demanded, his voice trembling underneath his bravado as he stood up, as well. Blaise raised her eyebrows at his question and laughed.

"You poor little human," she clucked, shaking her head. "You had the misfortune of coming between me and her."

"What do you want with me?" I hoped my voice sounded stronger than I felt.

Blaise smirked. "Stupid little Traveler. You're the one they want me to take. This one will just be a pleasant diversion for me."

"Screw this," Travis huffed, grabbing his bag off the floor and hoisting it onto his shoulder. "This is ridiculous. She's a hypnotist or some shit. You coming, Paige? Just stay behind me."

I wielded my history book like a weapon and followed Travis as he strode confidently past Blaise, who pursed her lips into a kiss as he walked past. We were close to the door when I felt myself being thrown through the air, my back smacking against the file cabinet in the corner of the classroom. I fell to the floor, looking up in time to see Blaise grip Travis by the throat one-handed as she pinned him against the wall.

"What are you?" he screamed, his eyes wide with terror as Blaise's face morphed, the menacing wide grin stretching across her face. He clawed at her arm, trying to break free from Blaise's iron grip.

I grabbed my history book from where it had fallen next to me, and hoisted it over my shoulder, whipping it right at Blaise's head.

Without taking her gaze off Travis, Blaise extended her arm and nimbly caught the textbook mere inches before it hit her face, her fingers curling around the binding. Black smoke wafted out from between her fingertips, and the book burst into a fireball, flaming scraps of paper fluttering to the ground as she incinerated it with her mere touch.

"Time to say goodbye," she growled, wrapping her other hand around Travis's throat. Glowing red veins, like trails of lava, spread out from where her fingers gripped him. Travis made a strangulated choking sound as the crimson lines criss-crossed across his skin. Blaise threw her head back in ecstasy, the red trails forming a web between her and Travis, sucking the life out of him.

"Stop it! Let him go!" I shouted, charging at Blaise. She lazily removed one hand and shoved me in the chest, blasting me several feet backward where I fell to the floor again. I looked up to see Blaise release her grip, and Travis slithered to the ground, limbs askew as he collapsed into a heap. His skin was gray, chalky—a loose pile of Travis-molded ash on the floor. Blaise poked him with her toe, and he slowly crumbled to dust, wisps of powder wafting across on the linoleum. I scrambled to my feet as Blaise turned to me with that wide, inhuman grin, her black tongue darting out to lick her thin red lips.

"That was glorious fun," Blaise purred, her eyes twinkling as she glared at me. "Now you're coming with me, little Traveler."

"Why are you calling me that?" I screamed. I gripped the desk nearest me and flung it in front of her. It skipped across the floor before Blaise reached out her hand, stopping it by merely placing her palm against the back of the desk.

"Cute. Nice try." She smirked, raising an eyebrow at me.

"You're fun. Much more lively than I originally gave you credit for."

Blaise rested both hands on the back of the red plastic seat. It exploded into flames, burning pieces of wood and molten lumps of metal and plastic scattering across the floor. Blaise stepped through the fire, unfazed, and I ran to the windows on the far wall, flinging one open. I grabbed the weak iron bars and shook them, the screws rattling in the weather-rotted wood frame. If I got the bars off, maybe I could survive the jump—aim to land in a snow bank or a Dumpster. I'd rather be alive with two broken legs than suffer an excruciating, fiery death in this classroom.

The door to the classroom swung open, the knob slamming into the plaster wall with a loud bang. I whirled around to see Blaise staring at the door with an entertained smile on her face—probably expecting another student to murder—but her smile faded when she saw Logan standing there, fists clenched at his side.

"Get out of here! Call the cops!" I shouted, slamming my palms onto the desk nearest me in frustration. *First, Travis, now, Logan. How many more, because of me?* But Logan merely held his hand up, giving me a slight nod—he never took his steely focus off Blaise.

"Stay away from her, *incindia,*" Logan ordered, a hateful look on his face as he spat out the unfamiliar word. Blaise took a hesitant step toward him.

"I wondered if you were to blame for Viola's sudden disappearance today." Her voice was full of bravado, but her once-arrogant movements were cautious, almost tentative, as she crossed the length of the room to confront Logan. "The *proditori,* isn't it?"

Logan's eyes narrowed as she spoke.

"You're about to find out how I earned that nickname," he said, striding toward her. She scrambled back into the corner of the room, her back pressed against the file cabinet as Logan reached over his shoulder, pulling a sword from behind his back. But there was nothing strapped to his back—the sword Logan brandished materialized out of nothing.

Logan expertly twirled the sword—Blaise's sparkling eyes tracking its movements as it gracefully sliced through the air. The weapon looked like it was made of ice—long, translucent and pale blue, rising from an intricate silver handle that curled over his knuckles.

This wasn't the quiet, somewhat shy boy from the back of the class. Instead, Logan was a commanding presence, his back straight and his voice confident and controlled as he ordered me to hit the floor. I crouched on the other side of the classroom, against the windows. Ducking behind a desk, I peeked out to watch as Blaise held her hand out, a massive swirl of smoke, red mist and flames churning above her palm until it condensed into a fireball—which she hurled at Logan.

He deftly blocked the fireball with the broad side of the sword, sending licks of fire raining onto the linoleum. She conjured another fireball, and I could hear a slight hiss as the frosty blade again sliced through the whirling flames, scattering burning embers on the floor. Blaise began to panic, her sparkling black eyes searching the classroom for an escape as she quickly created another fireball. Logan closed the gap between them, arms held high as he adjusted his grip on the sword, pointing the tip of the blade down until it was just a few feet from the base of Blaise's throat. She reared her arm back, but switched the fireball's target at the last moment— to me.

I scrambled backward on the floor, pinned against the corner of the classroom.

*This is it. I'm going to die. Again.*

The fireball exploded, temporarily blinding me with a burst of heat and light as Logan sent his weapon spinning in my direction, the blade cutting across the fireball's path mere seconds before it would have hit me. The sword embedded itself in the French class poster on the wall between the two windows.

"Get behind the desk!" Logan yelled. I scrambled to the front of the room and dove behind Miller's desk, flames raining around me as a fireball smashed into the desk, then another. I huddled against the gray metal desk, which began to burn my back as it absorbed the heat of the fireballs.

The shower of fire stopped, and I cautiously peered out from behind the desk in time to see Logan pinning Blaise against the file cabinet. She clawed for his face but he was quick—too quick—blocking her hands. She spit a wad of fire in his face, and he turned his head quickly, the flames singeing his cheek as he grimaced.

"Paige, hand me my sword, will you? I need to teach this *incindia* some manners," Logan asked calmly, holding her immobile. I ran to the spot where the blade was embedded in the wall and grasped the handle of the sword. My body jolted at its touch—the sword hummed with power in my grip. I braced my foot against the wall and yanked the sword free, stumbling a few feet backward.

And then I felt it, the burning, searing pain in my side as I was hit with a blast of heat and fire. I fell on the ground, trying to make sense of the agonizing pain, trying to extinguish the flames that felt like they were boring through my skin, tearing through muscle and bone before settling in my very cells. I heard Blaise's voice and tried to focus on her, on something—anything—to force myself out of my pain-induced stupor.

"Killing you should make up for killing the Traveler." Blaise was gloating. *She thinks you're dead.* I heard a pained grunt from Logan, and I forced my eyes open to see that he was wrestling with Blaise, who had him pinned on the ground. She was sitting on his chest, her mouth stretched even wider in a triumphant grin as her hands closed around his throat. The brilliant crimson veins began to form a web around her hands, spreading up his throat and across his face as his mouth opened in a silent scream.

I crawled along the back of the classroom, staying out of Blaise's eyeshot as I dragged the sword behind me. I used it as a crutch to push myself off the floor, fighting back the agony in my right side as I stumbled behind Blaise, who was straddling Logan's chest, blanketing him in those glowing ruby veins that were sucking the life out of him. Killing him.

I raised the sword with trembling arms, wincing in agony as I aimed the tip of the blade down. Using all the strength I had left in my withering muscles, I rushed toward them, plunging the blade between Blaise's shoulder blades. She threw her head back, her wide mouth opening in a scream that sounded more like a feral roar. She dropped her hands from Logan's neck, and the fiery red trails slowly receded. Blaise began convulsing, and Logan pushed her off him. I stumbled forward with her body, still keeping my grip on the handle. The blade began to glow, changing from the frosty blue to crimson, yellow and black, colors which undulated like lit firewood that was dying out.

It started at my hands—a scorching burn that raced through my veins and colored the edges of my vision. Everything shimmered, like pavement on a hot day. I screamed in agony, my chest pitching forward as a sudden blast of heat ripped through my heart, which beat painfully against my ribs. A red filter had been dropped in front of my vision—everything appeared in dizzying shades of crimson.

I yanked the sword out of her back, staring at Blaise's face-down body where it lay sprawled out next to Travis's ashes. Her body was the same dusty gray color, and plumes of sickly sweet smoke rose from her joints.

Travis… *Just stay behind me.* Travis, who tried to protect me from Blaise. Travis, who saw her hellish eyes and let me know I wasn't crazy. Travis, who was only seventeen. And now he's dead.

"I got someone killed. I killed someone," I whispered, gripping the handle of the sword tightly. It vibrated with power in response.

"No, you didn't get anyone killed. And you killed a demon that was about to kill me," Logan corrected me, wincing slightly as he pushed himself off the floor. He took a few steps toward me, and I reflexively held the sword out.

"What do you mean, a demon? And stay right there! Don't

move!" I ordered. I probably would have been more intimidating if the sword wasn't shaking like pudding in an earthquake, thanks to my trembling hands.

"Paige, I'm on your side," Logan said, holding his palms out in a defenseless gesture that was supposed to be reassuring as he took two small steps forward.

"What are you, Logan—if that's your real name?" I eyed him suspiciously, slicing the sword through the air wildly, and Logan shuffled backward.

"Logan is my real name," he said, keeping his hands up. "Blaise was an *incindia*—a fire demon—sent here to kidnap you," Logan explained, his voice soft and even. I stopped waving the sword, and he took a few steps toward me.

"And what about you? Are you a demon? How do I know you didn't kill her to do something horrible to me?"

Logan dropped his hands and took another cautious step toward me. "I'm not here to hurt you. I'm supposed to protect you from them."

"Protect me? Who's 'them'?" I asked, dropping the sword at my side as Logan inched forward. "What the hell are you? And—" I barked, raising the sword again. Logan took a step back, his hands resuming their inoffensive in-the-air position. "Stop coming closer! I know what you're doing. You're not that smooth."

Logan took off his baseball cap and ran his hand through his messy brown hair, which looked dark auburn through the reddish haze that coated my vision.

"I'm a demonslayer, Paige."

"Excuse me?" I definitely didn't read about that job description in my research on the paranormal.

"Yes, a demonslayer. And we have to get out of here. Now. You just need to trust me on this," Logan implored, his eyes sincere. "Look, I could have killed you a thousand times if that's what I wanted to do."

"Well, that makes me feel all warm and fuzzy."

"It's also the truth. Now, please, give me back my sword."

Logan reached out his hand for his weapon. I took a deep breath, ignoring the part of me that wanted to superglue it to my hand so I'd never be defenseless again. I closed my eyes and held it out, feeling the weight of the sword leave my hand as Logan—the shy, quiet cute boy who was apparently a demonslayer, of all things—took it back. I dropped my hands to my side and opened my eyes, just in time to see Logan sliding the sword behind his left shoulder. It disappeared, as if he were slipping it into an invisible case slung on his back.

Without the sword, I felt powerless. Raw.

"I got someone killed," I whispered as I tried to process the two deaths I'd just witnessed—one of which was at my own hands.

I stared down at my hands, expecting to see them covered in blood.

Instead, they were covered in fire.

I screamed as I began swatting at myself to extinguish the fire that seemed to be painlessly covering my body.

"Paige, listen to me." Logan bent down to meet my eyes, his voice calm. Maddeningly calm. He placed his hands on either side of my face and forced me to look at him. I could see my reflection in his pupils—I was an inferno, covered in flickering flames.

"I'm on fire! How can I listen to you when I'm on fire? And

why am I not in pain?" I continued swatting at the flames. "I think I'm supposed to stop, drop and roll, right?"

"You killed a fire demon. And now, you've absorbed her powers."

"So I'm going to be on fire forever?" I fretted, shaking my hands and sending little embers fluttering to the floor, the linoleum extinguishing them with a small hiss. "How do I stop burning up? Am I going to be some kind of friggin' eternal flame for the rest of my life?"

Logan's lips quirked up in a brief smile before he composed himself. He stood up straight, removing his hands from my face. "No, it fades after a while. And you'll learn to turn it on and off. Look," he began, his voice getting agitated, "I'll explain it all. But right now, we have to go because that dead fire demon on the floor is a few minutes away from exploding. And you won't survive that."

"What about Travis?" I asked in a small voice, and he frowned, his eyes darting to the pile of ash that had been my classmate.

"A casualty. I'm sorry, Paige," he said gently before assuming a more businesslike tone. "I know it doesn't make it any better, but he's not the first in this war."

War? My mind reeled over the word, but before I could ask, Logan continued talking, his words coming more quickly as he got more frantic.

"I don't feel like adding your name to the list of casualties, since I pretty much got my ass handed to me today protecting you. So we need to go now." Logan snatched up my backpack and coat, then grabbed my hand and hauled me out of the classroom into the hallway, which was empty save for the overly sweet smoke that was making it difficult to see. We ran to the staircase, briefly pausing only once for Logan to smash his elbow into the fire alarm, breaking the glass and sounding the siren. And then he was pulling me up the stairs, to the roof.

"Why are we going to the roof?" I yelled over the loud alarm as Logan ripped down the "No Exit" sign that dangled off a loose metal chain, blocking off roof access in the stairwell. I glanced down the stairs to the third floor, wondering where Dottie was and oddly grateful that my best friend was already dead. At least she couldn't get hurt.

"Quickest way to get out of here," Logan shouted back before practically dragging me up the stairs. "And we can't risk taking you through the school looking like that."

I looked down at our intertwined hands and saw that mine were still engulfed in red flames—flames that didn't seem to burn Logan. He pressed his hand against the red alarm box next to the door.

"*Reclax ne aperik,*" he muttered, repeating the harsh words several times. It didn't sound like any language I recognized. The long silver bar across the metal door clicked quietly as it unlocked, and Logan pushed open the access door to the roof, the dark gray of an advancing winter night greeting us. A blast of cold wind set the flames covering my body to dance and flicker as we trudged through the ankle-high snowdrifts that had piled up on the roof. Well, Logan trudged. I melted all the snow in a three-feet radius as I stared down at my feet. I should have been shivering from the freezing weather, but, you know, I was on fire. My foggy head was clouded with questions. Fortunately, Logan spoke up and addressed an un-spoken one.

"Let's go to my apartment. We'll explain everything."

"We?"

"My uncle and me." Logan stopped, and I stared at the six-foot wall that separated the roof of the school from the apart-ment building next door. I wondered if Logan was going to do some kind of spell to knock it down—I was working with the general assumption that demonslayers had magical powers, given the whole invisible sword and all—but he put his hands on my hips, pulling my back close against his chest. I blinked in surprise, not sure exactly where he was going with this.

"Hop over," he ordered, lifting me quickly. I grabbed the concrete rim of the redbrick wall and hauled my leg over it, waiting for Logan, who hoisted himself over the wall easily. Then, we both toppled forward, the snow barely cushioning our fall as the school shook with an ear-shattering explosion.

"Blaise," Logan said, answering another unspoken ques-tion before standing up. "Decomposing fire demons are just as annoying dead as they are alive," he added with a grimace.

"Do you think anyone was hurt?" I asked, screwing my eyes shut as I thought of Travis. "Anyone else, I mean?"

"No, the school was empty. Friday after midterms, remem-ber? The fire will burn off quickly—it'll likely stay confined to the classroom," Logan said, holding out his hand to help me up. I grabbed his snowy hand and pulled myself off the roof, grunting when I tugged against the wound in my side. The agonizing pain had stopped, leaving me with a pierc-ing, throbbing sting.

"Just a few more roofs, and we'll be around the corner from

the school. Should be far enough away that no one will see us," he said, before gesturing to my side as we stepped around a cell phone tower. It shimmered as it reflected the fire that still covered me. "My uncle can fix that for you. We're lucky you only got hit with a spark." Logan frowned.

"All this from a spark?" I asked, wincing as I remembered the blinding pain. My fingers—that weren't intertwined with his—reached around to my side, where there was a gaping, burned-out hole in the fabric of my shirt, exposing the side of my pale pink bra. I clutched the singed edges of the fabric, trying to pull them closed.

"Does it hurt less now?" Logan asked, reaching out his hand to look at the wound—and then stopping short when he realized that part of my bra cup was exposed. He quickly looked away, dropping my hand. I could have sworn he blushed, but then everything looked pretty red to me at that moment.

"Sorry, I didn't realize—because you're on fire and all that...." Logan stammered, turning his head.

I awkwardly folded my arms across my chest, trying to keep my voice at a normal tone so Logan wouldn't feel uncomfortable.

"Yeah, it doesn't hurt as much. Why is that?"

"You absorbed Blaise's power," Logan explained as he pulled off his blue sweater, standing in the cold in his white button-down shirt. "You'll be more tolerant of heat and fire—that includes burns," he explained, meeting my eyes before deliberately forcing himself to stare anywhere else. He awkwardly held out the sweater, his elbow locked straight as he gripped the balled-up fabric. "You'd make an excellent fireman—um, firewoman. You know, because you're immune to fire now," he rambled. "Put this on. You know, because of the, um…half-naked…just put it on."

He waved the sweater at me, and I reached for it before pulling my flame-covered hand back.

"Won't this burn? Wool is really flammable."

"No. The fire only hurts flesh."

"But it melted the snow."

"Yeah, because they're opposite elements. You have to focus to set fire to something nonliving. Please, just trust me and put the sweater on," Logan said quickly, keeping his eyes aloft as he pushed the sweater closer to me. I grabbed it and slid it on quickly, careful of my injured side.

"Are you, um, covered?" he asked, and I nodded before finding my voice.

"Yeah, I'm decent." I pushed up the long sleeves on the navy sweater, the extra wool bunching up at my elbows.

"Okay, let's go." I followed him as he led the way across the building, his steps swift and steady. I realized Logan had my backpack on, my coat tucked into the straps. The bag hung normally, not at all affected by Logan's magic invisible sword. *Probably because the operative word there is* magic, *genius.*

"Hey, thanks for grabbing my backpack," I said, my face burning with embarrassment—and, you know, fire—when I realized that I also hadn't thanked him yet for saving my life.

"Couldn't exactly leave evidence that you were there." Logan shrugged dismissively as fire truck sirens began to wail nearby.

"Okay, we just have to make this one jump, and we're set." Logan had stopped talking and was waving a hand to the five-foot gap between the building we were currently on—and the roof of the building next door.

"No," I whispered, terrified. I backed away from edge.

"No?" Logan's brows pulled together in confusion.

"I'm—I'm afraid of heights," I confessed, wringing my flaming hands together.

"Seriously?" His lips quirked up in an amused smile.

"Yes, seriously!" I retorted, looking around the roof for another way out. Maybe I could go back to Holy Ass and leave through the front door.

*Yeah, right, like they won't think the girl on fire has something to do with the inferno on the fourth floor.*

Logan chuckled, and I narrowed my eyes at him.

"It's not funny! I'm going to be stuck on this roof."

"Paige, I just watched you fearlessly kill a fire demon, and you're going to tell me you're afraid of heights?" Logan crossed his arms and cocked his head to one side, a thoroughly entertained smile on his face. "It's a little funny."

"I just watched a fire demon kill a classmate while I stood there, powerless," I replied quietly, staring down at the rivulets of melted snow running past my feet. "There's nothing funny about any of this."

Logan was instantly contrite. "I'd bet that you didn't just stand there, but you're right. Look," he sighed, taking off his hat to run his hand through his thick brown hair, "I'm sorry. I'm just a little jaded. Blaise isn't my first demon."

"How many have there been?"

Logan's eyes looked up, and he bobbed his head from left to right, as if he were counting in his head.

"Let's just say, a lot."

"A lot of fire demons?"

"Quite a few of those, actually." He wrinkled his nose in disgust. "Arrogant, snide, just nasty."

"What other kinds are there? Tell me about the biggest, baddest demon you beat," I wheedled.

"As much fun as it would be for me to stand around bragging, you won't put off this jump by having me tell war stories. I know what you're doing. You're not that smooth." He repeated my words from the classroom back at me, and I blushed. "Look, this jump is really easy. I've done this a billion times."

"That's you, not me."

"You can do this. I'll go first. But we have to go soon before anyone sees us. It's dark out and, well, you kind of stand out," he added, and I looked down at my burning feet again, frowning.

"Can you try to calm down? That should calm the flames."

"I'll give it a shot."

*Calm down, calm down.* I slammed my eyes shut as I tried to relax, but images of Blaise's bulging eyes and hungry mouth and Travis's tortured face fought for dominance behind my eyeballs.

When I opened my eyes, the fire seemed actually brighter.

"Sorry," I whispered. Logan frowned and put his hands on my flaming shoulders.

"Okay, try this." Logan's voice was low, soothing. "Shut your eyes again."

I squeezed them tightly shut, screwing up my face in concentration, and Logan laughed gently.

"Just close them. You look like you're hurting yourself."

I could practically hear the smirky smile in his voice. With some effort, I relaxed my face.

"The thing to remember is that you control it. It's a part of you," Logan explained, his voice soft but confident. "Try to feel the fire."

"I can't feel anything," I fretted.

"I couldn't at first, either. I was on fire in the middle of a football field. I'm pretty sure there's a town in Michigan that tells stories about the flaming ghost of Novi High, running like a maniac through the high school, ripping his burning clothes off because he doesn't know what's happening."

"Seriously?" I asked, my eyes springing open.

"No, not seriously. Now, close your eyes again," he added, that amused little smirk still on his face.

I rolled my eyes before shutting them.

"Now, here's what worked for me. Think of it like a muscle that you didn't know you had, that you didn't realize you were flexing. Do you feel it?"

I shifted my weight from one foot to another, feeling gritty particles of wet grime on tar grind underneath my feet. I felt Logan's hands on my shoulders, strong and reassuring. And then I felt it—it wasn't quite like a muscle, but the sensation was similar to that of a muscle that ached and burned after a workout. I relaxed it, feeling cool, refreshing air hit my face.

"Wow."

"What?" I asked, my eyes popping open. Everything looked darker to me.

"You did it," Logan whispered, awed. I looked down at my hands in the darkness—I wasn't on fire.

"I could still explode into flames like a stupid firecracker,"

I reminded him, holding out my arms in wonder. They were again the same plain, boring arms, covered in an oversize dark blue sweater.

"Still, that's…pretty impressive." He grinned. "I was starting to wonder how I was going to get you the two blocks to my place without people noticing. I didn't think anyone would buy that you were a performance artist."

"I guess you didn't save my ass today just to ditch it on top of a building while it was on fire, huh?"

Logan gave me a wry smile. "So now you admit that I was trying to save your ass? You had me fooled with the way you threatened me with my own sword and all."

"Sorry about that," I muttered, as the sirens wailed more loudly. If it weren't for Logan pulling me out of that classroom, I'd have been burned to a crisp when Blaise imploded. "I don't think I said it yet, but thanks for saving my life."

"Some lifesaving. You ended up having to save my ass," Logan countered, poking me in the shoulder.

I opened my mouth to protest, but Logan turned around and stepped up on the wall between the two buildings. He crouched low, then sprang into the air. I rushed to the edge of the building just in time to see Logan land on the roof next door with a few feet to spare. He jogged forward a few steps from the force of his impact before turning around to beam at me triumphantly.

"See, easy. Just don't look down," he called.

"Why did you say that?" I moaned, my eyes dropping to the alleyway between the two buildings as if they had weights attached to them. I felt the world spinning, and I turned around, my back sliding down the wall until I was crouching in a puddle on the roof.

I looked up at the dark, cloudy sky, watching the lights of a helicopter soar overhead. Travis would never see the world. He'd never sit at the dinner table with his family again. He'd never go to college, or even graduate from high school. And it was my fault. Blaise had come to Holy Assumption looking for me—that much was clear. I automatically reached for my bracelet, momentarily panicking when it wasn't on my wrist before remembering it was in my pocket. I patted my left-side pocket through Logan's sweater, feeling a momentary rush of relief when I felt the lump of the bracelet through the sweater. The relief soon turned to revulsion, as I grew disgusted with myself. Disgusted that I could feel comfort at having my precious bracelet back—when Travis was dead. Because of me. Because whatever I had set into motion that day by running into the street to save Dylan now meant someone was gone, and the top floor of my school was on fire.

Maybe I was supposed to die that day, and these were the repercussions of fighting fate.

I heard a soft thud and looked up to see Logan standing a few feet away, an unreadable expression on his face.

"Overwhelmed?"

I nodded.

"Look, it wasn't supposed to happen this way," Logan said, walking closer to me and crouching down to meet my gaze.

"I was just thinking that."

"You were?" Logan's eyebrows pulled together in confusion, and I nodded.

"I probably shouldn't have lived. I flatlined, you know. But the doctors brought me back…and I started to see ghosts… and now I'm responsible for someone's death," I rambled bitterly, not knowing or caring if I made any sense. I just had to say it. I took a deep breath, steeling myself to say the awful truth out loud. "If I wasn't alive, Blaise wouldn't have come looking for me…and Travis would still be alive. I shouldn't have lived."

"Hey, don't say that." Logan's voice was firm but gentle. He timidly reached his hand out and rested it on my shoulder, giving me a squeeze. His hesitation was surprising, considering that he'd been holding my hand—but then again, that was mostly just to pull me away from the school.

"I know this is a lot to accept, but what happened to Travis isn't your fault."

"You weren't there when he died."

"No, but I saw the ash on the floor. I know what happened."

"Still, it's my fault," I insisted. "Blaise was there for me. She told me so."

"Yes, she was. But it's my fault Travis died, not yours," Logan argued, his voice grave as he dropped his hand from my shoulder. "I knew there was someone at the school who would eventually be attacked. But it took me a really long time to figure out that you were the one with a supernatural talent. I was expecting some forlorn, weepy person, speaking in tongues and wearing all black."

"I wear a uniform." I picked up a corner of my skirt as if to say, "See?"

"You also hold your head high when you walk down the hall."

Flashing siren lights whirled in pinwheels on the buildings across the street, bathing Logan's face in a yellow and red glow. He stood up, holding his hand out to me.

"Come on, Paige. We have to get out of here." I slid my hand into his, and he pulled me off the ground.

"I'll jump with you, okay? Just focus on the stairwell on the next roof." Logan pointed at the metal door, latched to a small structure with a broken chain. I nodded nervously as we stepped up onto the low wall, not taking my eyes off the door.

"On the count of three, okay?" Logan squeezed my hand before letting go. "One…two…three…"

I bent my knees, and with all my strength launched myself off the wall, keeping my eyes on the door. It was probably a mistake, since my right foot hit the snowy rooftop at an awkward angle, sending me facedown into a snowdrift. I pushed myself out of the snow and looked around for Logan, who was sitting about two feet away, brushing ice out of his face.

"Are you okay?" Logan asked, taking off his hat and shaking his hair out.

I nodded, wiping the frosty bits from my own face.

"See, you faced your fear, you jumped, and you're fine," Logan said triumphantly.

"I think we could be a little less heavy-handed with the metaphors, don't you?" I snorted, scrambling to my feet.

"Come on," Logan said, jogging to the door. A chain was loosely looped through a hole where the doorknob should have been, secured with a weak lock. Logan yanked the lock off easily, holding it in his hands before turning to me.

"Do you think you can keep the flames at bay for a few blocks?"

I shut my eyes, focusing on the heat building inside me. When I opened my eyes, everything was ablaze.

"We need you to *not* be on fire," Logan said dryly.

"I know, watch," I said. I shut my eyes again, concentrating on pulling the blaze back. When I opened them, the fire was gone—but even in the dark I could see that Logan was trying his hardest not to look impressed.

"Not bad," he said, sliding the chain off the door. "Let's go. Once we get to my place, we'll explain everything."

He held out his hand, and just the tips of his fingers were on fire.

"Show off," I muttered and Logan smirked.

But I took his hand anyway, and he led me down the stairs.

# 04

I STOOD NEXT TO LOGAN IN THE DIMLY LIT hallway of his apartment building. It could have been any nondescript hallway in any old brownstone apartment building in Manhattan—walls painted a muted pastel color that was some compromise between pink and beige, everything bathed in a faint yellow glow from the flickering fluorescent light above.

"Are you sure you want to know everything?" he asked me, his soft voice contradicting his intense stare.

"What do you mean? Of course I do!" I needed to finally know more about what I could do, what it meant…to finally have proof that I wasn't insane.

"I mean…" Logan looked down at the bits of frost on the tips of his Converse sneakers. "I could make you forget," he whispered, rubbing the back of his neck with his palm. "You wouldn't have to know any of this. You wouldn't have to know about the existence of demons."

He finally met my gaze, his brown eyes serious. "You wouldn't remember what happened to Travis."

"No, I—"

"All you'd have to do is look into my eyes. I'd say a little spell, and the memory would be gone. Think about it."

I narrowed my eyes as I studied him, and Logan shifted uncomfortably under my stare.

"Blaise did this mind control thing with Miller. It was like he was her puppet," I recalled, feeling my stomach churn when I thought of how she robbed him of his free will. "She controlled him and told him what to do. Is that what you're offering to do to me?"

"It's called a *somnorvik* spell."

"Whatever. It gets a different name in every vampire and witch show I've ever seen. It might as well be called mind-*vik* eraser-*vik* hypnotizer-*vik*," I scoffed, rolling my eyes. "I don't care what it's called in real life. But I do care that you want to mess with my head!"

"It's really not like that," Logan said defensively.

"It's exactly like that. Look, I'm so tired of not knowing why I can do what I can do. It's time I knew what's really going on."

He studied me for a moment, his gaze serious. Finally, Logan gave me one quick but decisive nod.

"Okay, you've got it."

I grabbed on to Logan's hand again as he began to walk down the hallway, afraid he would disappear—and with him, all the answers I so desperately needed would also vanish. But as we stood in front of his apartment, it felt like Logan was the one holding on to me for support, clutching my hand in a crushing grip.

"Is everything okay?" I asked. "Did you forget your keys?"

Logan chuckled and cocked his head to one side as he gave me a slightly amused look.

"This isn't the kind of door that opens with keys," he said.

"Why is that so funny?"

He shrugged. "Because it's such a normal question."

"Well, what's the problem? Did you forget which secret compartment to press?" I stuck out my finger and poked the metal frame of the door.

"No, I'm just stalling," Logan admitted with a sheepish grin. "I should warn you. My uncle can be a little intimidating. He's…well, he's a warlock."

"Warlock?" I repeated, my voice rising in pitch as my studies of the paranormal came rushing back at me. "I thought those were evil wizards."

Logan shook his head, smiling at my comment. "No, movies got that part wrong. Rego's not evil—although he can be an asshole," he said with a grimace. "He'll probably be in a mood. Especially since things didn't go the way they were supposed to today."

"I thought you were supposed to save my life. You did that," I reminded him, but was met with a wry smile.

"True. But you weren't supposed to know. I was supposed to be stealthy, follow the plan. But things kind of fell apart," Logan said before casting a sideways look at me. "I shouldn't have said anything. It's not your problem." He gave my hand a quick squeeze before slapping his other palm against the brown-painted door.

"*Reclaxarit ne bulsharak,*" Logan whispered. I didn't recognize these words either, all discordant consonants and unfamiliar, tongue-twisting syllables. The frame of the door glowed a brilliant white, and Logan stepped back, pulling me with him. Thin lines of light dripped down from the top of the door, appearing to slice through the metal. The door quivered, then shimmered to the floor in iridescent ribbons, which fell into nothingness in the almost blinding glow outlining the entryway to the apartment.

"Rego? Are you here?" Logan called, stepping inside and tugging me with him. I wasn't quite sure what a demonslayer's apartment with a magical entrance would look like. I briefly pictured a cavernous, candlelit stone lair—maybe a pet dragon would be hanging out in the corner. I sure didn't expect to walk into a small kitchen in a somewhat rundown old apartment. The walls were dingy white plaster, dotted with gouges and deep scrapes. Some surprisingly pleasant fruit-and-spice scented concoction I couldn't quite identify bubbled over on a hot plate, sending a frothy pink foam spilling onto a kitchen counter cluttered with papers and bags of chips.

Past the pink-stained mess was a wobbly-looking table, which was littered with books and scrolls. Mismatched chairs with shredded vinyl seat cushions sat around it, and a heavy, deep blue curtain blocked off access to the center room.

"I know it's not much," Logan said apologetically, his cheeks pink as he surveyed the apartment, clearly embarrassed. "You probably have an amazing home."

"No, this is great," I said encouragingly. He smiled self-consciously as the curtain was pushed aside. A lean young man strode out, clad in a rumpled black uniform with some kind of purple emblem on his left shoulder. He was boyishly handsome and looked barely old enough to torment a fraternity pledge, let alone be an intimidating warlock. He flashed a quick, dimpled grin at us as he ran a hand through his dark brown hair, which rivaled Logan's in its unruliness.

Nope, there was nothing immediately scary about the person that stood before us—well, except for the spiked mace that hung from his belt, swinging slightly as he gave Logan a friendly clap on the shoulder, a large, opal-like stone glowing on his index finger.

"Logan! I was hoping I'd see you. And you've brought a girl over?" He managed to load the four-letter word with innuendo, his arched eyebrows rising in surprise as he not-so-subtly gave me the once-over.

"Hi, you must be Rego—" I began, and the man recoiled in mock-horror.

"Rego?" he repeated, his voice saturated with exaggerated disgust. "Do I look like I forgot to take the hanger out of my shirt when I got dressed this morning?"

He gave me a sly smile as he stepped closer.

"Let me kiss the hand of the most beautiful creature I've seen all day," the man cooed, taking my palm in his and bending down with his lips pursed, only to flip our hands at the last moment and plant a big kiss on his own knuckles.

"Wow. So that happened." I stared, incredulous, as he winked at me, his lips still puckered over his own skin.

"Paige, this is Ajax," Logan said dryly, gesturing to the young man, who was grinning widely, clearly pleased by his own joke. "He's—"

"Devastatingly handsome, renowned for his wit, and thrilled to meet the lovely young thing Logan's told me so much about," Ajax said, winking at me again, his violet eyes sparkling above an impish grin.

I gave Logan a questioning look, and he pulled me away from Ajax.

"I didn't—it's not like that—I was talking about possible targets and your name came up," Logan sputtered, glaring at his friend. "You know, Ajax, you're embarrassing and completely inappropriate."

"And starving," Ajax added, hopping up to sit on the kitchen counter. He grabbed a half-open bag of sour cream and onion potato chips and began digging in.

"Mmph," he moaned around a mouthful of chips. "You guys get the best food, I swear."

"What are you even doing here?" Logan asked Ajax, leading me to one of the chairs. I sat in it, wincing at the dull ache in my side.

"And where's Rego? I need his healing balm," Logan told Ajax. "Paige got injured pretty badly dealing with an *incindia* today."

Ajax shuddered dramatically before cramming another handful of chips into his mouth.

"Nasty things. I hate dealing with them," he said after he swallowed. "I had some updates on a situation I've been monitoring for Rego, so I decided to swing by and deliver them personally." His voice dropped to a whisper. "I don't exactly trust his new messenger."

Ajax ate another chip and resumed speaking in a normal tone. "He's back there in his office, just wrapping up something."

"And now he's done." The stern, businesslike voice boomed through the small room, and I spun around in my chair to see the curtains get impatiently flicked aside by a tall, impressive man who strode out to greet us. Now, this guy was intimidating: Rego stood straight and confident, with flawlessly straight black hair that framed an angular face and fell just above his broad shoulders, which were draped in a long, military-style black coat. The coat reminded me of what people in 1776 might have imagined citizens of the future would wear during battle. Where Ajax's uniform looked lived-in, like functional fatigues, Rego's double-breasted outfit was sleek, trimmed in leather and shimmering with rows of X-shaped silver buttons. Pointed silver-toed boots splattered with some kind of dark liquid peeked out from underneath the long hem. The same liquid—blood?—was splashed on the sword slung into his low silver belt. "Hi, I'm—" I began, and Rego held a long-fingered hand aloft, cutting me off.

"I know who you are," Rego interrupted, giving me a polite smile that didn't meet his gray eyes. "A pleasure to meet you, Paige."

*Yeah, right, it's a pleasure to meet me. You look like you'd enjoy a hammer to the eyeball more.*

"But I must say, meeting our new friend is quite unexpected, as she shouldn't even know I exist, let alone Ajax here."

"Things didn't exactly go as planned today," Logan said, surprising me with how hesitant and unsure he sounded. "It started with the rage demon this morning—"

"And ended up with you revealing this place to the target you were supposed to protect?" Rego interrupted Logan. "What if she gets taken? She could expose us all."

Logan's brown eyes narrowed, and he took a step toward his uncle.

"She's not going to get taken. And she's injured. She got hit with a spark from the fire demon." Logan's fingers curled into fists at his sides, betraying his calm composure. "So, we're going to give her something to cure her burns, and then we're going to tell her what's going on."

"It's in her best interest if we erase her memory," Rego said, his sentence sounding more like an order than a suggestion as he took a step toward Logan. "Knowledge will make her a liability. She shouldn't know—"

"No!" Logan shouted, and Rego stepped back in surprise. "She saved my life. And she doesn't want her memory erased."

"She doesn't get to make this decision."

"She's also in the room," I volunteered, and was rewarded with a venomous glare from Rego. *Dial it back, Paige. Don't poke the bear. Don't poke the angry, warlock bear.*

"I refuse to erase her memory. And, Ajax—" Logan pointed at his friend as he dug for crumbs in the bottom of the chip bag "—you're not doing it either."

"Are you sure you don't want the spell?" Ajax interjected, his full lips curled in a teasing grin. "They say ignorance is bliss. Don't you want to be blissful?"

"I think I'll pass," I replied, hesitantly taking my eyes off Rego and Logan's standoff to look at Ajax, who had crumbs down the front of his shirt.

Ajax merely shrugged in reply. "Just as well, my bliss-less friend. I'm really bad at it, so I'd probably turn you into a chicken or something."

"I'm definitely going to have to say no, then."

"My sweet, I'm sure you'd make a lovely chicken," Ajax replied.

"No one's doing any spells on Paige," Logan shouted, his voice determined. "So, Rego, unless you've learned how to pull off a *somnorvik* spell lately, this discussion is over. I owe her. And you know I always pay my debts."

Rego arched his eyebrow as he appeared to evaluate his nephew.

"Very well." Rego turned on his heel and disappeared behind the dark curtain. As he pulled the fabric back, I got a better look at the living room. Well, in a normal apartment, it would have been the living room. Instead, the walls in this room were lined with dusty, ancient-looking treasures and medieval-looking weapons—ornate, slightly tarnished brass and steel sharing shelves with brilliant, shiny gold.

Rego returned with a small, scratched mason jar, filled with a bright blue gelatinous cream that quivered in the glass.

"Apply this to the affected area. It should heal immediately. Your skin will be unblemished, as if you'd never been injured," Rego said, arrogantly adding, "It's my own brew, so it truly works wonders."

"Thanks," I said, opening my bag and stuffing the jar inside.

"Paige, don't you want to take care of that now?" Logan asked me. "We'll wait."

"No. It barely hurts anymore," I fibbed. My side still stung, but I was anxious to finally get some answers.

I leaned forward in my chair and folded my arms on the table. Rego sat in another chair and pulled a massive scroll off the stack on the kitchen table.

"Paige, why do you think you were attacked?" Rego asked,

one black eyebrow arched as he dismissed the scroll and pulled out another one. The question felt like a test.

"I assume it was because I can…well, I can talk to ghosts," I said, my tone very businesslike and matter-of-fact. After all, I was talking to a demonslayer, a warlock and a…whatever Ajax was. My talent, for once, didn't make me the weirdest one in the room.

"That's half-right. You don't talk to ghosts exactly," Rego corrected, "although I can understand why you're under such a misapprehension. You can speak to spirits that are trapped in an alternate version of your world." He spread his palms, gesturing to the apartment around him.

"There's the world that you know. The human world, so to speak. And then there's the other world."

"The Dark World?" I asked, then hastily explained, "My friend calls it that—but I thought she was just stuck in purgatory or limbo or something."

"Your blonde friend, right?"

I met Logan's gaze as he leaned against the wall nearest me. "You can see Dottie?"

"And hear her. I told you I didn't think you were crazy," he reminded me.

"Can we focus, please?" Rego demanded, and I turned my attention back to him just as he was unrolling a scroll in front of me. It was an aerial map of New York City—a surprisingly vibrantly colored and accurate map, considering how ancient the parchment looked. There was even an illustration of a high-rise that was under construction near my school.

"This is the world you know. The one you live in every

day." As we studied the map, the building shimmered, growing taller, and I gasped in surprise.

"It's an active map," Logan explained, seeing where I was looking. "It reflects the changes in this world."

Rego placed a piece of cloudy vellum on top of the scroll, and the map morphed. The buildings became more angular, with warped, sloping sides. The colors were darker, gloomier. A building on the East River crumbled into ash as I stared. My eyes reflexively sought out my street—West Forty-Fourth was a blazing inferno.

"May I present to you the Dark World," Rego said, waving his hand with a dramatic flourish over the grotesque distortion of New York. As he spoke, the landscape continued to undulate and change, the vibrant reds and oranges of the inferno in Hell's Kitchen reflected in flickering tongues of flame in Rego's gray eyes. "It's been known by many names throughout centuries, of course, but your friend's nickname for it is actually the English translation for the Old Demonic name for it. She was surprisingly accurate in her terminology," Rego said, clearly reluctant in his praise.

"The Dark World is an alternate version of your world, connected to it by its very nature. What happens in one world can impact the other. If the death of someone in your world is prematurely caused by an inhabitant of the Dark World— namely, a demon—the victim spends the duration of what would have been his or her life trapped on the other side. A demon played a hand in your friend's death, yes?"

"Actually, no. She—" I stopped short, not wanting to tell Dottie's secrets.

"She died in the fifties. She killed herself because she was pregnant," Logan finished.

"What does that matter?" I asked, indignant. "And her name is Dottie."

"I had to know who she was—is," Logan corrected himself, giving me an apologetic look. "After I realized you could hear her, I did a little research in the school archives after hours. I said I'd made that jump between buildings a thousand times," he added, that confident smile flashing quickly across his face. Then his smile faded as he continued. "I'm positive that Dottie was the victim of a male lust demon—an incubus. The mother is unable to resist his advances."

I mulled over what Dottie had told me about her ex. "She did call him a dreamboat."

"More like a nightmare boat," Ajax griped before explaining. "The mother never survives the birth. As soon as she's pregnant, the demon disappears, returning only to take his offspring back home." He pointed at the map, indicating the horrific home in question.

"But, wait a minute—Bobby didn't kill her," I pointed out, tracing a crack in the table with my finger, and it wobbled underneath my fingertips.

"A demon intervened in her life, directly bringing about her death. That's all that matters," Rego explained cavalierly, as if he were talking about dinner plans, not the victimization of my only friend. Seeing the aghast look on my face, he softened his tone—slightly.

"It's not surprising, given the timing of your friend's demise," he explained. "The lust demons really built their numbers in the fifties, rising to prominence in the sixties. Their numbers were so great, they influenced your side, actually. I trust you've heard of the hippies and their belief in free love?" Rego grimaced in disgust, and I nodded, thinking about the goofy Cinderella play my dad had dragged me to. It suddenly seemed a lot more sinister.

"It happened with the greed demons, too," Ajax interjected. "Ugh, in the eighties they were everywhere. Wasn't that an era of greed on your side?"

"Big-time. While I can't say I'm surprised to hear that there's a demonic influence on Wall Street, what does all this have to do with me?" I asked. "Why would a demon attack me simply because I can talk to people like Dottie?" I stared at the map as it undulated before me.

Rego folded his hands on the table, regarding me gravely as his silver rings clacked against the marked-up surface.

"That talent is precisely why. It means you can do more than simply talk to people. It's why the ruler of the Dark World, the Regent Queen, sent her minions to kidnap you. It's quite arduous to cross between the worlds. Very few portals exist—and most of those are one-way passages. It's a brutal journey full of unspeakable pain. No one can survive crossing over alone. You must travel in a group, so the energy is absorbed by multiple bodies."

"Why is it so painful?" I asked.

"Ripping a hole in one universe to visit another? Oh, dear Bliss, that's going to unleash some serious energy," Ajax answered with a low whistle.

"Where are these portals?" *Hopefully Antarctica, because I want to live as far away from these things as possible.*

"The demons have destroyed most of them. The remaining ones are not exactly convenient. One portal to the Dark World is in the ocean, for example. There's one that leads to this side in the demon queen's palace, heavily guarded, of course," Rego explained with a flick of his wrist as his iron eyes studied me. "But to have a Traveler like you at your disposal?" My skin crawled at the easy way the term Blaise had used rolled off his tongue.

"You're connected to both worlds. Your ability to talk to Dottie is proof of that. A demon or a warlock could use you to open a portal anytime he desired, and cross back and forth as often as he wants," Rego marveled, and my stomach turned at the way he regarded my value, like I was some supernatural bus pass.

"Why would you ever want to go there?" I asked, shuddering.

"It's not that bad," Ajax said, but Rego just brushed him off.

"We're at war here, Paige." Rego's tone was solemn, mouth set in a serious, grim line. "Warlocks are the rightful heirs to the throne—a throne that's been sullied by thousands of years of demonic reign. But now, we're closer than ever to taking back control. With your help, we could travel back and forth for supplies—there are herbs in the Dark World that cure injuries. I use salt from the seawater on that side in my healing elixir."

"And cocoa butter, because you can never underestimate the power of soft, touchable skin," Ajax chimed in, earning another of Rego's glares. The warlock pinned Ajax with his hard gaze until he muttered, "Ooh-kay, then," and focused on his chips.

"But beyond that," Rego continued, turning his attention

back to me, "you could travel to a safe point in this world, cross over and find yourself standing in the queen's chambers. If you knew the exact coordinates, it would be the perfect assassination."

Rego studied me speculatively. "And I'm sure you'd love to help us get revenge on the demons who arranged the attack on you today."

"No, Rego," Logan interrupted, glaring at his uncle. "Don't even think it."

"What?" I asked, looking back and forth between them.

"There's a slight potentiality that it could be something of a minor drain on your life force to cross into another dimension," Rego begrudgingly revealed.

"Put it in English, Rego," Logan said, before turning to me. "Paige, it could take years off your life."

He pressed his lips together in a thin line as he thought about how to explain.

"Think of opening a door," Logan said. "You shove, and the door opens, right?"

I nodded. "Now think of the exertion it takes to open a heavy door." He paused. "Now imagine trying to open the steel door to a locked bank vault. Think of pushing all your strength behind that door."

"This is like that?"

"This is a hundred times harder."

Rego leaned back in his chair, his steely eyes appraising me as he tapped his index finger against his lips. "But that would be after making several trips. One or two wouldn't hurt much if you were willing to help our cause."

"Rego," Logan warned, giving his uncle a stern look. "It could kill her."

"We don't know that for sure. If it's for the greater good, she could consider it. She's the one who didn't want her memory erased, after all," Rego replied, arching his eyebrow at Logan.

"So, is everyone who had a near-death experience a Traveler?" I asked, changing the subject.

"Can you tell us more about the accident?" Logan asked, crouching down next to my chair. "How you got the ability to talk to spirits trapped in the other world?"

I nodded numbly. When I was finished telling them the story of how I saved Dylan, Rego actually looked impressed. He even chimed in with, "Fascinating. It sounds like a fear demon got loose."

"What? Are you saying Dylan's a demon?" I blurted out. The kid was annoying as hell, but I couldn't imagine him actually being from hell.

"Nothing like that," Logan said. "It sounds like a fear demon transported Dylan to the middle of the street, since it was his mother's greatest fear that he'd run away like that."

"It's kind of their thing," Ajax chimed in, licking sour cream and onion dust from his fingertips as he swung his feet from his perch on the countertop.

"And you intervened and subsequently died—but were brought back. Had you not been resuscitated, you would have been trapped in the Dark World for the rest of your natural life, just like your friend Dottie," Rego surmised.

I stared down at my fingers as they mashed together in my lap, the news of how I narrowly avoided being a wandering soul, lost in a nightmarish dimension, sinking in and, not surprisingly, making me nauseous. Logan plunked a generic can of lemon-lime soda down in front of me, and I jumped back in surprise.

"Sorry, but you look a little pale," he said apologetically. "I thought you could use some sugar." I took the can gratefully, downing a couple of huge gulps.

"One thing I don't get is, why now? Why attack me at school and kill Travis?" I asked, my voice cracking over his name. "Why not just sneak into my bedroom and kidnap me—not that I want them to get any ideas."

Rego stood up and placed another piece of vellum, this one with a golden hue, over the map. Tiny pinpricks of light dotted the city—several in Central Park, a few in lower Manhattan—but there was a brilliant light marking where Holy Assumption stood.

"We've been looking for places where the membrane between the worlds is thin—places we could use to attempt opening a portal to strike against our enemies on the other side. My spies learned the Regents were doing the same thing. See, every time you've pulled a spirit out of that side into ours, you've impacted that membrane," Rego explained, jabbing each point of light.

"Every time you've talked to Dottie, you've kind of sent a big flare in the air." Logan circled the bright golden light at Holy Assumption with his finger tip. "So we knew there was someone with your talent in this vicinity—and it had to be someone at the school."

"Please don't tell Dottie that!" I begged. "If she knew that talking to me put a big fat glowing target on my back, she'd never forgive herself."

"Wow," Logan said, giving me a half smile. "That's really...nice...of you to look out for her like that."

"Oh. Um. Thanks," I muttered, fidgeting uncomfortably as I caught Rego's suspicious glare. "But it won't really matter, will it? I'm gonna get kidnapped and end up in some demonic version of Holy Ass."

"Look, Paige, no one's going to get you." Logan crouched down again so we were eye level, his voice low and sincere. "Two demons down. I've only got two more to kill."

"They're the new kids, right?"

Logan nodded. "Della's a lust demon—she's here to assist in your capture. She can simulate feelings of attachment, make you think you want to go with them. Aiden's a Regent."

Seeing my confused face, Ajax oh-so-helpfully explained, "They're the most powerful ones. Regents are the ones in charge."

My panic at hearing that a member of the dominant demon race was hunting me must have shown on my face, because Logan quickly grabbed my hand, giving it a squeeze. "I know how to kill a Regent. Trust me, I can protect you."

I took a final gulp from my soda and slammed it on the table, which tilted, and a lone scroll rolled off and hit the floor.

"No."

"No?" Logan's eyes widened, and he dropped my hand and stepped back.

"No?" Ajax repeated. "Did you hit your head, and did all your common sense fall out?"

"No—I mean, teach me. Teach me how to defend myself

against them. Please." I waved my hand toward the living room. "You have a billion weapon-looking things in there. Give me a sword. Teach me to fight. Please."

"While that's admirable, this isn't your war. Now it's time for you to step back and let Logan do his job," Rego said, a bit condescendingly. Logan didn't even acknowledge that his uncle had spoken, and just continued to stare at me.

"Give me a fighting chance," I pleaded, trying to make my voice sound strong—which was a futile task, considering how much it was trembling. "What if you're not around?"

"I'll teach you," Ajax offered, hopping off his perch, only to rest his elbows against the counter behind him, stretching his legs out and crossing his ankles.

"Where? In the kitchen?" Logan scoffed, rolling his eyes at Ajax before turning back to me. "I'll help you," he said, and Rego scowled.

"Logan, if she wants to help, she can by opening portals for me. Having an untrained civilian battling demons is not beneficial to our efforts to take back control of the throne."

Logan stood, turning to face his uncle. "She wielded my sword and killed the *incindia*. I think Paige can handle it."

"Paige isn't the one I'm concerned about," Rego said coolly. "You don't need the distraction." His last word was overflowing with innuendo, and I tugged at my skirt self-consciously, trying to make it longer. Jeez, what did he think I was, a lust demon? I wanted Logan to show me how to use his sword, not show me how to use his *man* sword.

If Logan picked up Rego's insinuation, he ignored it. He turned to face me. "Start tomorrow?"

I gave him a grateful smile and whispered, "Thank you."

"Just let me know if you need a sparring partner," Ajax said flirtatiously, and Logan shot him a withering glance.

"What?" he asked, blinking his eyes innocently. "She's going to be fighting demons, might as well practice on one."

"Practice on one?" I repeated, staring at Ajax, who raised his shoulders, giving me a guilty smile.

"Wait...you're a demon?" I gaped at Ajax, who watched with mild interest as I shot out of my seat, scrambling backward and knocking over my chair. It hit the floor with a loud bang, and Ajax, Logan and I all startled at the noise. Only Rego remained unflustered, his arms folded as he watched the scene with mild interest.

"He's not going to hurt you," Logan said, coming to stand between us, and Ajax shook his empty bag of chips, frowning.

"Oh, I don't know," he sighed. "I could kill for another bag of chips."

"You're not helping," Logan groaned.

"Paige, please, rest assured, Ajax is a trusted comrade, redeeming his reprehensible demonic nature by helping us. He's a double agent, if you will," Rego said, standing up and righting my chair in one swift, smooth move.

"It's because I'm doubly adorable," Ajax said playfully, not seeming at all offended that I'd freaked out when I found out he was a demon. "But perhaps I should leave. My good looks are already terrifying enough—I don't want to give the poor girl a heart attack."

Ajax bowed my way. "Goodbye, dear Bliss. I hope to see you again." Ajax nodded at Rego, promising briskly, "I'll be in touch."

Ajax slapped his palm against the front door, repeating the

words Logan had used. But instead of a white light, the entrance was framed in a purple glow before the door fell in ribbons, revealing a murky, swirling darkness. I could barely make out the faint outline of a hallway; it was like I was staring through polluted, cloudy water. With a crisp salute, Ajax stepped into the abyss, his form obscured by the muddy atmosphere before the door shimmered back into place.

"Where did he go?" I asked nervously.

"Back to his world," Rego said matter-of-factly. "He's got work to do."

"His world? I've never been to Europe, but now I'm in an alternate dimension?" I squeaked.

"You aren't in the Dark World," Logan reassured me, fighting back a smile. "Rego set this place up as a meeting point—but you can't actually use it to cross over." As Logan spoke, he tapped the tips of his fingers together to illustrate his point. "Here, the worlds touch, overlapping in a way. It's useful when you're trying to get allies in both worlds together for strategy sessions, pass supplies along…watch someone eat all your potato chips. But if we tried to follow Ajax through the doorway to the Dark World, we'd be stopped by an invisible barrier."

"So it's like standing on the border of New York and New Jersey, talking to each other?"

Logan grinned at my analogy.

"Something like that. Except the New Yorkers stay in New York and vice versa. Rego will unlink the worlds when we leave town."

"Any other surprises?' I asked, turning to Rego warily. "You're not a zombie, or a vampire? You're just a wizard?"

Apparently, that was the wrong thing to say. Rego frowned,

looking insulted, and his nostrils flared so wide I could have driven a truck through them.

"I'm not just anything, little girl. And witches and wizards are inhabitants of your world who play with potions and perform parlor tricks," Rego corrected me. "Warlocks are an otherworldly race, the true heirs to the Dark World throne. And we will be on that throne again, once this war is over."

He pounded his fist on the table for emphasis, and the rickety old thing wobbled on its shaky legs.

"Sorry," I muttered. "I didn't know any of this existed until a few hours ago."

"And if Logan had done his job correctly, you wouldn't know it existed at all. But what's done is done, and we're here now."

Logan tilted his head toward the door.

"Paige, if you're ready to go, I'll take you home now."

I nodded and stood up, wincing slightly when I pulled my backpack on. And then I had to face Rego.

"Thank you—for everything. I really needed to know. It was…it was hard not knowing the truth," I finished lamely, unsure of what to say to him. Rego was probably the most intimidating person I'd ever met, but then again, he was a warlock fighting to overthrow a demonic dictatorship. I couldn't imagine that kind of life turned you into a warm little cuddle monkey.

"It was enlightening, Paige. Perhaps you can be a useful ally in our fight." Rego shook my hand and bowed majestically, and I was surprised to hear that he sounded sincere.

I nodded and followed Logan, who did the same trick to open the front door, and we walked into a brilliant white glow. Once we stepped through the void, I looked behind me and was surprised to see the metal apartment door back in place. I touched the painted surface, half expecting my hand to go through an illusion. But the brown door was solid underneath my fingertips, the gritty imperfections in the cheap paint job scratching my skin.

"You doing okay?" Logan asked.

"I can burst into flames. Warlocks are real. There's an alternate universe full of demons and monsters. And I'm really freaked out by the fact that I just sat across from another demon while he stuffed his face with potato chips."

"Ajax is harmless," Logan said with a dismissive wave of his hand.

"A demon tried to kill me today, and more want to kidnap me. I'm sorry if I'm not super trusting of them."

"I've known Ajax for years."

"How do you know for sure that you can trust him?" I asked, my hands balling into fists. "He's a demon, and he knows what I can do. What if he's just using you to get to me?"

"We didn't even know you existed when I met him. You didn't exist—not as a Traveler, at least, when I met him," Logan explained, sighing heavily as he leaned against the hallway wall. When he saw I was waiting for him to continue, he took off his hat, staring at his hands as he rolled the brim between his palms.

"Out of all the demons I've ever battled, only three have gotten away. Ajax is one of them." Logan finally met my eyes, and an embarrassed look spread across his face.

"Look, I don't really talk about this kind of stuff, but I'm telling you because I want you to know you're safe, okay?"

He waited until I nodded before he continued talking. "Before I met Ajax, I'd killed every demon I'd faced. And I wanted to make Rego proud, make him see what I could do, you know? So when he got word of a hive of demons in the next town over, I snuck out and attacked them. Solo mission. I thought I was a badass." Logan rested his head against the wall, his eyes studying the ceiling as he remembered. "There were ten. I killed seven. I thought I had gotten away with it until someone grabbed me around the throat in a choke hold. I thought I was done for. Dead Logan, bye-bye." He laughed, and I gaped at him, astonished at the casual way he discussed his near-demise. "It was Ajax. He just kind of stared at me for a minute, and then slaughtered the other two demons who were racing toward me. He killed them, just like that," Logan said, snapping his fingers.

"Then he said he wanted to join up with us. I arranged a meeting for him with Rego, and he's been feeding us information ever since he crossed back over years ago." Logan grinned, his eyes lighting up at some memory. "It took him forever to find the portal back, too. It's his own damn fault for partying too long in Puerto Rico and bringing along rum punch for the trip." He paused, shutting his eyes and chuckling at some memory. "Ajax really likes this side."

"What was he doing in Puerto Rico?"

"Oh, sorry—I didn't explain. The portal's in the western part of the ocean—in the Bermuda Triangle."

"The Bermuda Triangle?" I repeated, my eyebrows practically shooting off my face in surprise. "The real Bermuda Triangle, where planes and boats and ships disappear?"

Logan just nodded. "Yeah. Ajax and two warlocks Rego was sending over to infiltrate the Dark World had a lot of fun before crossing over. Ajax calls it his Spring Break, but I think he was just stalling, because crossing over is supposed to be so painful," Logan revealed.

"I can't believe the Bermuda Triangle is real." I ran my hands over my face and stared at Logan, who just gave me a self-conscious smile.

Who would have thought that the quiet, sweet pen-stealer would be a font of supernatural information with a demonic BFF? I mulled over what Logan had just told me and realized one bit of information wasn't making sense.

"You said he crossed back over years ago?" I repeated, and Logan nodded.

"So, when did you meet him?"

"I was about thirteen." His tone was nonchalant, as if he were sharing what he'd had for lunch. "Ajax was seventeen."

"You were killing demons when you were thirteen?" I yelled in shock.

"Keep it down, I do have neighbors." Logan huffed, adding with a hiss, "Normal, human neighbors."

"I'm sorry," I hastily apologized. "Just…thirteen. You were a little kid, fighting monsters."

Logan pushed himself off the wall, holding his palm out as he began leading me down the hallway. "Give me your bag. Don't think I didn't see you wince in there," he added, tactlessly changing the subject, his tone brisk. "You should have put on the healing balm. Trust me, it works."

I wondered how many times Logan had used the healing balm and how young he started needing it. I snuck a look at his profile as we walked—there was nothing menacing about him, even with the tense set of his jaw. *And it's probably tense because you just insulted his childhood, moron. He's a demonslayer, he's probably been killing monsters since kindergarten.*

I slid the bag off my shoulder and held it out, but kept a tight hold on the strap as Logan grabbed it, and he gave me a questioning look.

"Hey, I'm really sorry. I didn't mean to sound like I was judging the way you grew up."

The guarded expression slid from Logan's face, and for a moment he looked lost and so deeply sad. But he quickly flashed me a grin.

"Don't worry about it," he said, tugging on the strap. "Now, let go and give me the bag. I can be really annoying and persistent when I want something. Just ask Rego."

I dropped my hold on the bag as Logan pushed open the front door of the apartment building, holding it for me.

"Your uncle Rego. He's…interesting." I kept my voice causal as we jogged down the short stoop to the sidewalk. I didn't want to accidentally offend him again, but I was curious—really curious—about who Logan really was.

"I know he can seem difficult, but you have to understand, Paige—Rego is a warrior." Admiration for his uncle colored his voice. "He's a soldier—no, he's more than that. He's leading the charge. He's doing what's right. And what's right is to put a warlock back on the throne.

"But," he added, giving me a sly sideways glance, "I could

see where he's an acquired taste. Rego totally has a chip on his shoulder."

*He has a whole family-size bag of chips on his shoulder.* But I kept my thoughts to myself and just nodded as we continued to walk.

"I don't understand one thing, though."

"Only one thing? You're handling this better than I thought!"

"Okay, I don't understand a lot of things," I admitted, shoving my hands into my coat pockets. "But this one is screaming the loudest for an answer."

"What's that?"

"What's with all the comments about you not doing your job? I mean… You. Saved. My. Life." I paused between each word, trying to drive the point home. "From where I'm standing, still breathing air in a human world, you did your job."

Logan glanced at me, an embarrassed smile on his face as we turned south on Amsterdam Avenue. I was relieved to see fewer fire trucks clogging the street.

"I have a confession to make," Logan said guiltily, looking down at his sneakers as we walked. "I stole your bracelet this morning."

"What? Why?" I asked, stopping short on the sidewalk, pulling Logan off to the side in the alcove of an apartment building.

"Rego had a very clearly defined plan—one I was supposed to follow," he explained, leaning against the glass door. "Find out who's the target, cast a protection spell on something they wear every day that makes them undetectable to demons. Then, I'd pick off the demons, and once you were safe, I'd go wherever Rego needed me next. I'm pretty much his go-to assassin," he added casually, like he'd just described his day shift at the local fast-food joint. Flip a burger, stab a demon, same difference.

"Just like that?" I asked, snapping my fingers.

"Just like that."

"So, what happened?"

"I had a particularly nasty battle with a rage demon in the school basement this morning. I was late in returning your bracelet to your locker after I put the protection spell on it." Logan scowled at the memory.

"Are you okay?"

"I'm fine. Just hit my head a little."

Before I could stop myself, my hand reached up to touch his face. Clearly, my hand had a mind of her own, and she was a big, face-touching flirt.

"Don't worry about me," he insisted, grabbing my wrist to stop me. Once his fingers had circled my wrist, he gave me a disapproving look.

"Paige, where's your bracelet?" Logan asked, exasperated, giving me a hard look. "Make it a little harder on me to fight off demons, why don't you?"

"Because I knew that when I took my bracelet off, right?" I retorted, pulling my wrist back and shoving my hand back in my coat pocket. "I thought the clasp was broken. Or maybe that I had imagined taking it off in the first place. Everyone thinks I'm crazy, Logan. I guess I started to think they were right."

I stared at the buttons of his coat as it hung open, embarrassed by my outburst.

"Sorry," I muttered to the scratched third button on his coat. "I didn't mean all that."

I felt his fingers underneath my chin, and Logan lifted my face to meet his.

"Yeah, you did. And it's okay," he said, keeping his eyes on mine as he let his hand drop from my face. "I didn't mean to make you think you were crazy. I'm sorry."

I paused, taken aback by his sudden change in demeanor.

"It's cool. Um, yeah, no problem." I brushed it off, giving him a bright smile before fishing the bracelet out of my uniform shirt pocket.

"Do you want to get it on?" I asked innocently, trying not to smirk when his words from earlier left my mouth. The corner of Logan's mouth twitched slightly, but he kept a straight face as he fastened the clasp around my wrist.

"Now, don't take it off."

"Does it really matter? They know who I am."

"Only two demons know who you are. Two demons stuck on this side. But they can always send more, Paige," Logan said gravely, and I felt a chill run down my spine. I nodded, staring at the thin platinum swirls that were standing between me and possible indentured servitude in a demonic universe.

We resumed walking home and had just cut behind Lincoln Center when an alarming thought hit me.

"The ones who know me—what's to stop them from coming to my home?" I asked, panicked. "What if they try to hurt my parents?"

"They won't," Logan said, his voice confident.

"How can you be sure?"

"Protection spell on your apartment," Logan said, giving

me a proud smile. "Wasn't even Rego's idea. That one was all mine."

I had a sudden image of Logan wearing a pointed wizard hat and a cloak, standing in the middle of Forty-Fourth Street waving a wand at my apartment building, and had to bite back a laugh.

"Wait—how'd you find out where I live?" I asked, and Logan gave me another smile, this one guilty.

"Like I said, I made that jump a lot. Once I realized you were the target, I found out your address from the school office and went from there."

I mulled that over in my head. "You could have just asked me where I live."

"I guess. It's just that Rego was adamant that I stay in the background, remain insignificant, all of that," Logan continued. "If someone overheard me asking where you lived, and then you disappeared—"

He stopped short, and I finished for him.

"At least no one would suspect you."

He nodded grimly.

"You did talk to me, though," I reminded him.

"I did," he agreed. "At least now I don't have to pretend to be such a quiet, forgettable lump."

"You're not forgettable," I immediately said, and Logan blinked before pressing his lips together in a bashful smile.

"I mean, I don't think I could ever forget the mental image of you writing history notes with a pink pen with jingle bells on top," I quickly added, and Logan squeezed his eyes together at the memory.

"Those things were so loud," he sighed. "I felt like Santa's elf."

I walked a little more closely to Logan, keeping my voice low.

"Can I ask you a question?" I asked, and Logan chuckled.

"What's so funny?"

"You hit me with an Inquisition earlier, and now you want to know if you can ask me a question," Logan said, his brown eyes sparkling with humor. "It's funny."

"This is all really new. I'm not sure of the protocol."

"I'm not sure there is any. You're the first to know the truth. And it's…um, it's nice having someone to talk to about all this," Logan stammered, giving me a slightly shy smile before adding, "Well, someone other than Rego, who's a barrel of fun."

"That's what I wanted to ask you about. Can you tell me about him? All I know is that he's a warlock. But what exactly is a warlock? Are they human?"

Logan adjusted my backpack on his shoulders as we walked. "Warlocks are humans who reigned over the Dark World centuries ago. Think of them as the Dark World version of wizards."

"No, thanks," I snorted. "He seemed insulted when I mentioned the word *wizard*. Like he wanted to bite my head off and ask for seconds."

Logan rolled his eyes. "He's a little precious about how warlocks are regarded—when it's their own damn fault that they aren't in power anymore."

"What do you mean?"

"They thought they could rule both worlds—that nonmagical humans would easily bend to their wills," Logan revealed, shaking his head disapprovingly. "They discovered a few portals to this world and began crossing over, testing how their powers worked in this world. You'd be surprised how many myths and legends in this world are actually about warlocks."

Logan leaned over, his voice a conspiratorial whisper as he spoke into my ear. "The Pied Piper? Totally real, and totally a warlock."

"Get out!" I yelled, then lowered my voice. "Seriously, are you kidding me?"

"Nope." Logan stood straight again, holding a finger to his lips.

"So, where was I? Oh, yeah—half the warlocks were in the Dark World, and the other half were running amok in this one. But they didn't protect their stronghold on the other side all that well. They were overthrown by Regents pretty quickly, and the warlocks that survived were banished to live in this world."

"What exactly are Regents?" I asked, confused. "Are they called that just because they're royal?"

"Yeah, some are royal, but they're also the most powerful race of demons." Logan frowned, rubbing his jaw with his palm as he spoke. "Most demons derive their strength from one naturally occurring element—basically, nature, or strong emotions. You've got fire demons, ice demons, fear demons, lust demons, and so on. But the Regents aren't bound by these rules. They can channel all the elements. They're an ancient clan—descended from the ones who banished warlocks. They're the ones who destroyed most of the portals—

the ones that were easy to get to, at least. And Regents have been in power ever since, with the warlocks working on rebuilding their numbers, intent on taking back the throne someday. And someday is coming up."

I opened my mouth to ask Logan why he decided to fight for the warlocks—after all, they didn't come out smelling all that rosy in his little history lesson. But then Blaise's barbaric murder of Travis flooded my memory, and I realized it wasn't hard to pick a side. But it did make me wonder something about Logan.

I paused. "Can I ask you another question?"

Logan gave me a cautious look. "Since you're asking again, I have a feeling this is a serious question."

"Yep."

"Sure, shoot."

"Your uncle is a warlock."

"That's not a question," Logan replied warily.

"I know you're a demonslayer, but are you also a warlock? Since your uncle is one and all. Or is he a demonslayer, too?"

Logan stared at me, confused, until a playful smirk tugged at his lips.

"Do you think demonslaying is something I was born into? Like, I have some weird birthmark on my foot that marks me as the chosen scourge of demons?" He made his voice deep and dramatic, like he was narrating a movie trailer.

"Something like that," I admitted sheepishly.

"You watch too many movies," he teased, nudging me with his shoulder as we crossed the street.

"You have an invisible sword strapped to your back and can open doors with magic spells," I countered, nudging him back, and he nearly stumbled into a parking meter. "What was I supposed to think?"

"Well, to answer your question, demonslaying is a profession. It's not a kind of person. All my skills are the product of years of training. And Rego's not actually related to me."

I frowned. "Then why do you call him your uncle?"

He just shrugged, causing my backpack to bounce around. "We travel around a lot. It's just easier to say he's my uncle. I can't exactly tell everyone, 'Oh, that's my dad's childhood warlock buddy who's been taking care of me ever since my... well, ever since I was eight.'"

"Your dad is a warlock, too?"

Logan sighed heavily, his breath coming out as white smoke in the cold air. "Yeah, he is...was." His face twisted with sadness and anger as he spoke. "I'm half-warlock, technically. If it wasn't for Rego, I don't know what I'd be. Dead, probably. Can we change the subject, please?" he asked, whipping his head to face me as we walked. His eyes were again ringed with a deep sadness, and the tortured look on his face made me nod quickly in agreement.

We walked in silence for a few more chilly blocks, until Logan finally spoke.

"Your bag is vibrating. I think your phone is going off."

"My phone?" Oh, crap. I missed my dad's usual check-in phone call. "Oh, no. This is bad."

"A missed call? *This* is bad? Yeah, this and heights make you tremble, but you want to learn how to fight demons and already took out an *incendia* like you were swatting a fly." The teasing tone had returned to his voice, to my relief, and

Logan turned around so I could fish my phone out of the back pocket of my bag.

"Yeah, this is bad." I looked at my phone screen. Five missed calls, plus a very angry, very worried all-caps text.

"Your boyfriend?" Logan asked casually, and I laughed.

"Yeah, right. Bellevue Kelly's beating them off with a stick," I said, calling my dad and pressing the phone to my ear. "And if you listen to the gossip, I probably had a conversation with the stick."

Logan opened his mouth to reply, but I quickly interjected, "It's my dad. When your kid's me, you tend to worry."

My dad answered on the first ring.

"Dad, I'm on my way home—"

"Where have you been? You're more than four hours late!" Oh, crap. The words poured out of my dad with such urgency that my phone actually shook from his frenetic tone.

"Dad, I'm just a few blocks away." I sighed. "We're walking home now."

"Who's this 'we'?" Oh, crap squared. What was I going to tell my father?

"Just someone from school, Dad. Please," I pleaded, sneaking a look at Logan, who was deliberately pretending to look in the windows of a bodega as we walked past, feigning interest in the expired boxes of crackers on display. "Can't you just trust me?"

"How can I when I've never even heard of this friend before?"

"Dad, he's real, I swear," I hissed into the phone.

"He?" Oh, crap to infinity. Maybe I should have gone with an imaginary friend.

"Just a friend, Dad. Um, is Mom there yet?" I really, really hoped my mom was there.

"Paige, we'll talk when you get home." My dad unceremoniously ended the phone call.

"Well, that went really well," I said, shoving the phone into my coat pocket.

"Your dad sounds really, um—" Logan paused, his eyes casting upward as he searched for the right word "—protective. I could overhear his side of the conversation." He gave me an apologetic smile. *Of course he heard him. The demons in the Dark World probably heard him.*

"Well, he's used to a crazy daughter who talks to imaginary friends, so right now he thinks I'm off somewhere talking to a wall."

"It's not so bad. Your parents care about you, that's all. You're lucky." The ghost of a wistful look crossed his face, but it disappeared so quickly I couldn't be sure if I'd seen it.

"Your dad really thinks you're off talking to a wall?" he asked, and I nodded, rolling my eyes.

"Or a parking meter."

"Maybe a squirrel?" Logan cracked a hesitant smile.

"Don't laugh, that happened once," I said, thinking of my date with Chris by the carousel in Central Park.

"Well, we can't tell your father that you fought off a demon, but—" he paused, giving me a hesitant glance "—maybe if he met me he'd know you weren't talking to squirrels."

"It was just the one squirrel."

Logan paused. "Who was it, really?"

"Just a really nice woman. She had flowers in her hair," I murmured, remembering how happy she was to be back in our Central Park. She told me all about her afternoons taking strolls in the park with her boyfriend. I originally thought she was simply ditzy—especially since she introduced herself as Feather and twirled around as she spoke, her long pastel skirt rippling around her in a bell, like petals on a tulip. I was suddenly hit with overwhelming sadness for her, being stuck in a warped version of Central Park. I changed the subject as quickly as possible, talking with Logan about movies, music and the most non-demonic topics I could think of until we got to my apartment.

My father must have been watching for me through the peephole, since he yanked the door open while my keys were still in it. His face was the color of his bright red hair— something I would have teased him about if I hadn't been the cause of his crimson complexion.

"Where the hell have you been, young lady? We've been worried sick!" The vein in his forehead throbbed so violently I thought it might reach out and flick me in the ear. "You know you're supposed to check in. Did you know there was an accident at school?"

"Dad, I'm fine," I said, holding my palms out in surrender as my mom joined my dad at the door. "I was hanging out with a friend." I jerked my thumb next to me, where Logan was a few feet down the hall, tying his shoelace out of my dad's line of vision.

"What friend?" my dad asked, the color draining from his face as his anger developed into concern.

"Sorry," Logan mouthed, quickly getting up and coming to stand by my side.

"Hi, Mr. Kelly," Logan said, his smile fading when he saw the suspicious look on my dad's face. "It's nice to meet you."

"And you are?" Dad asked, giving Logan a possibly lethal glare.

"Logan. Um, I go to school with Paige?" he replied as if it were a question, causing me to stare at him incredulously. Logan held out his hand tentatively, a nervous smile plastered on his face. I couldn't believe it. Demons were no problem for Logan Bradley, but two seconds with my father and he needed a hug and some hot chocolate.

I gave my mom my best pleading look, and she gently whacked my father on his arm with the back of her knuckles before she shook Logan's hand warmly.

"Logan, it's lovely to meet you. Won't you come in for a moment?"

"Thanks, but I have to get going. We were talking and let time get away from us," Logan said, looking visibly relieved to be addressing my mother. "I just wanted to make sure Paige got home okay. But, um, Mr. Kelly? What did you say happened at school?"

My father, who had relaxed slightly when Logan said he had to leave, sighed heavily. "There was some kind of accident at school—huge explosion in one of the classrooms."

"Did they say what caused it?" Logan pressed, and my dad frowned.

"No, all we got was an email from the school that there was a fire and it was contained. The news is starting to cover it."

"I wonder what happened. Maybe school will be canceled next week," I suggested cheerfully. *That sounds like something someone who had absolutely nothing to do with the fire would say, right?*

"That would be pretty awesome," Logan agreed, picking up my angle and giving me a sideways smile.

"Well, miss, you're already late for dinner." My father held the door out farther and ushered me inside, barely giving me a chance to take my backpack from Logan. As I grabbed the straps, Logan pulled the bag a little closer.

"I'll call you later, okay?" he whispered. I nodded, but his reaction was blocked by my father letting the door slam shut.

"Dad, why are you being so rude?"

"Me, rude? Young lady, you were extremely late. You didn't check in, didn't let us know you wouldn't be home for dinner—" he ticked my crimes off on his fingers "—and then you show up at the door with that kid."

I folded my arms across my chest. "That kid, as you call him, has a name. And Logan is just a friend." Who saved my life.

"Peach, listen," my dad began, and I stiffened. When I was a little kid, I mispronounced my name as "Peach"—and once upon a time, it was a term of endearment. Now, my dad only used it when he was about to say something I wasn't going to like.

"I think you need to be careful," Dad said, folding his arms as well as he leaned against our navy couch. "We don't exactly know what that boy's intentions are."

"It's not like that. We're just friends, Dad."

"Paige, you're fragile and—"

"Fragile?" I interrupted him, annoyed. Fragile? The word

always triggered a negative reaction from me. But after today, it ignited a rapidly shortening fuse. "Dad, seriously. Come on."

"Richard...." my mom began, his name sounding like a warning. But my dad ignored her.

"I don't want someone taking advantage of you or pressuring you into something," my father said. "You know that you're troubled."

And at that, my fuse ran out, and my frustration exploded.

"Oh, right, Dad, he walked me home so I'm going to go throw myself at him, have unprotected sex and drop out of school to have a bajillion of his babies because I'm fragile and crazy and need to be locked up!"

"Paige, watch your mouth!" my dad scolded, standing up. Fire trucks would have been jealous of the shade of red he turned.

"Dad, give me a little credit!" I mimicked his tone.

"Richard, I think you and I need to have a little conversation," my mom said through pressed-together teeth, and motioned for my father to follow her to their room.

I stomped away to my room, angry at my father for treating me like a naive, crazy little girl when, as far as he knew, the biggest crime I'd committed was making a new friend.

"If only he knew the truth," I muttered to myself as I peeled off Logan's sweater and my uniform, surveying the damage done to my side. A six-inch-wide swatch of skin was already puckered and shiny, as if the burn was already months old. I grabbed the healing balm, wrapped myself in my robe and was almost in the bathroom when I heard my mom's persuasive tone coming through my parents' door. I paused outside to eavesdrop. I couldn't help it—my mom could sell fish to the ocean, so I had to know what she was telling my dad.

"—hasn't had an episode in months. Maybe we've finally found the right combination of pills." Go, Mom! Even though I was careful to flush the pills every single morning, instead of taking them.

"It doesn't matter, Anna. I don't want some hoodlum taking advantage of her." I clapped my hand over my mouth to stop myself from laughing at the thought of Logan as a hoodlum—the feared leader of the infamous pen-stealing gang.

"I saw the way he was looking at her. Don't tell me they're just friends. And that attitude? Where did that come from? Him?"

"Really, Rich? That's perfectly normal teenage girl behavior, especially after what you insinuated. We raised our daughter better than to go off and boink the first boy she meets." I shuddered at my mother's use of the word *boink,* especially in relation to me.

"We're going to support her new friendship—" My mom's voice got louder—meaning she was coming closer to the door—and I scurried off to the bathroom, slipping inside just as I heard their bedroom door open.

I rested my back against the bathroom door, my head lightly thunking against the wood frame even though a thick yellow towel was hanging on the back to cushion the blow.

"Better get this over with," I muttered, grabbing the jar out of the pocket of my robe. I popped open the lid and skeptically sniffed the gelatinous goo. It had a faint odor, briny and slightly sour, like stagnant water near a beach.

I dipped a finger in the mix, half expecting it to burst into flames or melt my skin off. Maybe Rego added a dose of *som*—whatever that hypnosis spell was. Instead, my fingertip met a slightly oily cream, thick like butter only bright blue. I slid out of my terrycloth robe and swabbed my fingertip at the center of the burn, which tingled at my touch.

And then I heard a slight fizzing sound as the cream began to bubble on my skin.

Frantic, I grabbed a washcloth and scrubbed at the spot, making the surrounding skin even more tender. And then I stared at my rib cage in shock.

There, in the center of the burn, was a dime-sized section of perfectly healed skin.

# 05

I SHOULD HAVE BEEN ASLEEP. MY DAY SHOULD have left me exhausted, passed out in my bed with my cat at my feet and my pillow covered in drool. But instead, I was eating Hershey's Kisses and sitting on the hardwood floor of my room, my back resting against the pink and pale yellow comforter on my bed while a mix of my happiest songs played. Usually, the music put me in a better head space. At the very least, it helped mask the grating voices of the slightly drunk people who often walked down our block, headed home from the bars on Ninth Avenue. The slurred conversations wafted into my second-floor bedroom because my street-facing windows were open, letting blasts of wintry air cool my fire-demon-heated skin.

I wanted to talk today over with someone, but I didn't know who. Dottie was my go-to, but she couldn't exactly pick up a phone. My dad seemed to think that a boy walking me home was a federal offense—no matter how many times my mom had scolded him over dinner. My mom was rooting for Team Normal Paige—hell, she was the captain of the cheerleading squad—so how could I tell her everything I'd learned today? I had cousins in Long Island and Jersey, but they were all older and had dismissed me as some attention-seeking kid going through a phase. Every year for Christmas they gave me their old goth CDs and bell-sleeved lace tops, calling them "vintage." I knew they meant well, but it felt like they thought I was depressed. And, apparently, trapped in the nineties.

And I couldn't exactly talk to Logan—not that I had his number. But part of what I wanted to talk about was Logan. I felt my cheeks get hot as I thought about what my father had said. How *did* Logan look at me? What was he talking about?

"Ugh, don't you lose your mind over it. Dad would freak out if a boy so much as breathed in your direction. That's it," I whispered, even though I couldn't stop the indulgent smile that crept across my face as I thought about the sweet way he held my hand to comfort me.

*What are you doing, Paige? Swooning?* I banged the back of my head against the mattress. I couldn't find one legitimate reason not to trust Logan, and yet, part of me was skeptical. I had to be. Even though, if it weren't for him, I'd be doing push-ups in a demon army or whatever it was demons made you do when you were drafted into service. Or, I'd be dead, a floating spirit with Dottie in a grotesque Dark World version of Holy Ass.

Stuck in high school for the rest of my natural life. Talk about hell.

"Maybe you're just naturally suspicious. Just like your kitty," I muttered, staring at my cat as he gingerly approached me, cautiously smelling my sock-covered foot before jumping five feet in the air when my phone rang. I grabbed it from my nightstand while Mercer retreated into the closet, hiding behind an old acoustic guitar that I'd never quite mastered, no matter how much I practiced.

I stared at my phone, puzzling over the unfamiliar number. It was a New York area code, but I didn't recognize it.

"Hello?" I answered, switching off my music.

"Hey, it's Logan." I could barely hear him over the sound of clattering plates and canned music in the background.

"Logan?" I called, not sure if he could hear me.

"Logan—um, Logan Bradley," he replied stiffly, sounding slightly official, as if he were talking to someone's parents.

"I know who Logan is. I just— Where are you?"

"A diner. I snuck behind the counter because I don't have a phone." He said it casually, as if it were inconsequential— something that would have been a dark source of shame to everyone I knew at school. Then again, Logan wasn't exactly like everyone else. "Hey, what's your roof like?"

"My roof?" I repeated, standing up from the floor and pacing around my bedroom. I could barely understand him with all the background noise.

"Yeah, the roof of your apartment building. Can you get up there?" His voice was difficult to hear—his words rushed, drowned out by shouting.

"The super locks it during the winter." I kicked a fuzzy blue sock that Mercer had earlier claimed as his into the closet, trying to bait him into coming out, and was rewarded with an evil kitty death stare.

"Then it's probably a good spot. Want to meet me up there tomorrow morning?"

"We can't get up there," I reminded him. "It's locked."

"Locks aren't a problem for me." Even with the background noise, I could detect the slightly smug tone in his voice, and I remembered how he had no problem getting access to the roof of Holy Assumption. Jeez, he really was arrogant when it came to all things magical.

"Show-off," I muttered, and I heard him chuckle before returning to his businesslike tone.

"The manager's coming, so want to meet up on your roof tomorrow or not?"

"Um…okay," I said. Crap, I hadn't cleared this with my parents. "If I can't, how can I reach you?"

"If you're not there at eleven, then I'll know you—" It sounded like he said, "can't come," but the cacophony in the diner increased, drowning him out.

"Okay." I paused. "Um, thanks, Logan."

"I'm getting kicked out," he nearly yelled. "See you to-morr—"

The call disconnected, leaving me staring at the slightly warm phone in my hand as I sank onto my bed, puzzled by Logan's abrupt goodbye. Why didn't he have a phone? Did he seriously just get thrown out of a diner for calling me? And what does someone even wear to learn to fight demons?

I was glad I had a plan—even a plan as basic as Demon Defense 101 with Logan. It made me feel less weak, less powerless, less a victim of what was happening. The memory of Travis's brutal last moments flashed in front of my face, and I shut my eyes, trying to mentally force the image out as I took a long, deep breath.

"You saw some horrible things today. But you cheated death again, and you're still alive," I reminded myself aloud.

"If you want to stay that way, suck it up, get some sleep and learn how to kill demons tomorrow."

My voice echoed slightly against my pale pink bedroom walls.

"Those are probably the most unexpected words anyone ever put together," I whispered, flopping down on my bed and burying my head under the pillow.

But I was wrong: the most unexpected words were uttered by my father the next morning over breakfast. When I announced that I was going to hang out with Logan that day, my father simply—and a tad begrudgingly—told me, "Have a good time."

I nearly dropped my forkful of spinach omelet in shock, and I darted a quizzical look at my mom, who just winked at me and patted my father's shoulder.

"Your father and I are going to dinner, and then to that play—" my mom stifled a groan as she mentioned the theatrical torture in store "—so we'll see you later on tonight."

"Okay, Mom." I smiled, mouthing "thanks," since my dad's drastic change in demeanor was clearly all her doing.

"So, what exactly do you have planned for your day?" my father asked, trying his best to sound unconcerned as he repeatedly smacked the bottom of a hot sauce bottle. He was so busy studying my face, awaiting my answer, that he ended up drowning his eggs in the spicy goop.

I was glad I had an answer prepared. "The Museum of Natural History. Our school IDs get us in for cheap, and Logan's never been there." I assumed. Unless some of those relics in Rego's room were stolen artifacts.

"Well, have fun," Mom said cheerfully, handing my father a spoon to scoop up the extra hot sauce. "Bundle up, it's cold out!"

But until the fire demon powers wore off, being cold wasn't going to be a problem. I slipped on what I thought was a good uniform for demon-killing class: jeans, a tank top and my light blue hoodie—my favorite, because it was one of the few I owned that didn't have some kind of company's logo on it—*thanks, Dad!*

I barely made it to the third floor before I became so over-heated I ripped my coat off like it was a parasite attached to my skin. By the fifth floor, a slight but refreshing cold breeze wafted down the stairway. I kept climbing and found the roof access door being held open by a crumpled-up soda can.

"Hello? Logan?" I called. The rusty hinges squealed as I pushed the door open and stepped onto the tar roof, which was covered in a faint dusting of frost. Snowdrifts piled up on the west side of the roof, and a weather-beaten picnic table, left up here year-round by a charitable tenant, sat in the cor-ner. Logan, clad in jeans, a zipped-up hoodie and his ever-present baseball cap, was sitting on its bench, his forearms resting on his knees and a blue paper cup filled with some kind of steaming beverage in his hands.

"Hey, you made it." Logan grabbed a second cup from the table and got up. He held the cup out as I walked over to where he now stood.

"Watered-down hot chocolate, since I had to hang up so rudely?" he offered, swirling the liquid in the cup with a smile on his face.

"Well, when you make it sound that enticing..." I replied,

smiling back as I took the lukewarm cup of cocoa and sipped it. Yep, it was watered down, but still sweet.

"Thanks, I love chocolate."

"I know."

"How do you know?" I asked, one eyebrow raised. "Is this one of those 'All Girls Love Chocolate' things?"

"No, it's a 'You're Always Eating Hershey's Kisses' thing," Logan replied.

"Oh. Yeah. I guess I am," I agreed, surprised that he noticed.

"So, why did you want to meet here?" I looked around the isolated roof, confused, as I dumped my coat and bag on the picnic bench.

"It's a whole floor taller than the other buildings nearby," Logan explained. Seeing my puzzled look, he continued, "No one can see what happens on this roof. And we don't want someone calling the cops if they notice us battling with giant swords."

*Yes! I get a sword.* I internally high-fived myself.

"Makes sense." I nodded my head, taking another sip of the sugary cocoa as we walked to the center of the roof. "It is pretty private up here on Tar Beach."

"Tar Beach?" Logan repeated, frowning in confusion.

"Yep, Tar Beach." I tapped the blacktop with my toe. "My parents grew up in the city, and when they were kids, they hung out on the rooftops during the summer—you know, instead of the beach. They called it 'Tar Beach' and I just picked it up from them. I like lying out here in the summer. Just me, a bikini and my headphones. As long as I don't go too close to the edge, it's really relaxing."

"Um, yeah. Yeah, I bet." Logan averted his eyes, looking around the rooftop as he took another swig from his cup.

"Everyone does it," I explained, seeing the uncomfortable expression on his face. "It's not that weird."

I took another sip of my cocoa, frowning at his reaction.

"So, how are you doing? You know, with everything that happened…" His tone was casual, but his brown eyes were serious as he regarded me underneath the shady blue brim of his baseball cap.

"You mean, how, in less than twenty-four hours, I learned about the existence of an alternate universe full of demons?"

"Yeah. That."

"I'm dealing with it." I looked down at the pattern the soles of my Converse shoes left in the snow. I didn't want to dwell on yesterday; I wanted to move on. "It's not going to do me any good to sit around freaking out about it. But it will do me a butt-load of good to learn how to kick some demon ass."

Logan looked impressed, then drained the rest of his cup, crumpling it up and tossing it by the door to the roof.

"Well, that's what we're here for. One order of demon ass-kicking, coming up."

He then reached behind his shoulder to unsheathe his invisible sword. With one deft move, he twisted the sword so the silver handle was facing me.

"You'll be using mine for today," he explained, holding the sword closer to me.

"Do you always wear that thing?" I asked, stepping to the side to peer behind him. I still couldn't see anything but the beat-up fabric on the back of his black hoodie.

"Yes. Always." His voice was matter-of-fact. "And so will you."

Oh. Suddenly, the reasons for constantly having a sword around outweighed the cool factor of the sword itself. I must have been broadcasting my emotions all over my face, because when Logan spoke again, his tone was more soothing.

"Don't worry about it. You won't even notice it's there." He held out the sword and twisted his wrist quickly. My eyes followed the blade as he sliced it through the air in short bursts. "The sword doesn't have a form—no weight, no mass. It materializes when you need it. It's there to protect you."

He shifted his grip on the handle, so it was facing me again.

"Well, in that case…I've worn worse accessories," I weakly joked, reaching out for the weapon. As soon as I took the sword in my hands, Logan reached behind his other shoulder and revealed a second sword. It was a slightly smaller version of his, and Logan twirled it expertly, the blade whooshing as it quickly cut through the air in a figure eight.

"This one," he said, tossing the sword up high, where it spun twice before he caught it, his palm slapping against the handle, "is yours. But I'll be using it today." He whipped it into the air again, catching the handle behind his lower back with a smirk on his face.

I held my hands up and golf clapped around the sword handle for Logan, who bowed dramatically.

"Thank you, but I'm not that great." Logan affected an air of false modesty as he tossed the sword in the air again, this time catching it and balancing the silver handle on the tips of his fingers. His eyes glinted mischievously, and he loudly whispered, "Okay, maybe I am that great."

I scowled in mock annoyance, but I couldn't help giggling. Logan was entertaining when he was in his element, playfully confident to a point where it was almost conceited. But his little display wasn't off-putting—especially since I'd known him to be so shy. It was…cute. Really, really cute when he was showing off. And I couldn't help goading him.

"Pfft. I've seen better," I said.

"Oh, really? All right, tough girl, show me what you've got," Logan challenged, a glint in his eye.

I held his sword close to my face and inspected it. It looked different today—the blade was no longer ice-blue, but a cloudy purple, like a thin sliver of amethyst.

"Why doesn't this look the same as yesterday?" I turned the blade back and forth as I examined it.

"It reacts to the type of demon nearby. I don't think I have to tell you that it's something of a—" he paused, looking around the roof before continuing in an exaggerated whisper "—magic sword."

"The whole disappearing-behind-your-back-into-the-ether thing clued me in to that part," I replied, clasping the handle with both hands and holding the sword over my shoulder.

"So, what do you want me to do now?" I asked, expecting to run through drills or basic maneuvers. Instead, Logan oh-so-casually commanded, "Attack me."

"What?" I stared at him, dumbfounded, as I abandoned my stance, holding the sword at my side.

"You heard me." He tapped the sword in my hand with the one he was holding, and a wind-chime-like ringing echoed around the rooftop.

"What are you waiting for, Paige? Take that bad boy and try to ram it through me."

He tapped the blade again, and the handle slipped from my fingers, the sword falling on the ground.

"You want me to attack you? With a huge sword? I'm not going to do that!" I cried, staring at him in shock. "What, do you have a death wish?"

"You're not going to hurt me," he said confidently.

"How do you know? Maybe I'm a secret ninja." I crossed my arms and raised an eyebrow at him. "Maybe I took fencing lessons. You don't know. I could be lethal."

Logan flipped the sword upside down, crossing his ankles and balancing his palm against the handle like the blade was an old-fashioned cane.

"Oh, so you took Secret Ninja Fencing Classes?" He gave me an impish grin. "Haven't heard of those."

"Fine, I have no formal training," I huffed, "but you didn't know that."

"Look, Paige, it's not an insult to your skills. It's impossible to hurt me with my own sword. Magic sword, remember?"

"Seriously?"

Logan nodded. "There's no way in hell I'm going to lose my weapon in a battle and get killed with my own sword. That would just be…insulting." He shuddered in disgust. "It almost happened once. That's when I came up with the idea and had Rego charm the sword."

"What happened?"

Logan shook his head. "Story for another time. But it's a good tactic for battle. Pretend to drop it, demon grabs it—

you don't know how many demons try to take my head off with my own sword—only to let it be the last thing they do."

He chuckled at the memory, as I just smiled uneasily. *Demons trying to behead you? Yeah, that's hilarious.*

"Seriously, try to hurt me. You won't be able to."

I held the sword aloft and gently rapped it against his shoulder. It bounced harmlessly off his sleeve as if it were rubber.

"See? It's like attacking me with a teddy bear."

"A giant, magic, bloodthirsty teddy bear," I clarified, then shut my eyes, sighing heavily. *I bet those exist in the Dark World.*

"Now that you know you can't hurt me, try to get a good hit in, and I'll block you."

He waved the sword in the air with a flourish and held out his other hand, crooking a finger at me.

"I mean, if you think you've got what it takes. I know we're on a roof, and you're afraid of heights...."

I knew he was doing his best to taunt me, but still, I narrowed my eyes and held the sword with both hands, swinging hard at Logan's side. With a barely perceptible flick of his wrist, he blocked me, the swords crashing with the sound of shattering crystal mixed with wind chimes.

Raising the sword above my head, I tried again, and Logan stopped my blade with a minute twist of his hand. After about twenty more tries, my arms were getting tired, and the ground around me was a tapestry of my frantic footprints in the snow. Logan, on the other hand, had barely moved from his spot.

"I thought you were serious about this," Logan deadpanned, pretending to yawn as he simultaneously blocked what I thought was my best move yet.

"I am," I insisted, a little breathless. "I can't help that you're some kind of superstrong demon-fighting hero."

"Not a hero. Just well trained, that's all," Logan replied, a faint blush coloring his cheeks. He cleared his throat and assumed a more serious tone. "I think we should focus on how to block. It's not like you're going to be infiltrating hives of demons anytime soon—you just need to know how to defend yourself."

He took a step back, biting his lip as he studied me.

"You're holding the sword all wrong," he finally decided, slipping my sword into the invisible case behind his back before crossing the few feet to stand in front of me.

"Do you mind?" he asked, holding his palms up.

"No," I replied, not quite sure what he was getting at. And then he stood behind me, placing his hands on my hips. I was surprised that he asked for permission to touch me, considering all the hand-holding we'd done yesterday—but then I reminded myself that he'd merely been trying to keep me from bursting into flames. Still, I jolted slightly at his touch.

"Relax, Paige. Your stance is too rigid," Logan said, his voice in my ear. "Bend your knees."

I did as I was told, and Logan put his hands on my elbows, sliding his palms down my arms, until his hands covered mine, lacing his fingers through mine.

"You've been holding the sword over your shoulder like it's a baseball bat. You're not trying to hit a home run." Logan chuckled, and his breath tickled my ear. He pulled my hands lower in one decisive move.

"You want to protect yourself. The goal is to deflect my blade. You don't have to do big, elaborate gestures, okay?"

He guided my hands, slicing the blade through the air with deliberate, swift movements.

"Got it?" Logan asked, and I nodded stiffly, hyperaware of his chest being pressed against my back. Logan stopped moving the sword but didn't step away, keeping his arms around me, his hands over mine. I felt my heartbeat quicken, not sure if I liked him being so close—or if I was unnerved by it. The relief and disappointment I felt when he stepped away told me it was a little of both.

"Now, try to block me." Logan was facing me again, holding his weapon in the same deadly stance I'd seen him take in the classroom the day before.

"Don't worry—this is your sword, so the same rules apply," he reassured me before lightly whacking my arm. The blade painlessly bounced off my arm, and I yelped.

"Are you okay?" Logan asked, his eyes wide with concern.

"Yeah—just surprised," I admitted, embarrassed.

"I'll go slower," Logan promised, but I shook my head.

"No—a demon wouldn't. Don't go easy on me." I held my sword in the position Logan had taught me, and struck out at him. He blocked it, of course, but offered an approving, "Very nice."

"I'm a quick learner." I smirked, striking again as our blades collided with a deafening crystalline crash.

Several hours later, we were sitting side by side at the picnic table, eating take-out pizza as Logan offered up demon-fighting tips.

"Your sword is tangible as soon as you touch it, so don't

tip your hand by reaching for it until you need it," he cautioned. "You don't want them knowing that you're armed."

I bit into my cheesy slice, mulling over everything I'd learned about these mystical weapons—and realized something wasn't adding up.

"Hey, can I ask you a question?"

Logan's warm brown eyes widened in mock terror. "Uh-oh, you're asking again. This can't be good."

I gave him a withering look, and he bowed his head, holding out his slice of pizza as if to say, "Proceed."

"If I can't hurt you with your own sword, then why didn't you just take it from me yesterday in detention?" I asked, wiping pizza grease off my hand with a napkin. "It's not like I could have hurt you."

"That's true, but to just grab my sword from you? That would have been…I don't know—" he turned to face me, straddling the bench as he searched for the word "—rude. Yeah, I think it would have been rude."

"Rude?" I repeated, surprised. I had been expecting something a little more magically cryptic as an answer—certainly not something polite.

"Not chivalrous. I don't know." Logan sighed. He took off his hat, rolling the worn blue brim between his palms as his hair fell into his eyes. "You had just been attacked. You were so upset, and you were injured. You were also on fire," he reminded me, then paused. "And it's all my fault you were in that situation because I made you think you were crazy, and I didn't get there in time, and…"

Logan ran his fingers through his messy dark brown hair before setting the cap back on his head.

"I don't blame you. At all," I said.

Logan smiled a small, but genuine smile, before it spread into a more playful one.

"Don't tell your dad that. I think he wants to believe that you secretly despise me," he teased, and lightly kicked my sneaker with his.

"Shut up and eat your pizza," I said, wrinkling my nose at him.

"That's not a threat. This is so good," Logan moaned, giving his pepperoni slice a loving look. "You have no idea how so many places just get pizza wrong. Like cardboard covered in salty ketchup. It's practically abusive what they do to it," he added dramatically before taking a massive bite.

"The farthest I've ever been is Florida—and that was when I was a little kid," I admitted. "I don't remember the food, just Disney World."

"Chicago pizza is good," Logan said thoughtfully, peeling a piece of pepperoni off his slice and popping it into his mouth. "But just an average, everyday New York slice… damn, there's nothing like it."

"When were you in Chicago?"

"About two years ago, I think it was." Logan's brows pulled together in confusion. "Or maybe three. It was after we were in Texas."

"You don't remember when you lived in Chicago?"

"I'll be honest, time kind of runs together when you do what I do." Logan brushed crumbs off his jeans as he spoke. "It gets boring."

"Boring?" I gaped, nearly dropping my slice in surprise. "How is what you do boring?"

Logan shrugged out of his hoodie and turned around so he could rest his elbows against the table behind him. His current pose put the more aesthetic benefits of demonslaying on display, Logan's thin black T-shirt showing off what hoodies and his bulky uniform sweater hid. *That evil, terrible, selfish sweater.* I averted my eyes quickly before Logan caught me checking him out, busying myself with retying the broken lace on my otherwise perfectly tied Converse.

"It's just boring. Killing demons gets repetitive. If I have any kind of social life, it's because I'm tracking a demon to a party or whatever." As he spoke, Logan pulled at the tufts of brown hair sticking out from underneath the brim of his hat. "It's not like Ajax and I go clubbing. It's not like I make friends in every city and keep in touch with them after we move."

"Right. Of course not," I said hastily. I took another bite of my slice and chewed it silently, but I'd lost my appetite, now that I'd been reminded that this friendship had an expiration date.

Logan was quiet for a moment before shifting on the bench to face me.

"Look, Paige. I didn't mean it like that," Logan said. "It's more that I'm usually a ghost in people's lives. The person who comes in—and then disappears. I never spend more than a few months in any place. I can't keep in touch. There are no visits over Christmas break. There's no point in making friends."

"I can understand that—sort of." I pressed my finger on a bead of condensation on the outside of my soda cup, swirling the liquid in loopy, abstract patterns as I spoke. "Why bother getting close to someone if you're just going to get hurt, right?"

"When I leave, you mean?"

I stole a glance at Logan, and wondered if he was speaking in the abstract, or specifically about me.

"I'm just saying, I understand the impulse." I sidestepped his question, pretending not to notice how the thought of him leaving—the first living, breathing person to know the truth about me—truly stung. "I don't bother trying to get close to people, because they leave me or turn on me because I can't tell the difference between the living and the dead."

"There's something to be said for being self-sufficient, isn't there?" Logan shot me a sideways glance as he picked up his soda, and I nodded.

"It's safe," I admitted. "And smart."

"At least for the time being, we can be self-sufficient with each other," he said, holding out his cup in a toast. Our knuckles brushed as I tapped my cup against his, the ice slushing softly against the sides. Our eyes locked for a lengthy moment—too lengthy—in a gaze fraught with the kind of delicious tension and chest-warming rush of adrenaline that sets your heart pounding and your lips turning up into a smile of their own volition.

The kind of gaze that inspires trite songs that usually piss me off, because songwriters always rhyme "eyes" with "surprise," and I always considered it lazy songwriting.

Until now. Because I could have sworn I saw deep affection and sadness in Logan's eyes, and that surprised the hell out of me.

I stood up abruptly, nearly knocking my soda over. Logan

reached out to steady the cup at the same time I did, and our hands touched—which made both of us jerk our hands back, leaving the soda to spill all over the bench.

"Sorry," he muttered, flustered.

"It's fine—I was done with it anyway," I lied, equally as flustered as I busied myself by cleaning up, stuffing our garbage into the empty pizza box and mentally fighting with myself.

What was I doing?

*What was he doing?*

Had he just felt whatever moment passed between us—or was it all in my head?

*These moments only happen when he's trying to calm you down. You're overreacting.*

*If I am, so is he. We keep having moments, voice-in-my-head! You can't deny it.*

*Doesn't matter: he has a clear and defined exit date from your life, so admire those warm brown eyes and that smile—and those arms— from afar and that's it.*

I needed to take my own advice and listen to what I'd told Logan earlier: Why get close to someone when you're just going to get hurt?

"Let's practice some more," I suggested brightly. Logan nodded and quietly returned to the center of the roof where our earlier sparring had left slushy gray footprints in the otherwise pristine snow. We wordlessly fenced for almost another hour, the only noise breaking the increasingly overbearing silence being the discordant jingling of the swords clashing during our frenetic fight.

"Stop!" I finally called out, dropping my sword and rest-

ing my hands on my knees, breathing so heavily I was practically panting like a schnauzer on a treadmill.

"I just need a break." I held up a wobbly hand. "We don't
exactly work out the sword-wielding muscles in gym class."
And not talking to each other was really starting to grate on
my nerves.

"It's getting late anyway." Logan looked up at the darkening
sky. "It's going to be too dark to get much more practice in."

"Okay." I nodded.

"So, how did I do today?" I asked as Logan and I ex-
changed weapons.

"Honestly, you did good," he said, giving me an approving thumbs-up. "I wouldn't want you running off into battle
against a demon just yet, but you could hold your own in an
attack, at least for a little while."

"Maybe I'll practice a little more tonight," I said, swinging
my sword around before sliding it into its invisible case on
my back, which Logan explained manifests when the sword
is near—further proving that magic is a thousand kinds of
awesome.

"No plans? It's Saturday night," he said, surprised.

"I thought we covered this yesterday. Bellevue Kelly, remember?" I circled my face with my hands. "No one knows
just how sane I really am," I added dramatically, throwing
the back of my hand over my forehead.

I expected him to laugh, but instead Logan had his lips
pressed in a hard grimace.

"What? You look like something's wrong," I said.

"I was invited to a party tonight," he began reluctantly.

"Oh. Someone from school?" I did my best to sound casual, picking at a light blue string that hung off the seam of my cuff.

"Yeah. That girl Andie? She invited me to some party on Friday." The string snapped in my hand.

"Are you going? Her parties are supposed to be fun." I tried my best to sound detached, as if I didn't care what Logan did with the social life he suddenly cared about over demon killing. I guess when Andie Ward and her double Ds literally came bouncing by, your priorities shifted.

"Well, that girl demon—" He snapped his fingers as he tried to recall her name.

"Della," I offered, and he smiled, snapping his fingers again and pointing at me.

"Yes! Della. That's it! Anyway, I noticed she's zeroed in on a guy who hangs with that crowd. Lust demons get distracted easily, and it looks like she's found a diversion. I'm hoping I can kill her tonight."

"Oh."

"Anyway, do you want to do this again tomorrow?"

"Okay. Same time?" I asked, and he nodded. We picked up our trash and began walking to the door of the now very dark roof, illuminated only by the midtown skyscrapers just a few blocks away. Once we were back in the stairwell, Logan pulled the door shut, whispering yet another litany of words I couldn't quite understand. I heard the door lock click into place, and stepped down off the landing to make my way downstairs.

"Have fun tonight," I said as we arrived at my apartment, hoping I sounded friendly and casual and not at all jealous and ready to claw Andie's Logan-adoring eyeballs out.

"Paige, is that you?" I heard through the door, and I tried not to groan as I rested my forehead against the frame.

I took a deep breath, exhaling the words, "I should go," in one big, breathy, irritated sigh.

"Paige?" my dad called again. His voice was the urban equivalent of flicking the porch light on.

"I'll see you tomorrow," Logan mouthed, ducking behind me to head down the stairs as I put the key in the door.

"Yeah, Dad, it's me," I called, reminding myself that he'd actually been accommodating this morning. I pushed open the door, expecting to see my parents rushing around to get ready for their date night.

Instead, they were sitting in their go-to date night clothes on the navy couch, my mom's phone clutched tightly in her freshly manicured hand.

"What's going on?" I asked suspiciously, throwing my keys back into my purse.

"Sit down, Paige," my mom said gently, and I perched awkwardly on the end of the blue-striped armchair opposite them, sliding out of my coat and letting it pool around me as I did my best to keep a poker face. Meanwhile, my mind was racing. *They saw you on the roof.*

"Am I in trouble?" I asked, spinning my bracelet around my wrist. "I'm home pretty early."

"Oh, no, it's nothing like that," Dad said, and I relaxed, sinking back into the armchair.

"Don't do that to me, you guys!" I cried, slapping my palms against the seat cushion. But my parents didn't laugh.

"We got an email from the school. It turns out a classmate

of yours was killed in the fire at your school yesterday," my mom said. "Did you know Travis Moore?"

I wasn't sure how to sound. Horrified? Inconsolable? What was the accurate response to have? The aftermath of Travis's death sank in—not only had I watched him die, but I was going to have to act like I wasn't the last person to share his final moments.

"Yes. I mean, I knew who he was, but I only talked to him a few times," I said, truthfully enough. *Just stay behind me...*

"Well, on Monday there's going to be an assembly first thing." My mom reached across the coffee table, handing me her phone so I could read the email from the school.

"How are you doing with this, Paige?" Dad asked, searching my face for my reaction as I read the email. Suspicious fire...death of a student...fourth floor closed until further notice...

"I'm okay. Like I said, I didn't really know him but...he seemed like a good guy." I blinked rapidly, hoping to stave off any tears that threatened to push their way through.

"Are you sure you're okay?"

"Yeah..." My voice trailed off. "It's just sad."

I stood up to give my mom back her phone.

"Honey, we could stay home tonight," Mom offered, a sympathetic look on her face as she fidgeted with the phone in her hands. "It's not like we paid for these tickets."

"We'll stay," Dad mouthed to my mom.

"Guys, I promise you, I'm okay," I insisted. "You haven't had a date night in years. You're going to your favorite restaurant. And you got all dressed up." I fanned my hand to my mom, who sat in her nicest black pants and favorite green silk shirt, her long dark hair pulled back in an elegant chignon. I had inherited the same thick, wavy hair from Mom—I knew what a pain it was to put in an updo. The fact that she spent all this time on a complicated hairstyle was a big sign that she was looking forward to a night out.

"Dad, take Mom out," I said firmly, crossing my arms. "You'll gain at least ten husband points for it."

"Very cute, young lady," my father said, even though my mom laughed.

"Seriously, you guys. I'm not going to do anything tonight but watch TV."

But instead, later that night, I found myself in my bedroom, sprawled out on my bed with my old sketchbook and charcoal pencil, drawing random objects as I mulled over the past two days. The glowing oval ring on Ajax's index finger. Blaise's glittering eyes. Logan's hand, covered by the intricate lattice-work of the sword as he gripped the handle.

I giggled as I remembered how cocky Logan could be about his weapon-handling skills. He was fun to watch—and he was so playful when he was in his element. I'd almost think he was flirting with me, but sometimes, something so dark and sad would overtake his expression, and he'd seem so unsure.

"Maybe he's picking up on the fact that you like him and it's making him uncomfortable."

I scowled at the words, finally said aloud. I glanced over to where my cat had been batting a hair elastic. He was now sitting in the middle of my floor, staring at me, as if to say, "Told you so."

It was true: I liked pen-stealing, demonslaying Logan Bradley. But once the last demon was gone, so was he. He'd said so himself. Still, I couldn't help but mull over his shy smiles and the intense way he held my gaze while I absentmindedly sketched.

"Paige, stop it," I said aloud, before blowing some charcoal off my hand. "You have to stop reading into every time he touches you. Or every time he says something sweet."

I looked down at my sketch book and frowned at the illustration of slightly arched brows peering out from underneath a baseball cap.

"And you definitely need to stop sketching Logan Bradley."

## 9

"YOU'RE SEEING LOGAN TODAY? SO SOON?"

My mom did her best to keep her face impassive, but her voice shot up so high I'm pretty sure I heard a dog howling his reply in the distance. My mom and I were sitting around the small table in the corner of the living room on Sunday, talking about my alleged trip to the Museum of Natural History—and my upbeat chatter had put my mom in a pretty good mood. I really hoped that my announcement didn't change that.

"Yeah. I mean, if that's okay," I added hastily, taking a quick look at my father's empty chair as if he would materialize just to tell me no. Only my father would learn how to bend the rules of time and space just to stop me from seeing a boy.

"Of course it's okay. It's just a little...unexpected, that's all," she added, carefully picking her words. "I mean, we never heard of this boy until Friday, and now you'll have spent all weekend with him."

"Mom, we're just hanging out," I said, slathering the uneaten half of my bagel with a thick layer of cream cheese.

"I didn't imply that you were running off to Vegas and getting matching tattoos," Mom said with a smirk.

"You caught me!" I pretended to be surprised. "That's totally what we're doing. Face tat for me, tramp stamp for Logan."

We both broke into full-on giggle fits, until my mom wiped her mouth with her blue napkin before tossing it on the table. She arched her eyebrow and gave me her practiced stare.

"We're just friends," I insisted, squirming underneath her intense look.

"Just friends, huh? It always starts that way." My mom gave me a knowing smile and picked up her bagel again. I realized that the last time we had had a normal mother-daughter conversation was before I was hit by the car. Since then, all conversations had the cloud of my assumed mental illness hanging over them. And I do mean *all* conversations—even the sporadic ones about the opposite sex.

I'd missed our talks. My mom and I used to have an easy relationship. She had always been less quick to judge than my father. And I wanted to talk to her about Logan—I figured I could stay as close to the truth as possible as long as I kept all things demonic out of the conversation.

"You never heard of him before because he's new this year," I explained. "He transferred in and we only started hanging out outside of school this week. He kind of keeps to himself."

"Oh, where's he from?"

"All over. Chicago, Texas. He lives with his uncle. He's, um—" I fumbled for the words and leaned down to scratch Mercer's head as he pawed at my thigh, begging for some cream cheese. *What should I say Rego does? Saying "warlock" wouldn't exactly put a check mark in the Paige Isn't Crazy column.*

"He's what, sweetie?" Mom prompted me.

"He does something with the army." The warlock army. "Anyway, they move around a lot."

"That can't be easy on Logan."

"I got the impression his life was kind of…isolating." I frowned. I couldn't imagine Rego had been the type to tuck little Logan into bed at night.

"Well, how long is Logan here until?"

Good question. One that had kept me up for a few hours last night.

"He's probably leaving before the school year's out."

"Does he know about—" my mom paused, clearly searching for the words that I could have predicted she'd say "—how you've struggled in the past?"

I sighed, crestfallen. I had so desperately wanted my mom to talk to me like I was normal.

"You're doing great, sweetie," my mom rushed to say, reaching forward to place her hand over mine. "I didn't mean anything by it. I was just wond—"

"He knows," I blurted out quickly. "And he doesn't care."

I ripped off a big bite of bagel with my teeth, because I apparently eat like a bear when I'm sulking.

"Well, that's great. We all deserve someone we can be ourselves around. He seemed nice—in the brief moment I met him, at least," Mom said sincerely. "I mean, I don't think he's killed anyone."

My mom's comment promptly caused me to choke on the wad of my bagel in my mouth, my eyes tearing as she patted me on the back. She had no idea how wrong she was—and how acutely she reminded me of the fact that Logan was a demonslayer, here to do a job and kill the demons that wanted to kidnap me. My questionable feelings for him were insignificant compared to that.

"He's going to leave," was running through my head on a loop an hour later as I climbed the stairs to the roof. The door was already propped open.

Logan stood in the center of the rooftop, now damp from melted snow. He wore a pale gray button-down shirt with the sleeves rolled up, and had his back to me, his sword merely a blur as he showed off his considerable skills. Yep, he'd definitely been taking it easy on me yesterday. He was agile and swift, but strong—his sword slicing through the air with an audible whistling sound. When Logan heard the door open, he whirled around. He wasn't wearing his baseball cap for once, and the day was bright, almost warm, so his face was bathed in a soft glow from the winter sun. Logan's normally shaded eyes looked a much lighter brown in the sun, and they crinkled up at the corners as he gave me an easy smile.

*Are you deliberately screwing with me, sun? What's next? Is his smile going to sparkle as a bell-like "ding" chimes in the distance? Is a butterfly going to land on his shoulder? Give the boy a white horse and it's a wrap for poor Paige's heart.*

Not falling for Logan Bradley was going to be more challenging than I thought.

"Hey," I called in my best impression of "casual," but my voice just sounded slightly high-pitched and incredibly awkward.

"Hey, yourself," he replied, falling into step next to me as I walked over to the picnic table, dumping my coat next to his.

"So how was the party?" I asked, then hastily added, "I mean, is, um, Della dead?"

Logan scowled, reaching into his back pocket and pulling out his baseball cap. He rolled the brim between his palms before setting it on his head.

"No, she didn't show up. But from what people were saying, she's latched on to her victim."

I leaned against the table as he spoke, thinking of the lusty way Della had leered at Matt on Friday.

"Already? Wow, she moves fast."

"That girl Parmesan or whatever was crying in the bathroom about it."

"It's Pepper, actually," I corrected him, stifling a grin at his version of her nickname. "Did Matt dump her for Della?"

He nodded, sighing heavily as he also leaned against the table, which creaked under his weight. "If she's got her hooks into him, it's only a matter of time before Dottie gets another friend in the Dark World. After all, Della's the female version of the same demon that effectively killed your friend."

I ran my hand through my hair, grabbing a fistful at my scalp as I tried to process the news. The news that yet another innocent person would die—all because of me.

"So, what's going to happen to him?"

"She'll feed on him, and it will slowly suck the life out of him. After about two weeks, he'll look like an old man. He'll be an old man."

"Feeding on him? How does—" I stopped, noticing the pointed look Logan was giving me.

"Lust demon," is all he said.

"Oh. Ew." I shuddered. "How can we help him? Can we reverse it?" I asked desperately.

Logan blinked at me, taken aback.

"*We* aren't doing anything. Maybe when Matt sees his girl-friend, she'll trigger his memory and break Della's hold—if their connection is strong enough. Any reminder of a deep attachment can break her spell. But I'm not going to go run-ning off after Della to leave you unprotected from Aiden. He's a Regent, Paige. He's pretty powerful."

"But—that's not the right thing to do. We have to do some-thing to help Matt," I insisted, staring at Logan in shock. He merely gave me an indulgent smile that bordered on conde-scending. "Look, it's really admirable that you want to save him, but you have to understand that—"

"Don't talk to me like I'm an idiot," I snapped, irritated.

The muscle in Logan's jaw flexed as he gritted his teeth to-gether. "I don't think you're an idiot. You know I don't think that." He pushed off the table to face me, confusion and an-noyance flashing across his face. "But we don't how powerful your ability to move between the two worlds could be. You need to be protected. Why are you so worried about Vogel, anyway?" Logan spat his name out.

"Because Travis already lost his life. And now you're telling me Matt is in danger of losing his, all because I've got some weird supernatural ability to be able to open portals between two universes!" I cried, angry. "No. No! I won't be respon-sible for it. Della's death has to be the priority."

Logan shoved his hands in his back pockets and looked

down, his jaw clenched so hard I thought he might crack a tooth.

But when he turned his face up to meet mine, he merely nodded in agreement, one quick jerk up and down.

"Okay, fine," he said. "But if it's a choice of saving you or that jerk-off Vogel, I'm saving you."

"Well, I'm not going to argue with that," I agreed. "Obviously, I'm a fan of, you know, being alive and all that."

Logan waved his hand toward the center of the roof, quickly pulling out his sword as he walked.

"So, how was the rest of the party?" I changed the subject, hoping to dissolve some of the tension between us as I twirled my sword in a wobbly figure eight. Logan merely shrugged in reply before reaching out to swap our weapons.

"No good?" I asked, handing over my sword.

"Couldn't tell you." He grabbed my sword and stared up at the blade, balancing the tip of the handle in his palm. "I left after I found out Della wasn't coming."

"Seriously?" I asked, surprised. Logan flicked his palm upward, causing the sword to pop into the air, where he grabbed it and held the weapon at his side.

"Paige, I told you I was only going to see if Della showed up. She didn't, so I left. I was only there for about a half hour or so." He stopped, a devious smile spreading across his face. "I'm pretty sure I pissed off that Andie chick by leaving."

"I figured you'd stay if it was fun," I said, forcing my voice to sound casual and not like I wanted to jump in the air and do a victory dance. *Suck it, Andie!*

Logan stared at me as if I had fireworks shooting out of my nostrils.

"Seriously, Paige? After the way they talked—"

He stopped short, biting his lip as if he were trying to bite back the words.

"About me, right?" I finished for him with a resigned sigh. "It's okay. I'm used to it."

"Well, you shouldn't be," he said, his knuckles white as he gripped his sword handle. "They don't know you. Their small opinions don't define you. Being different doesn't make you worthy of scorn. And if I ever get to hang out with anyone, just for fun—" Logan continued, looking me straight into my eyes, taking a deep breath "—it's not going to be with them."

"Oh," I said, my voice slightly unsteady. *What happened to shy, uncertain Logan?*

"So, today, I was thinking I should just attack you," Logan began, then hastily added, "with the sword, I mean. Not, like, attack you. You know. I want you to work on your defensive skills."

*Oh, there's shy, uncertain Logan.*

"I'm also going to teach you some basic self-defense moves that are good to know in general."

I nodded, holding my sword up warily as Logan started his assault slowly, before building up to a furious attack. I managed to deflect one out of every five hits, but since he was using my sword, the strikes were merely surprising— not painful.

But he could have been clobbering me with a sledgehammer, and it still wouldn't have had the impact that his arms did when they were wrapped around me, holding me tight as he tried to teach me more self-defense.

"Try to head-butt me," Logan said, his cheek touching

mine as he held me from behind, holding my arms immobile. "Gently, though," he cautioned, and his breath tickled my cheek, causing my pulse to speed. "I will definitely bleed if you smash my nose in."

How romantic.

I squirmed in his arms as I tried to break his hold.

"If you can't throw your head back, try to smash my foot," Logan advised as I wriggled in his arms, causing his lips to brush against my neck. The accidental touch had me wanting to squirm for an entirely different reason, but Logan quickly released me from his arms.

I spun around to see him rubbing the back of his neck, looking down.

"What?" I asked, pretending that the last thirty seconds didn't happen—and that accidentally kissing my neck didn't make Logan practically flee to the other side of the roof.

*Remember this when you're tempted to read into the sweet things he says, Paige.*

"Um…throw a punch at me," he blurted out.

"Seriously?" I made a fist and held it up. "Why?"

"What if it's hand-to-hand combat? I want to know you can protect yourself."

"I doubt I can knock out a Regent, no matter how good of a teacher you are."

"It's a good skill to know, regardless," Logan said, defensively holding his palms out so I could punch them.

"You're recoiling your fist when you make contact with me. Don't do that," he instructed, taking hold of my closed fist and slamming it into his other palm. "Keep going. Really throw your weight into it. That's the key to a solid punch."

I nodded, and after the next three punches, he grimaced.

"Damn. That's good." Logan rubbed his palm on his shirt, then shook his hand, wincing. "Maybe you could take out a Regent."

"Take him out for pizza, maybe."

"I thought you were a secret ninja, remember? Show me what you've got. Or are your arms tired?" Logan frowned in an exaggerated pout as he held his palms up again. Oh, confident Logan had decided to show up again—and he was being merciless. "Poor widdle Paige."

"Fine, let's do this." I knew he was deliberately goading me, but still, I narrowed my eyes, quickly targeting Logan's palm again. Only this time, my aim was off—in my haste to show off, I missed his hand entirely and pitched forward, crashing into him like the smooth operator that I was.

"Whoa!" Logan exclaimed, grabbing me around the waist, stumbling back a few steps as he tried to steady me.

"Sorry!" I would have covered my face in embarrassment, except my hands were somewhat pinned between my chest and Logan. Considering how he reacted to the last accidental touch, I tried to bolt from his arms—but Logan wound his arms snugly around me, holding me upright.

"It's okay," he said, chuckling. "If you'd connected with my hand, I'd probably be in a lot of pain right now. That looked like a solid punch."

"Oh, yeah, the air around your hand is crying in pain right now," I muttered to the gray shirt button that was eye level.

"Totally has a broken nose," he agreed in mock serious-ness, giving me a barely perceptible squeeze.

"So much for my ability to beat up a demon."

"Oh, I don't know." Logan squinted at me, tilting his head to the side. "Maybe you could tickle them to death with one of those feather-topped pens you love so much."

"I don't hear you complaining." I pursed my lips, giving him a "so-there" look.

"You caught me," he replied with an infectious grin, and I found myself mirroring it, until Logan's smile faded, a somber expression taking hold of his face.

"In fact," he began, "I like them more than I should. I think I'll miss them a lot when I leave."

I had been holding myself rigidly against him—but I felt myself relax, my hands resting gently against his chest. His heart drummed out a soothing, steady rhythm underneath my palms—a light thudding that seemed to keep time with my own speeding heartbeat. I lifted my chin, locking eyes with Logan, who had a heartbreakingly sad smile on his face. Quickly, Logan dropped his hold, taking a step back as he shoved his hands in his back pockets and peered up at the sky.

"I should get going. Yeah. It's getting late."

"Not really," I replied, confused by yet another sudden change in his demeanor, and my earlier resolve to stop reading into things fizzled.

*There's no way he was only talking about your pens, right?*

"I should go," he said again, like he was commanding himself to leave. When he spoke again, his voice had the same authoritative tone.

"Tomorrow, I'll get to school early and save you a seat at assembly. Just stay in public places—hallways, classrooms, places where people are. I'll cut classes after assembly and try to take out Della before lunch."

"Okay." I nodded, still reeling from the one-eighty in our conversation. One minute, I'm in his arms—the next, we're talking about demonslaying.

"Don't be scared," Logan said. "You've had some practice. And you have a magical sword. And me. You'll be fine."

But the next morning, I felt anything but fine as I slid in the worn wooden seat next to Logan in the front of the auditorium—a new vantage point for me, since I was used to sitting in the back.

"It's all about visibility—demons don't want an audience," he explained in a low voice. I glanced back at the darkened rear of the auditorium and realized anyone could be hiding in the shadows underneath the balcony. Anyone who wanted to kill me or kidnap me.

Students in varying degrees of melancholy trudged in. Some were visibly upset and sniffling—others were subdued but nevertheless consumed by whatever was on the screens of their cell phones. Andie sauntered in, undeterred by the somber mood, and glared my way—a glare more venomous than her usual panicked "Paige is a psycho, everybody run" schtick. And then a loud sob echoed through the auditorium, followed by the muffled slapping sound of shoes running on carpet as Pepper fled from the assembly, her hands covering her face, as Matt made his entrance with Della.

"How does he not remember his feelings for Pepper?" I asked, awed. "I thought any memory of a strong emotion could break her spell?"

"Maybe it's one-sided. There has to be a deep connection between the two—something genuine, you know what I mean?" Logan explained, turning his back to me as his head swiveled to follow Pepper's sprint out of the auditorium. "But whatever, it doesn't surprise me that their link to one another is weak."

"Well, Dottie did catch Pepper hooking up with her ex," I whispered, and Logan huffed in reply.

"I've seen some variation of Pepper and Matt in every town I've been to. He's the popular guy, she's the popular girl." He gave me a thumbs-down and blew a raspberry. "It's like they have to be together or else the world will explode."

Logan pointed toward the middle of the auditorium, where Matt clutched Della's hand with both of his, devotedly following her to their seats.

"She's already started feeding on him," he observed. I gasped when I saw Matt; his skin was dull, a sickly shade of gray except under his eyes, which were ringed with purple bags. Matt sank into his seat next to Della and sighed in relief, as if the mere act of standing were painful. Meanwhile, Della looked even more radiant—all glossy hair and lush curves and seductive glances. She cast one of those signature looks at Matt, and they promptly began pawing each other like cats fighting over a piece of tuna.

The students in the row next to Della and Matt grimaced at the display and shuffled over a few seats, looking away in disgust.

"Aww, poor Matt."

The unfamiliar voice came from the previously vacant spot next to me, and I twisted around to see Aiden casually sitting there, his violet eyes sparkling with mirth as he draped his arm along the back of my seat.

I sprang to my feet, and Logan moved quickly to put himself between us, his left arm reaching behind his back to protectively curve around me.

"Get away from her," he snarled, and Aiden laughed delightedly, languidly stretching his long legs in front of him.

"Oh, really? What are you going to do? Threaten me in front of all these witnesses?" He waved his palm to the row of freshmen sitting behind us, who were openly gaping at us. "Really, *proditori,* that's hilarious. I can barely breathe, I'm laughing so hard!"

"Don't worry, you won't be breathing much longer."

"Ooh, you really burned me there," Aiden said sarcastically, wiggling his fingers in the air before turning his eyes on Logan. "Do you practice one-liners in the bathroom mirror? Or did you hire someone to write those zingers for you?"

Aiden leaned back and jerked his thumb toward Logan as he loudly whispered to the freshmen, "He's spent too much time with Bellevue Kelly. I guess crazy is contagious." He spun his index finger in a circle around his temple while crossing his eyes.

"You don't talk to her, you don't even look at her," Logan growled, taking a step forward. Aiden jumped to his feet, his eyes popping open. I couldn't see Logan's face, but judging by the look on Aiden's face, it had to be menacing. It was enough to prompt the freshmen to scurry away, finding new seats far from Logan.

"Is there a problem here?" Vice Principal Miller waddled up to us, an angry frown on his sweaty face. "Are you boys aware that we're at a memorial for a classmate? Or do you think we're here for our health?" he bellowed, his ruddy face glistening with exertion.

"Of course, sir. We're just sharing stories about the dearly departed. Such a shame." Aiden sighed dramatically, sticking out his lower lip in a pout. I shuddered—I couldn't believe I'd ever thought he was attractive—everything about him was sneaky, sleazy and just plain vile.

"You were one of the last ones to see poor Travis alive, right? In detention?" Aiden asked, his violet eyes open wide with innocence, and the color drained from Miller's face.

"Take a seat, Adrian…Abe…whatever," Miller growled, waving his hand toward the back of the auditorium. Aiden mimed tipping a hat to Miller, shoved his hands in his pockets and strolled away—turning back once to wink at me, mouthing, "See you soon."

"Do we have a problem here?" Miller's question was directed not at me, but at Logan. I hurried to stand at his side and saw that Logan wasn't making any attempt to hide the venom on his face as he glared at Aiden's retreating figure.

"Logan, answer him," I said, elbowing his side. "We don't want detention again." At that, he snapped out of it, shaking his head quickly.

"No, sir. Sorry, sir." Logan sat down quickly as Miller glowered at him one more time before shuffling away. As soon as I'd taken my seat, Logan twisted to face me, gripping the armrest so hard, I thought he might splinter the wood.

"Aiden's bold—I'll give him that," Logan seethed, scowling at where Aiden had strutted away to join Della and Matt, who were fused at the mouth. Even from several rows away, I could see the thin veins trailing from Matt's mouth, a dark spiderweb across his ashen skin. Aiden winked at me from his seat, and I turned away, a sickening shudder shooting through me.

I nervously pulled the sleeves of my blue sweater over the heels of my palms—a gesture I'd picked up from Dottie. "He didn't seem that afraid," I whispered. "Why didn't he seem afraid?"

"He should be," Logan scoffed, before a more thoughtful look crossed his face. "I shouldn't have reacted—it's not like he would attack you with all these witnesses. But instead, I gave him exactly what he wanted. He wanted to know how to set me off, and now he does. Ugh!" Logan leaned back, rubbing his face with his hands.

"Get it together, idiot," he mumbled into his palms.

"What?" I asked, not sure if I'd heard him correctly.

"Nothing," he said, dropping his hands from his face and folding his arms in front of him.

The lights in the auditorium dimmed, and Principal Branyan, clad in a smart, tailored business suit, took the stage, where a foam-board portrait of Travis from last year's school yearbook stood on an easel. She spoke of the fire, Travis's contributions to the science department at school, and the restriction on entering the fourth floor, until it was deemed safe by the city. A few freshmen cheered—the mandatory music class was held on the fourth floor, a mind-numbingly dull, forced mastery of the recorder—and Miller hurried over to threaten them with detention.

But as she spoke, I found it hard to pay attention. All I could think about were the two demons sitting just a few rows away—the imagined pressure of their eyes on me was like two weights pressing into the back of my skull.

After the assembly, students somberly filed out of the auditorium, headed to the next class. Logan stayed next to me, keeping his eyes trained on the demons, who ducked out the side door quickly with Matt in tow. Matt, whose previously dark hair was now lightly threaded with white.

"Remember, stay in public places. Hallways. Classrooms. Don't go into a bathroom if you're the only one in there," Logan cautioned me in a low voice. I felt light pressure on my backpack and realized Logan was resting his hand on it as he helped usher me through the crowd to my next class. The chivalry was unnecessary: thanks to Logan and Aiden's showdown, students gave us a pretty wide berth, avoiding us as if we were serial killers with the plague and a scorching case of head lice. Andie in particular scowled at me with remarkable hatred.

"Andie super-hates me today," I commented, and Logan's cheeks turned pink.

"What? Do you know something about that?" I asked suspiciously, and he just shrugged.

"Where's your last class before lunch?" Logan asked, deflecting my question as we arrived on the second floor, huddled against a row of lockers.

"History, room three-sixteen," I said, before remembering something, exclaiming, "Oh, damn it!"

"What? Are they here?" Logan's eyes opened wide in alarm as his head whipped around, surveying the area as his hand automatically reached over his shoulder.

"No—no. Nothing like that," I quickly said. "I just don't have my history book. Blaise, um, incinerated it when I chucked it at her head."

"Way to give me a heart attack, Paige," Logan huffed, slumping against the locker and leaning his head back with a dull thud against the metal door.

"Sorry," I said sheepishly as Logan slid his backpack off his shoulder to rummage around in it.

"Here, use mine." He held out a battered copy of *America: Our History I* and gently shoved it into my hands.

"Are you sure? What will you use?" I asked as I slid the weighty book into my backpack.

"Oh, I think I can convince Malhotra to give me another one without fining me." Logan grinned impishly. "I have a way of making people do what I want."

"That hypnotism thing? *Som*-nom-nom or...whatever?"

"*Somnorvik.* And, yes, that's what I'm going to do," Logan said with a laugh, moving closer when a freshman interrupted us, needing to get into the locker Logan was leaning against. "I'll be outside three-sixteen. Don't worry, okay?" he whispered in my ear, and I nodded.

But I didn't have anything to worry about in math class. Blaise was the only demon scheduled to be in Dr. Walsh's class—but I knew firsthand that her name would never get a check mark in attendance again. Instead, I scanned the classroom for Dottie, who always made an appearance in Walsh's class. It was right across from the third-floor bathroom, after all. I was tempted to make a midclass bathroom trip, but Logan's words cautioning me to stay in public places echoed in my ears.

Matt's seat was suspiciously empty, causing more than a few people to murmur about his appearance that morning. Shani Robinson, the news editor for the *Holy Assumption Observer,* was telling Tabitha that she'd heard Della had introduced Matt to some kind of scary new pharmaceutical, and she was planning an exposé in next week's issue.

As the teacher droned on, I pulled out the letter I'd written for Dottie the previous night. I figured she could stand over my shoulder and read all about Dark Worlds and demons and, yes, demonslayers that were too charming and quick-witted and adorably shy for my own good—but my best friend didn't make an appearance until fifteen minutes into history class.

Dottie peeked around the wood-frame doorway of three-sixteen just as Mr. Malhotra turned to the board to write in loopy penmanship about The New Deal.

"Paige. Paige! *Paige!*" she stage-whispered from the doorway, gesturing wildly for me to join her in the hallway.

I pursed my lips and jerked my head to the side, trying to indicate that she should come inside.

"Paige, come here!" she said. I wasn't sure why she was whispering—it wasn't like anyone except me could hear her. I shook my head briefly, one quick left-right movement.

"Please! It's important," Dottie pleaded, and then another blond head timidly appeared around her shoulder.

Travis.

My hand was in the air faster than you could say "guilty conscience."

"Yes, Paige?"

"May I go to the bathroom, Mr. Malhotra?" I stared nervously at the door—Travis's eyes were almost feral as they whirled around the classroom, stopping to lock on to mine in disbelief.

"Lunch is next. Can't you wait?" Mr. Malhotra looked as uncomfortable asking me the question as I did hearing it.

"No, it's an emergency," I said, eliciting snickers from some classmates and a visible frown of discomfort from my teacher.

"Fine, Paige." He hastily wrote me a hall pass, and I had to remind myself not to run to the front of the room to grab it.

"Let's go to our bathroom," Dottie said once I was outside, but I shook my head.

"No. We have to stay in public places," I whispered, leading her down the hallway away from Mr. Malhotra's open door, near the stairway. It was still close enough that one good scream would send teachers and students pouring out of the classrooms.

"Because of that psycho monster chick, right?" Travis spoke quietly.

I nodded, and Travis looked down at his scuffed brown uniform shoes—the shoes he was destined to wear until the time his natural life would have ended.

"Travis, I'm so sorry about what happened to you," I said, my voice hoarse with regret.

"It's not your fault." He shrugged weakly, and I slumped against a locker at the end of the hall, guilty. "I'm just glad one of us escaped."

Then Travis's blue eyes popped open wide, spinning around the hallway in panic. "Is she here? Blaise?"

"She's dead. She can't hurt you anymore. I—I killed her," I admitted in a shaky voice.

"Good. Because I would have messed her up," Travis said with false bravado, cracking his neck from side to side. I steeled myself for what I had to say, my fingers clutching the fabric of my plaid uniform skirt so tightly, I thought it might tear.

"She was there for me, Travis. It's my fault." I braced for some kind of verbal assault, since a physical one was out of the question. But instead, Travis gave me a rueful smile.

"Like I said, it's not your fault. We're cool. She's the one who kill—who put me here," he said, unable to utter the words. Dottie gently squeezed his shoulder, earning a grateful look from him and an audible gasp from me.

"What?" Dottie asked, then followed my eyes to where her hand was and gave me a knowing smile. *Of course Dottie can touch him. They're on the same side now.*

"Dottie, I have so much to tell you. I even wrote it all down in a note so you could read it over my shoulder in class."

"I was with Travis all morning, trying to convince him to come over to your side." Dottie gave Travis another sympathetic shoulder squeeze, but he just continued to stare at the floor, his shoe tracing patterns in the cracked checkered floor.

"Wait until you hear what I found out about your side. Blaise, and others like her, came from the Dark World," I revealed in a hushed voice. Dottie's pink-painted mouth dropped open in surprise. Travis looked paler—if such a thing were possible.

"What else did you find out?" Dottie asked, eagerly reaching for my arm, then pulling back before her fingers could pass through my skin and give us both chills.

I had only begun telling Dottie about the Dark World and demonslayers when Travis lifted his head with a low, pained moan. He wasn't just pale—he was transparent, the marked-up beige walls of the hallway visible through his form. Dottie began to waver, too. She flashed me a panicked look, her brown eyes glistening with terror before she vanished.

The last time Dottie had disappeared, it was because a demon was near. So I screamed, feeling my voice painfully rip through my throat as I unleashed my loudest, shrillest wail—the kind of screech that would be heard at the end of the hallway, and on another floor. In my panic, I thought I could even see it leave my mouth, wispy white curls of smoke that spun through the air, twisting with the ferocity of my shriek even though it wasn't even cold in the hallway.

But no sound came out. My scream should have echoed down the empty corridor, bouncing off the dull metal lockers and sending teachers and students streaming into the hallway. Instead, the hallway remained empty—so I screamed a second time, so forcefully I could taste blood on my tongue, but again the scream floated through the air, until it swirled in a tight spiral, coiling in the outstretched hand held in front of me. Aiden's hand.

"Neat party trick, isn't it?" Aiden asked, closing his fist around the smoke and shoving it in the pocket of his navy pants. "A particular talent of mine. I have to say, it comes in so handy sometimes!" he added with a conspiratorial wink, as if we were old friends.

If I couldn't scream, I could run. Which I did. I made it about ten feet before I collided with Della, who grabbed my arm.

"We don't have much time. I tried to slow him down, but he's coming," Della growled, taking her hand off her slashed-open face and scowling at the powderlike blood staining her palm—an injury I had no doubt Logan had given her.

I reached over my shoulder for my sword, but Aiden grabbed me from behind, pulling me back into the stairway at the end of the hall. I tried to scream, tried to yell—but even my grunts were silent.

"She's feisty for a little brat," Della sniffed, watching me struggle against Aiden, who wrapped his arms around my torso. I clawed at his skin, my nails breaking off in his forearm as he dragged me up the stairs, the loud banging of my heels against concrete echoing in the stairwell. I flailed in his arms, hoping to make enough noise to get someone's attention. Once they got me alone, I'd be gone.

Reaching over my shoulder, I grabbed the handle of the sword, which materialized instantly. I yanked it down over my shoulder as hard as I could, sending the broad side of the long sword flying upward into Aiden's chin with a forceful smack.

He cried in pain, releasing me as he reached up to cradle his face. I stumbled forward, tumbling down the few steps Aiden had hauled me up. I landed hard on my right side, ignoring the agony in my shoulder as I scrambled to my feet, lurching for the staircase door.

"Della, stop her," Aiden grunted, clutching his sore chin. Della caught up with me as I flung the door open. She grabbed a fistful of my hair and yanked me back, shoving me against the wall as the door slammed closed. I swung for her face, but Aiden caught my hand and grabbed my other wrist. He held both of my hands tightly behind my back as Della gripped my chin and stared into my eyes.

"Listen to me," Della began in a low, commanding voice, wrapping my hair around her fist and pulling down, so I was forced to look into her eyes. "You want to come with Aiden and me. It's so much better with us. So peaceful.

"Look at me!" she ordered, and something in my brain yelled—screamed—at me to keep my eyes shut. I felt her thumbs pressing on my eyes, pulling my eyelids up as I thrashed against Aiden's grip, my throat raw from my silent screams. I struggled to turn away, to tune her out—but those hypnotic eyes that seemed so cold earlier now looked warm. Inviting. Safe.

"Stop fighting it, Paige. You don't remember anything—just us. We are what you want." The words swirled around me like a soft blanket, like fleece and down wrapping me in warmth on a cold day. I felt like I was falling—but when I saw the depths of her deep black eyes, I felt stable again. She was right. Della was always right.

"Give Paige her voice back. She needs to speak her assent."

Suddenly, I could talk again. Della made Aiden give me my voice back. And there was only one word I wanted to say.

"Yes." Agreeing to go with her was almost nourishing.

The pain in my wrists disappeared as whatever was holding them immobile released me, and I happily followed Aiden and Della up the staircase.

# 07

"HURRY UP," DELLA ORDERED, PACING THE floor of a classroom that faintly smelled of sweet smoke. I sat on the tall stool where Della had told me to sit, swinging my legs as I studied the large beige room. It seemed familiar to me. Foamy, black noise-proofing strips were bolted to the walls, and the chalkboard was dotted with the simple three-note scale of "Hot Cross Buns" and other childhood rhymes. The melody echoed weakly in my head as I peered out the door window at the classroom across the hall. It was blocked off with yellow tape, the walls outlining the door blackened with soot. Something had happened there. I couldn't really recall what, but I knew it was important. Significant. I vaguely remembered someone screaming....

Della nervously stared at the door of the classroom, jumping at every imagined noise.

"Can't you go any faster?" she hissed, impatiently tapping her stiletto on the floor.

"It's not like I'm hot-wiring a car here, Dellica. Opening portals into other worlds is a bit complicated," Aiden shot back, raking his hands through his black hair as he studied the tattered scraps of parchment on the desk in the front of the room.

"He's going to come for her. He interrupted me in the basement. I was in the middle of feeding, too," Della said, anxiously prodding the jagged, still-bloody wound that marred her left cheek and wincing at the pain. "I made Matt attack him to keep him busy, but it's not like he's going to be hard to get past. He's just a stupid human."

"Well, if you would shut the hell up and let me do my job," Aiden yelled, his hands clenched into fists, "we'll be long gone before Logan shows up."

That name…that name stirred something in me. Something I needed to hold on to.

Aiden collected the bits of paper and shoved them into the canvas bag slung across his chest, then strode across the room to where I was sitting.

"Get up," he ordered, taking my hand to roughly pull me into a standing position, and I stumbled forward.

"Repeat after me, do you understand?" he demanded, and I nodded. Aiden extended his other hand, whispering clashing, foreign sounds that my tongue stumbled through pronouncing. But the cadence of the words sounded familiar. I could picture someone holding his hand in front of a door to unlock it. The image of flame-tipped fingers reaching out to me flashed across my mind before disappearing into vapor.

"We're losing her." The low, whispered statement came from Della, who stared at me with contempt as I tried to grab these fleeting images that danced across my consciousness.

"She's fine," Aiden said, taking my hand to pull me closer to him. I snatched my hand back and shook his touch off.

It felt foreign—unnatural. I didn't understand why, though. Wasn't I supposed to stay with him and Della?

"I thought your particular set of skills was supposed to make her more docile, Dellica," Aiden snapped, staring at me in confusion as I instinctively recoiled from him.

"I hate my real name." She wrinkled her perfect nose in distaste as she flopped onto a stool, swinging her legs. "Why do you insist on using it?"

"Because you hate it. And it amuses me to annoy you." Aiden smirked, grabbing for my hand again. I pulled it back and stepped away, and his smile faded. "Now tell me why this one isn't being so agreeable anymore when your little pet Matt is so devoted he'd eat kibble out of your hand."

"Who cares? Can't we just kill her and leave before he kills us?" Della begged, stomping her heel on the floor. "Look, we don't even need to go back! Just kill her and we'll stay on this side. We could rule over here. Listen to me!" she screeched, but Aiden dismissed her with a curt wave of his hand as he stared ahead, enthralled, a greedy smile slowly spreading on his face.

"What a prize she is for me to bring back," Aiden whispered in awe. I squinted at the scene. Thin cracks spiraled out of a small, pulsating dark oval that hovered a few feet above the floor.

"She can do it. She really is a Traveler," Aiden murmured, staring at me in reverence as I slumped against the desk, exhausted. Every impulse to stand up straight faded away as I watched the fragmented scene expand. The larger the portal grew, the more drained I became, overwhelming fatigue settling into every pore. I looked to Della for her approval, but she wasn't watching me. Her panicked gaze was directed beyond the portal—to the doorway of the classroom, where a shadowed form stood.

Suddenly, I was pressed against Aiden's chest as he held me close, roughly stroking my hair as this new person ran into the classroom, diving underneath the portal. He hit the floor with his shoulder and rolled forward—coming to crouch before the portal with a sword drawn.

"Sorry, *proditori,* she's got a new boyfriend. One that will snap her neck if you come any closer—and she'll accept it with a smile," Aiden said with a laugh, running his nose along my jaw as he placed his palm against my throat. I flinched at the sensation—the revulsion I felt when he touched me contradicting the unexplainable loyalty I felt I owed him and Della. I tried to untangle myself from Aiden's arms, but he only held on to me more tightly, planting a loud, wet kiss on my cheek and announcing in a singsong voice, "He wants to kill you."

The boy's eyes narrowed, his face settling into a hard mask—which softened when he met my confused gaze.

"Paige, don't be scared. You know me. You know I'm not going to hurt you." His voice, and the familiar, but gentle way he said my name, assaulted my mind with murky images of rooftops and swords and warm eyes and sad smiles.

Logan.

The pictures floated through my mind, anchored by that name.... That name that echoed in my head almost painfully, tearing down the dark filter that had been obscuring my memories. And I began to remember.

"No!" I screamed, pushing Aiden away—but he grabbed my wrist and twisted it painfully, bringing me to my knees.

Logan's face contorted in rage as he raised his sword and rushed closer, poised to attack as the dark portal continued to grow behind him. It was spreading, then retracting, a pulsating vortex that opened a doorway to another dimension. Every time it expanded, I felt weaker, all my strength leaving my body to feed the growing hole in our reality.

"I'll break her arm off and beat her with it," Aiden said savagely, pointing at Logan, as he bent my wrist back even farther. I cried out, my body twisting at an unnatural angle as my wrist strained against Aiden's grip. Logan stopped in his tracks, his sword frozen in its offensive position.

"Aiden, let's go," Della urged, her hands balled into fists. "Just leave her here."

"Hey, Dummica, the portal isn't completely open yet. But feel free to try to make it out of this room without the *proditori* slicing you in half," Aiden snapped at her. I weakly tried to punch him in the back of the knees with my free hand, hoping to knock him off balance while he was distracted, but all I did was cause Aiden to swiftly kick me in the side. Groaning, I clutched at my ribs as a wave of agony washed over me, and I heard Logan shout my name.

"Dellica, watch her, will you?" Aiden said, shaking my wrist and sending spears of pain shooting down my arm. "She's almost as irritating to me as you are."

He hauled me to my feet and shoved me at Della, who grabbed me around the waist and quickly held a blade to my throat. I wrapped my fingers around her forearm, pulling at her arm with ineffective, feeble tugs. But I was sapped of strength and couldn't get a strong grip on Della, my fingers merely slipping from her skin as I tried to wrench the knife from my throat.

"No!" Logan shouted, his eyes wide with fear as Della pressed the blade into my skin.

"Oh, calm down, you big drama queen," Aiden sighed dramatically. "Della's not going to hurt her—much. But if you touch a teensy-weensy hair on my head, Paige will lose hers."

Aiden grinned innocently, batting his eyelashes. The room was bathed in a quick flash of light as the portal shuddered and expanded, and black spots whirled across my vision as I tried to remain conscious. Logan's eyes—panicked and yet full of rage—met mine, and I focused on him as he stood before Aiden, tall and powerful.

"Oh, let's have some fun, shall we?" Aiden purred, throwing his arms open and locking them straight at the elbow. The air around his clenched hands crackled, with fiery sparks exploding in a straight line from the center of his knuckles. The sparks fused together, forming a solid, shimmering gold spike rising from curled golden gloves that shielded his fists.

"Here's the story, *proditori*—ooh, that rhymed," Aiden said, giggling, bouncing up and down like a kid about to go on the Ferris wheel—a kid brandishing deadly spikes, which he clapped together excitedly, making a waterfall of bright sparks rain down onto the floor.

"You surrender to me—and we don't kill the little Traveler over there. Because right now, I'd love to see what her insides look like." As he spoke, Della traced the tip of the knife along my cheek.

"We could maim her, though," Della cooed, a hard edge under her babyish voice. "I don't see why she shouldn't have a scar like the one you gave me." She pressed the tip of the blade into my cheekbone, and I felt the sharp sting of the metal as it pierced my skin, sending a warm, sticky stream of blood trailing down my face.

"Don't you want to show the *proditori* how loud you can scream?" she wheedled, and I bit my lip against the cry building in my throat. *Don't give her the satisfaction, Paige. Don't distract Logan. Do not scream.*

"I said, don't you want to scream?" Della taunted, dragging the knife lower, tearing at my skin, and a low cry forced its way from my lips at the searing pain in my cheek.

"Stop!" Logan shouted, his eyes darting between me and Aiden. They locked on mine—and were filled with anguish.

"No," I mouthed—but Logan merely shook his head, his expression grave.

"Stop hurting her," he demanded, glaring at Aiden. "She goes free, and we'll have a deal."

"Logan—isn't that what you go by? Logan? Well, Logan, she won't go free," Aiden said. "Do you think I'm stupid, Logan? She can open gateways between the worlds! She's valuable currency for me. I'm not letting this prize stay in warlock hands. But I'll agree not to cause her further injury if you come with me."

Della tapped the tip of the blade against the corner of my eye, using just enough pressure to cause pain without breaking the skin. My eyelashes fluttered against the bloodstained metal, which glinted in my peripheral vision.

"Aww, but hurting her is so much fun," Della sulked, twirling the tip of the blade slowly as she held it against my skin. I winced, squeezing my eyes shut as I braced myself for the inevitable agony. "I've heard warlocks have healing medications. Can you replace an eyeball? Because I bet she'd look hilarious with an eye patch."

"Stop it! You have a deal! I'll—I'll go with you," Logan cried, his voice frantic over Aiden's merry giggle.

"The Queen is going to be so impressed with me when I bring you two to the castle! About time that bitch acknowledged my worth," Aiden spat, his words saturated with bitterness and resentment, before switching to a gleeful tone.

"I bet she's got all sorts of torture planned for you, demonslayer. You've been getting in the way for far too long. She'll probably flay you and wear your skin like a cape. Or maybe she'll burn you alive. Imagine that—the little warlock warrior, his flesh melting away on the floor of the throne room. Such a pretty sight."

He narrowed his violet eyes at Logan, his voice lethal. "Now drop your sword."

The image of Logan tortured and burned—to save my life—ignited a spark of rage. And with it, another memory slowly bubbled to the surface, breaking through the final mental barriers that Della had built.

I focused on the rage, letting it fuel the fire as it built inside of me. I let the burn flash over my skin, the demon flames racing over my body as Della screamed in pain, dropping the knife to the floor.

I whipped my head back, the crown of my skull smashing into Della's nose with an audible crunch. She clutched her nose and stumbled backward, knocking over a stool as puffs of ruby smoke billowed down her flame-pinked face. Della launched herself at me, shoving me backward with powdery red hands, and I slammed against the blackboard, sending bits of chalk to the floor, where they shattered with loud pops. I reached for my sword, weakly and wildly swiping it through the air between Della and me. She grabbed the nearest sheet music pedestal and held it up like a shield as I desperately swatted at her with wobbly, ineffective strikes, the little strength I had waning the more the portal expanded.

The jangled clang of metal striking metal echoed in the classroom, as Logan swung his sword at Aiden. The demon held his spikes in an X-formation, protecting himself as Logan relentlessly attacked, his sword a mere blur as Aiden deflected Logan's unyielding strikes, the clashing metal sending a light dusting of blue sparks scattering across the floor.

"Dellica, let's go!" Aiden ordered, his once-confident voice now laced with panic. She blindly threw the pedestal she had been cowering behind at me, and it missed me by a few feet and smashed against the wall, splintering into pieces. Della ducked behind Aiden as he shuffled backward under Logan's assault until they were standing in front of the oval-shaped portal, which whirled and hummed with energy. Through it, a foggy version of the classroom appeared—with mottled gray walls instead of beige, where fat, buglike red creatures skittered across the surface. Della's long hair blew backward, and a stack of sheet music swirled in the wind toward the hole—all being sucked in by the gateway's vacuumlike force.

Aiden grunted, stumbling as he blocked a side blow, and Logan moved too quickly for Aiden to recover his defensive pose. Logan swung his sword upward as his deft fingers flipped the handle, forcing the blade to point down. Logan charged forward, plunging the sword down as Della grabbed the back of Aiden's shirt. She yanked Aiden roughly, and he fell backward against Della—and Logan impaled the demon through his right shoulder instead of his heart.

The sword's length ran through Aiden—stabbing Della in the stomach. Inhuman howls of agony echoed in the classroom as the blade turned black, then a shimmery pearlized pink rippling color. Della unleashed a guttural wail, her flawless face twisted in agony.

A dark stain began to spread from where the sword was embedded in Aiden's chest, a deep purple color that was oddly pretty—considering it was the hue of demon blood. Aiden wailed again, his face morphing into something otherworldly. His eyebrows became more arched—slick black peaks over luminous violet eyes that seemed to glow in a graying face. His shoulders heaved with suffering as large wings sprouted behind him, diaphanous gray tissue and tendons stretched between shiny black bones that ripped through his white shirt, which fell off his body in tatters. His spikes crumbled in a row of sparks, revealing oversize gnarled gray claws—and Logan braced his foot against Aiden's stomach, simultaneously pulling his sword out of the wound and kicking the demon back a few feet, where he stumbled over Della. She shuddered as she clutched her hands to her stomach, where crimson puffs of smoke seeped between her dusty red fingers.

Logan raised his sword again as Aiden reached into his pants pocket with trembling fingers and pulled out an oversize gold coin.

"Kill me or save her, *proditori?*" Aiden grunted, flinging the shimmering circle at me like he was tossing a Frisbee. I ducked as Logan ran toward me, grabbing me around the waist and knocking me onto the ground, just as whipping spines emerged from the spinning disk. Logan crouched above me as the thrashing razorlike spikes effortlessly sliced apart the chalkboard above us, sending jagged shards of black slate and splinters of wood and chunks of plaster raining down on Logan's back.

"I will watch you die," Aiden vowed, his flippant voice layered with a deep, unsettling growl.

"You won't touch her again," Logan shouted as Aiden slid his hands underneath Della's arms, dragging her backward as they both got sucked into the fractured portal in the center of the classroom. A rush of wind spun around the classroom, sweeping sheet music, instruments and wooden stools into the rapidly shrinking gateway. Logan grabbed me around the waist with one hand, shielding me with his body. Items smashed into each other in the vortex, scattering debris around the room as objects fought for a place in the diminishing doorway to another world.

Guitars collided with cymbals and horns, creating a discordant, off-key cacophony. The portal continued to shrink, spinning in tight, rapid revolutions, as the wind whipped my hair around and blew the cap off Logan's head. Black spots dotted my vision; my consciousness began to slip away. I felt myself slumping in Logan's arms, and he pulled me against him, protecting me from the shattered, broken things taking flight in the wind whirling around the room.

"Stay awake. Stay with me, please," he begged, his hands clutching the back of my sweater as I tried to keep the heavy blackness at bay. With a flash of light and the grating sound of tearing metal, the portal snapped shut, leaving scraps of shredded paper fluttering to the ground around us like confetti.

I buried my face in Logan's neck as he held me, supporting me as I panted for air. My uneven, shallow breathing steadied as the strength slowly trickled back into my muscles. When my breathing had resumed a somewhat normal—if a little shaky—pace, Logan rested my back against the wall underneath the shattered chalkboard, hovering over me as his hand gently skimmed my cheek.

"Where else are you hurt?" Logan's voice was frantic but his touch featherlight as he crouched on one knee in front of me, his fingers skimming over my slashed cheek before tilting my chin up to inspect where the blade had bitten into my throat. I flinched when the pads of his fingertips gingerly traced the raw skin.

"I'm okay. It's no big deal," I croaked. I attempted to push myself up into a standing position as a sharp pain shot up my forearm from where Aiden had twisted my wrist.

"Will Rego's ointment work on sprains, too? I still have some at— Whoa." I fell back onto my rear as I was overcome with a woozy head rush. Logan grabbed me around the waist, his other hand cushioning my head before I whacked it on the wall.

I frowned, letting my hands drop uselessly into my lap. "I feel so weak. Why do I still feel so weak?"

Logan placed his hands on my shoulders, gently pushing me down as I tried to get up again, and gave me a reproachful look. "Just rest for a second, please. A demon just used you to open a portal to another dimension and sucked all the

strength out of you to do it. Please, Paige, take five stupid
minutes to sit down and recharge."

"But we have to get out of here. What if someone comes?"
I asked, studying the disheveled classroom.

"It's lunchtime. Everyone's in the caf in the basement. Besides, this floor is off-limits and this room is soundproof," he
reminded me, adding gently, "We've got to leave across the
roof again, and you're not strong enough to go anywhere yet."

"But—"

"But nothing. I'm begging you, just relax. I've got you."

I sighed, letting my head fall against the wall as Logan
pulled out his sword, lifting up his sweater to slice off a chunk
of his shirt. He snaked one arm behind me as he settled against
my side, his hand finding a place at the small of my back. He
gently pressed the cloth against my cheek, wiping away the
blood. I tried not to wince in pain.

"Am I hurting you?" he asked, remorseful.

"I'm okay," I promised, but I flinched as he touched my
cheek again.

"Don't worry. Rego can fix this. You'd never even know
Della touched you," he said, his gentle touch somehow softening the hard edge in his voice.

"She's dead now, right?" I asked hopefully. My cheek muscle twitched, and I squeezed my eyes shut when I felt the skin
tug against the gash.

"I doubt she'll make it to a healer in time. That is, if the
trip through the portal doesn't finish her off first."

"Good." I felt my shoulders relax at that, and I took a deep
breath, wincing when I felt a sharp pain shoot through my
aching side.

"I'm hurting you, aren't I?" Logan asked, quickly pulling the now-bloody cloth from my face and setting it down on his knee.

"No—it's my side. I guess Aiden kicked me harder than I realized." Now that I was focusing on the pain, my ribs throbbed, eclipsing the pain in my shoulder from when I fell down the stairs. I pressed my palm against my side, prodding my ribs and feeling the familiar pain that I'd endured after saving Dylan's life.

Logan scowled, biting his lip as he studied the bloody cloth in his hand. I could practically hear Logan beating himself up. And I'd seen him in battle—so I assumed Logan was delivering himself one hell of an ass-kicking.

"I'm so sorry," he said quietly, his eyes downcast. "I'm supposed to be protecting you, and this is twice now that you've gotten injured. I can't believe I didn't—"

"Stop it. Your insistence on blaming yourself is taking valuable time away from me thanking you for saving my life," I interrupted before he could start cruising down Self-Critical Highway. Clearly, it was a road he knew well.

"And, hey, you're the one who taught me the whole head-butting trick. So, high-five yourself or something, because that really worked."

Logan smiled, shaking his head as strands of hair fell into his eyes. Now that his hat had found a new home in another dimension, his dark brown locks were a riotous tangle on top of his head. I automatically reached my fingers up to brush his hair out of his face, awkwardly pausing when he blinked in surprise at my gesture. I quickly ran my hand through my own disheveled hair as if that was my intention all along, and

Logan's cheeks flushed slightly. *You're about as smooth as sand-paper, Paige.*

I chastised myself for nearly crossing the line—a line that got thinner with every minute I spent with Logan. At least my battles with demons were over…and just in time, because the unreadable expression on Logan's face, as he gazed at me with soft brown eyes, made it very easy to forget that the sweet boy holding me would be leaving, now that Della and Aiden were gone.

The realization slammed into me, and I shut my eyes, feeling my shoulders hunch forward, bracing myself against the loss as a dull ache echoed in my chest. This hurt more than it should.

"How bad is it?" Logan's voice was layered with concern.

"Pretty bad. I, um…I'm annoyed at myself for getting so hurt. I thought I was stronger than this," I admitted, screwing my eyes shut more tightly when I realized there were two ways to interpret what I'd just said. "I'm just really sore," I added, hoping to mask my slip-up. But who was I kidding? That line between friendship and…something more…had pretty much evaporated, at least for me.

If Logan grasped my double meaning, he didn't let it show.

"Seriously, you're annoyed at yourself?" he repeated, incredulous. "You fought two demons. Hell, you gave one third-degree burns and then broke her nose. You did awesome."

"I guess that means you're an excellent teacher. So, stop sulking, you big sulky sulker, you."

"Okay, but only because you asked so nicely," he replied playfully. I opened my eyes to see that Logan was grinning at me, all traces of his earlier remorse gone. I had to return his infectious smile, and he slid his hand up my back, over my bare neck and into my hair. My skin tingled in the wake of his touch, and I had to bite my lip to keep from moaning as his fingers massaged my scalp. *Damn you, Logan, and your stupid magic sexy fingers.*

"How's your head, by the way?" he asked, that impish smile still on his face.

*Uh, full of unrealistic thoughts about you, now that the threat of demons kidnapping me is over. Thanks for asking.*

I smiled ruefully, pulling my knees up to my chest. "It hurts. But then again, everything hurts." *You have no idea how much this hurts.* "Maybe next time I'll try to use a weapon and not my own actual body when I want to injure someone."

"Good idea." He paused, then said in a low, breathy voice, "I was so worried, Paige. I'm glad you're still here with me."

Logan's fingers untangled from my hair, his hand sliding down my back as he rested his other hand on my knee. His gaze dropped down to my lips briefly before his eyes met mine again, and he leaned in closer to me. Too close for someone who was going to leave. Way too close for someone who had just run a sword through two demons—one of which was Della. I wanted him to kiss me, but not like this. Not because of her. And the words were out of my mouth before I could stop them.

"Are you being touchy-feely with me because you just killed a lust demon?"

Logan dropped his hold on me and shot back about a foot, his mouth open in disbelief. And horror. Lots and lots of horror.

"I just mean…you're being really affectionate…and you had said that when you kill a demon, you get their powers… and maybe you're feeling really lust demon-y right now." The words tumbled out, colliding with each other like rocks in an avalanche. Except an avalanche would have been much more subtle.

"So, I'm overwhelmed by lusty feelings, and you just happen to be conveniently injured and unable to fight me off?" Logan said slowly, his tone matter-of-fact and almost clinical. "Is that what you think of me?"

"No! I don't think that at all! I just didn't expect it—you being like that. With me, I mean," I stammered. "I didn't mean to offend you."

"Apparently, I'm the one who offended you. Don't worry, I won't touch you like that again since it's so *offensive*." Hurt flashed across his face as Logan spoke in an icy voice, over-enunciating the word.

"I didn't mean it like that. I'm sor—"

"Don't apologize. I'm—I'm the one who should be sorry." Logan's shoulders sagged as he rubbed his face roughly with his palms. He laughed humorlessly, shaking his head before speaking again, throwing his hand in the air.

"I overstepped a boundary, and now you think I'm trying to feel you up while you're in a weakened state."

"But that's not what I meant at all." The truth was, I really wanted him to overstep all sorts of boundaries. But instead, I'd made him think I considered him a pervert. *Smooth, Paige. You should have just gone for it and worried about what it meant later.*

"Honestly, I wasn't—" I began.

"Please, just drop it," he interrupted, suddenly sounding

weary. "I promise you, it won't happen again." He leaned
his back against the wall, his arms resting on his drawn-up
knees. I stole a glance at Logan's profile—his jaw was set in
a hard line, his head slightly tilting from side to side as his
eyes alternately narrowed and looked up, the way mine did
when I was running through possible outcomes of conversations in my head.

I opened my mouth to try apologizing again, but the tense
set of his jaw had me rethinking that approach, and I shifted
uncomfortably next to him on the floor.

"So, where are you going next?" I blurted out, unable to
handle any more awkward silence. Logan turned his head toward mine, a puzzled look on his face.

"*We* are going to see Rego when you're feeling better."

"After that."

"How hard did you hit Della with your head? What are
you talking about?" Logan's tone was still frosty as he studied
me. A glacier would have been positively tropical compared
to this. Not that I could blame him. He'd saved my life—
twice—and now thought I'd accused him of trying to play
grab-ass while I was incapacitated.

"Do you know what your next assignment is? Almost all
of the demons are dead, and Aiden's back in the Dark World.
Your job here is done. You're leaving," I concluded, rubbing
my side to pretend that the pained look on my face came from
actual pain and not from Logan's impending departure. *Just
remember that you're going to live. The demons are gone, Paige. His
leaving is actually a good thing. No, really. Keep telling yourself that,
and maybe you'll believe it.*

"I'm not leaving yet," Logan said, his eyes wide as he turned to face me. "What just happened is *really* bad. Aiden knows that you can be used to open portals between worlds. Well, at least from this one to the Dark World. And I'm sure he's on his way to tell all his little demon buddies." Logan scowled at that.

I stared at the shredded paper strewn around the classroom, which was cluttered with overturned stools, sheet-music holders and broken-up corkboards. I'd thought it was over. I thought the threat to my life was gone.

Instead, it was worse—far worse than I could have imagined. And, of course, I'd insulted the one person who had done nothing but protect me.

Yet again, I'd managed to just make a mess. Story of my life.

I was desperate to make things right between us, but a stolen glance at Logan told me he still wouldn't be receptive to another attempted apology. I decided to change the subject instead.

"How did you find me, in the music room of all places?"

"I figured they couldn't go far," Logan said, lifting one shoulder in a casual shrug. "Della was pretty bloody. She'd attract too much attention."

"Yeah, she was really mad about her face, by the way. I don't remember a lot from when I was under her spell, but I remember that."

"How did you break her spell, anyway?" Logan asked, studying me with a curious expression on his face. "What made you snap out of it?"

"I don't know," I lied, grabbing a piece of torn sheet music off the floor and studying the beginning notes of "When the Saints Go Marching In."

"You don't know?" Logan repeated skeptically as I busied myself with twisting the corners of the paper in my hands, intently focusing on my crappy origami project as if I were getting graded on it.

"Paige?" Logan said my name the same way he had when he first came into the room, his voice wrapping around the word, reminding me of how seeing him had helped me tear down the mental blocks Della had put into place.

"If you have some other talents—if you're a spellcaster of some kind or a witch, please, tell me," he pleaded. "You know I'll believe you."

*Of course you will. Because you're the first person in years to talk to me like I'm not crazy. You're the first person to really talk to me.*

I took a deep breath, staring at the folded scrap of sheet music in my hand as I steeled my resolve.

"It was you," I confessed, running my thumb over the creases in the paper.

"Me?"

I forced myself to meet Logan's eyes, bracing myself for the rejection I expected to see. Instead, he merely looked confused, his dark eyebrows pulling together as he stared at me blankly.

"What do you mean?" he asked, guileless.

"When I saw you, and heard your voice, I just knew," I explained, trying to keep my voice even and nonchalant and not at all affected by the fact that this admission would lay bare just how much Logan meant to me.

"Just knew what?" Logan asked, that same bewildered look on his face. *He's gonna make me spell it out, isn't he?*

I took a deep breath and exhaled through my nose.

"Before you came in, I felt—I don't know—loyal to them. But that's not even a strong enough word." I fumbled through my explanation as I tried to describe what it felt like to be under Della's spell. "There was this unexplainable urge to stay with them. I didn't question it. It felt natural, and right. But when I saw you, suddenly I knew that Aiden was wrong. That the feeling of belonging to him and Della was wrong." I closed my eyes for the last confession. "You felt right."

I opened my eyes to see Logan's puzzled expression soften.

"But you didn't want me touching you. You don't feel that way about me...." Logan's voice trailed off as he studied me. I bit my lip and stared at the folded-up paper in my hands when I heard him inhale sharply.

"Do you?" He curled his hand around my arm when I didn't answer. His voice was soft, layered with some emotion that I couldn't quite identify and desperately hoped wasn't pity. I steeled myself to look at him—to face the rejection I'd undoubtedly see in his eyes.

"Paige! Oh, my goodness, there you are, Paige!" Dottie exclaimed, bursting into the classroom. Her hand was linked with Travis's, and she dragged him behind her as she hurried into the classroom, her uniform skirt swishing around her knees while her hair, of course, remained perfectly immobile. Both Logan and I jumped at the intrusion, and he dropped his hand from my arm.

"You're bleeding! What happened? Why aren't you standing?" she asked, lines of worry cutting into her forehead. "Why isn't she standing?" she demanded, directing her bossy question at Logan, who was now on his feet next to me. "I'm Dottie, by the way."

"I know," Logan said with an entertained smile. "Nice to officially meet the famous Dottie."

Dottie became flustered, smoothing her perfect hair as she beamed at Logan, and Travis scowled at her, dropping her hand to cross his arms. *Just how friendly had Dottie and Travis gotten in the past couple of days?*

"Paige will be all right. We have stuff that can heal her. She just needs to rest for a minute," Logan explained, adding a halfhearted wave. "I'm Logan, by the way."

"I know," Dottie replied, sizing him up through her curled lashes.

"What happened in here?" Travis asked, taking a few steps around the classroom.

"Just your usual, boring, everyday demon fight," I offered weakly as Travis strolled over to the shredded blackboard. He clasped his hands behind his back as he studied the violent, jagged slices in the slate—which would have been me, had Logan not saved me. Again.

"Wow, the school's insurance agent must friggin' hate you," he said with a low whistle as he attempted to kick a few crumbled shards with his toe. Travis frowned when his foot passed through the debris.

"I'm never going to get used to that." He grimaced.

"I'm sorry," I whispered, and Travis gave me a resigned shrug in reply.

"Listen, we have to tell you what we saw," Dottie said, sitting down cross-legged in front of me.

"So, we were in the library, and we heard this commotion outside. There was this big gray monster with wings." She spread her arms to mimic Aiden's wingspan and flapped them a few times. "It had this girl under its arm—but it didn't look like he was hurting her. It looked like he was helping her walk."

"Aiden and Della! You saw them!" I slapped my palms against the floor in disbelief. "Did they see you?"

"No, they had their backs to us. We hid against the wall inside the library," Travis explained, sinking down to join us on the floor.

"Anyway, they both sounded like hell, but the girl was worse. She was coughing up all this red smoke—weird, right?" Dottie shuddered at the memory. "And she was crying and the guy was getting angry with her. He told her that he'd promised to take her to a healer so she'd better, and I quote, 'Stop crying about getting stabbed in the stomach already, it's annoying me.' Then he complained about going through the portal and how he'd have left her there if he could have gone through alone. So the girl started saying she couldn't wait to tell everyone about the Traveler—you, I assume?" Dottie pointed a perfect pink oval nail at me, and I flinched at the term, nodding my head. "Anyway, she said the Queen would be so thrilled, that she'd be sure to get an army here immediately to get you."

I turned to Logan, terrified.

"It's as bad as you thought," I whispered, and Logan hesitantly reached his hand out to comfort me.

"Wait. But then the monster—Aiden, right?—said, 'We're not telling the Queen anything yet,'" Dottie continued.

"What?" Logan's head snapped to face Dottie, dropping his outstretched hand as he leaned forward on his palms. "That doesn't make any sense," he muttered, shaking his head in disbelief.

"Well, the girl agreed with you, because she said the same thing," Dottie explained. "And Aiden said that, well...."

"What?" Logan prodded her, and Dottie took a deep breath, visibly steeling herself to continue.

"Aiden said, 'I want to see the grateful look on the Queen's face when I drag the bodies of the demonslayer and his little bitch into her throne room.'" Dottie mouthed the curse word in an effort to take the sting out of it. My poor, sweet old-fashioned friend. As if calling me a bitch was the worst part of that statement.

Travis jumped in to continue the story. "But then the girl started saying that they had to tell the Queen, that you were too valuable a weapon to leave here." I flinched at his words; I was considered a weapon, a thing to be used.

"And Aiden told her to shut it, and then he went on this whole dramatic rant about how he's going to prove himself, and he'll reap all the glory of bringing you both in and finally be considered worthy—whatever that means," Travis said, adding, "He sounded like a whiny little bitch, if you ask me."

"Della said she was going to tell the Queen, and he couldn't stop her," Dottie said, picking up where Travis left off. "Aiden told her, 'I can't let you do that.' And then we heard this loud cry—" Dottie shrieked, mimicking what she'd heard, and Logan and I cringed at her earsplitting screech "—and then a thump on the floor."

My theatrical friend pounded her fist on the floor to re-create the sound.

"After we were sure he was gone, we left the library and

saw Della on the ground in the hallway," Travis continued.
"There was all this red smoke pouring out of her. It was
nasty."

"She started to disintegrate. She actually turned into
smoke!" Dottie added with an amazed whisper, spreading
her hands and wiggling her fingers to imitate the creeping
spread of the crimson smoke.

"Why didn't she explode?" I asked Logan.

"That's only fire demons. Every kind of demon bleeds and
dies differently," Logan explained before shaking his head in
disbelief. "He killed her. I can't believe he killed her."

"That's a good thing, right?" I asked.

"It's a surprising thing." Logan looked lost in thought.

"Well, he's a demon. You can't be surprised that he's a mur-
derer with zero loyalty," I reasoned, and Logan pursed his lips.

"That's not always the case," he said, quickly rising to his
feet. I cringed, remembering Logan's demonic buddy Ajax a
moment too late.

"Paige, I'll get your stuff out of your locker and then we'll
go." I looked up to see Logan standing in front of me. "Are
you feeling strong enough? We'll go to my apartment and
see what Rego knows."

"I'm fine," I replied automatically, nodding my head.

Once Logan was out of the classroom, Dottie's voice
dropped to a conspiratorial whisper.

"What is going on with you two?" Dottie asked, propping
her chin on the heel of her hand as she rested her elbow on
her bent knee. All she needed was the telephone cord from a
rotary phone coiled around her finger, and she'd be a poster
child for the fifties teen.

"Seriously? I'm attacked by a demon, the music room looks like this—" I waved my hand around the disaster "—and you want to talk about boys?"

"We can talk about demons when Logan returns," Dottie said, blinking her lashes at me. "What's going on with you two?"

"Well, I could ask you the same question, Little Miss Holding Hands with You-Know-Who," I hissed in reply, mimicking her pose by resting my chin on my hand.

"I'll tell you if you tell me," Dottie wheedled, her brown eyes sparkling. "Did Logan kiss you? You haven't kissed anyone since playing Truth or Dare with Chris when you were a sophomore. The *first* time you were a sophomore."

"I know, Dots. I was there. And thanks for bringing up my rockin' romantic history, by the way," I added dryly as Travis rolled his eyes.

"Well, maybe you'll have some new romantic history to write," she said, her eyes starry.

"It'll be a short book. We're talking pamphlet, here," I retorted, thinking of how I'd accidentally offended Logan repeatedly today.

"Hey, can I just stop you guys before you start talking about pantyhose or ribbons or some other girly shit?" Travis interrupted, plopping down to join us on the floor. "And can someone tell me what happened here? I'd like to know."

I quickly told them what had happened—and before Dottie could beg for more information about what was going on between us, Logan returned with my bag and coat.

"You were gone a long time." I twisted my neck to stare at the clock above the destroyed blackboard. I had started to wonder if Logan had ditched me in all my rude, unrequitedly affectionate and slightly aching glory. Instead, he just smiled arrogantly, puffing his chest out.

"All your teachers will think you were in class this afternoon. And you're going to get an A on the pop quiz in physics. You're welcome," he added with a self-satisfied smile.

"Oh. Thanks. That hypnotism thing comes in handy, huh?" I forced a friendly grin on my face, but it probably just looked awkward. I was too unsure of how to act around Logan once we were alone. Would he want to pick up our conversation where it left off? Pretend it never happened?

I was definitely a member of Team It Never Happened.

"Are you okay to move?" Logan asked, coming to stand before me. He hesitantly stretched his palm out, and I gave him my uninjured hand, letting him help me off the floor. I winced as the movement pulled against my sore side.

"Your ribs?"

"I'll be okay, though," I insisted, shrugging into my coat. "I should be able to make it a few blocks."

I reached for my bag but Logan refused, insisting on carrying it. Because he just had to do perfect gentlemanly things that made me like him even more. That bastard.

Dottie cleared her throat. "Take good care of her," she told Logan, giving him a warning glance which disclosed her real meaning. "Or else you'll have to deal with me."

Logan gave Dottie a small smile, and I followed him out of the classroom. A few minutes later, we were back on the school roof, beginning our quiet trek across the skyline.

It wasn't until we had climbed over the wall at the end of the school that Logan spoke, calling my name softly.

I stopped talking and turned to face him, wincing at the pull in my side.

"That hurts worse than you're letting on, isn't it?" he asked, concerned.

"I'll be fine. I can make the jump," I insisted through gritted teeth. "What did you want to say?"

Logan just shook his head, his face composed in a stoic mask.

"Nothing. I can wait until you're healed," Logan said. But he grabbed my hand and swiftly led me across the rooftops before my mind could whirl into overdrive on what he meant. *Does he not want to hurt my feelings on top of my hurt body? Is he looking to let me down easily when I feel better? Then why did it feel like he was going to kiss me earlier?*

Okay, maybe my mind went into overdrive a little bit.

I kept a tight hold on Logan until we'd crossed the magical threshold into his apartment, and then he pushed me behind him, against the now-solid door, as he drew his sword.

A rapid whirring sound hit my ears as a pink blur whizzed by, embedding itself into the door with a low thunk.

"Stay where you are," wheezed the unfamiliar, gravelly voice. I tried to peer around Logan, but he reached behind his back, his arm wrapping around my waist and gently shoving me behind him.

Logan took a step forward, his body tensely coiled and ready to strike.

"Where's Rego? What did you do with him?" Logan demanded, but his voice was laced with fear.

"I said, stay where you are," the voice said. "That was a warning shot. I must promise you, kid, I never miss."

Heavy footsteps sounded on the floor, and he came into view.

He was short and stocky, and dressed in simple dark pants with a long gray tunic and a scratchy-looking vest made out of a burlaplike fabric. He had a ruddy, rotund face and thinning, dark yellow hair that was pulled back into a stringy ponytail. He would have looked nonthreatening—like the purveyor of a shop that sold patchouli and healing crystals—if it weren't for the crossbow he brandished, keeping a steady aim on Logan with his violet eyes.

"Drop your sword," the demon ordered.

# 8

HIS SHOULDERS, RISING AND FALLING WITH each measured breath, were the only part of Logan that moved. Otherwise, he was statue-still, holding his weapon steady.

"I said, drop your sword," the demon repeated from his perch by the wobbly table. He shot again, sending a thin red arrow finished with a plume of pink feathers and red beads sailing through the air. I yelped as it pierced the door a mere six inches from my head, my hands flying to clutch my book bag as it hung off Logan's back.

"I hand-make these arrows, kid," he warned, lovingly stroking the next one he loaded into the crossbow. "I know every dip and curve—the slight imperfections that impact where it lands. I never, ever miss." The demon grinned proudly at his deadly creation as it sat, tensed and ready, in his weapon. "Now, do you want me to shoot you in your wrist and force you drop to your sword? Or perhaps ensure that the girl cowering behind you never walks properly again, with one well-placed shot into her kneecap? Your choice, unless you relinquish your weapon."

The door behind us shimmered, this time with the telltale amethyst glow that heralded an arrival from the Dark World. Logan grabbed me and spun me around, so I was against the wall, pinned behind him between this new demon and whomever—or whatever—was about to come through the door.

The outline of two figures could be seen through the swirling dark fog that obscured the portal to the Dark World. Logan shuffled me back even more, the hand that wasn't holding his sword reaching behind him to again wrap protectively around my waist. I heard heavy footsteps as our new visitors breached the threshold, and Logan's shoulders relaxed slightly.

"Well, if I knew we were having a party, I would have brought a bottle of sunwine. Seems like we could all use a drink," came Ajax's familiar voice. His words were flippant but spoken carefully, cautiously. I peered around Logan's shoulder and saw Ajax's eyes sweeping the room, locking on mine briefly before settling on the demon with the crossbow. A girl stood next to him, small but fierce and beautiful, wearing a rust-colored trench coat that hung open over skintight black pants and an equally tight shirt. Her hair was a beautiful mess of fire-truck-red and coal-black waves, parted in the middle and tumbling over her shoulders, where it bled into the long dark scarf that hung casually around her neck. She would have been effortlessly stunning, if not for her telltale inhuman eyes—a ring of black surrounding a yellow pupil—that exposed her demonic heritage. Eyes which raked over Logan so thoroughly, she was sure to leave his skin marked up.

"Cerus, want to tell me what you're doing?" Ajax asked dryly, leaning against the kitchen counter with studied ease.

He looked like he was waiting to order a martini at the bar at the end of the day, not questioning the demon who was threatening his buddy.

"I've discovered these two interlopers," the crossbow-wielding demon hissed, and Ajax merely laughed.

"Cerus, consider where we are, you pompous old ass. To him, you're the interloper—I'm pretty sure he's the one who lives here," he said, chuckling, gesturing to Logan as if he'd never met him before. "You've heard the rumors about Rego's protégé. I doubt he'd be thrilled with you if he came home to find you've impaled his charge with one of your fluffy little arrows."

I gripped Logan's hand where it curled around my hip as I stole another glance at Cerus. For some reason, Ajax didn't want to reveal that he and Logan knew each other. I already didn't trust demons—but a demon that other demons didn't trust? Clearly that's the worst kind of demon ever.

Cerus studied us, his gaze calculating and cold.

"Remember, kid, one false move and your little friend will taste my arrow in the back of her throat. I never miss."

Ajax nudged his friend, who finally turned her gaze on me. Her body twisted gracefully, and she vanished in a swirl of black and red, thin trails of the color bleeding into the air like ink dissipating in a glass of water.

"I'm not going to hurt you—unless you're into that sort of thing." A light breath in my ear tickled my skin as she materialized behind me. I screamed as the demon grabbed me in her arms, my ribs throbbing with pain as I struggled against her ironlike grip. The room whirled around, a dizzying pinwheel of color and light—and suddenly I was swaying on wobbly legs, sandwiched between Ajax and this new girl, who whispered, "Be very quiet" into my hair as she kept me locked in her arms.

Logan started toward me just as Cerus gasped at the distraction, letting his concentration falter. In three long strides, Logan changed direction, crossing the room and swiftly delivering a roundhouse kick that slammed into Cerus's wrist. The demon cried aloud as his crossbow clattered to the floor, and he fell to his knees to grab at his weapon. But he was too slow: Logan punted it across the room, where it smashed into pieces against the wall, falling to the floor in a limp pile of feathers and wood and metal.

Logan raised his sword and sliced it down swiftly, stopping the blade a mere inch from Cerus's neck. A weak cry bubbled up through Cerus's lips as he shut his eyes in fear.

"I never miss either. Do yourself a favor and remember that," Logan growled as Cerus whimpered. Logan took a step back, keeping the tip of his sword pressed underneath Cerus's jaw.

"Aw, what's wrong? Not so brave without your crossbow, are you?" Logan goaded sarcastically. "Now, listen up, you little troll, what are you doing in my kitchen, shooting arrows at me?"

"I am not a troll!" cried Cerus, glaring at Logan from where he remained kneeling on the floor. "I am a Regent, a member of the superior demon race, and you would do well to respect—"

"Please, go right on ahead and kill him," Ajax offered, a smirk on his face. "Cerus talks like this all the time. It's really annoying. 'I'm a Regent, I'm so great, durr, durr, durr,'" he imitated in a deep, doofy voice. "Who isn't a Regent? I mean, really?"

"Even your friend doesn't seem to like you." Logan spoke with menacingly cool detachment. "So, why don't you tell me what you're doing in my kitchen before I *accidentally* run you through with my sword?"

"I'm here to confer with Rego," Cerus said scornfully, "on matters that have nothing to do with you, child. Why are you so concerned with me, anyway? Don't you care about Ajax and his little friend? After all, they're the ones holding your little human friend hostage."

"They didn't shoot arrows at us. Now, tell me, who are you, and where is Rego?" Logan demanded, pushing the tip of his sword further into Cerus's neck, effectively erasing the arrogance from his face.

"Rego isn't here yet! I arrived for our meeting early."

"To snoop around, I bet," Ajax chimed in.

"You're not even supposed to be here," Cerus snarled in reply.

"And yet I managed to show up anyway," Ajax retorted, the disdain in his voice contradicting the innocent smile on his face. "Funny how you like having meetings without me these days, Cerus."

"What are we all, childhood friends catching up? I'll ask once more before I take your head off," Logan barked, using the broad side of his sword to whack Cerus in the ear. The blade struck his skin with a loud smack, and Cerus howled in pain as lavender blood streamed from his ear. I squirmed, uncomfortable at the brutal sight.

"Just stay still," Ajax whispered to me, his voice low and his mouth covered as he pretended to scratch his nose. I stopped wriggling but glared at him. I'd had enough of demons telling me what to do today.

"Why are you here for Rego?" Logan demanded, his jaw clenched as he dragged the tip of his blade across Cerus's throat. I blanched, gritting my teeth at the grisly scene. Logan was menacing, authoritative, threatening—terrifying, even. The soldier he'd said he's always been.

"The Regent Queen—she needs to be overthrown. Her reign is impure," Cerus stammered in reply to Logan's question, his violet eyes wide with terror. "I have information for Rego on her itinerary."

"And you tell him this why? For your health?" Logan continued his interrogation, smacking him in the ear again before returning his sword to Cerus's neck.

"In exchange for his protection! Once she's assassinated, the warlocks will reign again. And I'll gain a prominent position, money, power.... Please, don't kill me," Cerus babbled, his face shimmering with sweat and his neck streaked pastel as blood streamed down his skin.

Logan smacked Cerus again, and I winced, fighting the urge to look away. I didn't harbor any particularly warm and fuzzy feelings toward Cerus, but this inquisition was difficult to watch.

"This is a revealing scene, Cerus. A teenager threatens you with a little paper cut on your neck and a few taps to the head, so you divulge all our secrets. Remind me to put you in charge of nothing," Rego seethed, startling us all as he stepped through the now-glowing doorway behind us.

Rego's entrance triggered an emotional charge in the room:

Cerus paled, his eyes focused on the warlock as he appeared to forget the blade at his throat. Logan stood up straighter, his face composed and slightly defiant, with only the flexing of his jaw hinting at any unease.

After hopping up on the kitchen counter, Ajax gave Rego a cheerful wave and a big grin, but it looked forced. The demon gripping me held me more tightly, only this time I couldn't help but feel like she was using me as a human shield.

Rego gracefully slipped off his nondescript beige trench coat, and tossed it carelessly into a corner—revealing the same military-style uniform I'd last seen him wearing—and stood before me, his reserved glare even colder. The Rego I'd met earlier was positively snuggly compared to the intimidating man who now stood before me.

Ajax tapped the girl demon with the back of his hand, and she released me. I all but ran into Logan's arms; well, arm. He still held his sword against Cerus's neck with one hand but pulled me into his side as Rego took his place before the red-and-black-haired demon.

"Ajax, you bring strangers into my headquarters when I'm not here? Without my permission? Is this an ambush?" Rego asked coolly, whipping his head to glare at Ajax, the blunt tips of his pin-straight black hair barely brushing against the stiff line of his shoulders.

"Before you get angry," Ajax began, his palms raised in deference, "I trust her, and she really wants to work with us. She comes bearing news of the fire demons."

"And she is?"

"Evadia, sir," she said, her voice clipped and devoid of the smarmy tone it had held when she grabbed me. "Eva for short." Eva—a normal, nonthreatening, somewhat old-fashioned name. Certainly not the name of someone who can bend the rules of time and space and teleport you from place to place.

"I've never heard of you." Rego curled his long fingers around the sword hanging from his belt as he spoke, before turning to Ajax. "You could have brought her information to me without bringing this—" he flicked his hand dismissively at Eva "—intruder here."

"Eva wants to join with us. I thought you'd be happy," Ajax replied, nonplussed. "I vouch for her, Rego."

Rego turned away from the two demons to stand before Logan, his silver-tipped boots thudding heavily with purpose on the floor.

"Remove your sword from my comrade's jugular," Rego ordered briskly. Everything about him was calm and coolly authoritative—but his eyes were stormy, landing on me with a glare that could wilt flowers.

"Cerus shot at—" Logan began calmly.

"Now, I said!" Rego demanded, and Logan gaped at him in shock.

"Rego just doesn't want to have to clean the mess when Cerus soils his undergarments," Ajax called helpfully.

"If you must open your mouth, I suggest you fill it with some of the snacks you begged me to get for you," Rego snapped, and Ajax obediently grabbed a bag of tortilla chips and a jar of cheese sauce off the counter. The potent aroma of processed cheese and corn and salt soon filled the kitchen.

Keeping the one arm wrapped protectively around my shoulders, Logan slowly slid the sword off Cerus's neck, keeping a cautious eye on the demon. He scrambled to his feet, first glaring at the broken metal scraps that had once been his prized weapon before letting his heated gaze rest on Logan.

"Who are you to attack my protégé?" Rego asked Cerus. "You think you can take on the assassin of untold numbers of demons? Or perhaps you think me a fool? That I would allow merely anyone into my sanctuary?" His voice started out maddeningly calm, only to rise in volume and intensity as he spoke at Cerus, who cowered in his chair. Finally Rego boomed, "Do I need to remind you who I am?"

"I'm sorry, Rego." Cerus bowed his head.

"Oh, don't apologize to the person you actually shot at, though," Logan muttered, and Rego turned his attention back on Logan and me. He folded his arms behind his back, one hand gripping the wrist of the other as he raised his chin in a commanding stance.

"You're early." Rego issued the observation as if it were an indictment, keeping his eyes locked on Logan. "And another jar of healing ointment is needed, I see. Are the offending demons dead, or did you somehow get waylaid again?"

"The lust demon is dead. But I wanted to know what you'd heard about this final demon. His name is Aiden and he's—"

"Dragging this assignment out, are you?" Rego's eyes traveled to where Logan held his arm around me, and Logan clenched his teeth, the muscle in his jaw twitching at the implication of Rego's statement.

"I've never given any reason to doubt my dedication," Logan growled, his hand dropping from my waist. "And yet, your little associate over there decides to shoot an arrow at my head."

"Are you really sure you want to question me, after all I've done for you?" Rego snapped in reply. "You're a soldier, who does what I order him to do. I must say, I don't appreciate your audacity. It's a recently learned character trait—" his gray eyes flickered to me again "—that isn't very becoming or beneficial to the revolution."

"Hey, kid, did you mention the name Aiden?" Ajax interrupted from his perch on the kitchen counter. He was still pretending that he didn't know Logan, and busied himself by using one corn chip to carefully apply a thick orange stripe of cheese dip to another corn chip before cramming both into his mouth. Ajax clearly loved playing the jester—but for whose benefit? There was a calculating mind behind the mirth and easy smiles; I just didn't know who he was trying to fool.

"Yeah, Aiden. He attacked this girl today," Logan explained, his voice emotionless as he jerked his thumb toward me. I tried not to flinch at the cold expression on Logan's face, doing my best to keep my face impassive and go along with whatever facade Logan was creating, no matter how hurtful. "I want to get her healed and on her way."

"And here I thought you were the feared demonslayer, *proditori,*" Cerus sneered, earning a hateful glare from Logan.

Logan kept his eyes on Cerus as he popped his sword in the air, catching it without even looking at it. "You got a sharp tongue there, buddy," Logan said, pointing his sword at Cerus. "Be careful you don't cut your own throat with it."

"Logan, please continue," Rego said, ignoring their bickering.

"Aiden and a lust demon, going by the name Della, discovered my identity, so they attacked me today. He used this girl as bait to get to me, then sacrificed Della so he could escape," Logan lied smoothly, his delivery of this fable so confident that I was nearly tempted to believe it.

"He hurt this girl pretty badly—Rego, can you grab the healing balm?" Logan asked, and Rego excused himself briefly, returning with another glass jar of the blue ointment, which he set on the tabletop with a heavy thump. Cerus greedily reached for the concoction, but Logan stepped forward and swiped it from Cerus's bloodstained hands.

"This isn't for you," he said coldly, before turning to me, his back to the demons in the room.

"Go in the bathroom and put this on your wounds. Your ribs, your cheek, everywhere," he said in a persuasive voice, his eyes shut. The hairs on the back of my neck tingled at the smooth, almost seductive tone in his voice—it had the same alluring quality that Della's voice had, but without instilling the all-consuming compulsion to obey.

I felt a flare of anger and betrayal rise inside me when I realized what he was doing. He was trying to put that spell on me—to hypnotize me into being his puppet.

Logan opened his eyes and grabbed my hands, pressing the jar of ointment into them. He had an almost desperate look on his face, as his eyes bore into mine.

"Go," he mouthed, squeezing my hands before releasing me, adding in a loud, brusque voice, "Do it. Now."

And that's when I realized he hadn't tried to cast a spell on me—only make everyone else think he had. He'd kept his eyes closed—those dark eyes that secured the spell's success with one hypnotic look. I attempted to appear fully under his influence, nodding dully with a vacant look on my face.

It wasn't hard to fake it—I was already dazed and completely overwhelmed—and I quickly ducked into the bathroom.

It was small and windowless with no escape. Like everywhere else in the apartment, the bathroom walls bore the marks and scrapes of a dwelling that had seen scores of careless residents come and go throughout the years. I tried shutting the door, but the swollen, cheap wood bumped against the frame, forcing it to remain open a crack. I pressed my ear against the thin sliver of space, closing my eyes as I focused on the conversation outside.

"I know of Aiden. His reputation precedes him. What I don't know is why he'd be so interested in this little human girl in the first place." Cerus's voice was saturated with contempt. "Rego informed me you were searching for the Traveler. Is this her? Can she open gateways between the worlds? Because that would be most helpful in assassinating the Queen."

"That girl? Like I said, Aiden was simply using her to get to me. She's nobody," Logan said dismissively. I winced at his hurtful words and tried to convince myself he was somehow trying to protect me.

"She doesn't seem like anything special," Cerus scoffed, and I peered through the crack of the door again, scowling. From my position behind the door, I only had a view of Logan's back. He stood with his arms folded in front of the bathroom, as if he were guarding me.

"As if you're such a prize." Ajax's voice was muffled—probably because his mouth was crammed full of chips and cheese—but the sarcasm was evident. "You're twenty pounds of dung crammed in a ten-pound sack."

I quietly snickered. If he weren't an evil demon, I might actually like Ajax.

"As usual, you're full of jokes but have no real contribution to offer. I still want an answer to my question. What can she do that's intrigued you so much, *proditori?*" Cerus asked in a measured, calculating voice.

"Aiden has seen that I'm fond of her. I haven't identified the Traveler yet, so I've been passing the time with this one." Logan jerked his thumb over his shoulder toward me, his voice so dismissive that it stung.

"And that's all she is to you? A recreational activity?"

"What do you want me to say? She's hot. And she won't remember anything by the time I'm done with her. I erase her memory so often, I'm amazed she can still tie her shoe-laces," Logan said callously, his uncaring words slicing right through me. Had he erased my memory? I was working with the general assumption that Logan was lying to protect me, to hide what it was that I could do, but still…damn, that was harsh. My heart lurched at the thought of such a deep betrayal.

"I forget sometimes that you're still a teenager," Rego muttered, his voice, for once, not sounding angry. It was almost… indulgent. I had forgotten Rego was in the room. Why hadn't he interrupted Cerus's relentless questioning?

I bit my lip, realizing that I already knew the answer: Rego wanted to hear how Logan would handle himself. *And if he'd leap to defend your honor, or if you're just a distraction that keeps him waylaid, as he said.*

Well, according to these guys, I was keeping Logan *way* laid—and as long as it was nothing more, Rego was apparently fine with it. Suddenly, my dad's desire to keep me away from all males made sense. Even males of different species only cared about one thing.

"Ajax, does your friend have anything to offer me?" Rego asked. "Or do you plan on justifying this intrusion by eating all my food?"

I listened as Ajax and Eva began talking about a hive of fire demons that had pledged support to the Queen, but their words were muted and difficult to hear now that the conversation was no longer heated.

I rested my head against the wall, still slightly dizzy and completely overwhelmed, and found myself staring at my reflection in the medicine cabinet mirror. And I gasped in shock.

It's a good thing my jacket had a hood, because if I'd walked through the streets of New York uncovered, someone would have called the cops. My hair was a knotted mess, a soft halo of frizz surrounding the tangled snarls. Stiff dark lines curled across my slashed face, strands that had gotten caught in the blood and dried in a veinlike web that crept across my right cheek. Part of my face was stained red, a crimson mask that coated my skin, dripping down my neck and onto the white collar of my shirt. A thin red welt stretched around my neck, a tender line of skin that resembled a ropelike choker. My eyes were haunted, almost sunken, and ringed with deep shadows—which made sense, since I was completely exhausted.

But the worst was the sticky, two-inch gash on my face, a stinging reminder of Della's knife.

I grabbed the jar of healing balm, which opened with a satisfying pop, and greedily scooped my fingers into the oily ointment, smearing a healthy glob of it onto my cheek and neck. It fizzed, a barely audible hiss that stung along the lines Della had carved into my skin.

The water that came out of the faucet wasn't hot. It was the tepid, barely warm temperature that was the calling card of a landlord providing just enough heat to avoid any fines. But it felt like heaven as I splashed it on my face, rubbing my palm along my skin, feeling the raised, puffy wounds disintegrate like soap flakes underneath my wet fingertips. I quickly unbuttoned my shirt and slid it off, using it to scrub the remaining blood off my face. The shirt was ruined, anyway.

Turning in the mirror, I poked at my ribs, rubbing the balm on the shadow of a dark bruise that was already blossoming on the skin underneath my yellow-and-white polka-dotted bra, and along where my shoulder had taken the brunt of my tumble down the stairs. The deep ache in my side had almost disappeared when I heard Rego swear—loudly—outside. I slipped my shirt back on, the damp fabric sticking to my skin as I peered through the crack in the doorway.

"Either we find a way to have the *incindia* colony unite with us, or we destroy them," Rego said, and I heard a loud bang.

"Careful, Rego. Don't knock this table over while I'm sitting on it," Ajax said, his voice sulky from where he was now perched on the wobbly table. "I'm quite comfortable. But I guess I do have to leave soon…Eva and I are expected back shortly."

"I must take my leave, as well. I'll follow you out, Ajax. But first, Rego, you owe me something," Cerus said, walking into view, his head tilted up arrogantly. He regarded Logan dismissively, glaring at him down his nose as he sauntered off to Rego's office of sorts, that curtained-off room full of artifacts and mysterious trinkets.

"It was quite the joy to meet you," Ajax said loudly as he and Eva approached Logan, bowing with a playful flourish before adopting a more serious demeanor.

"Sorry about performing my little parlor trick on the young lady, but we had to distract Cerus and get her out of his way," Eva purred, resting one hand against Logan's chest. "She didn't look like she could take care of herself. Hope it doesn't affect your enjoyment of her."

I rolled my eyes as Logan stepped back from her, letting her hand drop. *The thought of being someone's magically induced sex slave is way more nauseating than your little physics-defying trip through space, lady.*

Ajax cautiously glanced to where Rego and Cerus had disappeared before leaning in to whisper to Logan in an impassioned voice.

"I really, really hate the way he talks to you, especially in front of people like Cerus," Ajax fumed, and Logan just shrugged, as if to say, "That's Rego." But Ajax grabbed his arm.

"If I don't see you again, please, believe me this—he is not to be trusted."

"What? Why wouldn't I see you again?"

"He'll use her against you, Logan," Ajax warned. "They both will."

"Cerus and Aiden?"

"No, Cerus and Rego."

Logan yanked his arm back and stared at Ajax in shock as I blanched behind the door.

"What aren't you telling me?" Logan asked, his voice suspicious.

"The final battle in this war is coming sooner than we thought, and we've lost the advantage. Get out. You have to get—" Ajax jumped back as Cerus strolled into the room, brandishing a new crossbow, this one a shimmering gold color. Both Ajax and Logan feigned casual, unaffected poses as Cerus interrupted their secret conversation, aiming his unloaded crossbow at Ajax.

"Aren't you due at the palace right now?" Cerus asked with false interest. "Ingratiating yourself to the False Queen is a full-time job, after all."

"That's true," Ajax agreed cheerfully, unaffected by Cerus's taunts. "But I think Eva and I will stop by Nebrio's Tavern first. I could go for a nice swig of sunwine, and Nebrio brews his own."

Ajax pulled Logan into a brief, but tight, hug, before stepping back, keeping one hand on his shoulder.

"I bet you're fun with a few drinks in you—and Nebrio's is close by, right on the river. Join us sometime," Ajax said, slapping Logan on the arm before linking elbows with Eva as he followed Cerus to the door.

"Come, dear, let's see if Nebrio's got those little twiggy snacks I love. I go there every day for them. I'm obsessed!" Ajax called over his shoulder to Logan as he walked to the door. I heard the unfamiliar words, the cadence similar to the phrases Logan used to open the front door, and a creeping darkness overtook the room. I put my hand on the doorknob, ready to leave, when I heard Rego's voice, and my hand froze in place.

"I must say, I'm impressed," Rego said once the room was awash in light, signaling that the demons had left.

"Praise, Rego? That's new," Logan replied sullenly, folding his arms. I was surprised at how familiar his petulant tone was—then I realized he sounded like I did when I argued with my dad.

"I know your attachment to this girl isn't as casual as you've let them believe. You feel indebted to her for saving your life with the *incindia,* and I respect that," Rego said. "But it is something of a relief that you hypnotized her and sent her to heal her wounds, regardless of her inane feelings about the spell. I'm gratified to see she's not the all-consuming distraction I had feared she was becoming."

"I know what my role is," Logan replied in a clipped tone.

"I think the young lady is still under your influence, because she's rather quiet in there. Get her healed and send her home. When you return, we need to put a stronger spell on the door. I don't trust this Eva. I'm pleased you didn't reveal that we've discovered a Traveler in front of her, but Ajax may have shared this information. I trust you'll be here to assist in this spell? We need to ban both of them from entering."

"What do you mean? We've known Ajax for years!" Logan argued. "He's my friend."

Rego stepped closer to Logan, nearly nose to nose with him.

"Need I remind you this is a war? There's no need for friends or emotional entanglements. You'd do well to remember that." Rego's voice was emotionless and cold, and it chilled me from several feet away and through a door. The warlock stomped off, his footsteps fading, until they suddenly stopped.

"Just remember how well things worked out for your parents."

I gripped the door handle in shock as Logan recoiled from Rego, a flash of white light flooding the apartment, obscuring Logan's wounded face and nearly blinding me as I peered through the small crack in the door. I stepped back, blinking as spots danced across my vision.

I was still rubbing my eyes when there was a swift rapping on the bathroom door.

"Paige, it's me." He paused. "Logan."

"I figured. I don't think demons would knock," I said, flinging open the door. Logan barged through it, surprising me by wrapping one arm around my waist and holding me close as he inspected my once-slashed face.

"Are you okay?" I asked.

"Are you okay?" he asked me at the same time.

"Me, first. Good, you're all healed," he murmured to himself before looking down at my appearance. "And...you're all covered in blood."

He released me, stepping back with alarm, his blue sweater now dotted with watered-down bloody splotches. "Why are you all wet and all covered in blood?"

"I used my shirt to clean off my face," I explained, holding out the front of my shirt that was now tie-dyed with blood. "It was ruined anyway."

He studied me with a grim look on his face, his lips pressed together.

"Hey," I began gingerly. "What did Rego mean about your parents?"

"Don't worry about it." Not surprisingly, Logan dismissed

the comment, his tone softening as he brushed the damp hair back from my face to inspect the now-smooth skin. "Tell me how you're doing."

"I'm as good as can be expected, I guess." I shook my head as I leaned against the sink. "I was eavesdropping, you know."

"I figured," Logan said with a knowing smile—which faded quickly, as a worried look overtook his face. "Paige, I swear I've never hypnotized you. I promise. I would never use someone like that. You know I was lying, right?"

*Well, I know now.* "I figured," I said quietly as I stared at the tiled floor, feeling a rush of guilt for having doubted him in the first place.

Logan tugged the stained hem of my shirt. "I'll lend you another sweater. Stay here."

He ran into his room, returning quickly with a black sweater and shutting the bathroom door so I could change. "I don't know where Rego went," he called, "but I want to get you out of here before he comes back."

I slid on the sweater and stepped out of the bathroom to find Logan leaning against the wall, staring at his sneakers with a pensive look on his face.

"Let's take you home," he said, surprising me by holding out his hand. I hesitantly took it, and he gave me a quick once-over.

"You look nice in black," he said quietly, tugging on my shoulder.

"Thanks. By the way, this is all just a plot to steal your clothes."

"It's a pretty elaborate plot. You could have just asked me," Logan said with a laugh as he led me out of the apartment.

"You know me. Go big, or go home," I said, reveling in the lighthearted—and short-lived—moment. As soon as we were a few blocks away in a Rego-free zone, Logan pulled me over to the side and leaned against an ATM outside of a bodega.

"I think you should cut school for a couple of days," Logan said.

"How am I going to get away with that?"

"I mean, fake sick for a couple of days," he explained. "You've probably got a temperature of about a hundred and two, thanks to the fire demon power. Look, Paige, you opened a portal to another world today. You got attacked. You're running on adrenaline. You look exhausted."

"I'm fine," I insisted automatically, trying to stuff my hands in my coat pockets and missing the openings entirely. Logan arched an eyebrow at me, an indulgent smile on his face.

"Fine? Paige, you're in a total fog and falling down on your feet," Logan replied, taking my hands and guiding them into my pockets.

"Pockets are here," he said, and I shot him a withering glance, removing my hands to give him the finger.

"Paige, come on," Logan implored. "Think of it this way, don't you want to be clear-headed in case you run into Aiden?"

"I do feel like I could sleep for a billion hours," I admitted as I yawned again.

"Besides, it'll be really helpful for me if, at least for a few days, I know you're definitely safe," Logan said, his eyes following a customer out of the bodega. "I have stuff to do with Rego—he and Ajax have clearly had some kind of misunderstanding. But Rego's stubborn, so I'll still have to put a new spell on the apartment." A sad, reflective expression crossed his face, and he shut his eyes, shaking his head, before continuing. "I'm going to help him make some weapons, too. And I also want to do a little more research into who Aiden is, see if he's got any other weaknesses."

"And there's no chance of him showing up at my front door?"

"The spell of protection around your apartment is something like a confusion spell. Even if he tried to find your home he'd never get there—he'd find himself walking in circles. Trust me, you're safe at home."

"I'm never leaving my bedroom again," I vowed, trying to hide another yawn.

"Let's tell your parents I walked you home because you didn't feel well. Milk it for three days and return to school refreshed on Friday."

"Will I see you at all?" I asked, trying to sound casual—like my question was an afterthought.

"Yeah, I'll bring your books over after school." Logan paused, taking a deep breath. "Besides, we need to talk."

"About what?" I feigned ignorance, and Logan answered with a wide-eyed are-you-kidding-me look.

"We don't need to talk," I muttered. "We're cool."

"Paige, come on. We need to talk."

"So, let's talk now," I said, leaning back and misjudging how far I was from the bodega window, hitting the glass with a thunk.

"That's why we should talk after you've rested up a bit," Logan said with a smart-alecky smirk, rubbing the back of my head. I pulled away from him, scowling. *Don't hit me with the dreaded "We need to talk" while rubbing me down, buddy.*

"Let me sort some things out first, okay? Just…promise me you won't hate me," he asked timidly. I forced myself to meet his eyes—cinnamon-colored eyes that seemed regretful, even though it sounded like he was the one about to break my heart, and I nodded. The problem was that I was far, far away from ever hating Logan Bradley.

## 60

"WE SHOULD WAKE HER UP AND FIND OUT IF she has a temperature."

"She feels hot, Richard. It's safe to assume she has a fever. We don't have to wake her up to stick a thermometer in her mouth. Just give her aspirin when she wakes and let her sleep."

"We should wake her up to go to the hospital."

Those words, spoken frantically by my father, penetrated the thick layers of sleep that wrapped around me, forcing me to open my eyes. My lashes felt like they were glued shut, and I rubbed them as I sat up in bed, my bleary eyes focusing on my alarm clock. It was around seven.

"No hospitals," I croaked through my cracked lips. My mouth was so dry it made sandpaper seem positively luxurious in comparison. I reached for the red-and-blue water bottle on my nightstand—another freebie my dad had collected, this time from some sneaker company during the marathon—and gulped the now-lukewarm liquid, cringing as I recalled the story Logan had concocted when he took me home a few hours earlier.

My father had been in the kitchen when we got home, slicing potatoes for a dish that was sure to ruin carbs for me forever.

"Want to help your dear old dad try out his new vegetarian shepherd's pie recipe? It's got boiled beets and kale in it— Oh, hello, Logan," my father had added coolly, his cheerful demeanor fizzling like my appetite when he saw Logan helping me out of my coat in the living room. I'd gotten progressively weaker as we walked home, and Logan practically had to carry me during the last five blocks, my bed taunting me as its pillowy treats got closer.

"That's not your uniform," Dad suddenly snapped, pointing at the oversize black sweater that fell far below the hem of my uniform skirt. I appeared to be wearing Logan's sweater— and nothing else.

"Where are your clothes, Paige?"

My dad addressed me but glared at Logan, his face matching the flaming red color of his hair. I quickly tugged the hem of my sweater up, letting the bottom of my blue plaid skirt show.

"I've got my clothes, Dad," I replied, giving Logan a panicked look. To his credit, he only briefly matched my expression before giving my father a wide-eyed, beatific look.

"Hi, Mr. Kelly. There's a bug going around school and I think Paige caught it. She, um, threw up on herself during last period," Logan added, wrinkling his nose as he laughed uneasily. "Her shirt was kind of ruined. So, uh, good thing I keep a spare sweater in my locker, right?"

"Paige, are you all right?" my dad asked, his suspicion quickly turning to concern. "Why didn't the school call us?"

"No one noticed...I just feel tired," I stammered truthfully enough, swaying on my feet. Logan reached out his hands to steady me, and Dad narrowed his eyes when he noticed Logan's hand gripping my elbow—because apparently, letting me face-plant into the television would have been preferable to Logan actually touching me, according to my overprotective dad.

I could have gotten a migraine from the effort it had taken to *not* roll my eyes.

"Dad, if it weren't for Logan I don't think I could have made it home," I said quickly, and Logan dropped his hold on my arm as he shifted underneath my father's withering stare.

My dad had grumbled something about his kale burning and stalked back into the kitchen. When he was out of eyesight, I turned to face Logan, who was nervously staring after my dad.

"Really? I threw up on myself?"

"I couldn't think of anything else!"

I grimaced now as I remembered the humiliating story, and my mom pressed a cold hand to my forehead, then to my neck, mistaking my sullen expression for discomfort.

"Does your stomach still hurt?" she asked. I studied my mom as she sat on my bed. Her dark hair was coiled into a no-nonsense bun, and she was in a classically tailored blue pantsuit—one of her "power outfits," she called them. She only wore them when she was expecting a particularly stressful day at work.

"I'm feeling a lot better," I said cheerfully, not wanting to worry my mom. She must have had a trying day at work if she'd dressed in her power armor. I stretched and yawned, my sore muscles twingeing. "Still achy and a little sleepy. But so much better."

"Still sleepy?" My dad's eyebrows practically shot off his face. "Paige, you've been asleep for fifteen hours."

My alarm clock didn't say 7:00 p.m.—it was 7:00 a.m.

"Oh."

"'Oh' is right," my dad replied, grabbing a thermometer off my nightstand. "Now, let's see how this fever's doing."

It was one hundred and two, just as Logan had predicted.

"I think it's this bug going around. It usually lasts about three days," I said, trying to ease the worry off my parents' faces that I'd put there. Again.

"We should take her to the doctor. She's got to have an infection for her temperature to be so high," Dad fretted to Mom, as if I weren't even there.

"No!" I nearly yelled, and my parents stared at my outburst in confusion. I didn't want to add antibiotics to the list of fake medications I was supposed to be taking. "Look, if it's not better by tomorrow morning, then you can take me. I promise you, I'll be ready to do jumping jacks by then."

"Paige, I think—"

"I already feel so much better than yesterday. It's only the stomach flu. Just let me rest. Please, Daddy?" I lowered my head and stuck out my bottom lip, gazing at him through my lashes. My pouty face was the one surefire weapon I had in my anti-Dad arsenal, so I used it rarely. But Logan and I hadn't counted on my father's overreaction to everything that had to do with my health in our It's So Easy to Fake Sick scheme.

"Fine, but if your fever hasn't gone down, you're off to the doctor," he said adamantly.

I agreed—making sure my face was extra-smiley for my mom's benefit. I didn't want her stressed out at work, distracted on my behalf. I knew it crushed her to leave me when I was sick. Craziness couldn't be cured with cough drops and chicken soup, but a fever was something my parents knew how to fix.

After a stomach-flu-appropriate breakfast of weak tea and toast, I convinced my father that I'd be fine at home while he picked up some rich kid in the West Village. But the front door had barely shut before I ordered a massive bacon, egg and cheese sandwich from the bodega, cursing the bagel hole as I ate for not being full of delicious bagel. Apparently, opening portals to other dimensions really burned calories, because I was still hungry—and contemplating pancakes from the diner—when my dad returned with lemon chicken soup and convinced me to join him on the couch for a movie marathon.

I curled up on one end of the sofa with a heaping bowl of soup, trying to sip it as slowly as someone recovering from a stomach bug would while my dad camped out on the other end. He'd changed out of his work suit so it wouldn't wrinkle, opting for jeans and a bulky, neon-blue sweatshirt from some travel website that had already gone out of business. We'd just finished watching some breaking news report about a sudden drop in the stock market and joking that "It's time to sell the yacht, Jeeves," when my dad asked in a practiced casual tone, "So, this Logan kid...I'd like to know what the story is."

*You and me both, Dad.* I glanced over to my father, whose

cheeks turned slightly pink as he waited for my answer. I decided the best defense was a good offense.

"Dad, you're blushing. With the blue sweatshirt, pink face and red hair, you're rocking a serious snow cone vibe."

"Really, Paige? A snow cone?"

"Just saying, your interrogation tactics are anything but subtle," I observed, turning back to my soup as I fished for a piece of chicken.

"Well, back in my day, you didn't spend all weekend with a girl, or walk her home from school, or give her your clothing to wear, unless you were courting her," my father huffed in reply. *Oh, Dad, if only you knew my clothing had been wrecked by demons.*

"Dad, really? Courting? I didn't know your day was the day of the Pony Express."

"And now you bring out the 'Dad's so old' jokes. Nice, Paige. You're wounding your dear father's delicate heart," he said, placing a hand over his chest as he pretended to sniffle.

"You're the one who said the word *courting*," I countered, pretending to gag. "Dad, I'd bet five bucks that when you were in high school, you never said court unless it was preceded by the word *basketball*."

"We courted young ladies in our day," Dad insisted, his face serious.

I snorted like the delicate flower I was, holding my soup with both hands so I didn't spill it as I shook with laughter. "Right, Dad," I said dryly. "I can just picture you saying, 'Yeah, I really want to court that girl. I want to court her so hard!'"

"Paige, watch it," my dad warned me. "Just because you're not feeling well doesn't mean it's a license to mouth off."

"Sorry," I huffed, frowning. *Mom would have laughed.*

We watched a few more minutes of the movie before my father tried again.

"Your mother tells me that Logan moves around a lot. Do you know how long he's here for?"

I stirred my soup, watching the chicken and rice as it swirled in a whirlpool.

"No," I admitted, adding, "but neither does he." That much was true. It's not as if we knew when Aiden would finally be killed.

"So, I take it he makes a lot of, um, new friends in every new city?" My father emphasized the words.

"Dad, seriously?" I asked, shaking my head, even though I had also wondered just how detailed Logan's romantic history was.

"Well, Paige, put yourself in my position."

"Not if I have to wear that blue sweatshirt."

My father threw his hands up in the air, exasperated, and pushed himself off the couch, pacing the small living room. "I'm trying, Paige. I'm trying to have a regular conversation with you. Your mom insisted that we treat you like you're normal—"

"I am normal," I retorted through clenched teeth, making an effort to keep my voice even. But my hands were another story, the green and white bowl clattering as I set my soup on the coffee table.

"I know you are, Paige," Dad relented, the cushions sinking under his frame as he settled back onto the navy couch.

"But I'm your father, so I'm going to give this guy the third degree. And your situation makes me worry that someone will take advantage of you. I can't help it."

Dad patted me on the shoulder. "I just don't want to see you get hurt, honey. Just promise me you'll be careful. I've seen the way that Logan kid looks at you."

"Oh? So, how does he look at me?" I asked with forced casualness. *He's just being overprotective. Dad hates the way everyone looks at you, right?*

"Like the sun shines out of your—" Dad grumbled, stopping short when he realized he was speaking out loud. "Just be careful, honey," he repeated, giving me a quick hug. He held me tightly before releasing me to my end of the couch, where I curled up again with my soup. I ate it quickly, hoping I could squeeze in a quick nap before Logan came over after school—opening portals between worlds was pretty draining, and I didn't want to face "the talk" with shadows underneath my eyes.

I flopped on my mattress, half dreading his arrival, and half desperate to see the one person who knew everything. Logan knew the real me, knew I wasn't crazy. He was the one person I didn't have to constantly lie to. I still had some questions for him, so I pulled my sketch pad out of my closet and turned to a fresh page, writing down every random question that popped into my mind. Serious questions about the concept of demon families followed curious questions about the variegated color of demon blood, but the biggest questions were ones I couldn't bring myself to write down: How did he end up in this life with Rego? What happened to his parents?

And then there were the questions I was afraid to ask him.

Like, what happens to us once Aiden is killed? Is there even an us to worry about? The way he'd left things made me think there wasn't…but he had definitely seemed like he was about to kiss me in the music room.

I put my pen down and bunched up my comforter, burying my face in it as Mercer curled up between my ankles. I knew I'd have to find out these answers, and soon.

My father woke me with a gentle shake on my shoulder. I rubbed my eyes as I blinked up at him, confused.

"Hey, kiddo, are you ready for dinner?" Dad asked, his eyebrows pulling together with concern. "Your mom will be home soon."

"Dinner? I just had lunch. It's still early," I replied with a yawn, even though my stomach rumbled at the thought of more food. I scratched my head, trying to remember when I fell asleep. I'd been writing questions for Logan and shut my eyes for one minute….

My sleep-bleary eyes tried to focus on the clock. *That time can't be right.*

"Early? Paige, it's a little after eight."

"But Logan—he was supposed to come by after school…." I stammered, feeling the color drain from my face as I gripped my comforter in my fists. What could I say to my father? That I was worried Aiden had shown up, full of rage and vengeance, and attacked Logan? That I was terrified he was no match for Aiden's murderous devices, like those vicious slice-and-dice coins that could torture and kill? Or that my dad had completely misread "how Logan looks at me," and he'd decided there was nothing to talk about?

"No one came by. He probably caught the flu," Dad said

when he saw my pained expression. "It sounded like you did everything except vomit on him yesterday."

"Right. The flu," I repeated dully, nodding my head.

"Don't feel guilty, kiddo. I don't think that'll exactly drive him away," my dad said, muttering something under his breath that sounded suspiciously like, "I need a shotgun and a front porch."

"Look, your mom is coming home soon, and she's going to make you some scrambled eggs and toast for dinner. Think your stomach can handle that?"

I nodded automatically, even though my stomach was now twisting with the fear that something had happened to Logan.

Over dinner, my parents chalked up my distraction to the stomach flu, and I raced to my bedroom promptly afterward, grabbing my laptop and scouring everything my classmates posted online, looking for mentions of Logan, Aiden, any kind of fight at the school…but I found nothing except snarky commentary about Pepper and Matt's apparently renewed relationship status and repeated posts about their never-ending love for each other.

I shook my head at Pepper and Matt's drama—when I was six, I would have aptly proclaimed it a Barf-a-rama—and shut my laptop, my imagination going into hyperactive mode, launching detailed scenarios where Logan was attacked by Aiden. The images blended together, assaulting my dreams as I fell into a fitful night's sleep, my phone clutched in my hand in case he managed to call me from a diner or something.

But Logan didn't call. My night was lost to bizarre dreams, nonsensical narratives full of demons and disapproving parents and Logan vanishing into mist when I reached out for him. And the next day, the hours after school came and passed again without any word from him.

"I think one more day and you'll be fine," my mom was saying after dinner, inspecting the thermometer in her hands. My temperature readout was only in the high nineties; I'd managed to slip it out of my mouth when my mom stepped away to say goodbye as my dad left for the night shift.

"Have you heard from your friend?" Mom asked, tapping my phone where it was charging next to me on the couch.

"No. He doesn't have a phone, though," I added, and my mom's dark eyebrows shot up in surprise.

"A teenager with no phone? Talk about a mythical creature!" Mom laughed in surprise.

"His uncle's strict," I offered as a means of explanation, and my mom gave me an understanding smile.

"Well, I'm sure you'll hear from your friend—" Mom loaded the word with innuendo "—very soon."

But he didn't call. And that night, I couldn't sleep again. I curled up in bed, the tears that had streaked down my face and soaked my pillow finally starting to dry. I hadn't heard from Logan in more than two days. Would Rego have bothered informing me if Logan were hurt? I laughed harshly to myself, pretty sure I already knew the answer to that. Maybe I could call the school tomorrow, pretending to be a relative with a family emergency, needing to speak to Aiden. At least I'd know if he'd come to school. If he'd shown up, Logan definitely would have fought him.

Thinking of the possibility that Aiden had killed Logan sparked a fresh round of tears, spurred on by more fears— that Cerus had ambushed Logan in the middle of the night, seeking vengeance for the earlier affront to his ego, or yet another nameless demon had shown up to end Logan's life.

And then there was the other completely selfish but completely real fear: that Logan was avoiding me. He knew that I had feelings for him—the fact that I had been able to break Della's spell was proof enough of that. So maybe the real reason why he hadn't shown up was that Logan had taken a one-way train out of Paige's Awkward Crushville.

My phone began buzzing, scaring my cat off the bed as it vibrated, the number of my corner bodega flashing on the screen.

"Hello?" I sniffled, wondering if I had underpaid for my bagel sandwich yesterday.

"Hey, it's me. Can you meet me on your roof? I know it's late, but can you sneak out?"

"Logan?" I cried, relief flooding my system. I ran to my bedroom door, shutting it. My parents' bedroom was on the opposite end of our apartment, but I didn't want to risk waking them.

"Are you okay?" I whispered, spinning my bracelet nervously.

"Yeah," he replied, his voice rising in surprise at my question. "Listen, I actually asked if I could use the phone here instead of, well, you know, using my talents. I don't want to stay on longer than necessary. Can you meet me?"

"You're totally okay?" I repeated.

"Yeah, I'm fine."

"Give me a bit and I'll be up there." Of course I'd be there. I'd been panicking for more than two days. He sounded okay, but I needed to see that he was alive and well. Maybe he was lying to me so I wouldn't worry before I saw him.

I splashed some water on my face, trying my best to hide my puffy eyes underneath my own baseball cap. I dressed quickly in dark blue yoga pants, a tank top and a hoodie, and pulled on my well-worn Chucks. I figured they were my quietest shoes, allowing me to stealthily tiptoe through my apartment. But what did I know? It's not like I had a storied history of sneaking out late at night. I stood before the front door, making a silent bargain with it.

*If you promise not to squeak too loudly, I won't let you slam shut behind me anymore.*

The hinges were silent until I'd opened the door enough to slip out through the narrow opening, and they unleashed one short—but shrill—screech, as if it were a warning sign to tell me they'd been my quiet accomplice long enough. I paused to listen for my father's snore, which fortunately didn't falter.

The door shut quietly, the hinges taking silent mercy on me, and I slowly started my ascent up the stairs to the roof.

The night was cold but clear, the moon and Venus piercing the cloudless black sky with bright white light. The roof was dark, illuminated with the soft hazy glow of traffic and streetlights below us. I braced myself to see Logan slumped in a corner, battle-scarred and weary.

Instead, I found Logan casually leaning against the low barrier over the air shaft that separated our building from the shorter one next door. He gave me a slow, easy smile as he pushed himself off the roof, holding out a blue cup.

"I brought you hot chocolate," he offered. Logan looked the same as he had last weekend; his messy brown hair was tucked underneath a Yankees cap—a different one, since his regular cap had been sucked into another dimension. His gray hoodie hung open over a black T-shirt, and a smile was on his face as he held out the cup, the fragrant, sweet smell wafting through the cold air.

He really was fine.

And now that I knew he was alive, I wanted to kill him for making me worry.

I took the cup, tracing my fingers over the white plastic lid before I set it back on the wall.

"You're okay," I accused.

"And that's a problem?" he asked, bewildered.

"Aiden never showed up?"

"No," Logan said, a flicker of annoyance flashing across his face. "What are you getting at?"

"Didn't it ever occur to you to let me know you were at least alive?"

"Come on, Paige. No one can get to you at home. It was just few days." Logan shrugged, as if his disappearance was no big deal.

"Just a few days? A lot can happen in just a few days, Logan." I touched my cheek, which had been slashed open mere days earlier. "Look at what happened to me the last two days I was in school! I've been terrified that Aiden got to you—that he hurt you somehow. I've been home with no way to get ahold of you, thinking something happened to you!"

Logan's face softened as he studied me, and he stood slowly, approaching me carefully.

"Paige, have you been crying?"

"No." I shook my head, and he came closer, tilting up the brim of my cap. *Damn stupid puffy eyes.*

"You have been crying," he realized, his voice barely higher than a whisper.

"Oh, of course I've been crying," I said, blinking as a few tears threatened to make an encore performance, blurring my vision. I ripped my cap off and tossed it on the picnic table. There really was no sense in trying to hide it; I looked like I had biscuits around my eyes.

"If something happened to me you wouldn't be unprotected," he said softly, rubbing my arm in an awkward attempt to be soothing. "You know that, right? Rego would make sure you had a protector. You're too important."

I rolled my biscuit eyeballs in reply. "Are you actually trying to be dense? I wasn't crying because I was worried about myself. I was crying because I was afraid you were dead!" Merely saying the word prompted the tears in my eyes to overflow, and I brushed them away, frustrated and embarrassed with my emotional display. I turned away from him and stared at the ground instead, focusing on the frayed ends of my graying laces.

"I don't understand." He sounded confused, but I couldn't face him at that moment.

"You said you'd come here. When I didn't hear from you, I had a thousand scenarios running through my head, replaying over and over again like they were stuck on repeat." I grimaced as I recalled my vivid fears, wrapping my arms around my torso.

"Maybe you were hurt, lying somewhere in pain and needing help. Maybe you were attacked on your way to see me, because Aiden got to you. Maybe you showed up at your house and surprised Cerus again, and—" I paused, taking a deep breath to steady my trembling voice "—maybe he shot you."

I shut my eyes, trying to clear the gruesome visions that had plagued my mind for the past two days.

"Or maybe you took Ajax's advice and you decided to leave."

"Paige, I wouldn't do that to you. I swear," he said, stuffing his hands in his back pockets.

"Well, you did, for almost three days." He paled, looking guilty. "I know things are…kind of awkward…between us right now," I stammered, "but you're still my friend. Even though it's not the same for you, I wanted to know that you were okay."

I buried my face in my hands, embarrassed and exhausted and deflated, all the fight gone out of me as I quietly cried over everything: Logan's disappearance, my constant but necessary lies to my parents, the stress of the past few days—hell, the past few years. Logan quickly crossed the few feet of distance between us, folding his arms around my shoulders and pulling me close. This time, I didn't fight back. I didn't return his hug, but I let my head rest against his chest, my face still buried in my palms as everything I said echoed in my head.

"You think I wasn't around the past few days because I don't care?" Logan asked, and I shrugged in his embrace. "Paige, this has nothing to do with how I feel about you," he said firmly.

"It's fine, you don't have to say that—"

"I'm serious." Logan dropped his grip on me to cup my face in his hands. "It has to do with me."

"Oh, please, don't say, 'It's not you, it's me,'" I scoffed, wriggling away from him, his hands dropping against his sides. "I'd rather you tell me that it is, in fact, me. Say, 'Paige, you suck.' But don't give me some trite, overused pity line."

"I swear it's not that. I'm just not explaining myself well." Logan's eyes bored into mine. "I live with Rego, but he's really more my boss. I haven't—I'm not—this is really hard to admit," he struggled, sighing heavily. "I barely remember what it's like to be accountable to someone for the simple reason that they care.

"I'm not saying that so you feel bad for me. I'm saying it because it's true. It's been true for a long time," Logan confessed. His face was open and honest, his words simply a statement of fact. "So, that's why I didn't think about reaching out. It has nothing to do with how I feel about you."

"So…how do you feel?" I asked, daring to hope that his answer wouldn't crush me.

Logan stared at the ground as he collected his thoughts. "You, Paige Dawn Kelly, are a wrecking ball to my routine, colorless life," he said, finally meeting my eyes, "and I couldn't be happier or more terrified about it."

He took a step toward me, lightly resting his hand against my tearstained cheek.

"I've only been watching you since I got here and admiring the hell out of you for what—three months? I justified it because I thought you were the target, but I was just lying to myself. I admired you because no matter what people say about you, you keep your head high. And you make me laugh with the most random statements ever." He paused, grinning at some memory, and the look on his face made me grin, too.

"I really like making you smile." Logan stroked my cheek with his thumb, and I smiled even wider. "And I'm really, really freaking out about saying all this right now," he added.

"Well, it's about damn time you did," I whispered, and he wound his other arm around me, pulling me closer.

"I don't know what I'm doing. This is all new territory for me," he admitted nervously, and I threaded my fingers through his as he cradled my cheek. "I'm not supposed to want this with you. I wasn't even supposed to talk to you. But I can't pretend I don't feel this way anymore, can you? You feel it, too, right? Paige?" Logan prompted, almost desperately, when I didn't reply immediately.

"I do. You know I do." I nodded, and he exhaled in relief, resting his forehead against mine. We just stood there for a moment, letting the weight of what we were declaring sink in.

"Why do you think I never bitched about you borrowing all my pens?" I asked innocently.

"Really? So...for that long, huh?" Logan pulled back with a proud smile on his face.

"Shut up." I poked him in the chest. "I denied it to Dottie and to myself, but...yeah. What can I say, the sight of you with a glittery pen is really hot."

Logan pretended to brush some dirt off his shoulder, and I whacked him lightly on his arm. He grabbed my hand and held it between us, resting our interlocking fingers against his chest.

"I have to say one more thing," Logan said, suddenly serious again. "I don't know what I'm doing, but I know I should have said something first, be a gentleman and all that.

At least, that's what all the books and movies say, right?" he added with a self-conscious shrug.

"Well, the books and movies say you would have kissed me by now."

Logan stilled, and I internally berated myself for my complete lack of a filter, until an impish smile flashed across his face. Logan bent his head down to mine, lightly brushing his lips over my cheekbone, and my skin tingled at his gentle touch.

"C'mon, I wanted to ask you first," he whispered in my ear. "At least let me get something right." He pulled back, gazing at me with serious eyes—and I felt my breathing speed up.

"Can I kiss you, Paige?" Logan asked, the corner of his mouth lifted into a boyish, almost shy smile.

My hands slid up his chest, my fingers locking around his neck to keep them from trembling. I shut my eyes and nodded, his body shifting under my hands as he pulled me flush against his chest. And then I felt him: his gentle, warm lips touching mine, timidly at first. I unclasped my hands and let my fingers slide into the dark locks of hair at the nape of his neck. He whispered my name softly and when he pressed his lips against mine again, his kiss was much less shy. Logan's hands knotted in my hair, before gently sliding down my back, his mouth soft and urgent.

I used to worry if I'd remember how to kiss a boy. It had been a while, and I was afraid I'd be an uncoordinated mess of clashing teeth and dry lips and flappy tongue, who'd forget how to breathe and probably slobber, sending the boy running off in horror as he wiped his mouth on his shirtsleeve.

The way he was clutching me close, Logan clearly wasn't

running anywhere. After a slightly clumsy start, we found a perfect rhythm that ignited a slow burn, a sweet kiss that gradually built into a heart-pounding embrace that I felt in my chest and stomach and down to my toes, which curled in my shoes as he kissed me deeply.

He broke the kiss first, only to leave a trail of smaller kisses along my jaw, setting my skin on fire, until his mouth met my ear.

"Wow," he exhaled, and I could only nod in agreement, my breathing far too unsteady to attempt talking.

"I've wanted to do that since the first time I borrowed a pen from you," Logan whispered shakily, clasping his hands at the small of my back. I felt my cheeks warm, and I ducked my head down, resting my forehead against his chest. Logan tucked his fingers underneath my chin again and forced me to look up.

"By the way, your pens suck," he said, his grave tone betrayed by the teasing sparkle in his eye. "Girliest things I've ever seen."

"Using my pink pens isn't going to make you grow a vagina, you know," I retorted, and Logan laughed.

"There she is." He chuckled, planting a soft kiss on my forehead. "That's what I'm talking about. You're a little intimidating, by the way."

"Me?" I stepped back as I let my hands slide down his chest, coming to rest at his hips. *Yeah, you've got the torso of an action figure and I'm the intimidating one?* I gripped fistfuls of cotton to keep myself from tracing the lines barely hinted at underneath his shirt.

"You." He paused, giving me a sad smile. "I really hoped

you weren't the target. I'd heard that you talked to imaginary people, but you hide it really well. I didn't know it was you until a few weeks ago."

"Dottie and I hang out in the girls' bathroom," I explained, toying with a loose thread on the hem of his shirt. "That's usually where I get busted talking to her."

"So that's the problem. I don't spend my free time in the girls' bathroom." Logan grinned.

"I wouldn't call that a problem," I corrected him, raising an eyebrow. "I'd call that a valid life choice."

"Well, you only slipped up once, in the library. And don't worry, it was very subtle. You pretended to scratch your cheek, but you were really giving Dottie the finger because she was trying to make you flirt with me," Logan recalled, his cheeks turning pink again. "That's when I knew you really could hear her and talk to her."

He smiled wryly at the memory.

"Of course, I took that as a sign that you were highly offended by her suggestion that you flirt with me."

"It's totally offensive," I told him, my eyes wide with mock sincerity. "I mean, I really want you to kiss me again, but flirt with you? Offensive, obviously."

Logan grinned, his eyes crinkling up at the corners as he gave me a soft kiss. But when he pulled back, he somberly asked me, "Am I forgiven?"

"Yes. Just don't disappear like that again," I ordered, narrowing my eyes and pursing my lips in what I hoped looked like a stern expression.

"I promise. Just stop making that weird face," he teased.

"That's my scary face," I pouted. "It's supposed to be terrifying."

"No, your scary face is when you're crying," Logan said seriously, all hint of teasing gone. "Because it terrifies me that I made you cry."

"I scare you?"

"Not in the way you think," he said. "I just don't know what I'm doing, and I'm terrified I'm going to screw this up. Hell, I already screwed up."

Logan was a study in dichotomy: fierce and brutal, an efficient killer saddled with so much self-doubt. I wanted to help him. I wanted to know him. And I was desperately afraid of wounding him. I stepped back, but Logan stepped with me, keeping his arms around me.

"Is this thing between us too intense?" I asked, proud that I kept my voice even in spite of my fear that he'd answer "yes." Logan cocked his head as he regarded me, looking confused.

"This is going fast. Maybe too fast."

"I've known you for three months. I've liked you for three months," Logan replied, sounding confused. "This could have gone a little faster for me, just saying."

"Well, I'm just saying, maybe this is too much." I began babbling, barely stopping to take a breath because if I paused, I wouldn't say what I thought needed to be said. "And maybe I care too much and I don't want to scare you and we've been all over the place with our emotions tonight and maybe this is what Rego meant about me being a distraction—"

Logan pressed his lips against mine, effectively silencing me. Unlike our first kiss, which built into a toe-curling, passionate embrace, Logan was tender, almost reverential in the way his lips moved softly against mine as he gripped fistfuls of my hoodie at the waist. He broke away only to gently brush his lips against my forehead, both eyelids, the tip of my nose and both cheeks before returning to place another soft kiss against my mouth.

I'd read about intense, emotional kisses in sweeping epic romance novels and seen enough movies where the music built to a crescendo as the star-crossed lovers found answers in each other's kiss, usually with the moon as an audience, as it was tonight.

This kiss shamed those kisses, making them dry pecks on the cheek in comparison. And this time, I was the one who pulled away, my heart pounding and my body quivering.

"Does that answer your question?" he asked breathlessly.

I nodded, not trusting myself to speak actual words at the moment.

"I want this, Paige. I want you in my life. I want this to work, whatever that means." Logan clasped his hands at the small of my back and squeezed me for emphasis. "And maybe that's selfish, because there's so much about me, and this world, that you don't know. And I want to tell you."

"So, tell me," I urged.

"I will. But this is all new to me, too. I'm trying to fig-ure out how to make this work. It's complicated on my end. Just...be patient with me, please?" he pleaded, his face open and trusting.

"I'll try," I promised. His answering smile was so endear-ing, I had to stand up on my toes to place a quick kiss against his lips.

"See you tomorrow? You promise you won't disappear again?"

Regret flickered across his face briefly before giving me a warm, reassuring smile.

"I'll be there," he promised, and leaned in for one more kiss.

# 10

DEMON FIGHTING WAS ABSOLUTE HELL ON MY manicure, I realized, filing down my rough nails as I sat on the couch with my father the next day, choosing cuticle care over rereading the next chapter in my history textbook. It was one of the few books that had been in my backpack on Monday, so I'd read it already. Besides, my father was distracting me, furiously flipping television channels, which were all covering the plummeting stock market. Finally, he landed on an infomercial.

"Hmm, if you order in the next thirty minutes, you get a tote bag that you can keep, even if you return everything," he muttered, reaching for the cordless phone as it rested on the cushion between us. I grabbed the phone quickly and held it out of his reach.

"No, Dad. Please! No more stuff with logos on it." I feigned sobbing, switching hands before my dad could get a solid grip on the phone. "Most girls dream of ponies. I dream of owning things you can't read."

"But it's a nice bag," he said. "Nice and roomy. You could use it for school."

"Dad, I am so not using a bag with the words *Deluxe Fat Burner 5000* on the side!"

"But—"

"Neither will Mom," I insisted. "And she'll think it's a hint, and then you'll be in every kind of trouble that ever existed." I held the phone aloft, and Dad returned to his end of the couch with a resigned sigh.

"I didn't think of that," he said. "Your mom might be really mad. Damn."

I sighed in relief, letting the phone drop on the cushion between us again.

"Might? She'd make you sleep on the couch, Dad. This teeny, tiny couch, with nothing but your free tote bag to keep you warm."

*And I won't be able to sneak out at night to see Logan.*

I glanced at the front door guiltily, as if it were going to come to life and rat me out for sneaking up to the roof last night. But so far, my secret was safe, with only me, Logan and my cat aware that I'd left the apartment.

I'd managed to sneak back in quietly, my dad's snores a victory cheer as I stealthily made my way through the rooms to my bedroom, where Mercer greeted me by sitting on my pillow and meowing at me knowingly.

Dad had resumed channel surfing when the building buzzer sounded, loudly reverberating throughout the apartment. I jumped off the couch and hurried to the intercom next to the front door.

"Did your mother order some— Oh." Dad's quizzical expression morphed into one of irritation when Logan's voice boomed through the apartment on the static-filled speaker.

"Be nice," I cautioned Dad. Normally I would complain about the earsplitting intercom system, but hearing Logan—unharmed and alive—calmed my lingering fears that he wouldn't show up today.

Clearly my father didn't share my opinion.

"He's too loud," Dad grumbled as I pressed the button on the ancient intercom, buzzing Logan upstairs.

"Dad, I'm pretty sure he didn't invent the technology behind this intercom. Everyone sounds loud on it. You could probably hear a mosquito fart on this thing."

He ignored my comment, switching subjects. "Aren't you going to put on clothes?"

I looked down at my gray T-shirt and black yoga pants. It was appropriate clothing for someone staying home from school with sickness.

"I'm in clothes. Pretty boring clothes, actually." I took a deep breath, trying to be grateful that my dad was acting stereotypically overprotective over something normal like clothing and not my mental state.

"Dad, I look like I'm going to the grocery store. I've actually worn this to the grocery store."

Logan rapped on the door as my father grumbled, "I still think you should put on a sweatshirt. And a sweater."

I ignored my Dad and opened the door to see Logan standing in the small hallway, shifting his weight from foot to foot.

"Hi," I greeted him almost timidly, resting my head against the door.

"Hi, yourself," he replied just as shyly, an endearing smile on his face. The brim of his baseball cap was sticking out of his coat pocket, his hair adorably mussed and his cheeks flushed from the walk over. Dark locks hung in his eyes, which spar-kled in spite of the swipe of shadows underneath.

*Had he looked this tired last night?* It had been too dim on the rooftop to notice, but in the harsh fluorescent light of the hallway, exhaustion and stress were evident on Logan's face.

But we'd overcome an emotional hurdle last night, and the effects of that were also evident, because we just stood there, staring at each other with starry-eyed grins.

"I brought you hot chocolate," Logan said, holding out a cup. "It's really good this time, I promise. You didn't drink yours last—"

"Weekend, right. Last weekend. Thanks, that's so nice of you," I interrupted loudly, before mouthing, "My dad is here, remember?"

Logan squeezed his eyes shut, gritting his teeth.

"Sorry," he mouthed, opening one eye with a pained ex-pression on his face.

I leaned against the door and pushed it open with my back.

"Come on in. Dad, Logan brought me hot chocolate. Isn't that nice?" I added pointedly, peeling back the plastic lid to take a sip, delighting in the rich taste.

"Did he bring your schoolbooks, too? Or is this just a so-cial call while you're still sick?" Dad asked, crossing the room and folding his arms to scrutinize Logan as he stood awk-wardly next to me.

I gawked at my father as Logan slid his overstuffed back-pack off his shoulders and lost his grip on the strap, letting it fall to the floor with a loud thunk.

"Yes—um, yes, I have her books, Mr. Kelly, sir," Logan sputtered, clearly unnerved by my dad. I stared in surprise.

Demonslayer Logan would have bounced the heavy backpack on his foot like a hacky sack before slicing it open with his sword, all the books magically falling onto the coffee table open to the correct pages. It's a good thing Aiden never attacked around my father, because he seemed to make Logan more skittish than my cat around a vacuum cleaner.

"Well, I guess you kids will set up at the table, right?" Dad asked before sitting back on the couch, resuming his rapid-fire channel flipping.

"Dad, I have a lot of work to catch up on, and there's not enough room on that table for all our books." I gestured to the small round table in the corner of the living room. "We'll study in my room."

"Paige Dawn Kelly..." Dad warned me, dragging my name out.

"Daddy Richard Kelly..." I repeated in a deep voice, imitating his tone.

"If your dad says we should stay here..." Logan began, and I shot him a surprised look.

"Dad, you're watching TV and it's really loud," I pointed out, grabbing Logan's elbow and ushering him out of the room as quickly as I could.

"We'll keep the door open," I called as I led the way to my bedroom.

"Paige?" Dad called.

"Yeah?"

"I'll check to make sure the door stays open."

"Of course, Dad." I sighed, a little annoyed. What did he think was going to happen in my bedroom while he was home, anyway? The last thing I needed was for my father to catch me in a compromising position with Logan. Forget the demon army—I'd be spending senior year in a military school.

"Why do you get so flustered around my dad?" I asked in a hushed voice as Logan followed me down the short hall to my bedroom.

"I don't know! I just get nervous," he hissed in reply, his brown eyes wide and adorably panicked. "He acts like he hates me! And apparently, today I'm extra hateable."

I rested my hand against his cheek and gave him a warm smile. "Okay, so you protect me from demons, and I'll protect you from my dad," I said sweetly. "And if he scares you, just remember that my dad is wearing a free shirt for a frozen fish company, and he's allergic to shellfish. This is the big scary man you're dealing with."

"I'm not trying to cook him a nice shrimp dinner. I'm trying to be respectful, so he doesn't forbid you to be my girlfriend," he mumbled, and I felt that twinge in my heart again, for the insecure, wounded side of Logan he hid so well.

I darted a quick look to the living room and swiftly kissed Logan on the cheek.

"Don't be afraid of my dad," I whispered, grabbing his hand. "Now, come look at your girlfriend's bedroom."

His answering smile was blinding, and he followed me as I strode confidently into my room, internally doing backflips over being "officially" boyfriend/girlfriend. I couldn't wait to tell Dottie, my eternally romantic friend. She'd probably say we were "going steady" and offer us a bunch of old-fashioned romantic advice. I wondered if she would ask Logan if he was going to give me his varsity jacket or pin me. *More like I'm going to pin him. To the wall. And make out with his face.*

I plopped on my bed, but my bravado faded as he hovered in the doorway before stepping in, slowly setting his backpack on the floor. I hadn't had anyone who wasn't a family member in my bedroom since my first sophomore year, when my then best friend Hannah accused me of faking insanity for attention before she stormed out, telling all our friends I was crazy.

Logan's eyes whirled around the room, taking in the music posters on the pink walls and the web of twinkle lights hanging along the ceiling before stopping to inspect my bookshelf.

"Who are these people?" he asked, picking up a silver-framed photo and studying it.

"Uh, just old friends from my old school."

"The ones who stopped talking to you after you saved Dylan's life?" he asked, arching an eyebrow.

I nodded.

"I never got around to replacing the picture," I lied, aware it was a weak excuse. How could I explain that I used to cling to these reminders of a time when my biggest problems were remembering if Amber and Hannah were still in a fight or if Chris Delaney only liked me, or if he *liked me* liked me.

Logan set the picture back, giving it one last look.

"Why replace it? You look pretty in that photo. Happy," he said in a measured tone. He next picked up one of my cat figurines, a bobblehead that resembled Mercer, who was currently curled up on the bed.

"Oh, didn't you know? I'm a future cat lady," I explained matter-of-factly, and he laughed, patting the black-and-white cat so its head bounced around.

"So, what do you think of my room?" I asked nervously as he sat down next to me on the bed, smoothing his hand over my pink-and-pale-yellow bedspread. And then Logan looked up at me, a mischievous glint in his sparkling brown eyes.

"Well, the pink pens make sense now," he said, leaning back to smack his palm against the pink-painted wall.

"Shut up," I muttered, turning my back to him and folding my arms. "I like pink."

"Well, I like you. And I like your room." Logan wound his arms around me from behind, pulling my back against his chest. "Very much, on both accounts."

"As much as I'd like to stay like this, my dad's going to come in here in about three seconds and ask us if we want soda or snacks," I groaned, "and if he sees us like this he's going to add castration to the menu."

Logan dropped me from his hold as if I were made of lava— a bold statement, considering he wielded fire demon power. He bolted to the opposite side of the room, settling in my pink beanbag chair with a textbook protectively over his crotch. He glanced warily at the door, his face pale.

Sure enough, a minute later my dad poked his head in just to check and see if we needed anything. Then he made sure the door was as wide open as possible. And tested the lock. And studied the hinges, possibly contemplating removing the door from the frame. And then he left. Probably to go collect his award for Most Embarrassing Dad of All Time That Ever Existed in the History of Everything.

"So what did you do today?" I asked, hiding a grin at the sight of Logan in the beanbag, which puffed out around him like a big pink pillow. And then his cheeks turned as pink as the poofy chair.

"I used my skills to get out of my afternoon classes," he

admitted, rubbing the back of his neck. "I fell asleep in two of my morning ones."

"Seriously?"

"Hey, I was tired," he said defensively, the very mention of exhaustion making him stifle back a yawn. He stretched out his arms, smiling in relief—but his smile soon faded, leaving Logan with an apprehensive, almost nervous expression on his face.

"What?" I asked, paling.

"So, I have to tell you something," Logan said, brushing his hair back and then clutching a fistful in his palm. "Apparently Ajax was right about the final battle coming up. Cerus was talking with Rego while I was home this afternoon. Something about how the greed demons are all shutting their shops, stockpiling their coins and prepping for the coming war."

"What did they tell you?"

"They didn't tell me anything. They thought I was at school. I was in bed—their voices woke me up and I eavesdropped. The greed demons operate out of what would be lower Manhattan, and they're slowly abandoning it. Not big fighters, those guys."

I traced the pattern on my bedspread as Logan spoke, mulling over his words.

"Logan, I think it's affecting this world."

"What do you mean?"

"The news is full of reports of the stock market dropping. We're talking at a crazy rate. And the greed demons' neighborhood mirrors the financial district," I explained. "I mean, Rego did say that the two worlds were connected, and what happens in one affects the other. A war on that side's definitely going to affect us."

"Who's going to war?" Dad asked, popping his head into the doorway. "Everything going okay? You having trouble with some kids at school?"

"Dad, seriously?" I cried, throwing my hands in the air and letting them fall onto my mattress with a thud. "Have you been standing there eavesdropping?"

My dad coughed awkwardly in reply.

"No." *Yes.* "I just wanted to see if you need anything."

"Dad, we're fine," I insisted, and he spun on his heel and walked out of the room. I followed him and peered out the door, making sure he'd gone back into the living room.

"I'm sorry about my dad," I said, pulling over an ottoman to sit next to Logan.

"Don't be. Your dad's scary, but you're lucky," he said wistfully, tracing a seam in the beanbag with his thumb. "You know he cares."

I studied Logan's pained expression. "Can you tell me about your parents?" I asked hesitantly, not wanting to push him.

"My parents…" He paused, steeling himself with a deep breath before he continued in a small voice. "My parents wanted me far, far away from that world. I remember they wanted a normal life for me. Giving me a normal name," he emphasized the word, "was the first step."

"What do you mean normal? Compared to what?"

"In case you haven't noticed, everyone who is somehow connected to the Dark World has a ridiculous name. They're all nicknames and titles, loaded with meaning and insight and Very. Heavy. Symbolism," he said in a dramatically deep voice, rolling his eyes.

"Aiden's a normal name."

"Because you're thinking of it as being spelled the human way, but the demon spelling is A-e-o-d-h-a-n. *Aeodhan*," he explained, pronouncing it in an affected tone. "Means fiery or some other forced complimentary spin on his temper."

"Does your name have another meaning, too?"

"Other than King Awesome?"

"Well, yeah. Other than the obvious."

Logan shook his head, a smile on his face.

"Logan's a pretty common name. My parents originally wanted something super normal, like John or Mike, but they liked what the name Logan meant. It means 'little hollow'— that dip of land between valleys," he continued, taking his left hand and swiping it sharply through the air in a V-shape. "I remember someone telling me I was named for the earth."

He paused. "This earth," he clarified. "This side."

Logan stared upward again, but his eyes grew unfocused, as if he wasn't seeing the strands of twinkle lights above his head. His brow twitched, and his lips turned down as he reacted to the memory he was replaying.

"I really don't remember much, to be honest. The first eight years of my life are really foggy. But I remember waking up one night and hearing my parents arguing. I was seven, I think. My father said he wanted me free of obligation, free to enjoy the gift of life. I remember him saying that—the gift of life." He repeated the words reverentially, a melancholic smile on his face as he remembered his father.

"I was a little kid, so of course I was excited. I was expecting a present, something wrapped up in a bow that I could play with. It was years later before I understood that he'd been trying to save me from this existence."

"What else do you remember about your dad?" I asked, and a hard, guarded mask overtook his face.

"Does it matter? I ended up surrounded by the war and death and duty I was supposed to be spared." His face was impassive as he rattled off the powerful words, words that should have been significant and symbolic but instead were merely routine for him.

I nodded, realizing that this topic of conversation was closed. Sensing that Logan needed a minute alone, I excused myself to grab my notebook from where I'd left it in the living room—and, of course, got caught in a mini-inquisition from my father.

"Just keep the door open," Dad cautioned me again as I headed back inside. My eyes rolled of their own accord at that reminder. My dad was nearby, and he was a walking, talking cold shower. What did he think was going to happen? I had my feelings in check.

But when I returned to my bedroom, I practically swooned at the sight that greeted me. We're talking resting-my-head-against-the-door-and-sliding-down-to-the-floor-with-my-hands-clasped-over-my-heart-level swoonage.

Logan was asleep in the beanbag chair, his hand resting on Mercer's belly as my cat stretched along his denim-clad thigh. Logan's lips were slightly parted as he breathed deeply, his dark lashes resting on the deep shadows that spread underneath his eyes, which were even more prominent as his face relaxed. He curled his legs and tilted his head toward me, his hair a messy dark tangle on top of his head.

I smiled at how, a few weeks ago, I would've never imagined that Logan, the Dottie-dubbed "potential dreamboat," would be in my life beyond stealing all my pens and making random conversation in class—let alone curled up in a warm, sleepy ball on my pink beanbag chair. But that was a time before demons and warlocks came into my life. Before I realized that there was no "potential" about it—Logan was beautiful to me, a complicated and wonderful person, who I was slowly realizing needed me as much as I needed him.

While my dad would probably love the fact that Logan opted to fall asleep in my room rather than make a move on his daughter, I knew Logan would flip out if Dad found him unconscious in my room. I gave his shoulder one gentle shake, and Logan's eyes flew open immediately, his hand flying over his shoulder to grab at his sword before his eyes focused on me, realizing where he was. Mercer shot off Logan's lap, scrambling to find refuge underneath my bed.

"And I thought I was irritable when I woke up in the morning. Don't take my head off. I mean that literally," I warned, wrapping my hand around his and pulling it down.

"I can't believe I fell asleep." He sat up straighter and rubbed his eyes as he tried to wake up, looking at me with adorably bleary eyes and messy hair.

"I can't believe how cute you look right now," I replied, the words out of my mouth before I could stop them, and we both blushed.

"I'll forgive you for calling me 'cute' since I fell asleep on you, but I should go." He pushed himself off the floor and clasped his hands together, raising them over his head in a stretch.

"It's okay. You looked tired. You don't have to leave."

"I actually have a bunch of stuff I need to get done with Rego. I just wanted to make sure I came by. I didn't want to disappoint you again." Logan stuffed his hands into his back pockets as he looked down, gazing up at me through his dark lashes.

"Thank you. I appreciate it," I said, squeezing his arm. "Anything specific got you so tired?"

"Just a bunch of stuff. Still helping make weapons." He brushed it off. "Now, I know your dad is here, so hook me up with a hug before I go."

Logan widened his stance, curling his fingers at me.

"Well, okay. I guess I can suffer through a hug," I teased, before grabbing him by the collar and surprising him with a kiss that I could still feel that night as I sat at my desk, finishing the assignments that I'd missed during my fake bout of the stomach flu. The kiss definitely distracted me during my Spanish homework. With the amount of time I spent reminiscing about Logan's lips, you'd think I was an honors French student.

Logan was picking me up in the morning—he insisted—and his arrival was barely seven hours away by the time I finally finished everything. My cat was gently snoring as he stretched out across the foot of my bed, so I hugged my pillow to my chest as I tried to find a comfortable position around the fur ball when I heard the soft rustle of paper.

I fanned my fingers out, running them underneath my pillow as I tried to find whatever scrap of homework had made its way into my bed.

*Stupid homework, taunting me in my dreams.*

But instead, my fingertips found a folded-up piece of paper, with my name written on the front in a neat, but definitely masculine handwriting. I turned on my light and started to read.

Dear Paige,

The art of the handwritten letter. It's pretty much lost, isn't it? Well, I'm bringing it back, because I don't have a phone and I'm not going to shout these words after finagling a phone call in a diner. Besides, my handwriting is awesome and everyone should be subjected to it at least once.

I wanted to tell you that last night was important to me. Significant. Life-altering, if you will. In the story of my life, that's where you cracked the spine of the book. The mark is there, forever tattooed on my narrative and I couldn't be happier. You have to understand: I've spent a long time being angry. I've been fueled by rage and vengeance. It's why I shut down whenever we get too deep: you and I exist in this perfect bubble. That might sound crazy, but to me, it's perfect. I don't want to taint it by bringing anything ugly from my past into it. And last night you reminded me of a life outside of all this ugliness—a life where the words *fulfilling* and *happy* and *rich* mean something. You reminded me what it feels like to have someone care.

You offered me an out last night, asking me if this

thing between us was too much for me. It's not. But considering everything I've just written, I'm wondering if it's too much for you. At some point, it will be too much for you, and you'll want nothing to do with me. I know it. And it's not fair to you. I'm in if you are. And if you're not, this is your out. I won't hold a grudge or be mad. I won't ever stop protecting you. I'll understand—hell, I'm offering the out. I see the reason for it and I'm sure you'll take me up on it at some point. But I'm a coward who has to put it in a letter, because I don't want to hear the words.

But, if you're in, please take my hand tomorrow morning, since I'd probably turn 900 shades of red if you mention it to me. And then we can go look for my man card, because clearly I've lost it, and am now a pathetic emo boy, asking for reassuring hand squeezes from a beautiful girl when I should be pleading for you to wear yoga pants more often.

I hope you're reading this at night, in your bed, so I can tell you to have sweet dreams. If you found this, Mr. Kelly…um…hi.
Logan

I reread the letter until I nearly had the words committed to memory. I knew we'd had some kind of emotional breakthrough last night, but I hadn't realized how significant—or to use his term, life-altering—it was for him.

It was scary. Scary that I could have that kind of effect on someone. Scary because I was afraid of hurting him. But he had the power to crush me, as well.

I rolled onto my stomach, burying my face in the crease between two pillows as I clutched the letter in my hand. Logan was the only person who saw me—the real me—stealing my pens and sparking random conversations as an excuse to get to know me.

I didn't have to worry about keeping a story straight with Logan. It was refreshing. Freeing. Relaxing—when he wasn't storming into a classroom to save me from a demon, that is. And at the same time, our connection was intense, developing into a deep friendship that turned into romance at what felt like a breakneck speed, even though I'd known him for nearly three months. If I continued down this path, I knew where it was going to end. It was going to end in the word that was way too soon to even be thinking about. The word Logan all but said in his letter.

His wonderfully poetic letter. *Damn, that boy can write.*

He promised to protect me no matter what, and I believed him. If I decided this was too much, and I needed to pull back from him, he'd understand. He gave me an out.

I rolled over and covered my face with my pillow—the pillow I'd cried into for two nights, terrified that he'd been taken from me, from this world.

*It's not going to get easier. Walk away now. Walk away and protect your heart—what little part of it you can salvage.*

The scared part of me found the idea tempting. I was standing on a cliff. Logan hadn't exactly promised to catch me. But he'd promised to hold my hand on the way down.

And the next morning, Logan replied with a shy, endearing smile when I squeezed his hand, and I knew I made the right decision to fall.

# 11

"CAN I BORROW A PEN?"

I looked to my left where Logan leaned across the aisle, his hand outstretched and his fingers flicking backward in a "gimme" gesture. I reached into my bag, my fist first closing around a boring ballpoint pen before dropping it in favor of the glittery pink one that I had stuck in my notebook.

This one had a fuchsia plastic flower on the top.

"Here you go," I said sweetly, returning his smirk as I dropped the sparkling pen in his palm.

"Oh, good. Pink flowers. My favorite," he drawled, turning back to face the front of the classroom where our English teacher, Miss Doyle, was droning on about Shakespeare.

It had been a month since Aiden attacked me and disappeared. A month since Logan had left me that letter. And my life had been pretty normal for the past four weeks.

Well, if by normal you meant that my demonslayer boyfriend spent every spare moment teaching me self-defense, sparring with me on my rooftop with our magical swords, and my dead best friend spent most of her free time making out with her brand-new, also-dead boyfriend.

When it came to my life, normal was a relative term.

After English we headed to the library to meet up with Dottie and Travis. My last class was a free period, but the school wouldn't allow students to leave early for some ridiculously archaic insurance reason. The rule was annoying—especially because it was Friday, and I really wanted to go home early with Logan. He had the same free period—actually, he and I had all the same classes now except for gym, which was split up by gender, thanks to another ridiculously archaic rule. After Aiden's attack, Logan had used his talents to have his class schedule rearranged so it aligned with mine. I teased him about being a stalker, but it was nice having someone to talk to in class. Even nicer when that someone had a way of making me laugh, melt and roll my eyes, all in the same five minutes.

And, you know, save me from demons—especially considering that we didn't know what had happened to Aiden, since Logan hadn't heard from Ajax since I was last at his apartment.

Rego had also been scarce, not that Logan complained about that.

We found Dottie and Travis making out behind the last stack in the library, his hands sweeping through her previously shellacked hairdo. Logan cleared his throat loudly, and they gasped, jumping apart.

"You guys really seem to love getting frisky in the reference section," I teased, crossing my arms and leaning against the bookshelf.

"Like you don't do the same thing when no one is looking," Travis replied, mirroring my pose and tilting his head to the side. I blushed furiously—not because we did, but because we *didn't*. While Dottie and Travis were setting up camp in R-rated territory, Logan and I were barely visitors to PG-13 land, sharing a few steamy kisses on my rooftop in between sparring with swords. Not that I was complaining, but...well, yeah. I guess I was complaining a little.

"What's up with your neck?" Logan asked abruptly, gesturing to Travis. I stared, fascinated, as the purple hickey on his throat slowly faded to red, then pale pink, until it disappeared entirely.

"Is something wrong?" Dottie asked, and then I was gaping at her as her disheveled hair slowly crept back into place.

"You—your hair is all neat again—and his neck—the hickey," I stammered, gesturing back and forth between them.

"Yeah, I've noticed that, too," Travis admitted, a faint blush creeping across his freckled cheeks, and I wondered just how many hickeys he and Dottie had seen vanish. "Guess we can't change our appearances for long."

"At least I died on a good hair day," Dottie said flippantly, patting her bangs and grinning. Her uncharacteristically cheeky comment shocked me, but Travis was unfazed, kissing her on the cheek.

"Damn, Dots. You're the best," he said, a love-struck grin on his face. She gazed back at him with an equally adoring look, and I suddenly felt like we were intruding on a very private moment.

"So...we'll be over at the usual table," I muttered, grabbing Logan's hand and leading him over to the corner spot that we'd come to claim as ours over the past month. After Aiden and Della had accosted me in the hallway, hanging out in the usually empty third-floor bathroom wasn't much of an option anymore. It was too deserted—and Logan couldn't exactly explain away his presence in the girls'-only room. The library was usually packed—and now that Logan sat with me, I could talk to Dottie without appearing to talk to myself.

"So, how long do you think until they forget about us?" Logan asked, his eyes twinkling at me as he stretched back in his usual chair. Always on guard, Logan preferred to sit with his back facing the corner—so he could observe everyone entering the library.

"They've already forgotten, I'm sure." I gave Logan a knowing wink as I pulled out my books, setting them on the table with a dull thud. I wanted to get some homework done so I wouldn't have to deal with it after Logan and I sparred on the roof, which usually wiped me out. Thanks to a healthy dose of my signature pout—I practically sprained my face giving my dad doe eyes and a mournful frown—my dad had finally agreed with my mom to extend my after-school curfew to seven-thirty.

Seven. Freaking. Thirty.

*Yay, I'm almost eighteen and I finally get the curfew of a thirteen-year-old. Go, me.*

"You don't seem annoyed by it," Logan observed, picking at the frayed edge of the wood-printed laminate that was peeling off the edge of the table.

"By what?" I asked, flipping through my notebook.

"By your best friend getting all wrapped up in her new boyfriend and starting to ditch you. I thought this was the kind of stuff that pissed girls off."

"This isn't exactly the kind of situation that gets played out in a 'very special episode of an important teen drama,'"

I said in a deep imitation of an announcer's voice, making finger quotes around the words. "I'm not going to tearfully confront Dottie, weeping something like, 'I want you to be happy! I just want to be important to you, too!'" I bit my knuckle dramatically and looked away with a fake anguished expression on my face.

"All right, I see what you mean," Logan said, biting back a smile.

"I'm happy for her. I'm glad she has a friend."

Logan raised his eyebrow as he gave me a pointed look.

"I think they're a little more than just friends," he said, holding his thumb and index finger a few inches apart.

"Just a little," I agreed, spreading my palms two feet apart, and Logan laughed—probably thinking of the billions of times we'd caught them sucking face in the library. "But, seriously, I think she'd be just as happy if she and Travis were platonic," I continued, feeling the need to champion my friend.

"Dottie was lonely before. Really lonely. She was so sad, so resigned to being miserable and scared and alone. The fact that she's actually making jokes about her death is so crazy to me," I said, frowning when I thought about how forlorn Dottie used to be. Now she had company—company she clearly enjoyed, based on her magically disappearing hickeys—and I supported it entirely, even though the smoochfests surprised me at first. I hadn't expected Dottie to throw herself with such…unrestrained abandon…into another romantic situation considering how the last one turned out. But she'd explained to me how it felt to finally have someone to share her life. Someone to understand how she felt. Someone to make the dark hours in that Dark World a little brighter.

"All I want is someone to hold me and tell me it's going to be okay. That's all anyone wants, I guess. He does that for me. And I actually want to do that for him," she'd explained to me when I asked her about her seemingly overnight relationship with Travis. I couldn't find any flaw in her logic. I didn't know how long they'd be trapped there together, but at least Dottie and Travis had each other now.

"Hey, guys!" Travis called merrily, causing both of us to jump—Logan literally, since he scrambled to his feet, his hand flying behind his shoulder to grab his sword. The sudden movement caused the students at the table next to us to stare in surprise, and Logan hopped from foot to foot, pretending his leg fell asleep.

"Chill, dude. I didn't mean to ruin the moment," Travis said, his palms raised defensively.

"Right, because we're the ones giving each other mouth-to-mouth every chance we get," Logan retorted, and Travis puffed out his chest in reply.

"Don't hate. Besides, can you blame me? My chick's hot." he said, throwing his arm around Dottie's shoulders, causing her to giggle.

"Get a room," I teased. The table next to us began whispering again, and I sighed, twirling my bracelet around my wrist as I waited to hear the inevitable "Bellevue Kelly" nickname get dropped.

"Oh, Pa-ige," Dottie said, her singsong voice stretching my name out to two syllables. "They're not whispering about you."

She pointed toward the entrance of the library, where Pepper and Matt hovered by the door. It had been a month, but

Matt's very public betrayal—and Pepper's apparently immediate forgiveness—was still one of the most popular topics
of discussion. It sure was at the table next to us, where they
talked about Pepper and Matt as if they were characters on TV.

"I can't believe she stayed with him!" sniffed a girl from
my physics class with shoulder-length blond hair.

"Yeah, get thome thelf-rethpect!" lisped Tabitha Nakamura, who'd recently added a tongue ring to her catalogue
of piercings.

"You know how the girl Matt cheated with disappeared?
Well, I heard it was because Pepper had her jumped by some
gang. And Matt's still in love with the other girl—that's why
he looks like crap," Shani Robinson added, nodding her head
knowledgeably as she repeated what sounded like the plot to
another "very special episode of an important teen drama."

They weren't the only ones talking about Pepper and Matt
as they made their way to the front desk to return some books.
Matt—whose dark hair was still threaded with some strands of
white—at least had the decency to look embarrassed, casting
wary looks in our direction, but Pepper held her chin aloft,
her face emotionless. I found myself begrudgingly respect-
ing her for it. I knew how hard it was to act like the gossip
and words didn't hurt, when, in fact, they chipped away at
all your confidence and sense of self until you felt like every
day was an act. And then you were merely numb.

"I feel sorry for Pepper," I admitted in a hushed voice. "Is
that wrong?"

"Yes," Logan, Dottie and Travis all replied in unison.

"What? I feel bad for Matt, too. It's not his fault that he was hypnotized by a demon," I maintained, peeling back another piece of the laminate. "Does he even know what happened?"

"He just thinks it was an uncontrollable attraction," Logan explained, then clenched his teeth, the muscle in his jaw twitching. "And don't waste your time feeling sorry for him. You're not stuck in the locker room with him. He's loving this. Cheats on his girlfriend who takes him back. He's the hero of the douchebag brigade at this school."

"It still doesn't excuse what that succubus Della did," I maintained, and Travis snorted at my comment.

"Seriously, Paige. You should hear what Matt and some of his friends have said about you—"

Logan silenced him with a look, and I felt a creepy chill down my spine. I was used to people talking about me—I was Bellevue Kelly, after all—but something told me this locker room conversation would make me want to gag.

"I mean, they talk about all the girls," Travis hastily explained.

"Not anymore." Logan's voice was low and lethal.

"What did you do?" I turned to face Logan as he slouched low in his chair, glaring across the library. He kept his arms crossed over his chest, and I'm pretty sure he cracked a knuckle.

"Logan? Why are you doing your best impression of a mafia enforcer right now?" I asked, both amused and confused by the sudden display of testosterone.

"Don't worry about it," he replied, sitting up to adopt a less threatening pose. He grabbed my backpack and took out my physics book, idly turning pages.

"Now, Travis, you're good at physics, right?" Logan said,

not-so-subtly changing the subject. "There's some stuff I don't understand with, um—" he looked down at the random chapter he'd flipped to "—electromagnetism."

I narrowed my eyes at Logan.

"What did you do?" I repeated, and he just ignored me, pointing to the physics book with an innocent look on his face.

Scowling, I returned to my English homework, vowing to find out what Logan had done as he pretended to struggle through an old physics assignment he'd already aced. He rarely attended a normal school, but Logan studied on his own, saying he wanted to know more than just "demonslaying stuff."

Twirling a curl around her finger, Dottie mooned over Travis as if he were explaining the wonders of the galaxy. Which I guess he sort of was, but...still. *I really hope this works out, because if there's a way to make hell worse, it's by throwing a scorned ex into the mix.*

I finished English and wanted to get a head start on math, since we still had about twenty minutes left before the bell rang. I'd left my textbook in my locker, so I excused myself from the table, heading to the front of the library where copies of all our texts were kept.

"If I were a math book, where would I be?" I wondered aloud as I scanned the row of books, finally finding the bright blue cover shelved incorrectly among the art history texts. My fingers had barely brushed the spine as a hand reached out and snatched it before I could get it.

"Hey, I was about to— Oh. You," I said dryly as Pepper held the math book to her chest, a smug look on her face.

"You," she replied, pursing her lips as she regarded me.

"Talking to an invisible person again?" she asked, a satisfied smile on her face.

"Actually, I was talking to myself, wondering where the textbook I found first could be." I braced myself for a classic Pepper retort—probably something about how I might as well be invisible because I had no friends, blah blah blah. *Been there, done that, took the souvenir photo.*

Pepper tilted her head toward the back of the library, where Logan was balancing his chair on its back legs, glancing up at us from underneath the brim of his cap. His eyes were suspicious as they focused on Pepper.

"You seem cozy over there with the hot weirdo," she said, brushing her hand through her chin-length brown hair.

I narrowed my eyes, my temper flaring protectively as she eyed Logan. I wanted to fling myself in between them, to shield him from her calculating, judgmental stare.

"Don't you dare talk about him like that," I growled, and her eyes widened as she took a step back. Pepper quickly regained her composure, though, and graced me with her trademark condescending sneer instead.

"So, aren't you going to say something bitchy to me? No Little Miss Know-It-All comment to me about how I deserved this from Matt after—" she dropped her already low voice even more "—the whole thing where I kissed Diego?"

"No. I'm not the one who goes around judging people and making fun of them and assuming that I know everything about them," I retorted, and Pepper sucked her teeth, gripping the edges of the math textbook more tightly.

"This isn't the first time he's cheated," she said abruptly, a challenging tone to her voice as she tilted her chin up. "It's just the first time he's done it so publicly. But I'm not stupid."

"I never said you were."

"I know. You're actually the only person who hasn't talked shit about me."

I blinked slowly as I stared at her.

"The very definition of ironic, don't you think?" I asked, gesturing back and forth between us.

"Whatever," she huffed. "Just...just know that I'm not stupid."

"Why do you even care what I think?"

"I don't. I just don't want you thinking you're better than me. You're a loser."

"Loser, wow." I held my hand over my heart, pretending to hiss in pain. "Don't hurt yourself trying to come up with snappy comebacks, Paprika, I'm not here to gloat. I can't make you feel any worse than you make yourself feel. All I want is the math book."

She leaned against the bookshelf and exhaled through her nose, a frown on her face.

I held my palm out and sighed.

"Can I have it or what?"

Pepper dropped it into my waiting palm but gripped the sides as I tried to walk away with it.

"What?" I shut my eyes and exhaled. At this rate I was going to get five math problems done, at most.

"I'm not stupid, Paige. I'm going to get him back good for this."

"Why bother? Just break up with him." I knew I should

just walk away, but I couldn't help it—the insight into her weird little mind was too intriguing.

"I have to have a boyfriend," she explained, as if it were the most obvious statement in the world. "You don't get it. You don't have the friends I do."

Normally that would be an incredibly bitchy comment, since it was about my lack of friends and, of course, the fact that it was uttered by Pepper. But instead, I didn't take offense. Her statement was too revealing, too sad.

"Maybe you shouldn't have the friends you have either, then," I replied, and Pepper's perma-scowl was back on her face.

"You don't get it."

"Obviously."

I wrenched the book from her hands and returned to my friends. Sure, two were invisible and one was half-warlock, but I wouldn't trade them for all the "cool kids" in the world.

"What was that about?" Logan asked, his eyes shifting to stare at Pepper.

"I honestly have no idea," I said, pulling on the end of my ponytail and curling a lock of hair around my knuckle as I relayed the odd encounter.

"I don't get what she means about how she has to have a boyfriend, though. What's the big deal?"

"Might I remind you that you have a boyfriend? A pretty great guy, by the way," Logan interjected.

"He's all right," I said flippantly, but I squeezed his hand, earning a playful scowl in reply. "But seriously, you're my boyfriend because you're awesome. Why stick around with someone who sucks? This isn't a play where you're casting for the role of 'boyfriend.' Find the person first and then build the role around them."

"That's easy for you to say because you've always been on the outside," Travis said.

"I wasn't always," I corrected him. "And besides, why does Pepper care what I think?"

"Because you *are* on the outside. And because, at the end of the day, Pepper is jealous of you," Travis said, glancing back to where Pepper and Matt had taken up residency at a table with Andie and their usual posse of sycophants. They'd probably all dress alike even if we didn't have to wear uniforms.

"Other than my grades, which are barely a fraction higher than hers are," I pointed out, "what could she possibly be jealous of?"

"Pepper's whole identity is wrapped up in her image. Being the popular girl, having the good grades, having the right boyfriend."

"So why was that my problem?"

"Because you don't give a shit, and everyone knows it. You aren't mired in high school drama. You know, Paige—" Travis leaned forward, whispering even though Logan, Dottie and I were the only ones who could see him "—half the school thinks you make up being crazy just to avoid dealing with people. That half thinks you're brilliant for it."

"And the other half?"

He leaned back. "Oh, they think you're crazy and they're terrified of you. Remember, you did threaten to smack Pepper. No one else can see Dottie, so of course they think you're nuts."

"Yeah, I always forget about that when she's slamming

doors in my face and calling me a freak." I pursed my lips as I considered this.

The bell rang, and I watched as Pepper and Matt silently gathered their things. He grabbed her around the waist and she kissed him on the cheek, giggling as her forehead knocked against the glasses he'd started wearing after Della. When Matt turned away from her to grab his backpack, though, her smile faded to a petulant little pout.

And I thought the act I put on for my parents was exhausting.

Perspective was an amazing thing. From where I'd been sitting—usually on a lukewarm radiator in the girls' bathroom—my situation wasn't enviable. I'd been held back a year, stuffed with pills, and until recently, the only person who believed that I wasn't crazy was my dead best friend. I'd felt trapped in my situation—but apparently, I was the poster child for freedom.

"What's got you so quiet?" Logan asked, throwing his arm over my shoulder as we walked down the stairs, headed toward the front door of the school.

"Just thinking about what Travis said—about how I have all this freedom, because I don't care what people think."

I sighed, yanking my hair out of its elastic, and raked my hands through it.

"The thing is, though, I'm such a fraud," I admitted, coiling and uncoiling the black elastic band in my hands. "I'm sitting here judging Pepper in my mind, when I'm no better. I pretended not to care, but I did care. I used to want so badly for my biggest problem in life to be something dumb, like finding a date for a dance like the stupid Spring Fling, which Dottie swore up and down was the most fun thing that ever happened. So I think I just convinced myself that I didn't care, because it was easier than being disappointed all the time. I mean, it's not like Bellevue Kelly's ever actually going to have fun at a dance, right? So it was easier to just shut off all those daydreams where I was normal, even though that's what I wanted."

Logan pulled me closer, tucking me into his side.

"You were scared, and you found a way to cope," he said, leaning into me as we walked down the hall.

"Being numb isn't the same as being brave, and I'm getting credit for the wrong thing." I rubbed my face with my hands. "Ah, I don't know. I'm probably not making any sense."

Logan regarded me silently for a moment before nodding his head, agreeing with whatever decision he'd made.

"Come with me," he ordered, grabbing my hand and directing me back the way we'd come, weaving against the flow of exiting students as he led me to the auditorium. He opened the door and peeked inside, looking at me with a giddy smile on his face.

"What's up? Are you thinking of joining the Drama Club?"

"Not exactly," he said, leading me into the darkened theater. The stage was bare, save for the backdrop of a forest at dusk for the recent production of *A Midsummer Night's Dream*. Logan led me through the seats, stopping briefly at the lighting board to flip a few switches. Tiny lights pierced the background on the stage, slowly twinkling on and off.

"Who knew Holy Ass had such high production values?" I stared in awe at the enchanting set. Logan hit one more button, and turned a few knobs, and the faint strains of classical music filled the air.

"I don't know what this is, but it's pretty," I said, resting my forearms on the front of the lighting board as I watched Logan work.

"It sounds familiar," Logan admitted, and I cocked an eyebrow.

"Are you secretly a connoisseur of classical music?" I asked, sliding off my backpack and setting it on a nearby seat.

"No, but I've seen a lot of car commercials," he said, laughing. "Nothing sells a sports car like some old dead guy banging away on a piano."

"So, why are we in here?" I tapped my hands on the ledge, but Logan merely replied with a cryptic smile.

He stepped away from the lighting board and took my hand again, leading me up the aisle to the front of the stage.

"Logan? What's going on?"

"Get on stage," he said, grabbing me by my hips and effortlessly lifting me up so I was sitting on the front of the stage. I scrambled to my feet as Logan gestured for me to take a few steps back before running to the front and leaping, bracing his palm against the boards as he effortlessly vaulted his body on the stage.

*Damn, that's hot.*

Logan tossed his hat to the side, running his hands through his hair in an effort to tame it before holding his right hand out to me and bowing.

"Dance with me?" he asked sweetly, tilting his head up, the twinkle lights reflecting in his warm brown eyes.

"Here?"

"Are you going to take my hand and dance with me or what?"

He wiggled his fingers at me, and I placed my hand in his outstretched palm. Logan quickly tightened his grip and spun me into him, my back hitting his chest with a thud. He held me tightly as we began to sway slowly to the music.

"You said you would never go to a school dance," he whispered in my ear, his breath warm on my skin. "Well, you're now dancing in a school. So technically, this is a school dance. And I think this is a lot nicer than dancing around some balloons in a gym, don't you?"

I nodded, squeezing his hands as I snuggled back against his chest.

"Especially right now. The wrestling team is in the gym. Slow dancing to the soundtrack of their grunts might be a mood killer," Logan said, taking my hand and spinning me once, so I faced him. Well, more like I face-planted into his chest with a thud, and I stepped back, rubbing my nose.

"Sorry, I guess I don't have any fancy moves down," Logan apologized, and I clasped my hands around his neck as his hands settled on my hips.

"I don't need them." We swayed for a bit, until the song ended—and then continued dancing without music, slowly moving around the stage.

"So, can I ask you a question?" I gave Logan a hopeful smile, and he groaned.

"Oh, no, you're asking. That means it's gotta be bad." He took my hand and spun me away from him. I twirled back, landing against him with a thud again, and we both laughed.

"No way, buddy. You're not going to distract me with these sensual, smooth dance moves."

"But they're the sensual-est and the smoothest. Watch this," he teased, turning me and trying to dip me. Instead, we ended up with my back against his chest as he held my hand over my shoulder, attempting to dip me backward.

"This isn't right," he muttered. "It looks easier in the movies."

I spun around and placed my hands around his neck again. "So my question...."

"Yes, dear?" Logan asked with a resigned sigh.

"What was Travis talking about with the douchebag brigade?"

Logan bristled, and we stopped swaying for a moment.

"Please?" I asked, and Logan relented.

"They talk about the girls in school."

"And?" I prompted, and Logan gritted his teeth.

"And they rate them on their, uh, presumed skill set. When your name came up—" Logan paused, shutting his eyes and tensing as he recalled whatever they said about me "—I couldn't stand by quietly. I told them to stop."

"And they listened?"

"Well, I may have driven my point home by knocking one of Vogel's friends on his ass. Oops," he said with a self-satisfied grin.

"Sounds like he deserved it," I murmured, and we began swaying again.

"Oh, he did," Logan said, kissing me on the top of my head. "There was some bullshit bro talk after, like 'Sorry, bro, didn't realize you guys were together.' They stopped talking about you, but every girl they talk about is important to *some-one*. So I just said something about learning to have respect for women and to stop talking about all the girls like that."

"You just said?" I repeated, arching an eyebrow. "That's all it took?"

"Well, it helps when you're really good at blocking a punch." Logan shrugged, spinning me again, this time more smoothly. "I mean, these guys aren't exactly assassins, so it wasn't hard to thwart their lame attempts at fighting. I never had a rep at a school before. I think they're all afraid of me." He raised his shoulders, giving me a guilty smile.

"Someone has the hot bad boy with a heart of gold image down."

"I'm clearly better at that than I am at dancing."

I rested my hand against his cheek.

"I can't believe you did that," I whispered. Logan stiffened, his face tense.

"Are you mad?"

"Mad? You took on a locker room full of guys to defend my and every other girl's honor. I'm a second away from falling to the ground and swooning. I'm talking legit romance movie swoonage."

"It wasn't a big deal," he said, turning his head to kiss the palm of my hand.

"It's a very big deal," I replied softly. "Why are you so perfect sometimes?"

"I'm not." Logan took my hand from where it rested against his cheek, lacing our fingers together. He rested his forehead against mine, his eyes downcast.

"I want to be worthy of you, but I'm not perfect. Paige, I'm so far from it."

His voice was heartbreakingly sad, causing my chest to ache.

"What are you talking about? Logan, you're the best person I've ever met," I insisted, squeezing his hand. "You're the only one who knows the real me."

He shut his eyes and took a deep breath.

"What is it?" I asked.

"I have to tell you something." His voice trembled as he gripped my hands, as if he were trying to keep me rooted to my spot. As if I were going anywhere.

"So, tell me," I said, desperation creeping into my hushed voice.

"I'm terrified you'll hate me, even though I deserve it. But I—"

"Is this a private party?" Travis called, interrupting us with an exuberantly cheerful voice.

"Great timing, Travis," Logan hissed, dropping his forehead to my shoulder before releasing my hands, turning to glare at our towheaded dead friend as he sauntered down the aisle, dragging along a reluctant Dottie.

"We're interrupting them," she loudly whispered, pulling Travis back a few feet.

"Can you give us a minute?" I asked as Travis grinned devilishly at Dottie, knowing exactly what he was doing.

"Come on, they're always interrupting us," Travis replied, dragging her back and wrapping his arms around her. "Payback's a bitch."

"So am I if you don't give us some space, Travis," I retorted, darting my eyes to Logan. His face was guarded—whatever he was about to tell me now locked away beneath his steely expression.

"Oh, please, like you guys aren't going to go up to your roof and have tons of alone time all weekend," Travis said as Dottie stared at the stage in awe.

"This is so romantic," she cooed, clasping her hands together.

"It *was* romantic," I muttered, resentful that the moment had passed—and Logan was clearly not about to open up to me with an audience. He stood there with his arms folded, the muscle in his jaw twitching as whatever he'd been about to tell me churned behind his stormy eyes. Dottie frowned, and I noticed that she was slightly transparent—giving me a first-class ticket for a guilt trip.

"Dots, you don't have to leave," I said apologetically. It's not like she'd known Logan and I were about to have a breakthrough before stupid Travis barged in. "It's okay."

"No, it's not," she replied faintly, her voice slightly panicked.

I looked up at Logan in terror, and he quickly pushed me behind him, withdrawing his sword as he assumed an aggressive stance.

"Is it Aiden?" I whispered, gripping on to the back of Logan's shirt as Travis and Dottie disappeared entirely.

And then everything in the auditorium went black.

# 12

ADRENALINE FLOODED MY VEINS, A SICKENING tension chilling my body as I grabbed the back of Logan's shirt more tightly, needing to stay connected to him in the darkness. He spoke quickly, repeating *"Luserna Illuminabit"* in that unfamiliar language. His voice was confident and strong—reassuring me in the darkness. If he was afraid, he was hiding it expertly.

Brilliant flashes streaked over our heads, summoned by Logan's spell. They spun in tight whirlpools, quickly taking the form of dusky orbs of light that hovered in the air, illuminating the auditorium in an eerie, acidic yellow glow.

Something darted through the seats in the darkened rear of the auditorium, a shadowy alcove underneath the balcony. I stepped back, dropping my hold on Logan's shirt to draw my sword, holding it in the defensive stance I'd tried to perfect over the past month.

"Just stay behind me," Logan said, one arm outstretched to the side as a barrier to protect me. Those words bounced around in my head—the very same words that Travis had spoken before Blaise killed him.

I took a deep breath, gripping the handle of my sword more tightly as I tried to steady my trembling hands. *Logan isn't Travis. He's killed hundreds of demons.*

A sudden cracking sound broke the silence, with sharp, rapid pops and snaps echoing through the empty auditorium. One of the seats came flying down the main aisle, shattering into splinters of wood and twisted metal joints.

A seat that until now had been bolted to the floor.

Another seat followed it, and I heard a deep, feral grunt from the back of the auditorium, as a hulking figure lumbered out of the shadows.

Even if you didn't know he was a demon, you'd cross the street when you saw him coming. He looked like a cage fighter, close-cropped hair capping off a mass of solid muscle. A leather patch covered his left eye, and a long, puckered red scar pulled at the skin of his cheek. Where Aiden was lean and graceful, this demon was stocky, a mountain of muscle that tested the limits of the thin, yellowed T-shirt and holey jeans straining to cover him. His hands were clenched into fists as he strode purposefully down the aisle, his massive chest heaving as he turned to grab another seat. In one swift move, he slammed his hands down, smashing the seat to pieces before ripping the base from the ground and hurling it toward the stage. I let out a strangulated cry, and Logan's arm reached back to me, his hand curling around my hip as he gently shoved me back behind him.

"Remember when I said only three demons have gotten away?" Logan whispered. "This is one of them."

He gave my hip a reassuring squeeze before walking forward. "You still have quite a few anger issues there, Bor,"

Logan called to the demon calmly, spinning his sword the way someone might casually swing an umbrella or a cane.

"How long ago did I take your eye? I was what, thirteen? I wasn't even that good back then," Logan said, laughing—as Bor let out another grunt, his body appearing to vibrate with hostility and anger.

"Rage demon," Logan whispered in a clipped tone. "Do not step foot off this stage until I tell you to run. Go home. Don't go backstage—stay visible."

"What about you?"

I heard his faint yet frustrated sigh.

"Don't worry about me. I'll meet you. Midnight, your roof."

With that, Logan ran and leaped off the stage, landing in a crouching position a mere few feet in front of Bor.

"I can smell you from here, Bor." Logan laughed harshly as he stood before the hulking demon. "What's wrong—can't find the soap with only one eye?"

Bor unleashed another loud, inhuman roar, his jaw seeming to unhinge with the force of his howl, and he effortlessly ripped out another chair, sending bolts scattering as he raised it over his head and rushed at Logan, bringing the heavy wood crashing down. A cry stuck in my throat as Logan ducked to the side mere seconds before the chair exploded in a burst of shattered wood and twisted metal—right where he'd been standing. My eyes finally found Logan, balanced on top of a nearby aisle seat, one foot on the armrest and the other on the back of the chair.

"Your aim sucks. Try to get me, cyclops," he taunted, crooking his finger in Bor's direction. The demon rushed toward Logan, who deftly ran across the row of armrests, luring the demon farther away from me.

"I'm right here," Logan called in a singsong voice to Bor, whose bulky size was too great for the narrow aisles. The demon brought his massive fists down on the chairs, smashing them as he cleared a path to chase after Logan. A trail of splinters and debris followed Logan, who was in full überconfident demonslayer mode. He kept turning around and provoking Bor, making sure the rage demon was following him.

"C'mon, stinky. I'm right here," Logan called, ducking as Bor flung a broken piece of wood at him.

My hands began to cramp as I clenched my sword, desperately praying that Logan didn't stumble as he precariously balanced on the thin slivers of wood. One fall was all it would take for him to lose momentum, for the rage demon to catch up to him.

Bor lurched forward, his meaty arms swinging out to grab Logan, who launched himself off the last chair, coming to face Bor with his sword drawn and raised.

"Paige, now!" Logan shouted, and I jumped off the stage, running to the exit, sword in hand. I heard a series of grunts and cast one quick look back, seeing Logan's sword splashed with dark blood, the front of Bor's shirt slashed and stained brown. And then I slammed into something hard.

I stared ahead of me, rubbing my sore shoulder as I gaped at the large golden bars that had appeared out of nowhere in front of me, blocking the aisle as they formed what looked like a gate, topped with razor-sharp spikes that pierced the air several feet above my head.

I raised my sword like a bat, swinging at the bars as if I were trying to hit a home run. Instead of knocking the bars down, the blade ricocheted off them with a dull clang, throwing me off my feet as my sword vibrated in my hand.

And then I heard a soft chuckle from the balcony above.

"I knew I needed a gilded cage to catch this little bird, but I had no idea she'd run so willingly into it."

That familiar voice floated over the sounds of Bor's angry snarls—that familiar voice that clawed my already raw nerves to shreds. Trembling, I scrambled to my feet, retreating away from the golden contraption, this creation of Aiden's designed to somehow torment me. Would it electrocute me? Impale me with those spikes? Unleash whiplike spines intended to slash me to pieces like his last little invention?

That was the problem with magical torture devices invented by demons—the possibilities for inflicting pain really were endless.

I looked up, finding Aiden leaning forward on the balcony, his chin resting in his hands as if he were watching a cute scene play out in the theater.

In a sick way, that's exactly what he was doing.

"Oh, no, little bird, I don't think you're going anywhere," he purred, grinning at me with his calculating, confident smile as he rubbed his shoulder. He appeared to be wearing some kind of armor over his right side, where Logan had stabbed him previously, and he tapped it, mimicking a beating heart.

I screamed for Logan, but he didn't hear me over Bor's savage howls, which reverberated in the auditorium. Logan's back was to me as he furiously hacked apart the bloodied demon. Bor's left arm was gone at the elbow, his right arm a dark, pulpy patchwork of deep gashes as it wildly clawed for Logan. Bor was nothing but a relentless, ruthless beast, tasked with distracting Logan so Aiden could get to me. And it was working.

"He can't help you now," Aiden cooed, a delighted smile on his face. "I just love how useful a rage demon can be. I'm sorry to have kept you waiting, but it took me forever to find just the right guy for the job."

A shimmering, spark-filled mist coiled around the bars on both ends of the gate. The sparks condensed into a vertical line, solidifying into another golden pole. Then another. The mist was everywhere as the golden bars began multiplying, one tall, spike-topped pole after another materializing at a rapid pace, lining the aisle where I stood.

Caging me in.

Logan's shouts echoed in my ears as I turned on my heel and started racing toward the stage. I had to outrun the bars that kept appearing, forming an expanding cage that threatened to wrap around me, trapping me in this magical jail. The bars made a sharp turn inward as I reached the end of the aisle, and I flung my sword on the stage, the blade hitting the floorboards as I launched myself forward. My fingers gripped the high edge of the stage and I hoisted myself up. I'd just managed to swing my other leg up, and I rolled across the boards as the golden bars crashed into the stage with a dull clang before disintegrating into mist.

I heard a loud swear from Aiden, followed by a slamming door as I grabbed my sword again, pushing myself into a standing position with one hand. My eyes first fell on the now-empty balcony before searching for Logan, who was taking one final swing at Bor's neck. The demon's furious roar sputtered—turning into a sickening gurgle as Logan sliced through his throat. Then Bor was silent, and the only sound was the hollow, dull thud of the demon's head landing on the floor, where it unevenly rolled down the sloped floor of the auditorium. Bor's body remained standing, his weight swaying back and forth. With the tip of his sword, Logan poked Bor's chest, and the beast fell back with a weighty thud that reverberated in the auditorium.

Logan spun around quickly and ran toward me, leaping on the stage and joining my side in mere seconds.

"Paige, are you hurt?" he asked, his tone agitated but his face full of nothing but concern as his eyes roamed over me, checking for injuries.

"I'm okay," I said in a trembling voice, my body shaking as I tried to come down from my adrenaline overdose. "But Aiden was here. He was in the balcony, he almost trapped me," I told him, and Logan's eyes narrowed as they darted from the now-empty balcony around the auditorium.

"Come on, we're getting you out of here." He wrapped his arm around me as he started swiftly ushering me to the edge of the stage, his head swiveling around as he glared at all the darkened corners of the auditorium. I knelt down to hop off the stage when I noticed movement on the balcony.

"He's here!" I yelled, pointing up at the balcony, where Aiden had his arm pitched back, a bulging satchel slung across his chest. He pulled out his fist and flung a handful of coins at us, light glinting off the shiny metal discs as they flew through the air. The spines unfurled, lashing at the air with audible whipping sounds as Aiden reached back into his bag for more ammo.

Logan grabbed me around the waist, spinning and pulling me into his arms as we ran into the wings. As if they could see where we were hiding, the discs sharply turned to seek us out. The small, deadly weapons whizzed above, and we dove to the floor, the discs embedding themselves in the wall behind where our heads had been moments earlier.

We huddled on the floor, Logan's body covering mine as the projectiles flew overhead. They pierced the forest backdrop, shredding the painted canvas into long, heavy sheets that tumbled to the stage alongside sparks from the severed electrical wires.

The discs relentlessly flew overhead, glittering gold whips lashing at the walls backstage and shattering them like they were made of thin crystal, not thick concrete. Metal crunched loudly next to me as the coins found the door to the dressing rooms, the thrashing spines effortlessly carving the steel into slivers.

I burrowed my face into Logan's neck, my fingers clinging to his shirt as his hand rested against the exposed side of my face, keeping me shielded. And then he cried out, his head falling to my shoulder. I felt him shudder in pain as one of the gold discs sliced into the wall just inches over his shoulder.

I tried to disentangle from him, desperate to check his injury, throw myself over his wounded back—protect him in some way—but Logan braced himself above me with one palm over my shoulder. His other arm wound around me, keeping me close against his chest.

"You're hurt!" I cried, but Logan merely gripped me more tightly.

"I'm fine," he grunted, still protecting me in spite of his pain. I shut my eyes as chunks of black-painted concrete rained down, the coins scarring the walls with deep gouges.

And suddenly it was over—the auditorium grew quiet again, and the only noises piercing the silence were the faint, steady sounds of concrete chips dropping on the floor, the flapping of the shredded canvas and the popping sound of sparks from the severed wires on the stage.

Logan pressed his finger to my lips as we listened for Aiden.

"He's gotta be out of ammo. He won't face me in hand-to-hand," he whispered, wincing as a bolt of pain shuddered through him.

I tugged on his collar, begging him with my eyes to let me up, but he just shook his head. Logan took a deep breath before shouting, "Nice try. Wanna come face me so I can skewer you again?" His voice sounded strong and clear, but his face told another story, his features twisted in agony.

We heard the unmistakable sound of a door slamming, and Logan relaxed slightly. Still, we remained crouched against the floorboards, tangled up in each other until we heard the indisputable sign that Aiden truly was gone: Dottie and Travis were back—and they were frantically calling our names.

"Back here," I called, running my hands over Logan's face and chest as I tried to find out where else he could be injured.

"You're hurt," I fretted. "Is it your shoulder? Do I need to go get Rego?"

"No," he said, his jaw clenched and his eyes tightly shut

as he tried to take a deep breath that ended in an agonizing shudder.

"Let me see," I begged, trying to unwind myself from his hold. But Logan merely pulled me tighter to his chest, burying his face in the crook of my neck.

"Just give me this moment," he asked plaintively, clutching me tightly—and I began to panic.

"How badly are you hurt?" I whispered, my eyes wide as I wrapped my arms around him. A sticky wetness soaked the back of his shirt, and I pulled my hands back in shock, staring at Logan's ashen face as tears began filling my eyes. He quickly grabbed my wrists, covering my fists with his hands as he pulled us to a standing position.

He grimaced at the movement, the agony plain across his pale face.

"Logan, please. You're scaring me," I said, the tears that were blurring my vision now streaming down my cheeks. "Let me see. Let me get Rego. Please, I can't lose you."

"It's just a deep scratch," he insisted, his voice rough as he held my hands. "I swear. Please, don't look."

Dottie's and Travis's faces appeared behind Logan, their expressions perfectly synchronized as they transitioned from worry to relief—and then to confusion.

"Aiden attacked. Logan's hurt," I choked out, and Travis's brow was furrowed as he stared at Logan.

"What's all over you guys?"

"What?" I asked, puzzled. Logan dropped his hold on my wrists, and I looked down at our hands, missing his touch.

And then I stopped.

Everything stopped.

My palms were splotchy with Logan's blood. He watched me carefully for my reaction, but I could only stare at him. Without saying a word, he shifted his stance, turning his back toward me but continuing to watch me over his shoulder for my reaction.

There, on his right shoulder blade, was a curved rip in his white shirt, where a lash had sliced through the fabric and into his skin. It wasn't wide, but it was deep—he was bleeding profusely, and the blood glued his shirt to his back and stained my hands.

Stained them a deep purple.

Logan turned to face me again, wincing at the movement.

"I wanted to tell you. I tried to tell you so many times," Logan began, but he let his voice trail off.

"Tell you what?" Travis asked, but Dottie just shook her head at him. She knew what it meant.

"Paige, you should leave," Dottie ordered, giving Logan a suspicious look that would normally have made me laugh. "I don't think you're safe here."

"You think I'm going to hurt her?" Logan sputtered, twisting to stare at Dottie in shock. The movement caused pain to shoot across his face as he reached his hand behind his back, bracing his injured shoulder.

I felt numb. Foolish. Naive. Blind. A thousand words for how I felt raced through my head as I stared down at my hands, colored a rich purple from demon blood—Logan's blood. I raised my eyes to meet his, those brown eyes that I thought I knew so well, and I could only think one thing.

*How can I love you if I don't even know you?*

"Paige, please, say something." Logan took a step toward me, and I reflexively flinched backward.

"It's still me," Logan insisted, gazing at me with those mournful eyes.

The same eyes that sparkled at me playfully in class, teasing me about my pens. The same eyes that were serious when we sparred on the roof, narrowing with focus as he taught me how to swing a sword. That peeked at me over an adoring grin, before sharing a sweet kiss.

*I don't know who you are.*

I backed away from him as more images assaulted my mind. Logan defending me. Standing up for me. Saving my life.

Lying to me, telling me he was a half-warlock. Instead, he was a demon—part of the race of creatures that wanted to kidnap me and hurt me.

"This is what you wanted to tell me. This is why you gave me an out." My voice sounded foreign and hollow, and I felt disconnected from my body, like I was watching someone else react.

Logan took another step toward me, and I stepped back again, not trusting myself to touch him. Not trusting him to touch me.

My gaze met his briefly, the regret and sadness that had always been brimming in his eyes suddenly making sense.

I wondered what he was seeing on my face, since every nerve, every emotion was at once numb and overloaded. I got my answer when he finally spoke.

"You want to go," Logan said softly, his eyes never leaving my face. "You should go, Paige."

It was all I needed to hear. So I ran—leaving Dottie and

Travis and Logan standing there on the stage as I rushed up the aisle, grabbing my coat and bag and pushing the doors open. I kept running, my mind flooded with memories of the past six weeks with Logan. The letter he'd written me. How he'd offered me an out—an out I probably should have taken. But then I wouldn't have the memories I do have, like us curling up on the picnic table on the roof every Friday and Saturday night after my parents went to bed. Cushioning ourselves against the unforgiving, splintered wood by wrapping ourselves in a soft, thick blanket that I'd smuggled from the linen closet, and sharing soft, unhurried kisses in between talking about everything and nothing...

But we never talked about the one thing we should have talked about—his past, and who he really was. I never asked him, hoping he'd open up in his own time since he'd begged me to be patient with him. Would he have answered me if I'd asked about his parents?

*Oh, your uncle once got arrested? Talk about embarrassing relatives—I'm related to a bunch of demons. Sorry if I didn't bring that up earlier.*

I braced my hands on either side of my front door, panting. I had no recollection of my run home, vaguely recalling horns bleating at me on Amsterdam Avenue. I'd probably run right through an intersection and didn't even notice it. I could hear the TV through the door, the rapid-fire flipping of channels indicating that my father was home. I tried to steady my breathing—I just wanted to curl up in my bedroom and think. Or not think. Or swipe the bottle of Irish cream my dad thought I didn't know was hidden with his cookbooks, and drink it until I couldn't spell my own name.

I slid on my coat—I'd somehow run here with it in my hand—hoping it would hide my disheveled appearance. The last thing I wanted was my father to notice that anything was wrong. I'd just found out that I didn't really know the one person who knew me best. I couldn't face an interrogation about it.

"Hey, Dad," I said, giving my father a tight-lipped smile and wave as I walked into the apartment, trying to stealthily head straight into my bedroom.

He didn't fall for it.

"Paige, what the hell happened to you?" Dad asked, and I paused, looking down at my hands and feeling my heart drop when I realized they were, of course, still stained with Logan's blood.

"My pen exploded?" I said, holding up my hands.

"Not the ink!" Dad replied, muting the TV and sitting up straighter as he scrutinized me. "What's in your hair?"

I gingerly patted my stained fingers on the crown of my head, feeling gravel-like bits of concrete coating it like a veil.

"Oh, I don't know. Construction site near the school?" I lied weakly. *Why not keep lying, Paige? Everyone's doing it.*

"Are you okay, honey?" Dad asked, scrutinizing my face. "You're home really early. Where's your shadow?"

I frowned at my father's nickname for Logan, and Dad's blue eyes narrowed as he studied me.

"What's wrong? Is it Logan? Did that boy hurt you?"

"Dad, no," I insisted as my father folded his arms, clearly not believing me.

"Paige, you look like you're in a daze."

"I'm fine," I said, smiling brightly to make up for the trembling in my voice. "Just tired."

My father paled as he studied me, getting up from the couch to stand before me.

"You didn't have one of your...episodes again, did you?" he asked gently, his eyes searching my face. "You've been doing so well, but maybe having a boyfriend is too much stress on you."

I winced at his mention of a boyfriend—and Dad noticed.

"Maybe you need to go back to therapy—"

"Dad, no. It's nothing like what you think. Please, just let me wash this b-b-bright ink off me," I stammered desperately, wringing my hands together as I stood on display in the center of the living room. *I can't believe I almost said blood.*

Finally I just strode into the bathroom, desperate to get my hands clean as I used a nail brush to scrub the blood off my hands, trying to hold back the tears as the violet-tinged water swirled down the drain. There was a lot of it. And suddenly I was terrified for Logan. I stifled a gasp as his agonized face flashed behind my eyelids. *Is he okay? How bad is that wound?*

"Something is wrong, I know my daughter," my dad insisted, standing in the entrance to the bathroom. "Did Logan do something to you?"

"No, Dad."

"Are you sure? I never liked the looks of that boy," my father said, folding his arms as he leaned against the doorframe. His comment sparked a flare of protectiveness in me. Dad already tormented Logan every chance he got. *Don't make it worse on him the next time they're in the same room. If there is a next time.*

I barked out a short laugh at the irony of it all. The only reason I knew Logan was a liar was because he'd gotten injured protecting me.

"What's so funny, Paige?" my father asked suspiciously. "What did he do to you?"

"The idea that Logan would lay a finger on me is what's funny. It's nothing he's done," I said, gripping the edge of the sink with soapy fingers. No matter what, I couldn't let my dad have a bad image of him. Logan didn't deserve that. I didn't know what he deserved right now, but he didn't deserve my father's scorn. I could at least do that for him.

"Are you sure? Did he say something ungentlemanly—" he growled as he pronounced the word "—about you? I know how locker room talk goes."

"Dad, Logan hit a guy who said something ungentlemanly about me in the locker room. Logan's the last person to say or do anything like that to me."

My dad's eyes opened in surprise.

"And you're mad at him about it?"

I shook my head no.

"Well, I don't know if I agree with using violence to solve anything, but in this case—" my dad bit the inside of his cheek as he tried to hide a smile "—Logan's gone up a few points in my estimation."

"Glad to hear it," I said, brushing past my dad to go back into the living room. He followed me.

"Paige, what happened? You come in here upset, you don't even notice that you've got gunk in your hair. I thought teenage girls lived and died by the condition of their hair."

I whirled around to face my dad, a smart remark ready to

burst through my lips. But when I saw the earnest, concerned expression on his face, I felt my shoulders sag.

It was hard enough trying to sort through my feelings about what I'd just discovered about Logan. Part of me felt betrayed. Another part of me felt like he had to have a reason for keeping it from me. And then there was the rational part of me, which told me to move to Canada and change my name, because Logan was a demon and all demons were evil.

All those warring parts of me agreed on one thing: this was the deepest hurt I'd ever felt, and I couldn't handle trying to defend Logan to my father anymore.

"Can't I just have a bad day and not get the inquisition over it?" I pleaded.

"Okay, kiddo," Dad said, coming over to give me a hug. "Go wash this crap off, and just remember, I'm here to talk," he said, awkwardly patting my debris-dusted hair. "Or if it's really, um, womanly stuff, you can talk to your mom when she gets home," he reminded me.

And she sure tried to get me to talk, especially after my father had gone to work. So much for holing up in my room all night. My mom dragged me into the living room, wanting to know why Logan hadn't joined us for dinner—as he had every Friday since I first squeezed his hand.

*For one night, couldn't my parents forget that they cared about me and leave me alone?*

"Mom, it's just a—"

"Bad day. I know that's what you told your dad. But I know the difference between a bad day, and a bad day over a boy," Mom replied, staring at me wisely as we sat on the couch, the laugh track of an old sitcom sounding in the background.

"So, what did Logan do?" she asked, holding her white mug, absently running her fingers over the raised red logo for some bank. "And don't even try to tell me it has nothing to do with him."

"Fine, it does," I finally admitted, taking a sip of my tea. It was loaded with sugar and milk, just the way I liked it. But it was doing nothing to calm my nerves.

"What did he do? I've heard it all before. You should hear the things the younger girls at work talk about." My mom raised her eyebrows and let out a whistle.

"Logan's different from those guys." If only she knew how different.

"Sweetie, it doesn't matter how old they are. There are some universal truths when it comes to men," Mom said wisely.

"He, uh…he didn't tell me something he should have," I said, deciding that was true enough.

"About what?"

"Um…you know. Stuff." I shrugged. *Way to be literate, Paige.*

My mom pursed her lips, pulling them to one side of her face as she studied me.

"Does it have something to do with things he's done in the past, maybe? Perhaps other girls?" she asked, arching a sculpted eyebrow, and I groaned.

*Oh, great. Now Mom thinks this is about sex, and I don't even know if we're physically compatible.* Aiden had wings. Who knew what other differences existed between us?

I shuddered at the thought of the surprises that could be

hiding down below, and my mom nodded sagely, thinking I'd just confirmed her suspicions.

"It's not what you think," I mumbled, holding up my mug and trying to hide behind it, feeling my face flush.

"Have you talked to him about why you're upset?" she asked, and I shook my head.

"No. I just—" left him standing there, injured and bleeding, as I ran away "—needed time alone."

"Well, maybe you should call him tomorrow," my mom continued.

"You know, Dad would probably like nothing more if I never spoke to him again. Why are you taking Logan's side?" I asked, studying my mom curiously.

"I'm taking *your* side, Paige," my mom corrected me, reaching for one of the butter cookies that sat on a plate on the coffee table. Instead of biting it, she simply studied it, running her finger along the sugar crystals baked into the top.

"I know you've had a hard time of it ever since the accident," Mom said, her dark eyebrows pulling together. "The past three years haven't been easy. We did what we thought we should do to support you, but nothing seemed to help you get over what happened. You're always so careful of what you say around us. So guarded."

I bit the inside of my cheek as my mom spoke. And here I thought my parents believed my little normal act.

"We try not to force you into things, to let you talk to us in your own time, and you're still so cautious. But you're not like that around Logan. He's given you back something—this little light. I don't know if it's that you feel like you can be yourself around him or what, but I'd hate to see you lose that. So that's why I say I'm on *your* side, because I do think he's been good for you. But if you feel like your trust was permanently broken, well, that's another story. Just think things over before you make any final decisions."

My mom punctuated her statement by biting into the cookie and brushing the crumbs off her fingertips.

I thought about what my mom said as I stared at the glow-in-the-dark stars on my ceiling, lying in my bed fully dressed in jeans and a top. Guilt washed over me as I thought about how I fled from Logan—as he was injured, pleading with me to listen. Well, I may have run away then, but I wouldn't walk away from us now. Not without giving him a chance to explain.

Of course, tonight was the night my mom decided to stay up late watching a movie, so it was nearly one before I could sneak out of the apartment. I didn't know if Logan would be on the roof as usual, but I hoped he was. I wanted to know that he was okay. I had to hear his side—and he deserved to tell it. And as angry and hurt as I was by his lying, I finally admitted to myself the real reason I was going to meet him. The words had burst into my head before, but I knew it was true: I loved him. I couldn't help it. I loved Logan, and I had to find out if he was really the person I fell in love with, or just a carefully crafted facade.

# 13

AS I CLIMBED THE STAIRS, MY BRAIN SPIRALED with fake but elaborately detailed conversations. Maybe Logan would turn into a demon, spewing hateful, hurtful words at me about how it was all an act to win my trust. Or maybe Logan would explain that he'd killed so many Regents, he'd taken on their blood as well as their powers—but he was still definitely a human.

I was really rooting for that scenario to be real.

And then I remembered something Logan had said, right after he was injured. He'd held me close, begging me to let him have this moment.

At the time, those words had been like an icy injection in my chest. My heart had dropped, and I'd started to panic, thinking that he'd been mortally wounded, holding me for one final embrace.

Instead, now I knew what he really wanted was one final moment with me—with us—before I left him. The out he'd offered me in that letter hadn't been for my benefit. It had been for his, to protect his heart when I turned him away.

Logan had known I'd run from him the moment I discovered what he was. And that's exactly what I'd done.

So I wasn't really surprised when I pushed open the rooftop door and found that I was alone. It was just me. Me and the memories of where we'd practiced fighting with swords. Me and the ghosts of the kisses we'd shared, cuddled up on the picnic table.

I wrapped my arms around my waist as I walked as near as I dared to the low wall that edged the rooftop, watching how midtown's lights illuminated the low, heavy clouds, making them seem almost bright against the dark sky. The night was crisp but not cold, not that chilly temperatures bothered me these days. It had been a frosty night two weeks ago, and Logan had used the weather as an excuse to wrap his arms around me from behind. We'd stood there, not kissing, not talking…just being. I slumped against the picnic table, rubbing my face with my hands.

It couldn't have been an act. If he wanted to hurt me, he'd had countless opportunities. It was real. It had to have been real.

"You're here."

His voice startled me, and I stood up straight, my head whipping to the side to see Logan standing in the doorway. Taking measured, slow steps, Logan began walking across the rooftop, keeping his eyes on me. He was dressed comfortably, in a dark gray T-shirt, black hoodie and dark jeans. He looked cozy—like he was well suited for travel. Especially with the big duffel bag slung over his shoulder.

My mouth went dry, and my heart lurched at the sight.

I'd expected us to fight. I'd thought we would argue. But I never imagined he'd just leave.

"This is goodbye," I said, my voice a harsh whisper.

"You're telling me to leave?" Logan asked. I blinked in surprise at the expression on his face. He actually looked hurt.

"Aren't you already?" I flicked a finger toward his bag. He dropped it off his shoulder, taking swift but cautious steps, closing the gap between us quickly.

"Paige, I've got a sleeping bag in there. I was planning on staying up here all weekend in case you came up to speak to me."

I slumped against the table again, this time in relief. He wasn't leaving. My bruised heart was momentarily soothed by the idea—and it kind of pissed me off.

"That's not fair!" I cried, frustrated, and he took a step back, standing about four feet in front of me.

"Not fair?" Logan repeated, looking confused.

"No, it's not fair that you can make these big, wonderful, romantic gestures straight out of a movie—but can't tell me the truth. You've been lying to me since the moment I met you."

"Technically, I wasn't really lying," Logan said defensively. "If anything, it was a lie of omission."

I rolled my eyes. "It's right in the title, Logan. It's a lie of omission," I said, crossing my arms. "It's not called a truth of omission. If it wasn't a lie they would have called it something else, like…the poodle of omission."

A brilliant—but brief—smile flashed across Logan's face.

"Only you can make me laugh when you're in the middle of telling me how much you hate me," he said ruefully as he raked his hands through his hair, his ever-present baseball cap missing.

"I don't hate you," I told him, and Logan's eyes brightened—until I continued. "But I hate that you lied to me. I hate how hurt and betrayed I feel right now."

I felt tears start to prick my eyes, and I pressed the heels of my hands into my eyes, willing the traitorous tears to stay back.

"You were the one part of my life that wasn't a lie. The best part," I admitted, keeping my hands over my face as I spoke. I felt his fingertips circle my wrists and gently tug as he spoke, his voice soft and pleading.

"Don't hide. Look at me. Please."

I let Logan pull my hands from my face, and he quickly dropped his hold on my wrists. He stepped back a few feet, giving me space, but he kept his eyes locked on mine.

"Paige. Talk to me."

"What do you want me to say? I practically had a script written of what I wanted to say to you. But now…" My voice trailed off weakly as I ran my hands through my hair, gripping fistfuls of it at the scalp.

"Just tell me what you're feeling."

"I'm feeling like you should have told me the truth!" I cried, throwing my hands in the air before letting them drop, bringing my shoulders drooping, as well. "And honestly, I feel like everything you said or did must have been a lie."

Logan swiftly crossed the distance between us, cupping my jaw in his hands and gently tilting my face up so my eyes met his.

"Paige, I swear to you on my parents, I have never once lied to you about how I feel about you," he said gravely.

"Then why didn't you tell me the truth?"

"I could give you a whole speech about who I am, and how it was for your own protection that I didn't, but honestly, that would just be an excuse. The truth is, I was a selfish coward. I didn't want to lose you."

He brushed his knuckles along my cheek as he spoke, his eyes staring intently into mine.

"You know what, that's not entirely accurate. It's not that I didn't want to lose you. It's that I can't lose you," he confessed, his eyes glistening with unshed tears. "I don't know how I can go back to a life without you in it. I don't want to be without you."

He squeezed his eyes shut and dropped his hands from my face, stuffing his fists into his back pockets.

"Funny how that worked out, huh?" Logan asked bitterly. "I lost you anyway."

"Why did you lie to me and say you were a half-warlock?"

"I am a half-warlock," Logan maintained, somewhat indignantly. "I just happen to be half-demon, as well."

"And you don't think I deserved to know that we're a different species?" I hissed, gesturing between us with my hand. "I mean, how do I know we're even compatible in that way?"

Logan arched an eyebrow at me, and I blushed. Of all the things to bring up right now, this was what came shooting out of my mouth. *Way to go, Paige. You're as discreet as a dump truck.*

"Paige, how do you think I even got here? Warlock dad, demon mom. Trust me, we're compatible. In, um, that way," he added, his pink cheeks matching mine as he rubbed the back of his neck.

"Oh." I stared at my sneakers, focusing on the same broken lace that I'd never bothered to fix.

"I'll tell you what happened to them, if you want."

My head jerked up, and the pleading expression on his face shocked me.

"You actually want to tell me about your parents?"

"I've always wanted to tell you. You're the one person I want to talk to about everything. But I didn't know how to bring it up without scaring you away with who I really am," he admitted, his eyes downcast. "But I guess it doesn't matter now, since I've lost you anyway."

"Not yet," I whispered, and Logan's eyes snapped up to meet mine.

"No?" he breathed, his eyes shining.

"We need to talk, but…I don't think so. No."

The words had barely left my mouth before Logan had me wrapped in his arms—and my hands snaked around him, squeezing him back.

"We still need to talk," I reminded him, my voice muffled by how smushed I was against Logan's chest.

"About anything you want," he promised, but he kept me snugly in his embrace. Finally, I pushed away from him—I needed answers before he started kissing me, since Logan's lips were a proven distraction technique.

He walked over to where he'd dropped his bulky bag, rooting around in it for a thickly folded plastic blue square.

"I figure we might as well get comfortable. This could take a while," Logan said, shaking out the square to reveal a waterproof tarp. I helped him spread it out on the roof, and he pulled out a black sleeping bag, unzipping it so we could sit on it like a blanket.

"This is cozy," I said, patting the thick nylon quilting of the sleeping bag as I sat on it, cross-legged.

"I was going to call you and tell you I'd be up here all weekend, and every day after school, whenever you wanted to talk," Logan explained, reaching in the bag and pulling out two bottles of water. "I figured I'd be spending a lot of time up here."

Logan unscrewed the cap on a bottle of water before replacing it and handing it to me. I stared at the water bottle, momentarily derailed by the gesture. It was one of a thousand little things he'd do to show he cared—opening my drinks so I wouldn't have to struggle with the stubborn plastic cap. Indulging me in my chocolate obsession. All little tokens of affection that made me feel cherished.

And I knew that no matter what he was about to tell me, I could believe him. I should believe him. Logan's feelings were truly genuine.

"So, you know how warlocks and demons are at war for control of the Dark World," Logan began, resting his elbows on his knees as he sat cross-legged in front of me.

"Ever since the warlocks lost control centuries ago, they've been fighting to get back on the throne," he explained. "They've had hundreds of years of rebellions. Think constant, brutal fighting—whole villages destroyed, families massacred—and it never accomplished anything. The warlocks never took the throne from the royal Regents."

"That's what you are, right? Your blood is the same color

as Aiden's. You're a Regent?" I asked, tracing the stitching on the sleeping bag with my fingernail.

"Half-Regent," he corrected. "Anyway, the Regents were powerful, wealthy and smart. A Regent's biggest physical asset is that they—um, we," he said, giving me a self-conscious smile, "are able to absorb and wield most demon powers. Like, if a fire demon tries to burn us alive, we just absorb the flames, and use them on someone else later. It makes us really hard to kill."

"So, what can kill you?"

Logan arched an eyebrow. "You looking for ideas?"

"Yeah, me and my army of sparkly pink pens are coming for you. Oh, no, look out," I added dryly, waving my hands in the air.

"Oh, those are definitely lethal," Logan said soberly, his eyes wide and sincere before crinkling up in a smile. "But it takes a warlock or another Regent to kill a Regent. I'm not as impervious to injury, since I'm only half-Regent. But it still takes a really strong demon to take me down. And I can't absorb every power. I can't incinerate someone from the inside like Blaise can, for example. But I wouldn't want to, either." Logan scowled as he repeated her name.

"But apart from having the coolest demon power," Logan added with a smile, "the Regents are smart, calculating politicians. About twenty years ago, they called for a summit meeting in the Dark City with the heads of the warlocks, saying they wanted to end the rebellions, end the bloodshed."

"What's the Dark City?" I asked.

"It's the other side's version of New York City," Logan explained, waving his hand toward the midtown skyscrapers that surrounded us. "It's essentially the capital of the demon world. Every demon race is represented with their own zone, which is really just a neighborhood, and whoever sits on the throne there rules the world."

"Really?" I asked, surprised. "One demon, in charge of an entire world, just because they sit on the throne in some city?"

Logan snorted. "Have you met a New Yorker who doesn't think the world begins and ends with this city?"

"Very funny." I gave him a withering look, before adding, "And for the record, it does."

Logan grinned, spreading his palms as if to say, "See?"

"Anyway," he continued, "centuries of rebellions had decimated numbers on both sides. Most demons aren't fighters, you know. They just want to live their little demon lives."

"What, with a house, two kids and a dog that can eat your face off?" I asked sarcastically—before realizing that this was Logan's family I was mocking. Fortunately, he chuckled at my comment.

"Something like that. Although demon dogs are actually quite well-mannered," he added thoughtfully. "They don't eat your face off unless commanded to do so."

I gawked at him, and he shrugged.

"You brought it up," he said, rubbing his slightly stubbly jaw, and I vowed to keep my own jaw clamped shut until he was done talking. "Anyway, the summit proposed the establishment of a council, made up of warlocks and Regents, to handle all disagreements, grievances, dole out punishments, set up laws…. You get the idea," he explained, and I nodded. "Rego was on this council, obviously."

Logan got more agitated as he spoke, coiling the white

string of his hoodie around his finger. I reached out my hand to steady his, where his skin was starting to turn bright red from the cord being wrapped too tightly.

Logan clutched my hand in his, threading our fingers together as he brought our joined hands to rest on his knee.

"The other warlock in charge was Rego's best friend, Maxim Rex," he said. "He and Rego were the new leaders of the warlocks—the smartest, most effective leaders they'd had in centuries. Maxim Rex was brilliant. Fast. Lethal. And he was the logical choice to rule the Dark World—way more than Rego." He paused. "Maxim Rex was my dad."

I noticed he said *was,* but I remained silent, simply holding his hand and letting Logan continue his story.

"Rego and my dad believed that warlocks belonged in power—that this council wouldn't solve anything but keep the warlocks from asserting their rightful place on the throne. So the plan was to get close to key members of the council, gain their trust, learn their secrets—and then slaughter them.

"It didn't go as planned," Logan said with a sly smile.

I gave him a questioning look, and he continued, a faint blush coloring his cheeks.

"My dad was apparently renowned for his—how can I say this?—other skills." Logan coughed nervously. "He had quite a reputation, if you know what I mean."

"Since he's your dad, I guess we'll go with the term *heartbreaker?*" I suggested, and Logan exhaled, relieved.

"Yeah, that works," he agreed, giving me a grateful smile. "I can't think of my dad as a player. I mean, the man wore turtlenecks."

We both laughed, although Logan's was more a nervous chuckle. "Anyway, my dad's assignment was to woo the daughter of the Regent king. See what secrets he could wheedle out of her, and then kill her when she wasn't useful anymore."

Some memory tugged at the corner of Logan's lips—a memory that was in stark contrast to the brutal story he was telling—because an adoring smile spread across his face.

"What happened?" I prodded him.

"What do you think happened?" Logan asked, sadness coloring his sentimental smile. "They fell in love. The demon princess and the warlock tasked with killing her. Also known as Mom and Dad."

Logan's eyes darted to mine, studying me for my reaction. Even though I'd assumed this was where the story was headed, it was still a shock to hear my boyfriend's supernaturally scandalous parentage confirmed.

"That's why my blood is that color. All Regents are some shade of purple, but only members of the royal line bleed that deep purple color," Logan continued when I didn't freak out.

I did my best to keep my face calm, even as I realized this meant Aiden was somehow related to him, and squeezed his hand to prompt him to continue with his story,

"As you can probably guess, their relationship didn't go over well." Logan frowned, his eyebrows pulling together as he ran over the next part of the story in his head. "Obviously my father wasn't planning on killing her anymore— especially after they found out that I was on the way. But my parents were young and stupid and idealistic. They thought I was proof that we could coexist peacefully."

Logan picked up my hand from where it rested on his knee, clasping it between both of his as he gritted his teeth.

"Yeah, right. Coexist peacefully, my ass. The news that I was on my way wasn't exactly cause for celebration. The warlocks considered the infallible Maxim Rex to be a traitor. And of course, once the Regents discovered the plot to kill the council, they wanted to slaughter all the warlocks. So, my parents escaped. They abandoned everything, disguising themselves as regular humans to raise me here."

Logan spread one hand around him, indicating our world.

"They left it all behind?"

"For me." His voice was hollow as he spoke, guilt coloring his face.

"Logan, that's what good parents do. They sacrifice for their kids," I said, clutching his hands tightly. "They wanted to save you. They didn't want you to be a part of that war."

"No, they didn't." Logan pressed his lips together in a line. "But after Regents took my parents, I didn't have much of a choice."

We were both sitting cross-legged. I scooted closer to him so our knees were touching, and reached out, resting my palm gently against his warm cheek. He shut his eyes and leaned into my touch, folding his hand over mine before bringing our clasped hands between us again.

"Rego had kept in contact with my parents. He didn't agree with my dad's decisions, but he said he respected them. Maxim Rex—well, actually, at this point, he just went by Max, because it sounded more 'human,'" Logan explained, emphasizing the word. "Anyway, Max taught Rego how to set up places like the apartment I live in now—areas that straddle both worlds. My parents wanted to keep tabs on what was happening in the Dark World—my mom especially worried about her family—so Rego would report back to my parents with any news from the other side.

"Nine years ago, there was a huge warlock rebellion on the other side. It was brutal." Logan emphasized the word, letting out a low whistle. "The armies of both sides were nearly destroyed. The Regents won, but only barely. So, the warlocks were ready to reconsider the idea of a ruling council."

Logan kept his eyes on our clasped hands, linking and unlinking our fingers, seeming to memorize the way they fit together as they rested between us. He inhaled deeply, steadying his breathing, and I knew whatever event separated him from his parents was coming.

"It was right after my eighth birthday. I don't really remember a lot about being a little kid, but I remember that my parents threw me this big, elaborate party. It was like they knew it would be the last one. My mom sat me down and explained that she had to leave for a few months, that her family needed her. I threw such a fit," Logan recalled with a short, bitter laugh. "I was a spoiled brat. My mom and dad had gotten me this radio-controlled car for my birthday, and they'd promised to take me out to play with it. I was so pissed that she wouldn't be around to do it. Like I said, brat."

"All kids are brats," I said, squeezing his hand, and Logan gave me a grateful look.

"I was too little to understand what they were telling me. My mom and dad really wanted peace in their world," he continued, his voice reverential as he spoke of them. "With no peace in that world, we'd have none in this one. Mom was a member of the royal family in charge, and she obviously had credibility for wanting an alliance between the warlocks and demons. So it made sense that she return to the Dark World to reassume her role with the royal family, and Rego came to stay with my dad and me, as added protection, since some Regents still wanted all warlocks to die, and vice versa."

Logan abruptly dropped my hands, folding one arm over his chest and bringing his other palm to cover his face. He rubbed his eyes, and when he finally met my gaze again, his brown eyes were bloodshot and bleary.

"I didn't even smell the smoke," he whispered, his eyes resting on me but unfocused. "Rego shook me from my bed. I was coughing. My eyes stung, and I couldn't breathe. He said we had to leave. Someone had given me this little back-pack for my birthday. They told me never leave home with-out it—I think it had some kind of little kid tracking device on it. Anyway, I grabbed it and started throwing stuff in it. Mostly toys I had gotten for my birthday. A framed picture. The remote-controlled car. I was still grabbing stuff when Rego just picked me up and ran out of the house with me."

We were sitting on a rooftop in the middle of Manhattan, but all I could hear was Logan's uneven breathing as he told his story, the sounds of traffic and people chattering six stories below blending into a low, dull, insignificant buzz.

"I didn't know what was happening. I was screaming for my parents. I finally passed out from exhaustion and stress. We had lived in Connecticut, and the next thing I remember was waking up in a hotel room in Pennsylvania. Rego told me what he'd learned—the Regents ruled that my mother was a traitor to her kind. They took her as their prisoner. Her own family." Logan angrily dashed away the few tears that had leaked onto his cheeks with his knuckles, his movement so aggressive I was afraid he'd bruise his skin. "That night, the fire was supposed to kill me, the unholy, unnatural spawn." He spat the words out, his voice shaking with rage.

"Instead, it killed my father. Of course, there were rumors that he got out, was in hiding—because it's not enough for the Regents to kill my father, they have to destroy his integrity after he's dead."

Logan stopped speaking after that last comment, but he was anything but quiet. His breathing was ragged, rough with emotion, and my hands twisted in my lap, desperate to comfort him in some way. I'd known whatever happened to his parents had to be bad—but I had no idea it was this heartbreakingly brutal.

I hesitantly reached my hand out to him, and placed it over his heart, which beat rapidly under my palm. Logan covered my hand with his, but held it there, and when his breathing steadied, he continued speaking.

"Rego isn't my father. He isn't nurturing and he sure isn't the kind of guy who read me bedtime stories or bandaged my skinned knees. When I turned eight, I wanted that remote-control car. But by the time I turned nine, the only thing I wanted was revenge. And Rego helped me with that."

Logan was stone-faced as he spoke, his slightly damp cheeks the only evidence of his earlier emotion. He even dropped his hold on my hand, and I let my palm drop from his heart, my hand casually resting against his leg instead.

"How did he help you?"

"Rego started teaching me stuff immediately. We were

on the run. Someone had just tried to kill us. I had to learn how to defend myself," Logan explained with a matter-of-fact shrug. "I helped him, too. My particular genetic makeup made me very valuable for certain spells that the warlocks could use against the Regents. Whatever Rego wanted from me, he could have."

Logan reached behind his shoulder and slowly pulled out his sword, resting it flat across his knees.

"Like I said, Regents are hard to kill. Regular warlock-forged steel can injure, sure, but you need a powerful weapon to conquer such a powerful creature. Something created with a part of the monster you're trying to destroy."

Logan ran the tip of his finger down the smooth amethyst blade.

"Every warlock who uses one of Rego's weapons has something made with my blood," Logan revealed.

"Wait," I snapped, reaching out and grabbing his wrist, causing Logan's eyes to pop open in surprise.

"What?" he asked.

"So a few weeks ago, when you disappeared and said you were helping Rego make weapons, you were tired because he had been bleeding you?" My voice rose in pitch as I spoke, and Logan gingerly grabbed my hand, removing it from his wrist.

"Um, you're about to draw blood with your nails. Ow, Paige," he said, and I jerked my wrist back, holding my hands up.

"I'm so sorry!" I yelped, and Logan merely laughed as he put his sword away.

"It's nice to see that you still get angry when you feel like

I've been wronged," he remarked, rubbing his wrist. "Even if I'm on the wrong end of your temper."

"I said I was sorry! It's just the thought of you as a little kid—and now—bleeding to make weapons..." I slammed my eyes shut, shuddering.

"It's okay," Logan said, putting his hands on my shoulders and giving me a little squeeze. "Look, I wanted to help in any way I could. Back then, it was with weapons. My blood made Rego's weapons lethal. And Regent blood added the nice little perk of stealing the demon's powers when you kill them."

"So that's why I absorbed Blaise's fire power," I realized. "Your blood."

"Yeah, it, um..." Logan paused, suddenly looking very uncomfortable. "It also makes me aware of the presence of any sword," he added rapidly, the words running together.

I stared at him suspiciously as he ducked his head.

"Can you repeat that, please? And why do you look guilty?"

"If I focus hard enough, I can pinpoint your location—because you've always got the sword." He flinched, anticipating my response.

As I realized the implications of what he was saying, my jaw dropped in horror, and Logan quickly put his hands up in defense.

"Before you get mad, you have to understand that it's an involuntary thing. It's not like I asked for them to be homing devices. But the more blood used to make the sword, the more powerful the sword is...and the easier it is for me to find it. I wanted your sword to be really powerful, in case you ever needed to use it. Technically, you could argue that what I did was kind of a nice thing." He gave me an angelic smile, and I just glared at him in response.

"Yeah, it's really nice that I'm essentially microchipped like a prized schnauzer."

"It's not like that, I swear," Logan insisted. "I understand why you're pissed. It's why I'm telling you now even though I knew you'd be mad. But it helped me find you when Aiden and Della had you. And I promise you, it's not like there's a blinking tracking light above your head or anything."

"Still, I should have known," I maintained, indignant, and Logan nodded, giving me a sheepish look.

"Are you sufficiently creeped out and pissed off yet?"

"You know what? I am all pissed off," I said, narrowing my eyes at him.

"Sorry," he mouthed, and I sighed heavily. *At least he's telling you everything now. And if it weren't for that sword, you'd be hanging out in a demon dungeon somewhere.*

"I'm sure Dottie would love it if you ranted to her, all pissed off about me. Now that she knows what I am, she's not my biggest fan." His eyes looked up as he shook his head, and I wondered what Dottie had said to him after I left. "I can only imagine what she's going to say to you about me," he muttered.

"Um, hello? You can see and hear her. Anything she says about you, you're probably going to know about it."

I paused as I considered that statement. Logan could see and hear my best friend and Travis—but all the other demons seemed to chase them away.

"How come you can see her and Travis, anyway? You're a demon."

"Half-demon," he replied automatically.

"Yeah, but still, why don't you chase her and Travis away like Blaise and Aiden do?"

"Are you asking me to? Because I'd love to tell Travis to take a hike sometimes," Logan said with a snarky grin, relishing the change in subject, and I poked him gently in the leg.

"They're trapped over there because a demon caused their lives to end prematurely. When a demon's in the area, it sends them back to where they belong, so to speak."

"But you're a demon."

"Half-demon," he stressed, sounding exasperated. "I'm only half. I can see them because I have ties to that world, was conceived on that side—but I was born on *this* side. My energy is strictly Light World, baby."

I studied Logan's face as he grinned rakishly at me. His energy was anything but dark, especially when that boyish grin made his eyes sparkle like that, underneath his disheveled mess of brown hair.

He was nothing like Blaise or Aiden…Blaise with her glittering eyes and inhuman teeth, and Aiden with those huge wings and gray claws. Aiden, who was a relative. I inhaled sharply, studying Logan's face for an indication that he was anything other than what he professed to be.

"What are you thinking?" he asked warily as I spun my bracelet on my wrist. "You look…well, you look terrified right now, and your bracelet is going to start smoking, you're spinning it so fast."

Logan reached his hand out and pressed his palm on top of my wrist, effectively stopping my nervous tick.

"What do you really look like?" I asked in a whisper.

He was silent for a moment.

"Do you want me to show you?" His reply was just as quiet.

I nodded, and Logan pushed himself off the sleeping bag, unzipping his hoodie as he stood. He shrugged out of it, and then pulled at the hem of his shirt.

"What are you doing?" I asked, scrambling to my feet and covering my eyes with my hands. "I meant your demon form. Not, um, what I mentioned earlier. The whole human and half-demon compatibility thing, I mean. Oh, please don't take your pants off, I am so not ready for that conversation tonight."

"Paige," Logan called with a soft chuckle, and I peered out at his body from between my fingers. He was wearing his dark jeans—and a very self-indulgent grin.

"I should have explained. I have wings. I didn't want to rip my clothes."

"Wings?" I squeaked. *Forget that, take your pants off instead.*

"Yeah, wings."

"Like Aiden?" I asked, my voice hoarse.

"I'm nothing like him," Logan vowed, his body tensing as he gripped his shirt tightly in his fist.

"Okay. Do it," I ordered weakly as I kept my eyes on the ground.

A hushed fluttering sound drew my attention, and I looked up. Logan stood before me, his hands clenched into fists at his side, broad shoulders lifting slightly with his measured, steady breathing. While shirtless Logan was a very nice sight, it wasn't what made me lose my breath: it was the black wings beating softly behind him, slowly enough that they made a faint sound but not quickly enough to take flight.

Logan's eyes—which had been closed—opened when he heard me gasp, and they anxiously searched my face for my reaction.

I took a step closer, studying his eyes—the irises were now a crystal-clear violet, ringed with his familiar brown. But where Aiden's were cold and frosty, Logan's eyes held the same warmth I'd always found there.

I rested my hand against his heart again, feeling it beat rapidly in his broad chest. Aiden's skin had turned gray and corpselike, but Logan's skin remained the same pale, peachy tone. His muscles were slightly more defined—the cut of his stomach a little sharper, his biceps more rounded—but not in an inhuman, exaggerated way. My hand slid to his shoulder, curving over the sculpted muscle as I slowly walked around to his back, to study the wings that he brought to a stop.

I trailed one finger along the edge of his wing, feeling the smooth black bone beneath my skin, and Logan shivered.

"Does that hurt?" I asked, my hand stilling.

Logan shook his head, turning his face to the side to watch me over his shoulder as I stroked his wing, the smooth, glass-like texture contradicting its unfathomable strength.

I let my fingers travel down, to the diaphanous black wing that felt like delicate silk, stretched tightly between the bones. I crossed behind Logan as I continued my exploration, letting my hand gently press against the center of his wings, at the swirled knot of black bone between his shoulder blades.

*You're standing behind your boyfriend, exploring his wings.*

*His wings.*

*Your boyfriend has wings.*

My fingertips shook slightly, and I willed them to stop,

trying to reconcile the Logan I knew with the one standing bare before me. Logan was otherworldly, in the literal sense of the word. But he also was a pizza snob who lived in hoodies and baseball caps.

*You're either all in, or you're out, Paige. When you face him again, you need to let him know one way or another. He deserves that.*

I pressed my hand on his back—home, human territory— and caressed the expanse of smooth, unblemished skin that, hours before, had been painfully injured. Logan's agonized face, struggling with pain as he held me close, protecting me, flashed before my eyes, and I laid my palm against his shoulder, thankful that he was healed.

I took my final steps as I finished circling his body, coming to face him again.

Silently, we stood before each other, my eyes searching his and seeing nothing but love—and fear. Logan was standing naked before me, after all, in more ways than one.

"Thank you," I whispered, and Logan merely nodded his head in acknowledgment, his dark eyebrows pulling together with some unspoken question.

"Do you hate me like this?" he finally asked, his voice rough.

I shook my head, clasping my hands around his neck as I rested my head against his chest. I was all in. I wanted to heal what was there, now more than ever. Now that I knew the real him.

"All of you is beautiful. But especially your heart," I murmured, planting a soft kiss where it beat in his chest. They were words I would normally laugh at, or repeat in a mocking tone, making fun of anyone who would say something so cheesy and trite. But I couldn't help it; the words were true—all of Logan was beautiful. And he did have a beautiful heart.

As soon as my lips touched his skin, Logan's arms circled around me, and we both relaxed more deeply into each other.

"It's yours, you know." His voice sounded deep and low in his chest, rumbling against my cheek, and my pulse sped at his admission.

"I hoped so," I confessed as I snuggled into his embrace. They were the same, familiar arms, but at the same time, they felt different. They felt stronger.

"Hoped so?" Logan repeated, and he tilted my chin up with two fingers, urging me to meet his eyes. "Paige, you have to know by now that I love you." His eyes were brimming with emotion, a shy smile on his face as he brushed a lock of hair back behind my ear. "I started falling for you the first time I heard you speak, and I don't think I'll ever stop falling in love with you."

My heart, which had been keeping a speedy rhythm along with his, might have stopped at that statement. That wonderful, perfect statement, spoken in a voice that managed to be confident and tender at the same time, promising me his past, present and future all at once.

"When everyone else says I love you, they make it sound like a punch line. You make it sound like a promise," I said as Logan moved his hands down to my back, softly rubbing in circles.

"It is."

"It is for me, too," I said. Logan's hands stilled on my back, and I lifted my eyes to meet his.

"Really?" he asked, the beginnings of the brilliant smile on his face.

I stretched up on my toes to kiss him, but Logan met me halfway. He leaned down to press his lips against mine, the words he'd just spoken repeated in breathy tones amid gentle touches.

"Can I ask you one more thing?" I asked after we'd broken apart, punctuating my question with another, albeit brief, kiss—which earned a chuckle.

"When you ask if you can ask a question, I know to brace myself. Those ones are the worst," Logan reminded me, and I snorted.

"Well, can I ask it or what?"

"Can I put my shirt back on and, uh, my wings away?" Logan bargained, and I pretended to think it over.

"Deal," I said, keeping my eyes on him as I walked backward toward the sleeping bag. His wings fluttered lightly, appearing to shrink behind his back, where they disappeared into nothingness. He pulled on his shirt and joined me on the sleeping bag moments later, only this time Logan stretched out on his side, his head propped up by his hand. I mirrored his position as our hands intertwined between us.

"So, your question?" he asked.

Ah, yes. The one I'd wanted to ask for weeks.

"What's supposed to happen now? With us, I mean?" I braced myself for Logan to tell me how he'd eventually leave, but instead, he started laughing.

"Are we having The Talk?" Logan emphasized the words, grinning at me playfully. "Oh, no, it's the infamous Talk!"

"Don't make fun, we were supposed to have The Talk

weeks ago." I swatted at him, and he caught my hand, giving my fist a kiss before setting it back down.

"Well, what do you want to happen?" he asked me. "I don't think what's *supposed* to happen really applies to us."

"It's selfish, but…I don't want you to leave." *Sorry, everyone Logan would have saved from demons. I wanted him to stay with me, so sucks to be you.*

"Why is that selfish?" he asked, bewildered.

"Well, Aiden's not going to be a threat forever, so I know your time here has to come to an end at some point." I frowned. "And besides, I can't ask you to make that sacrifice."

"It's not a sacrifice if I want to do it."

"You just told me about how you've wanted nothing but revenge since you were nine," I reminded him. "I don't know what the protocol is here, but I'm pretty sure you shouldn't give up your lifelong mission for vengeance because your girlfriend is being extraclingy."

Logan ran his thumb over my hand before rolling onto his back, tugging me with him.

"Come here." He caught me as I fell onto his chest, his right arm curling around my waist, keeping me snug against his side.

"You were too far away. This is better," he said matter-of-factly, cushioning his head with his other arm. We lay like that for a moment until he spoke again.

"What if I've already talked to Rego about this?" he asked quietly, and my head popped up to stare at him. His face was a perfectly composed, serene mask.

"I'm leaving him. Them. All of it. They can fight their own war. I'm done."

"But—I thought you were—I thought revenge was what you wanted," I stammered, shocked. "Your mom, she's a prisoner."

Logan blinked his eyes slowly, exhaling a long breath.

"Paige, both of my parents are dead."

He sounded so defeated as he said those words, and I wrapped my arms around Logan as far as they would go.

"I'm sorry," was all I could say.

"I was about fifteen, and I was just exhausted. I was burned out—my life was nothing but kill, move on, kill, move on," he said, his fingers idly running down my back as I rested my chin on his chest, facing him as he spoke. It would have been a sweet embrace, if not for the gruesome conversation topic.

"We'd just moved to some new place, again, and I found this photo of me and my parents that I hadn't even remembered in that old backpack. It was from my last birthday party. They really played up the part of human parents, you know? We looked normal. And I'd looked so happy with them, holding up that stupid toy car. I started to remember things—things I'd suppressed under a fog of revenge. I remembered how much they didn't want me to be a part of this life, and here I was, some kid slaughtering demons. I was tired of being a killing machine and never hearing anything about how it was helping get my mom back.

"So I went to Rego and proposed we make a deal for my mom. I had a pretty fearsome reputation at that point. After all, I was the big bad *proditori,* right? The Regents couldn't have been happy that I was running around, some nameless, faceless killer, infiltrating hives of demons and assassinating them all. I suggested that if they returned my mom, they could strip me of my powers."

Seeing my confused face, Logan explained, "There's a spell that can strip warlocks and demons of their powers. It's painful on the part of the spellcaster and the subject of the spell. And apart from the loss of magic, it would make me physically weaker than your average human. But," Logan said with a wistful smile, "it would have been worth it to free my mom. I figured we could live as humans somewhere on this side, start a new life. Good plan, right? I mean, it's not like my mother had been some terrifying warrior to begin with—she was just sitting in their dungeon. What did they have to lose?

"Rego finally got word that she'd been killed months earlier—a public execution to caution demons against associating with warlocks," he revealed, his hand stilling on my back, clutching the fabric of my shirt in his fist. "I thought I wanted revenge before, but after that, it was all I lived for. I had nothing and I hated everyone. I hated Rego, for not being my father. I hated myself, for being the very thing I hated. I hated my mom, for being idealistic and going back to help, for picking the greater good over me. And then I hated myself all over again, because I was mad at my mom when she was dead. I begged Rego for assignments, so I could kill as many demons as possible. But it didn't dull the pain."

Logan sounded lost, his voice taking on a desperate tone. "After a while, I just felt hollow—like a shell that was filled with nothing but death and rage. No wonder this isn't the life my parents wanted for me. Hell, this isn't the life I wanted for me," he said, his palm rubbing against his stubbly jaw again.

"Nothing I do will bring my parents back. What do I think

I'm doing? Avenging them? I'm disgracing them. They didn't want this for me. Spending my life fighting, killing, seeking revenge—this doesn't honor them. It's the worst thing I can do to their memory.

"But this," Logan said, taking my hands in his, "this is living. This is what I want."

I looked down at our joined hands, at the way they fit together perfectly.

"Are you sure?" I whispered, trying to keep the hope out of my voice.

"I'd finally have a life worth living," he said, squeezing my hands for emphasis. "I could stay in school, figure out what I want to do with my life. I like English class, so maybe I could be a writer. Replace the sword with a pen, see which one really is mightier," he added with a wink.

"I think both are pretty potent in your hands," I muttered, remembering his letter, and Logan smiled modestly in reply.

"I could actually take you on a date," he said wistfully. "Besides, someone's gotta protect you."

He'd bared his soul and more tonight. He'd told me he loved me. And that should have been enough to kill the toxic voices that had started questioning the prospect of Logan staying here. For good.

*He's only staying to protect you. He's making all the sacrifices. He's going to get tired of you and resent you.*

"Don't do this just for me," I mumbled, giving voice to my insecurities. "What if we don't work out?"

"Yeah, we're going to break up because you didn't text me back quickly enough," he said sarcastically, squeezing my side. "You know, it would be nice if you had a little more faith in us. Life-altering relationships don't come around all that often."

Logan pulled me closer, his lips just inches from mine. "This is my decision, and you're the one overthinking it. Your initial reaction was happiness. Go with that."

My head and heart warred—with my heart screaming to let Logan leave it all behind and stay with me while my head whispered that he'd resent me later. But when I closed the distance between us, kissing him fiercely, I realized that logic never stood a chance against my heart.

# 14

"YOU TALK IN YOUR SLEEP."

Familiar arms wound around me as I stood in front of the bookshelves in the school library on Wednesday.

I narrowed my eyes and whirled around to see Logan standing there with a playful grin. Ever since I fell asleep in his arms last Friday night, he'd been telling me that I called his name in my sleep. And walked in my sleep. And did a strip tease in my sleep.

Fall asleep for five minutes, give the boy *hours* of entertainment.

"Logan! Oh, Logan! You're so sexy!" He mimicked my imaginary sleep-talk in a high-pitched fake girl voice, throwing his head back and shaking it from side to side as if he were in the throes of passion.

"Is this joke ever going to get old?" I sighed, patting him in the center of his chest before pushing him away, and he pulled me back against his body, lowering his head to nuzzle my neck. Good thing we were out of sight of the librarian— since Friday night, Logan had gotten a lot more affectionate, his earlier aversion to PDA having evaporated. He'd admitted that he felt too guilty about keeping his true nature a secret—"You didn't know what you were kissing. I felt like I was stealing!"—but now that everything was out in the open, he wasn't shy about grabbing kisses before class. Or after class. And once, during class, when the teacher's back was turned.

Yep, we were one of those annoying, so-in-love-it-makes-others-want-to-vomit couples, and I loved every nausea-inducing minute of it. He even held my hand in front of my parents—making my mom smile sentimentally, and my dad, of course, turn a previously unseen shade of purple. I think it was called puce.

"So listen," Logan began, resting his hands on my hips as I leaned against the bookshelf behind me. "I'll walk you home, but I won't be able to hang out after school. Something's going on—Rego's asked me to stay for a meeting. I think it's important that I be there."

I raised my eyebrows in surprise. When Logan first told Rego he would quit after killing Aiden, Rego's reaction was volcanic. He accused Logan of deserting the cause. He questioned his loyalty. And although Logan didn't delve into details, opting to skim over the particulars of Rego's tirade—probably because it had to do with me—Logan did tell me that Rego made it a point to bring up his father.

"Going off on his own didn't end so well for Maxim Rex," he'd reminded Logan, insisting on using his dad's "warlock" name instead of the name Logan knew he'd preferred, Max. "He was a far superior soldier than you are. What makes you think you'll fare any better?"

That, particularly, was a low blow. It had backfired on Rego—and merely confirmed Logan's decision.

But in the past few days, Rego and Logan had worked out an arrangement. Logan would become something of a mercenary for the warlocks—an assassin for hire—when the warlocks were faced with a particularly difficult demon. And Logan would train a replacement, a young warlock named Tristan who was doing work for Rego in the Dark City.

In the meantime, Logan planned on renting an apartment by hypnotizing the landlord—I'd had to talk him down from a penthouse, since people might notice the teenager with no income living like a mogul—but Logan argued that he wanted to get a job and save for college, so he had to ration out his limited funds somehow.

Rego financed his war through alchemy; he could turn metal into gold. That's what was hidden behind the curtain in his living room—a secret lab that gave him an endless source of income in the human world. It would be no skin off that straight, permanently-in-the-air nose to turn a friggin' toaster to gold and hand it to Logan. "Here you go, buddy. Thanks for the years of work. This should pay for college, an apartment, and maybe buy you a new baseball cap."

But no. Rego just had to keep ties to Logan, and it alarmed me to no end. But Logan was so entranced by his plan for college and a normal life that I kept my mouth shut.

"Do you have any idea what the meeting could be about?" I asked, and Logan's hands tightened on my hips.

"It has to be about you. Even if I hadn't planned to leave after this mission, keeping you safe is still the most important thing right now."

Logan shut his eyes and pressed his forehead to mine.

"But…I'm afraid they want to use you."

"But what can I do, other than be used to open a portal?"

"Cerus seems to know the Queen's itinerary. If he finds out where the Queen is going to be at a certain time, you can be used to open a portal on the corresponding point this side. She'd be ripe for assassination," he explained, and I shuddered at the memory of the last portal I opened. I'd been so tired...I could feel my life fading away. But if I did this one last thing—one last thing for Logan—maybe he'd finally be free of it all.

"Maybe I should let them," I suggested, and Logan stepped back, his face twisted in horror as he clenched his fists.

"I'm just saying, then it would finally be over," I reasoned, but Logan glared at me.

"Do you honestly think it would ever end there?" he asked, squeezing his eyes shut as he pressed his fingertips to his temples. "Someone will eventually kill the person who replaces her. And then they'll get assassinated by someone else. And so on. It will never end."

He opened his eyes, and they were bleak, empty. "You'd be used, and used, and used, until you were nothing."

"Okay. So let's not do that, then," I said hastily, and he let out a weary chuckle before pulling me back into his arms.

"Yeah, let's not," he agreed, kissing the top of my head before drawing back.

"Come on, it's time for lunch." Logan took my hand and led the way to our usual table in the back. "I know the perfect corner that's a great spot for sneaking sandwiches and dealing with annoying dead friends."

But Dottie and Travis were nowhere to be found at lunch. It wasn't entirely surprising: while Dottie had gotten over Lo-

gan's demonic side pretty quickly, Travis seemed to be holding a grudge, suspiciously watching Logan when he thought
no one was looking.

"They're probably off somewhere, enjoying their privacy.
Lucky," Logan muttered under his breath, glancing up at the
security camera in the corner—one of several dozen now
scattered throughout the school. After the fire in the detention classroom, reported vandalism in the music room—and,
of course, full-on destruction of the auditorium—the school
had hastily installed security cameras throughout the building, citing evidence of gang activity. Shani Robinson's impassioned editorial in the *Observer* called it a "forced police state
punishing the many for the evil actions of a few."

If only she knew just how evil.

"Some privacy would be nice," I agreed, my glance landing
on the table next to us, where Princess Pepper and her ladies-
in-hating congregated. Of course, Pepper's eyes kept shooting my way—but I realized she didn't have her usual "Paige
Sucks" expression on her face. She looked stressed out and
anxious. And that's when I realized that her perfectly coiffed
hair was messy and uncared for, her eyes ringed with shadows. She was fidgeting, shifting in her seat as she twisted the
massive gold ring on her hand.

"Wow, Pepper's looking kind of...rough," I commented,
and Logan gave her a passing glance before waving his hand
in a dismissive way.

"Looks the same to me. Wake me when she looks like the
person who hasn't been a total bitch to you."

I snorted at his comment, and Logan gave me a beatific
smile before curling his lip in disgust in her direction.

"She's probably got the flu. I'm sure she'll use her last bit of energy to injure you somehow in gym before collapsing into a germy heap on the floor."

Gym was my first class after lunch, but Pepper—who usually took every opportunity to spike the volleyball at my head or blast the hockey puck right into my knees—hung back when we ran laps around the gym today, missing a prime opportunity to trip me as I rounded a corner.

I had just finished changing when she approached me in the locker room.

"Paige, can I talk to you for a second?" she asked as I tossed the terrycloth wristband that I wore over my bracelet back into my locker.

"No."

"Please?"

"No."

"It's important," she said, shifting her weight from foot to foot as she looked around the locker room. We were alone in this row, but I heard voices on the other side of my locker and the slamming of metal doors as my classmates headed out for their next class.

"Then talk to me as we walk to my next class," I replied, not wanting to be left in an empty locker room while Aiden was on the loose—or be left alone with Pepper.

*Really, which is worse?*

"No, I have to talk to you alone!" She held her palm to her chest, frowning.

"If it's so important you can suffer through being seen with me in public," I snapped, resting my palms on either side of my locker as I took a deep breath.

"It's not that," she said, her voice small. "I screwed up. I screwed up so bad."

She rubbed that giant ring on her hand and quickly shoved it underneath my nose. I slapped her hand away, but not before a heavy, bitter scent filled my senses. I instinctively held my breath as I tried to pull away, but my limbs immediately grew heavy, my shoulders dropping from the weight.

I started to collapse, and I felt Pepper catch me, shifting me so I collapsed onto the bench in between the row of lockers, my head in my lap.

"Hey, Pepper, you coming?" Footsteps, followed by Andie's unmistakable voice, rang in my ears. "What's up with Bellevue Kelly?"

*I can't move! Why can't I move? Help me!*

My thoughts screamed, echoing in my head, but my limbs wouldn't budge. My muscles ached as if I were trying to move a brick wall, my body unresponsive, my lips still and parted slightly.

"She said she got dizzy. Go on, I'll get her to the nurse," Pepper said, her voice shaking and weak.

"Ew, don't help her. Just leave her here and send the nurse in."

*Can't she see I can't move? Andie, don't leave me with her!*

"No, it's okay. You should go," Pepper urged.

"Yeah, I guess if you just left her there, you'd get into trouble." I could picture the eye roll that accompanied Andie's statement, lips curling into her signature snotty expression.

"Want me to stay with you?" Andie asked, sounding like she'd rather do anything else.

"No, it's cool," Pepper insisted, anxious. "Just go on ahead."

I felt Pepper sit next to me, where my dead limbs rooted me to the bench. My breathing was slow and labored—but I was still alive. At least for now.

I heard Andie's steps fade, the hiss of the air brake to the locker room door and then, the sound of metal on metal as the door closed. We were alone in the locker room—and I was a prisoner in my own immobile body.

*Logan, please, please come find me!*

"I'm sorry, Paige. I had no choice," Pepper was saying, her voice thick with sobs. "Aiden made me do it."

My stone body didn't react, but inside I began to crumble at that name. I wanted to run and scream and shake Pepper until her teeth chattered, but I couldn't move. My eyes were frozen open and starting to ache.

"He was so charming. I thought I'd dump Matt for him— really show Matt, you know? Do it in public, right in front of everyone, and embarrass him the way he'd embarrassed me," she confided in me, as if we were friends—as if she hadn't just guaranteed the end of my life. "But Aiden—he's so horrible, you don't even know what he's done to me."

*Pepper, you fool. You don't know anything.*

She whimpered, her voice thin with the terror she felt. And I was forced to listen to it, bound by a lifeless body made useless by whatever potion he'd instructed her to use on me.

"He was so nice, until he gave me this ring." She shoved it under my face again. The movement jostled me, throwing my dead body off balance. I slid to the floor, hitting the cold tile floor with a thud. I was dimly aware of a painful ache in my back, but I couldn't feel much. It was like my entire body had been given a shot of Novocain, making me aware of my motions but feeling nothing.

"I'm so sorry! I didn't mean to knock you down!" Pepper dropped to her knees next to me. "The ring—I can't take it off. And it hurts so much." She sniffled, sounding like she was convulsing with sobs, but I couldn't see her. I couldn't see anything except the exposed steel pipes and the water-stained, pale green ceiling above my head.

I wished I could close my eyes and force some other image into my head, so the last thing I'd see wouldn't be this grimy ceiling, which grew blurry as my eyelids remained open.

"He made me do it," Pepper was whispering. "If I didn't do this, he was going to kill me. I'm sorry. I'm just in so much pain—"

"Well, that was the point."

Aiden was here. I tried to scream, but of course the only sounds were his footsteps echoing in the empty locker room, and his smug voice as he explained his invention.

"When you put the ring on, it pierces your skin with a microscopic metal wire. It finds a vein and shimmies through it, until it reaches your heart. Brilliant, isn't it?" he gloated, and his footsteps stopped. Probably because he paused to admire his own ingenuity.

Pepper's sobs grew louder, nearly drowning him out.

"I would calm down if I were you," he snapped. "Your heart is wrapped nice and snug in wire. Think of your heart like a little baby, wrapped in a soft cuddly blanket. Only if that wire wraps any more tightly around your little heart, it'll slice it into pieces."

Pepper whimpered loudly, and then her cries were quickly

muffled, as if she had clasped her hand over her mouth. I desperately tried to burn, searching for my fire demon power and feeling nothing, not even a spark.

"You screwed up, Pepper. You were supposed to wait until she was completely separated from her little protector, and he's somewhere in this school," he growled. "Now where exactly is he?"

"I did wait!" she cried. "Logan's always with her. This is the one class he doesn't have with her, and everywhere else has security cameras! Getting Paige alone in the locker room was the only option, and there's an emergency exit you can use."

"Where is he? How long do I have?"

"He waits for her outside of her next class. He'll be here in a few minutes if she doesn't show up. Logan's always with her."

The mention of Logan's name made a sudden, but powerful, sense of calm surge through me.

*He'll find me. He always finds me.*

But that calm quickly turned to terror when Aiden's blurry face came into view, hovering over mine as my eyes remained fixed on the ceiling above me.

"Lights out, Paige," he whispered, placing his hands on my forehead and shutting my parched eyes. Something was placed over my nose, and I heard Pepper scream before everything faded away.

# 15

THE FIRST THING I NOTICED WAS THE SMELL. IT was musty and dank, like an abandoned building that spent more time wet than dry. The distinct scent of garbage hung heavily in the air—that same sharp, sour aroma that all trash had, a rancid heaviness that burned your nostrils and settled on your tongue. There were more smells, too—like the smell of exhaust, thick with acrid chemicals and smoke.

The sounds hit me next, the rapid grinding of metal on metal and the bleating of a loud horn as what sounded like a train roared by, stirring the air and pelting my cheeks with grit. I flinched and realized I could move again. I flexed my fingers, twisting my hands and feeling that my wrists were painfully bound in my lap.

I forced my heavy eyelids to open, dusky slits of vision widening as I blinked, trying to focus on the scene before me.

I was curled up at the base of a tall, graffiti-splashed pillar in an alcove adjacent to what appeared to be a train tunnel. The recessed room was lined with industrial-looking pipes, and dust danced in the slots of light beaming down from an overhead grate.

"She's awake!" The peppy cheer—and burst of solo ap-
plause that followed—reverberated dully in the cavernous
tunnel. I looked up to see Aiden skipping over the tracks to
meet me, his shiny boots scattering the rocks that covered
the floor of the tunnel.

"You have given me quite a lot of trouble," he said, wagging a finger at me. Over his thin black shirt, he wore that
shiny armor, which I could now see was comprised of several overlapping circular plates that started at his wrist, covering his arm and shoulder and spreading out like a fan over
his right pectoral.

"Cute accessory," I grunted, and Aiden's impish grin faded,
his eyes growing dark and menacing.

"Your little boyfriend did a lot of damage to my shoulder.
Do you want to repay the favor?" he growled. He braced his
right fist at his side, those fiery sparks shooting out of his
knuckles until they solidified into his weapon of choice—
that long gold spike. He rushed forward, sliding to his knees
and grabbing a fistful of my hair. Yanking my head back, he
forced me to look at him, pressing the tip of the spike into
my shoulder.

"Do you want to know what it felt like when his blade
sliced through bone and tendon and muscle?" he seethed.
Aiden pushed the spike into my shoulder more forcefully, the
tip easily penetrating my sweater and shirt—and only after I
cried in pain as the tip pierced my skin did he drop his hold,
withdrawing his spike with a satisfied smile.

"That's what I thought. Keep your smart little comments to
yourself, if you have any sense of self-preservation. I need you
alive—but they never said you couldn't be writhing in pain."

He pressed his index finger into my forehead. "Just ask your little friend Pepper," he sneered, pushing hard and making my head jerk back. "She's a bleeder, that one."

Her scream—the last thing I'd heard before waking up here—echoed in my head.

"Is she dead?"

"I stabbed her in the stomach, so by now, probably." Aiden just shrugged, casually and carelessly dismissing another life.

I bit the inside of my cheek, trying to keep the tears filling my eyes at bay. I didn't want to give Aiden the satisfaction of seeing me cry. It was the one thing I had left.

He stood up again, folding his arms as he studied the narrow space between the tunnel wall and the train tracks. He bent down, setting three gold pyramids in the shape of a triangle on the rocky floor. Aiden moved with precision, taking care to adjust each pyramid until the gilded tips all appeared to aim toward the same focal point somewhere above the center of the triangle.

"This might make you a teensy bit tired." His voice dripped with false concern as he gave me an exaggerated pout, leaning down to adjust one of the pyramids again. "This is a special kind of portal, you see."

He strode over to me, his steps graceful in spite of the uneven, rocky ground. With an evil grin, Aiden squatted in front of me, grabbing my chin tightly with the hand not covered by a lethal spike.

"Let's see your little protector try to stop me now."

"He'll stop you—and then he'll kill you," I vowed, but Aiden merely laughed as he stood up before me, shaking his head in amusement. Reaching down, he grabbed my wrists where they were bound by a thin gold wire, and I cried out as it sliced into my skin. He yanked me to my feet, and I stumbled forward, falling onto my knees on the rocks, which tore through my tights and cut into my legs.

Aiden hauled me forward, the tips of my shoes scraping across the jagged rocks as he dragged me in front of the triangle he'd set up before dropping me onto the ground.

"I don't know how much you know about crossing over, little girl, but it's too much energy for one body. Crossing over alone is suicide. It would turn you inside out." As he spoke, he casually hooked the tip of the spike into the sleeve covering his other arm, pushing the fabric up over his elbow.

"It's preferable to travel with more than just one person, spread the energy around, you know," he added matter-of-factly, as if he were explaining something mundane like fractions and not interdimensional travel. "I'm telling you this now because I don't want a lot of screaming when we come out on the other side. I'm going to be tired and you're going to be in a lot of pain. It's harder for humans than it is for my kind to cross, and I really don't want to hear your whiny mouth."

Aiden gently traced my jaw with his spike. "I don't even need you to speak for this spell. So keep your mouth shut or I'll start breaking bones." I kicked at his legs, and he merely laughed, dodging my feet and stepping around me to grab me around the waist. He pulled me up, holding me in a viselike grip with my back against his chest.

I struggled against Aiden's clutches, thrashing in his arms and screaming, my desperate cries dying as echoes in the tunnel. Only hours before, Logan had held me like this in the library. And now his warm arms were replaced with Aiden's, whose breath hissed sharply in my ear as he began to chant in the demonic language. The pyramids began to glow, bathing the entire tunnel in a honey-colored light.

Immediately, I felt weak. The brighter the glow, the more faint I felt. My knees began to buckle, but Aiden held me tightly, clutching me against him as my life began to drain from me. I flailed in his arms, fighting for consciousness, but it was like holding water in my fist—it all dripped away.

Pictures flitted in front of my mind as I fought to stay awake. My dad teaching me to ride a bike...my first Yankees game with my mom...Logan's eyes as he told me he loved me. I held on to these images as I forced my eyes to keep open. *Was this my life flashing before my eyes?*

A gold mist curled out of the pyramids, meeting in the center of the triangle. The mist dipped and swirled, a serpentine fog that undulated to the tune of Aiden's chants.

*"Mekus cruor, mekus de cruor!"* Aiden wildly repeated the phrase, his voice morphing into a savage, beastly growl.

Aiden dropped his hold on me, and I collapsed to the ground, pushing myself onto my side to see him stand at the base of the triangle, holding out his arm. He dragged the top of the spike along the inside of his forearm, gritting his teeth as he tore a thin line in the pale skin. His hand dropped, deep purple blood streaming down his arm and pooling in his closed fist.

He thrust his dripping fist into the mist, which hungrily curled around it, as if it were consuming the blood. Purple veins branched out from his hand into the fog, wrapping around the mist and feeding it. Aiden's face contorted in agony as he shut his eyes, his mouth open in a quiet wail, as the mist pulsated before bursting open. A blast of wind knocked both of us back, sending rocks scattering as we sprawled on the ground, gaping at the small, ripped-open hole above the triangle.

It looked like someone had violently torn open a painting, leaving rough, tattered edges hanging around the hole that uncovered another painting underneath it. The edges of the canvas glowed, flashing white before it got bigger—a gaping wound that offered a peek into the world on the other side.

I rolled over onto my stomach with a grunt, trying to push myself up with my bound hands and falling down. My bones felt like chalk—like they'd snap with the simple act of pushing my body off this bed of rocks. My vision blurred, and I wondered if this was what Travis had endured before Blaise turned him into ash. Logan had saved me that time. But this time…

*Logan…where are you?*

Aiden crouched before me, stroking my cheek with his bloody finger. I summoned the scraps of energy I had left to jerk away as forcefully as I could, stumbling back and falling against the rocks. My wasted eyes saw a shadow flickering behind Aiden, and I flinched as another train roared by, drowning out all sound except Aiden's voice as he pulled me to my feet, gripping me by the throat and pinning me to the pillar. I gasped for air, his fingers closing tightly around my neck.

"The first thing I'm doing when we're on the other side," he purred into my ear, his breath moist and invasive on my skin, "is arranging the assassination of your protector. You'd be surprised how many in the warlock army would give up their little warrior for the right price."

Aiden stepped back, still gripping me around the throat.

Dark spots skipped around in my vision, drawing together to form a curtain of blackness that closed over me.

And then Aiden's fingers loosened their grip, keeping only a light hold around my throat as I slumped to the ground. I was dimly aware of shrieks echoing around the tunnel. I grabbed his wrist between my bound palms and pulled his arm off me, his fingers easily slipping off my skin with just a feeble tug. The stale air in the tunnel was a welcome, fresh rush of oxygen to my deprived lungs as I crumpled against the rocks, taking huge, gulping breaths.

Panting, I forced my blurry vision to focus and stared in confusion at Aiden's arm—his arm, which was no longer connected to his body, but lying about a foot from me, staining the rocks a dark purple where it had been sliced from his body.

I heard a low whine, and I pushed myself up into a sitting position, looking toward the source of the weak cry. I could see the silhouette of Aiden, cowering on the ground, blood gushing out of the stump that had once been his left arm. He scrambled backward, his heels ineffectively scattering rocks as he kicked wildly, trying to find some purchase to get away from Logan.

Logan, who stood before Aiden, his chest rising in anger and sword gripped tightly, dripping with blood.

"I told you not to touch her," Logan snarled, slicing his sword through the air with an audible whirr. Aiden held up his shielded arm in protection, giving birth to a spray of sparks and light as Logan's sword clashed with the metal. A malevolent smile tugged at the corner of Logan's mouth as he studied the demon, writhing in pain and panic at his feet.

I'd seen Logan bleed an unnatural color, watched him cast

spells in an otherworldly language, and hell, I'd even seen and touched his wings. But he'd never looked demonic until this moment.

Logan held the tip of his sword against Aiden's throat, a slow grin on his face. The portal expanded again, showering the tunnel in another blast of bright light and spotlighting Aiden's face, which was twisted in terror.

"You can't kill me!" Aiden cried, his eyes appearing a pale violet in the blinding white light from the portal.

"Oh, but I can," Logan told Aiden. "I'm just trying to figure out which way will be the most painful."

Aiden used his armored hand to swipe at Logan's sword, sending another spray of sparks scattering around the rocks as Logan let his sword be pushed to the side. Logan looked almost amused as he shadowed Aiden's movements, following closely as the demon scrambled to his feet, clutching at his bleeding stump.

Logan sauntered behind Aiden as he stumbled forward a few steps before kicking him in the back of the knee, sending Aiden sprawling down on the rocks. In two steps, Logan had Aiden pinned on the ground, his foot pressed against Aiden's neck.

"You can't—you need me," Aiden sputtered, his usually artfully messy black hair now stringy and hanging in his face. "You need me to close the portal."

"I'm pretty sure killing you will do the job," Logan said. Aiden's hand wildly flung in the air, and I saw the gold disk reflect the light from the portal as it flew in the air.

"Look out!" I tried to scream with the last surge of energy I had left; but the words left my mouth in a weak croak as

Aiden's signature weapon unleashed its deadly whips, which lashed in the air as the disk spun toward me. The spiny whips whirled, and I tried to move, struggling to my feet only for my legs to collapse underneath me, my body drained of all strength as the portal expanded again—devouring my life to sustain its own.

Logan rushed toward me, his sword drawn—and quickly hacked through the disk midair. It imploded with a flash of gold smoke, an almost musical tinkling sound heralding its destruction before fragments of the feared weapon rained down ineffectively on the rocks.

Aiden had struggled to his feet, his head whirling from side to side before picking a direction, and he began staggering off balance in search of an exit. Logan raced toward him, launching himself off the rocks and knocking into Aiden, forcing the demon onto the ground with a heavy thud. Aiden yelled in pain as Logan stood up, kicking the demon in the ribs, the force of his kick sending Aiden rolling onto his back. Logan raised his sword, and with one swift move, impaled the demon through his good shoulder, pinning him to the ground.

A retching, gurgling sound escaped Aiden's throat, and he clawed ineffectively at the sword with his one hand. Logan gripped the handle, jiggling it slightly to test how firmly it was lodged in the ground—earning another wet-sounding cough from Aiden. Logan grinned, taking obvious delight in Aiden's agony.

"That should keep you in place. I'm looking forward to killing you slowly, *Aeodhan*. Every mark you left on her is another hour you'll scream in agony."

And then Logan turned to me, beginning his slow approach. His head was tilted down, his hair hanging in his face as his dark eyes fell on mine—once-familiar eyes that were now cold and bloodthirsty, bathed in the harsh white glow of the portal. And I was afraid.

Afraid—until Logan fell to his knees in front of me and cupped my face, and the warmth and love I knew was back. I exhaled in relief, my shoulders relaxing at his touch.

"He'll never hurt you again," he murmured, his eyes searching mine as his hands slid down my neck, inspecting the bruises that were likely already forming from Aiden's constricting grip. Logan gently took my bound wrists in his palm and slid his index finger in between my raw wrists, whispering harsh words from that shared demonic language.

The wire fell away, disintegrating into mere gold flakes that fluttered to the ground like celebratory confetti. Logan cradled my wrists as the portal flashed again—and I gasped, doubling over in pain as the doorway to the Dark World grew.

"The portal," I choked out, my hands wrapping around my stomach. "It hurts worse than last time. Every time it gets bigger, it hurts. It hurts so—"

My words were cut off as I braced myself against another wave of pain—a searing burn that felt like it started in my bones and radiated outward, settling into my skin and leaving my body desiccated in its wake.

The savage look returned to Logan's eyes when he saw how much I was suffering. He stood, taking one long, last look at me before crossing back to where Aiden was pinned to the ground, his bloodied fingers clutching at the sword.

And Aiden was laughing.

"You have to let me go! Don't you want me to close the

portal?" he asked, a delirious smile on his face—a smile that morphed into screams when Logan removed his sword.

Grabbing Aiden's collar in his fist, Logan lifted the demon up and slammed him against the pillar.

"You don't have any special weapons. You don't even have all your limbs. It's over, Regent." Logan slammed Aiden back into the hard concrete for emphasis, but the demon just smiled in reply.

"But you don't get to kill me, so it's worth it," Aiden sneered.

"Wrong," Logan replied. His elbow thrust upward, and I heard the grating sound of metal on concrete as Logan skewered the demon, the point of his sword scraping the pillar as Logan's sword found an exit through the demon's back.

Withdrawing his sword, Logan stepped back as Aiden held his hand to his stomach, purple seeping through his fingers. The portal expanded again, a forgiving burst of dazzling light that seemed to leach the color from the macabre scene, making it appear in black and white.

A slow smile spread across Aiden's face before he began choking out blood.

"I still win," he whispered hoarsely before collapsing to the ground. Taking no chances, Logan raised his sword and in one quick move brought it down on Aiden's neck, beheading him.

And just like that, Aiden was gone—the demon who had terrorized me was now a nonthreatening collection of pieces on the ground.

"I'm so sorry." I heard Logan though my foggy brain, his fingers gently touching my skin.

"I found Pepper. She was in bad shape but she—she man-

aged to tell me what she did." Logan's voice was more pity-
ing than angry at her foolish actions. "I found you as fast as
I could. I'm so sorry he hurt you."

"You're here now," I told him, and he pressed his forehead
to mine. The portal flashed again—sending me into convul-
sions as it sucked the life out of me to grow even bigger. All I
felt was pain. Pain—and the feeling that I was slipping away.

"Why—why isn't it closing?" My voice sounded very small,
and I realized Logan had his arms around me, supporting me.

"It should have closed when I killed Aiden," he said, turning his head to stare warily at the portal, which was about
three feet wide at this point. I could clearly see the world
beyond ours. It looked similar enough—pale gray walls that
were decorated with jagged marks, much like the looping
graffiti that colored the walls of this tunnel.

And then I heard a roar as something moved in the portal—something that reminded us we needed to close it immediately. A pair of skeletal legs, all white bone and stringy
beige tendon, tall and strong and terrifying, slowly ambled by.

"Why isn't it closing?" I asked, my fingers gripping Logan's shirt.

"I don't know," he admitted, his eyes wide with fright.
"Did he do something differently to open it?"

The portal flashed again, and I felt my consciousness slip
away for a moment. When my eyes opened, Logan was kneeling before me, his hands brushing my hair away from my face.

"Paige, please, remember. How did Aiden open the portal?"
Logan's voice was calm and soothing, but his eyes were frantic.

"He did a spell, like last time. Except, he put down those
gold pyramids first," I said, pointing to the three glimmering

points. "He was really careful about their placement. And then they gave off this gold mist that he used to open the portal."

Logan stood quickly, rushing over to the pyramids and kicking them out of formation. The gold triangles glimmered brightly in protest before fading to a dull gold, but the portal continued to swell.

"Paige, what else?" Logan returned to crouch before me, panic beginning to creep into his voice.

"He cut his arm," I remembered, taking my index finger and tracing a line down the inside of my forearm. "It was like the mist was alive, and Aiden fed it his blood."

Logan leaned back on his heels, the color draining from his face.

"No wonder he said we needed him," he muttered.

"What does that mean?" I asked, frantic.

Logan stood, pacing a few steps before the portal shuddered again—reminding him that we were out of time. He quickly knelt in front of me, pressing one hand against my cheek.

"Paige, he opened a blood portal. Aiden used his blood to open it. He thought he was the only one who could close it," he explained gravely.

"So, throw his head through the damn thing!" I cried. "I wanted it on my bookshelf, but do this instead!"

Logan laughed—but this time, it was tinged with sadness.

"You have made me smile more in the past few months than I have in my entire life, Paige Dawn Kelly. Never forget that," he said, his thumb brushing my cheek.

With those words—coupled with the adoring but heartbroken expression on his face—cold panic began seizing me.

"Why do I feel like you're saying goodbye?" I asked in a trembling voice.

"Paige, the portal is going to keep opening. It's going to destroy both worlds. It's going to destroy you as it grows," he said, his other hand finding its way into my hair.

"So throw Aiden's head—"

"It has to be living blood, Paige. Living Regent blood will close the portal." Logan paused, taking a deep breath. And I felt that sickening chill—the one where you realize your life is about to change, and you desperately wish you could freeze time in that moment, to preserve your life as it was Before. Before whatever was about to annihilate and crush your heart hadn't happened yet.

"Don't say it," I begged him.

"I have Regent blood." His voice was hoarse, as if it were painful to say the words. It should have been painful, because those razor-sharp words cut me worse than any of Aiden's torture devices.

"Don't say that."

"I can close the portal."

"No."

"I have to, Paige."

"No!" I screamed, trying to hold him close and cursing my weak limbs when they slid uselessly against my side.

"I have to," he insisted. "This portal is going to kill you if it stays open much longer."

"And it will kill you if you go through it," I sobbed, grabbing his hand.

"Someday, you can tell the world about the demon who saved it." He gave me a rakish smile.

"Don't do that. Don't you dare do that! Don't you dare joke with me and tease me in the same breath that you tell me this is my last moment with you," I sobbed again, fresh tears pouring down my face as I realized the truth of what I said.

"Paige, I have to do this," he said, tucking his fingers underneath my chin and urging my eyes upward as he had countless times before. *This can't be the last time I feel his touch.*

"The portal is killing you, and fast. So, listen to me, I want you to do something for me, okay? I want you to live and be happy and have a life that's full and rich and everything you showed me life should be," Logan told me, his eyes glistening above that endearing, sweet smile that he showed only to me. My trembling fingers reached up to touch his lips, and he pursed them softly, placing one last kiss on them before my weak hand fell limply into my lap.

"Logan, please. I love you. Don't leave me," I begged. Logan took my hand and wrapped it around the back of his neck, holding it there before kissing my lips softly.

"If I don't do this, there will be nothing left."

*And if you do, there will be nothing left of me.*

"I don't know how to do this," I wept, my eyes scouring his face, every beloved line and curve. "I don't know how to say goodbye to you and tell you everything you are to me."

"Don't worry. Don't regret anything you did or didn't say," he said, absolving me of all my future remorse. "I already know. Because you are everything to me."

His brave facade began crumbing, and Logan pressed his lips to mine for a kiss—our final kiss—and I tried to memorize his every soft touch, every whispered word and every breath.

The portal flashed again—sending a quake rippling through our world. Metal creaked, bursts of dirt and concrete were dislodged from the tremor, raining down in the tunnel and on our heads. In the distance, I heard car alarms blaring overhead, and the nightmarish bone monster roared from inside the portal.

"Don't go," I pleaded. "I can't be without you. I can't not know you."

"You're the only one who ever really did know me. And I'll always be with you. I promise you," he said, his voice strong with conviction as he stood up, still holding my hand. As his first tear fell, Logan stepped away from me, his hand slowly slipping out of mine until it was just our fingertips that were touching. And then his touch was gone, sending a bolt of pain through my arm and into my heart, which truly and finally shattered.

Logan stood in front of the portal before turning and giving me that smile that melted me every time.

"I love you."

And with that, Logan began running into the portal, sacrificing himself for me and for our world.

# 16

THEY SAY LOVE GIVES YOU STRENGTH. BEFORE that day, I always thought that was a platitude, meant to be embroidered on a pillow or stitched onto an embarrassing sweatshirt worn by some weirdo aunt.

But when I saw my love about to take a leap into certain, agonizing death to save the world, whatever reserves of energy I had left pooled together, giving me strength.

It wasn't a lot of strength. It was just enough to launch myself from my collapsed position on the rocky floor. I stumbled forward—my fatigued feet tripping on the rocks as I wildly reached out for his hand. They also say the course of true love never runs smooth. Well, in my case, it runs like an uncoordinated, broken-down shell of a person.

But it didn't matter. Because as Logan jumped through the portal, I was there—my hand wrapped around his, his face turning to register in surprise and grief before we were sucked into the doorway.

And then pain. Pain that I'd always associated with a time before medicine, pain that came with scary medieval words like *disembowelment*. Somehow I kept Logan's hand in mine as our bodies were being ripped apart and soldered back together with fire, only to be shredded into pieces again. And then it was over—my body shaking with the aftershocks of the brief, but immeasurable pain—as I was sprawled, facedown, on a bed of rocks.

My fingers flexed, searching for Logan—and the movement sent another tremor of pain through my body. But before I slipped into blissful unconsciousness, I felt his warm hand twitch in mine.

Dimly, I became aware of movement—my body shifting, although not of my own accord. The burden of my weight fell to my back as something held me, rocking me gently.

"Why did you do that? Why?" I heard his pleading voice as he cradled me in his arms, soothing me with his touch before I faded back into the blackness.

"Wake up. Please, wake up. Paige, you can't be gone. You can't be gone and I'm still here. Please come back to me." His whispered voice was frantic, grief-stricken, pulling me again from my euphorically numb state. I felt my hair being brushed off my forehead as Logan's hands pressed against my neck and inside my wrist.

"Come back to me, please," he begged, repeating that mantra, and I felt his lips touch my skin as he continued pleading with me. I fought the lure of unconsciousness, forcing myself to face my pain to end his.

"Logan?" I whispered, and he pulled me into a tight hug, exhaling in relief as he stroked my hair.

"Are...we...alive?" I asked, and Logan pressed a kiss against my temple before answering.

"For now," he replied.

"Where are we?" My voice sounded foreign to my own ears. I opened my eyes to see that we were tucked behind a pillar, hidden in an alcove similar to the one we had been in minutes before. *Had it only been a few minutes?*

Chalky white rocks lined the ground underneath us, and I struggled to sit up in Logan's arms. Relief briefly flashed across his face as I came out of the pain-induced fog, before pure grief took over. He gently brushed my hair over my shoulder as he cradled me close.

"Why did you do that?" he asked, covering my face with gentle kisses before pulling back to stare at me mournfully. "You would have finally been safe. Why didn't you let me go?"

"I couldn't let you die." My answer was simple, but it was the truth.

"But—"

"You would have done it for me. Like you said, life-altering relationships don't come around all that often."

"But you're in the Dark World now." The words had barely left his mouth when a roar echoed in the tunnel, as if to drive his point home. Logan held one finger over my mouth, and we cowered behind the pillar. Something solid—and heavy— scuffled through the tunnel behind us, weighty footfalls hitting the rocks with a thud that reverberated with a dull echo. I could feel Logan's heartbeat matching mine as I buried my head in his chest, his arms wrapped around mine, relaxing only when the creature had moved past us.

"When we know those…things…aren't nearby, just use me to open up another portal," I said, looking up at him.

"Paige, I don't think you could open a book right now, let

alone a doorway to another dimension. It'll take days before you're strong enough."

"But I'm already feeling stronger," I insisted, sitting up straighter to illustrate my point.

"You've also been unconscious for hours," he revealed.

"Hours?" I repeated, panicking as I reached into my pocket, automatically looking for my cell phone among the spare change. "I have to call my dad. They're gonna…"

My voice trailed off as I realized what I was saying.

"I promise I'll find a way to get you home, Paige. I just don't know how to do it right now," he said, quickly pulling me into his arms, muffling my cries as the weight of what we'd done settled over me, crushing me.

"Can't we at least try to open a portal?" I begged, looking up at Logan with a tearstained face.

"I don't know how to do it," he admitted, shame reddening his cheeks. "I'm not a full-blooded Regent, and I'm not a full-blooded warlock. I only know basic spells—most of my training has been physical. Swords, weapons, hand-to-hand."

"So that's it? We're both going to be trapped here forever? I'll never see my parents again?" I asked, my voice very small.

Every bratty retort, every temper tantrum, every snide, ungrateful remark flashed through my mind, countered by my parents' desperate attempts to keep me safe and healthy, and it unleashed a fresh round of tears.

*When was the last time I'd told my parents that I loved them? Would they know? Would they think I ran away, abandoning them?*

Logan studied me, his eyes darkening with resolve.

"No. You're not going to lose your family," he said, his jaw set in determination. He gently unwound my arms from around him before standing up, unbuttoning his oxford and letting it fall into a puddle around his feet. Logan's forehead wrinkled in concentration as the subtle transformation took place—the enhanced definition of his muscles, his eyes paling from cocoa to violet, and those large black wings, which unfurled behind him in the dusky light of the tunnel.

Logan crouched before me, slipping his arms underneath me as he picked me up, curling me against his chest.

"What are we doing?" I asked, sliding my arm across his shoulders.

"We're going to fly to Rego."

"Fly?" I gasped. "You really can fly?"

Logan looked slightly offended.

"They're not just decorative," he replied, giving them a quick flap. "It'll be the fastest, and probably the safest, way to get to him. But I'm really out of practice, so hold on tight."

"But Rego—will he even want to help us?" I asked, panicked. "After what you told him—"

"What I told him won't matter. You're—" Logan paused, as his Adam's apple bobbed slightly when he swallowed back whatever it was he was going to say.

"What?"

"Over here, you're a threat to him. Just like you could be used to assassinate the Queen, now you could be used to kill him. It's in his best interest to get you home."

He tilted his chin up, his eyes steely with resolve.

"And I'll give him whatever he wants to make sure that you get home," he vowed, holding me tightly. "Now hold on."

Logan's footsteps crunched faintly as he stepped out of the alcove, making a sharp turn right as he walked along the tunnel, hugging the dingy walls, which were coated in faded but colorful markings, scrawled in a sharp handwriting.

"Graffiti?" I whispered, and Logan shook his head, his jaw tense.

"Warnings," he replied, and I gripped his neck more tightly as he picked up his pace. Red-tinged light beamed down through crevices overhead, dotting the tunnel with eerie spotlights which appeared as crimson splashes as they settled on the stark white rocks.

The only sounds I could hear were our raspy breaths and the crunching of rocks underneath Logan's feet as he steadily but swiftly carried me through the tunnel. His breathing grew heavier, and I realized we were on an incline, until finally, the ground leveled out, with a faint blush of light appearing ahead.

That's when we heard the first roar, the savage sound reverberating in the tunnel and making it even louder.

Logan began running, forgetting about trying to stay quiet in a race to escape the tunnel—and the bone monster that was somewhere behind us, patrolling the depths of the dark, cavernous space.

The second roar was a deafening, feral sound, a shriek layered on top of a primitive growl, and Logan began sprinting in earnest toward the light.

We could *feel* that second roar—our skin heated by the blast of hot breath that came out of the bone monster's mouth.

"Hold on," Logan ordered, his fingers clutching me tightly as he tilted forward, his wings beating rapidly—and I realized he was trying to gain enough momentum to take flight. I wrapped my arms around his neck and buried my face in his shoulder. And I should have left it there.

Because when I glanced behind him, I got a good look at what was following us. The immense skeletal face was a long white oval, punctured with gaping, empty eye sockets. Sinewy beige tendons held an underbite of spikelike teeth, which stayed low to the ground, snapping and snarling as the bone monster galloped in our wake, its gait almost canine.

With a rush of wind, we lifted off the ground, Logan's takeoff wobbly but fast. We careened around the tunnel, the monster's head swiveling and snapping as it tried to catch us, one large bony claw swiping at us in an effort to knock us out of the air. Logan dove low, skimming the ground as he dodged the creature, whose face took on a pinkish hue as we reached the exit.

Logan grunted with exertion as we flew upward, out of the tunnel.

"I think I've got this now," Logan said, flying more smoothly as we gained height.

Over his shoulder, I could see the bone monster emerge— the skeletal head followed by six pairs of bony legs and a massive tail, which swung in anger as the monster raised its head, roaring at the sky in fury.

I shut my eyes and gripped him tightly, my fear of heights— and, you know, nightmarish bone monsters from another dimension—wrecking havoc on my equilibrium.

*Just look at Logan. Just look at him and everything will be okay.*

But when I opened my eyes to look at him, the expression on his face told me that everything would not be okay. I followed his line of vision and gasped in horror.

The sky was gray—not the shade of an overcast or stormy day, but the color of death, the sickly hue of corpses and illness. Hanging high in the center of the sky was the sun. At least I think it was the sun—a meaty red orb visibly pulsed, as if someone had torn a hole in the skin of the sky, revealing the putrid flesh beneath. Somehow, this bloody crimson sun gave a blush-colored light to the Dark City, which spread out beneath us.

Elongated dark skyscrapers pierced the sky, almost gothic in their gracefully curved spires and elegant points. Winged creatures, much like Logan, flew around the twisted spires, dipping and swooping low, the flapping of wings a low hum that settled in my ears.

In the center of the darkness, where Central Park should have been, was instead a glacial wasteland, a stark ice-blue dead zone packed with clusters of brittle, frozen trees.

My eyes sought out my neighborhood, and even though I'd known it from the map Rego had shown me, I still gasped when I saw that it was on fire, shimmering with smokeless red-and-orange flames whose heat radiated out in undulating waves.

"I *will* get you out of here," Logan vowed. I pulled my eyes from the wretched landscape, meeting his determined ones as we hovered in place.

Logan shifted his grip to hold me more securely. His eyes turned back to the city that sprawled beneath us, his head lowering as his eyes targeted an area to the south.

And then we were off, Logan rapidly flying toward what would have been the Upper West Side. The nightmarish landscape blurred by as Logan picked up speed, the warm wind chapping my tearstained cheeks as Logan spread his wings, gliding downward like a hawk, flapping his wings to slow his descent as he came to stop on top of a building, jogging forward with the force of his landing.

He leaned down to let me slide out of his arms, my feet settling somewhat unsteadily on the rooftop, which looked like any other rooftop on the Upper West Side. It was covered in black tar, and the entrance to the stairwell was a nondescript red-painted door, housed in a little structure made of weather-beaten brown bricks. Wordlessly, Logan took my hand, leading me across the roof. He yanked the door open, the hinges creaking and causing me to jump at the noise. I peered inside at the dark stairway, before looking at Logan incredulously.

"It's just a stairway," Logan reassured me as he craned his neck to check out the shadowed staircase before taking a few steps down.

"*Luserna Illuminabit,*" he said, repeating the spell he had used to conjure light when the auditorium had been cast into darkness, and golden orbs of light raced ahead of us, illuminating the dark staircase. Logan pulled out his sword, holding it in one hand and gripping my hand with his other.

"Just a stairway?" I repeated, eyeing his sword.

"Doesn't hurt to be prepared," he muttered, before turning to face me. I was standing a few steps above him, making us eye level.

"I swear it to you, Paige. I will get you home, if it's the last and only thing I do."

With that, Logan turned around, and I let my love lead me down into the darkness.

★ ★ ★ ★ ★

# ACKNOWLEDGMENTS

YOU'D THINK WRITING A BOOK JUST REQUIRES an idea and a laptop, but the truth is, an author needs—and heavily relies on—his or her support system to get those words down. I'd like to give thanks to the following people who supported me on this journey:

Natashya Wilson and the brilliant team at Harlequin Teen. I have to especially thank my wonderful editor Annie Stone for her exceptional insight and guidance, and Tara Gavin, who gave me the opportunity to live my dream with *Spellbound*. I'll be forever grateful.

My fantastic agent, Lynn Seligman. I'm so lucky to have you in my corner.

Dawn Yanek. Paige and Logan would probably still be on a roof somewhere without you. Thank you for your invaluable advice, edits and, most of all, your friendship.

My husband, Dave. Thank you for your support and patience when I live in my head and leave my shoes in the living room as I get to know my characters. Mom, you read my first stories and instilled in me a love of reading and writing, and belief in myself. My Ponyville girls, Mindy Monez and

Catharine McNelly, you keep me crazy and sane in all the best ways. Melinda Oswandel, Ben Trivett, you guys rock. Kate Treadway, KP Simmon, Hannah McBride, Lisa Mandina and Alice Marvels, thanks so much for your support and kindness and, of course, 140 characters of entertainment. Brielle and Shaelyn, I can't wait to watch you grow up and see what books you love. I love you girls.

# Q&A with CARA LYNN SHULTZ

Q: What inspired *The Dark World?* How did you come up with the idea—and what came first, the characters or the world?

A: *I grew up in New York City, and I wanted to continue writing stories that were set in my hometown. I adore my city. But setting a book in New York can be limiting—there's only so much creative license you can take when everyone knows what New York looks like. Around the time I was wrapping up my last book, Spellcaster, and pondering ideas for a new series, I had an ocular migraine, which is really trippy, bizarre and more than a little scary. It makes your vision appear fractured. I told a friend that it looked like a portal to another universe was opening, and joked about how, with my luck, it wouldn't be a doorway to a word full of unicorns and magic kittens but a doorway to "another dimension full of demons that want to eat my face and steal my TV." And that's when the final scene of The Dark World popped into my head.*

*With this in mind, I started thinking more and more about an alternate version of New York City—where I could still write about my beloved hometown, but change it to suit my needs. I was obsessed with the mental picture of a distorted, grotesque version of New York, and I described the skyline with the pulsing red sun and corpselike gray sky to my cousin Jennifer, who told me, "Get some characters there, and I'll read that." The next step was figuring out how to get characters into that world. I wish* The Dark World *had a sexier origin story, but that's how it happened. A New Yorker with a migraine. Maybe my next asthma attack will give me something good, too.*

Q: You've already written two novels, *Spellbound* and *Spellcaster*. Was *The Dark World* harder or easier to write after having a few books under your belt? Was your process different this time?

A: The Dark World *was easier in that I had a better understanding of the publishing process. I knew the timeline of what to expect and when to expect it. And I knew some of my writing pitfalls at that point. The hard part was learning new characters and discovering what makes them tick. But that's also the most fun part.*

*My process remained the same, though. I've always listened to music when I write. And I prefer to write at night—2:00 a.m. is when I really get on a roll.*

Q: What inspired the different kinds of demon powers in the book? Where did the idea for Regents come from?

A: *In the early drafts of* The Dark World, *there was only one kind of demon, and they all had the same powers. But as I started writing, I had too much fun with Blaise and her powers, and she spawned the concept of fire demons. After that, I started breaking out the demons into groups. When it comes to* the demons who draw their power from nature, their powers are a little more obvious—e.g., fire demons can conjure fireballs. But for the demons who derive their power from emotions, I referenced extreme human reactions. Take a rage demon, for example. He has a single-minded focus: to obliterate his target, seemingly unaware of the destruction he causes, or the damage he does to himself, in trying to achieve his goal. Ever see someone when they're in a senseless fit of rage punching a wall? I amplified that for the rage demons.

As for Regents—originally they were that lone race of demons terrorizing my poor characters. An all-powerful demon race is scary and fascinating, especially the more we learn about them. And as for their name, well…Regents sounds regal. And Regents are also the names of standardized tests that I took in high school that were stressful and held way more power over my high school career than they should have. In fact, I had to take the French Regents and Latin Regents on the same day. That's six hours of language testing. You can't tell me that's not just a little demonic.

Q: I'm guessing you draw a lot of inspiration from your personal experiences in New York City, since you've lived there all your life. Did you go to a high school like Holy Assumption? Are there any landmarks in *The Dark World* that are from your past or your childhood?

A: *I always thread real-life references into my books. My high school, Dominican Academy, was similar to Vincent Academy—which is Paige's first school, and also Emma's school from* Spellbound, *except my high school was all girls. So the mentions of specific things that Paige did when she was in her first school—like hang-*

*ing out on the steps of the Met—are very real things we did in high school. And I had to nod to the carousel in Central Park, because my grandparents used to take me there when I was a little kid. Paige lives in Hell's Kitchen, where I grew up. In fact, Paige lives on the street my cousins lived on when we were teenagers. All the restaurants and specific meals Paige mentions are real— especially when it comes to ordering from your bodega. The relationship between New Yorkers and their bodegas is a very special and sacred thing.*

Q: Without giving away any spoilers, can you tell us a little about what's next for Paige and Logan?

A: *They're about to take a dangerous journey through the Dark City. Secrets will be revealed. Loyalties will be questioned. Things will get heated (in, ahem, a good way). And someone's world will shatter.*